The Mystics and The Mystery

Books by Cheryl Lafferty Eckl

Non-Fiction for Times of Dramatic Change

A Beautiful Death:
Keeping the Promise of Love

A Beautiful Grief:
Reflections on Letting Go

The LIGHT Process:
Living on the Razor's Edge of Change

Poetry for Inspiration & Beauty

Poetics of Soul & Fire

Bridge to the Otherworld

Idylls from the Garden
of Spiritual Delights & Healing

Sparks of Celtic Mystery:
soul poems from Éire

A Beautiful Joy:
Reunion with the Beloved
Through Transfiguring Love

Fiction for the Love of Twin Flames

The Weaving: A Novel
of Twin Flames Through Time

Twin Flames of Éire Trilogy
The Ancients and The Call
The Water and The Flame
The Mystics and The Mystery

The Mystics and The Mystery

Twin Flames of Éire Trilogy - Book Three

Cheryl Lafferty Eckl

FLYING CRANE PRESS

Library of Congress Control Number: 2020910302
ISBN: 978-1-7346450-6-4 (paperback)
ISBN: 978-1-7346450-8-8 (e-book)

The author wishes to gratefully acknowledge:

Content development - Paula Kennedy Kehoe
Cover and interior design - James Bennett
Publishing support - Theresa McNicholas, Janice Haugen
Irish translations - Dónall Ó Héalaí & Dr. Pádraig Ó Héalaí, CelticConsciousness.com
Cover photo - John Finn, unsplash.com, used with permission
Author photo - Larry Stanley

Printed in the United States of America

For the seers,
past, present & future

Walk the circle of my wisdom.
Climb the pathway, scale the mountains.
Inward, outward, forward, backward.
Time becomes as weaving garments,
Yet of light, not earthly matter.
They will clothe you if you faint not.
                              —Elder Brother

Dear Reader,

Éire, luminous home of many a Celtic heart, is a land of stone. And stone recalls its prehistoric past in megaliths and passage tombs. Mighty structures that some say are older at a date of 3000 BC than the pyramids at 2500 BC.

But what if the pyramids are ten times that old? Who built them and who began erecting Ireland's neolithic structures almost as soon as the last ice caps receded from Northern Europe?

Did refugees travel to desert climes following the sinking of Atlantis twelve thousand years ago, bringing with them pyramid-building technology? And did they, more than once, return from Egypt to the cool, green island their ancestors had passed on their way East—each time to escape persecution and leave their mysterious legacy in stone?

These are fascinating questions that our seer, Debbie, is drawn to explore. For she knows she was one who fled the destruction of Egypt's 18th Dynasty in the company of her twin flame, her soul's other half, known in this life as Jeremy.

In those long-forgotten days he promised her safety, but could not guarantee his own. She lost him then. Will she find him again? Is she even allowed to search for him?

Or must she wait for events to come full circle, as the Irish have always known they do—and which they made certain that future generations would perceive when they placed a Celtic circle of wholeness around the symbol that connects spirit and matter.

In this conclusion of the *Twin Flames of Éire Trilogy,* Debbie and her beloved Jeremy are assisted by the Ancients in the person of Masters Saint Germain, K. H., and others of the Great White Brotherhood—their elder brothers and sisters of the One Light, whose story this also is.

Come, let your imagination open to the numinous realm of Éire's past where mystics have always ventured to solve the mystery of being.

Is mise le meas (Sincerely yours),
Cheryl Lafferty Eckl

P. S. At the back of the book you will find a Glossary and Irish Language Pronunciation Guide, plus a few notes about the Ancients.

Prologue

Debbie was one of the last guests to leave Glenna and Rory's wedding reception that had been held at Fibonacci's coffee shop on Long Island, New York. Their grand Irish *céilí* had been a glorious celebration, shared among family and colleagues and members of the spiritual community known as Friends of Ancient Wisdom.

She'd felt guilty about not helping the owners, Lucky and Róisín, clean up. But by the time she and her spiritual master and teacher, F. M. Bellamarre, had concluded their conversation, the work was done.

"Go on home, lass," Róisín had urged, her green eyes bright with motherly affection. "I can see that F. M. gave you plenty to think about."

"He certainly did," agreed Debbie, who had been embodied as Róisín's granddaughter and fellow seer in first-century Ireland.

"Thanks for understanding. I'll catch up with you in a day or two. My sister is expecting a large shipment of herbs at her store on Monday, so I'd best be there to help her stock the shelves."

Debbie was pensive as she drove the few blocks from the coffee shop to her sister Cyndi's health food store, called Conroy's To Your Health. She parked in the spot reserved for her behind the building, let herself in, and climbed the narrow stairs to her one-bedroom apartment above the shop where she lived simply and rent-free.

Not quite ready to retire for the night, she made herself a cup of tea from the relaxing blend she had created for the store and sat in the upholstered easy chair she considered an essential luxury. She wanted to meditate, but her thoughts were still on the Master's comments that her twin flame could be in the process of making his way to her.

Who is he? she wondered. F. M. had said she would recognize him, though he would likely not remember her. At least not for a while.

"He's a bit blind at the moment," were the Master's exact words.

Debbie was tempted to go searching on the inner for clues to the identity of her beloved, but she already knew that her seer's sight would be closed on the matter.

Instead of probing where she ought not, she settled her awareness in her heart and visualized a beam of pure light and love radiating out to her soul's other half, wherever he might be in the universe.

She did not expect her love to make contact, so she was surprised when she felt a flash of acknowledgment. An image began kindling in her heart—and a vision of an ancient past life appeared as clearly as if the scene had happened only yesterday.

One

A strange wind was blowing through Egypt and it had nothing to do with the desert breezes that signaled the beginning of The River's life-giving flood season. This wind was sinister in a way that young Meke had never felt. At least, never so strongly as now.

She was not comforted by her mother's attempt at lightheartedness or her father's determination to distract her with the board games of strategy they had played together since she was very small.

There was danger in the capital and she was aware that all of her sisters knew it. With her being the youngest of Pharaoh's daughters, they sought to protect her.

But Meke had always been an observant child. She'd learned that from her grandmother, the Dowager Queen Mother. The one who had died suddenly more than two years ago. The one who had told Meke she thought the priests who practiced the dark arts had poisoned her.

Is that what had happened? If so, who was next? Her father? Her mother? Meke knew they had enemies among the priests of the hidden god, Amun. The ones whose temples her father had closed in favor of the Sun God, Aten.

Since the loss of her grandmother, her dearest friend and closest confidante, Meke had felt lost. And now she was very afraid. She couldn't identify exactly what or whom she feared. Only that she could feel an enemy lurking, unseen, preparing to strike without warning.

Had her parents been warned? They were certainly making their own preparations, though for what, Meke couldn't be sure. Again, no one was talking to her.

"I am old enough to be included. My older sisters were already mothers by my age of fifteen," she complained to Mau-Ba, her grandmother's gorgeous black panther.

Meke had been taking care of the silky feline, who had stopped eating when her mistress died. The granddaughter had coaxed Mau-Ba back to life, though she could tell the animal's will to extend her own advanced years had not fully returned.

It would be only a matter of time before the beautiful creature slipped away from this life. But Meke had vowed to give her love and the best of care for as long as she remained.

Somehow, telling her troubles to the regal panther encouraged Meke in her resolve to be included in matters of concern to Pharaoh's family. She sought out her mother and asked the questions of the elegant Queen that had kept her youthful mind awake at night.

"Mother, what is going on? Why are there whisperings behind pillars? Why are people leaving the palace and not returning? Are we going to leave? Should I be packing?"

"Oh, my perceptive daughter. You are my brightest seer. I should have known we could not shield you." Meke's mother could not hide the concern in her cool grey eyes.

"Yes, my girl, danger is upon us. The forces that oppose us have grown bolder since the death of your grandmother. The Dowager Queen retained enormous power, even at her age. Now that she is gone, a vacuum of influence and persuasion has been created with no one to fill it."

"Are you afraid, Mother?" Meke searched her mother's refined features. Truly, she was the most beautiful woman who had ever lived. The sculptors and artisans had all said so for many years.

"I will not give in to fear, but our world is shifting, Meke, and plans must be made. Your father will not abandon his work here, and I will not leave his side. Your older sisters and their husbands are committed to staying. But, my dearest daughter, you must go."

Meke shuddered. Hadn't she always known that her fate was to leave the glittering world of Egypt that her grandfather and great-grandfather had created?

Ever since she was a small child, she'd had dreams of herself sailing on a ship—out across The Great Sea into whose vast reaches The River emptied its blue waters in the delta that spread like a giant fan.

She wanted to burst into tears. But she was Pharaoh's daughter. She would prove her maturity and her worth. She straightened her spine and focused her unusual light green eyes on her mother's face.

"When must I go, Mother?"

"We do not know, my daughter. Perhaps weeks or months yet. Be brave and learn your lessons well. You will need all of your skills and knowledge in days to come. And, yes, you should pack a bag, just in case the time arrives sooner than we expect."

"Who will escort me if you or my father or my sisters cannot?"

"That remains to be arranged, my girl. Do not fret about these things. Your father will ensure your safe passage. You know you are his treasure. He grieves to know you must leave our side, though it is for the best."

"Thank you, Mother, I am content," said Meke as she departed from the Queen's presence.

But, of course, she was not content. Who would go with her? Would *he* be the one? She breathed a prayer to Aten that her friend, the soldier Jarahnaten, might be her escort.

He was ten years her senior, a strapping young man with a muscular physique that glistened in the desert sunlight as he stood guard at the palace.

Jarahnaten also had a tender heart. It was he who helped her bring Mau-Ba around. He had a way with animals as well as with people. They had become fast friends and soon discovered they had more than a love of animals in common.

He seemed to know much about palace intrigues. He listened to what was said and was observant of people's actions. Sometimes others gossiped to him. But mostly he just knew.

"You see things, don't you, Jarahnaten?" Meke ventured one day. She focused her luminous green eyes on his dark brown ones, willing him to admit what she suspected. "You see into the next world like I do. I can tell. Your aura changes. Does mine, when I am seeing?"

"It does, my bright friend. But do not share our secret. There are spies everywhere. You must do your best to be invisible."

"Yes, I know how to do that," said Meke proudly. "Grandmother taught me."

"Good, then see that you practice. You may soon need that skill."

A shiver went up Meke's spine and she suddenly did not want this handsome soldier to leave her side. "Will you keep me safe, Jarahnaten?" she asked urgently.

"I will," he promised. "To the best of my ability, I will protect you." He prayed to Aten that his best would be enough.

Less than two weeks later, Meke was crying herself to sleep in the loneliness of her private chamber. She had known the end of Mau-Ba's life was fast approaching. But, still, she had not been ready for the panther to fail to rise that morning from the foot of her bed where the magnificent animal had been sleeping.

The night before had been chilly, so Meke had wrapped a coverlet around the sleek black body that had grown terribly thin in only a few days. At her gentle touch, Mau-Ba had purred softly and looked up into Meke's face with her deep emerald eyes as if to say thank you.

In that moment, the princess had not dared to let herself realize that the panther was also saying good-bye. She knew it now.

Of course, the process was part of Nature's eternal cycles of birthing, growing, and dying. Meke understood that. She lived in a culture that depended on the annual flooding of The River for its sustenance.

Yet losing Mau-Ba was like losing her grandmother all over again. She was overwhelmed with grief and wept until sleep overtook her.

She had not bothered to undress, which was fortunate. The night was moonless and silent when she awoke with a hand on her shoulder and another covering her mouth, lest she cry out.

"Meke, do not speak," commanded a male voice in a whisper. "It's me, Jarahnaten. Be as quiet as you can. Get up and come with me. Bring your bag. We are leaving now. Make haste!"

Pharaoh's daughter rose up in an instant.

"My parents? My sisters?" She mouthed to her guard as she slipped on a cloak and left the chamber in her bare feet, carrying her sandals.

Jarahnaten held the small bag she had packed with a few belongings.

"They sent me for you. There is no time for farewells, Meke. Come with me. Now!"

His hand was strong and sure, but somehow gentle on her arm as he led her through a back corridor of the palace. As if by magic—her mother's magic, Meke was certain of that—they slipped out into the dark of night. Jarahnaten's inner sight and his soldier's sense guided them to a waiting vessel moored at a relatively unused quay on The River.

"Are you coming, too?" Meke was terrified his answer would be no. *Please, Aten*, she prayed in her heart. *Do not let him abandon me.*

"I will be with you, my dear Meke. We are meant for each other. I will not leave you, ever." He wrapped his cloak around her slim young body and held her close.

"Thank you," she sighed wearily and nestled against the warmth of his chest, which was more familiar than she had expected. She looked up into his dark brown eyes, searching for answers. "Can you tell me where we are going?"

"Far to the West," he replied as he led her to the cabin where they would be sheltered from the elements. "To a land that is misty and green, so I have been told."

"How I wish my family were on this ship with us." The ache in Meke's heart was almost more than she could bear, and she wept again for all the losses that had come upon her young life. And she feared for the fate of her loved ones who knew that fighting for the cause of the One God was worth the sacrifice they would surely be asked to make.

"I know, my sweet Meke." Jarahnaten stroked her hair and did his best to comfort her.

In the safety of her protector's strong embrace, Pharaoh's daughter willed herself to dream hopeful images of where she would awaken, and eventually drifted off to sleep.

Two

Debbie was wide awake now, her imagination sparked by the fear and sorrow she felt from her former self, Meke, and excited by the comforting love of Jarahnaten. She was certain this vision of a past life was showing her the man who was her twin flame.

She had seen snippets of their escape from Egypt before, but never with this much detail. She had a feeling that not even in her lifetime as Dearbhla, the first-century Irish seer, had she been so aware of her Egyptian past as she was now. It was almost as if the full memory had been sealed until she possessed the spiritual tools to transmute the record.

Debbie had always known she was a mystic. Even as a child she'd had a foot in the world of the unseen. She was fortunate to have been born into a family with seers in earlier generations. And now she was blessed to have a true friend in Róisín, a master seer who was acting as her mentor and as a second mother, since both of Debbie's parents had passed away when she was still in her teens.

Róisín often reminded her that not all is revealed at once—even to the most gifted clairvoyants. "When you are guided by the voice of your own inner teacher, you will perceive what you need to know when that perception is important for your soul development. Pray for divine illumination, my girl, not for gifts beyond your capacity to use them wisely."

Debbie agreed that the mystical laws of clairvoyance seemed to operate on a "need-to-know" basis. So what was it that she needed to know? She would have to ask Róisín her opinion the next time they saw each other.

When her parents were alive, she might have asked them. Neither of them was a seer, but they did have keen intuition. When Debbie used to perceive other realms as a child, they had taken a common-sense approach to her clairvoyance.

"Seeing has its challenges as well as its rewards," her father had told her. Fortunately, he'd made certain that his daughter knew how to protect her vision from negative or frightening images by praying to Archangel Michael. And her mother had taught her siblings, who did not have second sight, to respect their sister's special ability, even if they did not understand it.

Her sister Cyndi had come the closest to appreciating Debbie's gift. They were the nearest in age and shared many interests. In fact, those mutual interests had led to Debbie's first meeting with her teacher, F. M. Bellamarre.

With these memories on her heart, she decided to make another cup of tea and give herself up to recollection until she could finally sleep.

"I wish I could go with you to the Botanical Gardens today," Cyndi lamented one especially fine Sunday in July two summers earlier. "But I can't stop sneezing. Besides, I know you want to sit by the river and commune with your invisible friends. I would just be in your way."

Cyndi was right. Debbie really did want to spend time alone in the old growth forest that shelters the Bronx River.

"Thanks for understanding, Sis. I'll stop by the garden center on my way home. If they have any fresh herbs, I'll pick them up."

At the time, Debbie was still working for the powerful Manhattan politician, A. B. Ryan. But on weekends she liked to help her sister by making tinctures and essential oil blends for their personal use and for sale at Cyndi's health food store called Conroy's To Your Health.

Today Debbie was feeling an incredibly strong prompting that she should sit by the river to calm her mind. Working for A. B. Ryan was becoming increasingly difficult and she needed some inner guidance.

She felt certain that allowing herself to ease into Nature's healing rhythms and fragrances would provide that guidance. And she was quite sure the nature spirits would come out to play in the sun that dappled the river bank where it shone through the trees.

The Gardens were busy on this Sunday, and the shaded walking trails that wound through the forest were filled with individuals and groups as diverse as New York itself. Debbie accompanied them for a while and then made her way to her favorite meditation spot that no one but the most frequent visitors knew about.

As she eased down a slope where she could sit next to the river, the laughter of children and adults faded into the background. Totally alone now, she felt her body melt into the sounds of peacefully flowing water. A gentle breeze fluttered the leaves of enormous trees that made a lush canopy above her. Birdsong filled the air with their joyful trills.

Soon she was treated to the antics of the elementals her sister knew she could see. A group of gnomes was playing tag on the river bank. Undines were splashing gaily in the rills and ripples created by rock outcroppings which the river had carved into artistic shapes.

Debbie felt herself soothed by the sylphs who were making leaf music in the upper tree branches. And to her absolute delight, her favorite tree devas (whom she closely resembled) made an appearance, their tall willowy forms elegant as they stood serenely by, watching the activity of their fellow nature spirits.

She was deep into a meditative state, relishing this communion with the unseen world that was truly one of the rewards of her gift, when she detected the approach of an unusual presence that felt divine.

However, when she turned to her right she observed only a man in his mid-forties standing a few yards away. He was dressed for the heat of the day and was making use of a finely carved walking stick. His light brown hair, beard, and mustache were expertly trimmed and showed flecks of red and gold that glistened in the sunlight.

Most remarkable were the man's violet eyes. They sparkled when he smiled and conveyed to Debbie a vibration of refined congeniality.

For a moment, she was disappointed that her reverie should be disturbed, as she was certain her elemental friends would hide until this stranger continued on his way. But when she glanced back to her left, she was astonished to see that all of them had turned toward the mysterious visitor.

The undines were not splashing, the sylphs had ceased whispering through tree branches, and the devas were standing in an attitude of reverence. The gnomes doffed their little hats and stood with their heads bowed. As Debbie watched, each one of the nature spirits gave honor to the man in the way most appropriate to their evolution.

"Thank you, friends," he said and returned their deference with a bow of his own. "Please, do not let me disturb your play."

His voice was cheerful and rang with a sort of musical quality that Debbie had encountered on occasion when she'd been in the presence of angels or other spirit beings.

"I see that we share a mutual intention for our afternoon," said the man, addressing her amiably as he strolled over to where she had risen to her feet. "The joy of nature spirits who are free in their own element is inspiring to experience, is it not?"

"Yes, it is." Debbie found herself as intrigued in observing this visitor as she had been in watching the elementals. He did not seem to mind her attention.

"Allow me to introduce myself," he said, smiling again in a way that warmed her heart. "F. M. Bellamarre, at your service."

With a graceful gesture, he produced a business card that was printed on expensive ivory stock with a *fleur-de-lys* design embossed in dark purple ink. On the front she read:

F. M. Bellamarre, A., M. C.

"My name is Debbie Conroy." She offered her hand which he shook with an appropriate amount of firmness. As he was obviously a cultured person, this did not surprise her. What did surprise her was the feeling of a subtle electrical current that shimmered up her arm and lodged in her heart with a tingle that did not cease when they released hands.

For a moment she forgot everything but that sensation. Then she found her voice and managed to ask with the respect he obviously deserved, "I am not familiar with the initials after your name, Sir. Are you in the medical profession, perhaps?"

"As it happens, I am very interested in matters of health on all levels of body, mind, and spirit," he responded affably. "However, these days I am 'Alchemist, Master of Community'. And, please, call me F. M. May I join you as we watch and listen to our elemental friends?"

"Yes, please do," said Debbie. She smiled to see that F. M. had brought a square of water-proof material on which to sit, just as she always did. Whatever else he might be, she felt they were somehow birds of a feather.

Although she wanted to know what it meant to be a Master of Community, she was quiet for a while, as she could sense that her new companion was contemplating the beauty of the day.

She did the same—it was easy in this restful atmosphere—and remained silent until a family of mallard ducks floated past. When the females quacked their own greeting to F. M., he acknowledged them with a wave and a generous smile, and then turned to Debbie.

"This setting always reminds me of Ireland," he commented.

Somewhat surprised, she agreed. "I was there once and have always wanted to return. The land, the people, and their hospitality felt like my soul's home. Sometimes I have such a longing—I can't really explain it."

"I understand," said F. M. with comfort in his voice. "The soul yearns to go where the veil between worlds is thin, and Éire is such a place. And now would you like to know what it means to be an Alchemist, Master of Community and why I made a point of finding you today?"

"You made a point of finding me?"

"I did. You see I am in the early stages of an experiment in what you might call 'soul alchemy'. I am creating a community of individuals who, whether they realize it or not, are on a spiritual path. As you are a soul who is aware of living in both the unseen and the seen, you are one of my first contacts."

Debbie's eyes were wide in amazement, and yet something deep inside her said that she'd been expecting this encounter.

"We are calling our community the Friends of Ancient Wisdom," F. M. explained, "for we know we have been associates in all manner of relationships through many embodiments in many different eras. What bonds us is the love of the Divine that lives in each one's heart, and also our determination that the wisdom of great golden ages should be known to and practiced by more than a few adepts."

"That sounds marvelous!" exclaimed Debbie. "I've always believed that the knowledge of the ancients should be brought forward to modern times, but I had no idea it could actually happen."

"So, you are interested in joining us?"

"Yes!"

"Then let me invite you to one of our gatherings. On the back of my card you will see an address on Long Island. We meet at seven o'clock on Saturday nights at a bookstore and coffee shop called Fibonacci's, recently opened by my associates, Lucky and Róisín O'Connor. They are delightful people who possess considerable insight and wisdom. Róisín is an accomplished seer and someone from whom you may learn many valuable lessons."

When Debbie turned over F. M.'s card, her hand went to her heart. "This is very close to my sister's health food store. I'm surprised I've never seen it."

"Everything in its time," said F. M., his violet eyes twinkling. "And now I must leave you, my dear. I look forward to seeing you again very soon. Enjoy the rest of your afternoon."

They stood together and shook hands once more. Debbie had meant to watch her new friend depart, but her attention was drawn to the mallard duck family who were quacking at the undines splashing around them. When she looked back along the river bank to observe where F. M. would likely still be walking, he was nowhere in sight.

And here we are, a little over two years later, Debbie mused as she climbed back into bed. Many mystics had gathered and mysteries had been revealed since that first sunny meeting with F. M. Bellamarre, whom she now also knew as the Ascended Master Saint Germain.

Clearly, she and the other Friends of Ancient Wisdom were far from finished with the Master's experiment in soul alchemy, she thought as she drifted off to sleep. In fact, she had a feeling the biggest mysteries of her life were only beginning to unfold.

Three

Monday was an unusually busy day at Fibonacci's Tea Merchants and Coffee Roasters. Even more so for Lucky because of the message he had received from F. M Bellamarre in the morning and the astonishing registered letter that had arrived in the afternoon.

"Róisín, darlin', will you help me gather the Friends? I know we were all together on Saturday, but we need to have a meeting. You and me, Kevin and Sarah, and Debbie. Invite Glenna and Rory, too, if they're still in town."

"They are, yes."

"No honeymoon?"

"No money, they told me. Besides, Rory's never been to New York City. They're staying with her parents in New Jersey so they can go into Manhattan every few days. They've lots to see. And they have to find a place to live on their own. Probably out here since Kevin has asked Rory to manage the bookstore and help develop his academy."

"Good. Ask them all to be here at five o'clock if possible. I know Sarah puts her babies to bed early."

"You look worried, darlin'. What is it?"

Lucky handed her the letter. When Róisín started to read, her hand went to her throat. The color drained from her face.

"I can't believe my eyes. Surely this is some kind of trick."

"That's what I want to discuss with our team. This affects all of us. We'll say no more until they're all here."

"I've no words. But I will give the matter some thought."

"Thank you, darlin'." Lucky wrapped his arms around his wife of thirty years, the soul who was not his twin, though she had been his mate and partner for more lifetimes than either of them cared to count.

She looked up into his bright blue eyes. "Does it seem to you that our tests are becoming more complex?"

"It does. We're all being called to step up our attunement and our mastery. 'The game's afoot,' as F. M. likes to say. I wonder how we're meant to play this one."

Fibonacci's coffee shop was normally closed on Monday after lunchtime, so having a private late afternoon meeting at one of the library tables was no inconvenience. Debbie and Róisín had brewed a large pot of tea with herbs meant to enhance clear thinking, and there was fresh apple cake sliced for anyone who needed a nibble.

The Friends of Ancient Wisdom talked easily together and waited for Lucky to begin their meeting. We are so like a family, observed Sarah as she fed her baby Gareth a bottle. Glenna was feeding his twin, Naimh, a look of bliss on her face.

"Glenna, is your baby light going on?" Debbie teased her friend.

"What? Goodness, no. Not yet. Let me get used to being married first." She turned to Rory, who was seated next to her. He looked up from gazing at the tiny bundle in his wife's arms and gave her a sly smile. He was obviously quite taken with the baby girl.

"Lucky, are you stalling?" asked Kevin. The man seemed to be taking longer than usual to drink his tea and sample some of the apple cake, which he rarely ate.

"Guilty." Lucky brushed a few crumbs from his shirt and drew a deep breath. "Right. First the pleasant news. We're going to have a party." A few exclamations went up from the group.

"We just had a party," laughed Sarah. "Are you planning another céilí so soon? Is somebody else getting married? Debbie?"

"Don't look at me. I just turned down a proposal."

"What? Who?" Sarah asked as she smoothly shifted Gareth to her shoulder to burp him.

"Craig," admitted Debbie. "I didn't mean to say anything. He proposed on Saturday night and I politely declined. Sorry Rory."

"That's all right. I wouldn't recommend your marrying him, either, even if he is my brother." Rory grinned and they all laughed.

Lucky explained. "No weddings or *céilís*. F. M. wants us to hold a costume ball for *Samhaim*, upstairs in the ballroom."

"How exciting!" Glenna clapped her hands. "I've been to several Hallowe'en costume parties but never one with a Celtic New Year's theme. What is F. M.'s purpose? Did he tell you?"

"He said he has a surprise in mind and, with him, there's always a spiritual aspect. He wants all of the Friends to attend. Everyone is supposed to dress as a past embodiment where they manifested the greatest mastery. Or they can choose to come as an angel, master, fairy, or other spirit being. We'll make it a true pot luck, so people can bring whatever food they want to share."

"Sounds like a grand time," commented Róisín, "and no small amount of work to organize everybody."

"I'll do it. I'm a really good organizer," offered Glenna, her eyes bright with enthusiasm. She was tentatively patting Naimh on the back and giggled when the baby rewarded her efforts with a mighty burp.

"Good work," congratulated Kevin with a wink at Rory. "Don't say you're not ready for motherhood, Glenna. You've got the knack."

She wrinkled her nose at him. "As I was saying, I'm a really good organizer. Once Rory starts working with Lucky and Kevin, I'll be the only one here without a job. After years on Broadway, costumes are right up my alley. I might be able to borrow some, or at least get reduced rental rates from one or two of the costume shops in Manhattan. I know most of the folks who run those businesses."

"That's grand, *a chara*," said Lucky. "Let's meet soon and come up with a plan."

Glenna was beaming. "Thank you for letting me help. After being part of theatre companies for most of my life and meeting the Friends of Ancient Wisdom in Dublin, I'm eager to become an active member of the community here. You have no idea what this means to me."

"We're delighted to have you join us," said Sarah, and the other women nodded in agreement. However, Róisín noticed that Debbie had gone strangely quiet. What had disturbed the lass? she wondered. A question for another time.

"What else, Lucky?" urged Kevin. "Your brow has worry lines I've never seen before." He laid a hand on the big Irishman's shoulder.

"There's no way to introduce this matter except to read you the letter I received this afternoon by registered mail."

Lucky held up the single sheet of stationery. Everyone leaned in to get a closer look and gasped. "As you can see, the letter is written on official letterhead from Ryan Investments, Inc. and is signed by A. B. Ryan."

"What does he want?" said Kevin through gritted teeth. "I suppose trying to seduce Sarah, stabbing me, attempting to destroy the souls of Glenna and Rory, and stealing Fibonacci's is not enough."

Now it was Lucky's turn to console his friend with a hand on his shoulder. "Listen while I read. You wouldn't believe this if I told you."

"To: Lúcháir M. O'Connor . . ." The sound of snickers caused him to look up at several pairs of mirth-filled eyes.

"Yes, my name is Lúcháir. It means 'welcoming joy.' I have four older sisters. My mother was ecstatic to have finally produced a son so she could stop having babies. They were old-country, mind you. My father would have a son or know the reason why not. My mother considered me a gift from heaven." He rolled his eyes. "May I continue?"

"Yes, darlin', go ahead." Róisín patted him on the knee.

To: Lúcháir M. O'Connor
Fibonacci's Tea Merchants and Coffee Roasters
Dear Lucky:

Being a man of action like yourself, I will come right to the point. I know we have had our differences in the past. I think it's time we let bygones be bygones and come to a mutually satisfactory arrangement.

My sources tell me that the historical landmark status you are requesting cannot be granted. This is not my doing. The buildings don't meet the requirements.

I have an iron-clad deal with the owner of the other portions of the block your businesses occupy. You are the only hold-out, which means I could squeeze you if I wanted.

However, rather than lowering my offer, I am prepared to raise it by ten thousand dollars and give you up to six months to relocate.

I feel this is more than a fair offer. My attorney and I look forward to negotiating exact terms with you.

(signed) A. B. Ryan

Stunned faces stared at Lucky when he finished reading.

"This must be a trick." Kevin uttered what most were thinking. "I wouldn't trust that man as far as I could throw my SUV, even if he did limp away after Rory pierced him with a sword a few weeks ago."

"Fair play to you on that score, my brother," said Rory. The memory was still fresh of how his friends had descended to the astral plane in their etheric bodies as the druids Ah-Lahn and Alana to free him and Glenna from the murderous intent of A. B. Ryan in his guise as Arán Bán.

"Do you suppose he's been that significantly weakened that he's lost the power to harm us?" asked Sarah. "F. M. did say that our combined efforts on the inner had greatly diminished him."

"My only response to that has to do with leopards and spots," said Kevin grimly. "I'd rather not put any of us in a relationship with A. B. Ryan—financial or otherwise. I wish your brother could swoop in with a better offer, Sarah."

"Can't he? I know he's got the capital."

"No, A. B. is right when he says he's got an iron-clad deal with the owner of the block we're in," explained Lucky. "If he wanted to, he could squeeze us out of every cent Fibonacci's is worth."

He turned to his wife. "Róisín, darlin', you haven't spoken. What are you seeing? Anything?"

"I feel the hand of the Master at work here," she began. Her eyes were focused and thoughtful. "I can't tell you much except that I get the sense he's playing an intricate game of strategy. A bit like six-dimensional chess, if you can imagine. I know he can't tell us what to do. We're all players in this match and we must exercise our best discernment to make our choices."

She thought for a minute, then brightened with inspiration.

"Lucky, darlin', I think we should go upstairs and hold a service. Will you lead us? Once we invoke the guidance of *An Síoraí*, the Eternal One, I feel certain we'll know what to do."

"Perfect," he agreed. "Of course I'll lead us. Let's take a break and meet upstairs in ten minutes."

"Sarah, are you all right with the babies?" asked Róisín as she picked up empty tea cups and handed them to Debbie, who was clearing dishes.

"They're fine. I've noticed they have a way of arranging themselves to be asleep while we're doing spiritual work so they can participate in their finer bodies. They even managed to not be born until Ah-Lahn and Alana had finished rescuing Glenna and Rory from Arán Bán. They're not letting a small factor like infant bodies deter them from being a part of our mission for twin flames. I'm quite in awe, really."

Kevin was following Rory up the stairs to help Lucky prepare for their service. He clapped his friend on the shoulder as they entered the ballroom and said with a grin, "Straight into the fire, eh Rory?"

"Just like old times," laughed his druid brother. He turned to his wife who had followed them up the stairs. "This is how Ah-Lahn and I spent many an hour with Master Druid Óengus in his grove. I never would have expected to be back in this kind of spiritual battle, but here we are."

"And you're loving it, aren't you, *mo chroí*?" said Glenna, kissing him on the cheek. "You were made for this, Rory."

"Well, minus actually being captured and tortured by an evil druid, yes, I believe I was made for this fight."

Four

Róisín and Sarah were taking the babies and their gear upstairs on the elevator, so Debbie was the last one of the group to make her way to the ballroom.

One thing she profoundly appreciated about her Friends of Ancient Wisdom, she mused as she climbed the stairs, was their respect for one another's silences. She knew they had noticed that she'd gone quiet after Lucky's announcement of the costume ball, but they'd said nothing.

She had mixed feelings about this *Samhain* celebration. Of course, she would dress as Dearbhla, her first-century Irish incarnation. She had indeed been masterful in that lifetime—a prophetess as well as a seer and healer. But she wasn't certain she wanted to be reminded of all that had taken place at *Samhain* during the year of her most accurate and disturbing prophecy.

Dearbhla had not married. Like now, Debbie reflected ruefully. But she had been privileged to guide many apprentices from youth into their own mature vocations in the healing or seeing arts.

She had grieved over the death of her dear friend, Ah-Lahn, and had watched in dismay as her community floundered without his leadership. It had eventually righted itself, though not without many changes.

Although her niece, Alana, had gone to study with the master druid affectionately known as Uncle Óengus, Dearbhla had not been without emotional support. Some of her female apprentices remained with her, and Madwyn, the young male seer, had become her most able assistant well before he reached his own majority.

"I will not leave you, Dearbhla," he had vowed. He'd kept his promise and had cared for her in her dotage. She had died in his arms, his dark brown eyes filling when she reached up to brush a lock of hair from his brow. Her strength had failed in that last gesture, and he'd held that loving hand in his own until she took her final breath.

All of these recollections rushed through Debbie's mind as she joined her friends in a single row of chairs in front of the altar. Lucky lit the tapers in the standing spiral candelabra, signaling that he was ready to begin their ritual with an invocation.

O great beings and powers of Light. Beloved An Síoraí, the Eternal One, we call to you to send forth rays of illumination this night. Guide and guard us, we pray. Illumine us each one. Blaze your dazzling light rays into our hearts and minds, and show us the way to go.

Lucky immediately sounded the OM and all joined in as they had so many times in the past. Accustomed as they were to these rituals, they kept the chant going until a very high resonance was reached.

The future of Fibonacci's was important to all of them, the meaning of that future unique to each. They individually felt a particular attachment to the community, which was one of the main reasons for the existence of the coffee shop and bookstore.

As they poured their devotion, their hopes and dreams into the chants and mantras that Lucky led tonight with extraordinary fervor, they said their personal prayers for the positive outcome each one's heart desired for themselves and for the good of all.

What is my place in the community and where would I go if it were not here? Debbie wondered as she chanted. *Ireland,* came the immediate answer from her inner voice. She knew that was true, but tonight was not the time to entertain leaving when remaining and fighting for this outpost of the Great White Brotherhood was the need of the hour.

Lucky had taken a chair at the end of their row so that Debbie was seated directly across from the golden sun disc above the altar. As she and her friends chanted in exquisite harmony the ancient words that Ascended Master Saint Germain had taught them, she found her gaze transfixed by the presence of the face at the center of the disc. It appeared more distinct tonight than she had noticed in previous services.

The vibration in the room continued to grow more luminous. Her concentration deepened until she felt her soul rise out of her physical body and she stepped into the orb of golden light that had formed in front of the sun disc.

Without effort, she was transported to a land that glowed like a sunbeam. Everywhere was light, light, light. Scintillating, vibrating with a soundless sound of unconditional love and peace and joy, and with the power of Divine Wisdom's pure knowing.

She was bathed in illumination's golden light. She knew herself in her mastery. Not only was she wise, she was compassionate and strong. She had achieved that wholeness through many lifetimes of service and devotion to cosmic purpose.

As she walked in fields of gold, she suddenly felt the overwhelming power of a magnetic attraction that sent her running to greet the one she had longed for, the twin of her soul, the other half of herself she had yearned to reconnect with for eternity.

Yes, they had been together in many relationships. As friend, lover, companion on the path, parent, child, sibling. But their togetherness had never lasted. Always there had been cause for separation. They had never found the key to overcoming the external forces that opposed their oneness or the personal karma that kept them out of harmony.

But here, now, in this glorious golden etheric land their reunion had been achieved. They were united as they had not been since the beginning of their sojourn in the planes of matter. The same, yet different, for they each brought their individual wholeness to the final wedding of their souls.

"I will never leave you," he vowed.

"Nor I, you," she responded. "For we live in one another."

They joined hands amidst the radiation so intense they were nearly invisible. She reached up to brush a lock of hair that had fallen across his forehead. But, in that moment, his figure dissolved from her sight and the vision faded.

Debbie held her heart as she found herself once more in her seat in the ballroom, chanting with her dearest friends. Had she seen for the first time a prophecy of what might come to pass? Or had she experienced this vision of unity with her soul's other half many times between embodiments when they were shown what all twin flames were meant to accomplish? In this moment, she could not know the answer, so she willed herself to bring her attention back to the ritual at hand.

The manifestations of light that she and her friends were invoking by the power of sound had built to an incredible level of resonance, as if myriad spirit beings were reinforcing the discernment required for them to make the right decision.

The sun disc behind the altar glowed with a magnificent radiance until, with a great flash, the room filled with a stunning white light that filled the auras of the seven adults and two infants who remained peacefully asleep in their stroller.

Everyone sat in silence for several minutes, absorbing the answer that had come to them. At Lucky's signal, they stood and formed a circle, clasping hands and facing into the center. Solemn eyes looked intently from one trusted companion to the next, searching for the unity of purpose that could only be perceived with the heart. At last, they declared as a single, resolute voice, "We sell."

They squeezed hands around the circle to seal their decision. Lucky said a prayer for the sealing of the light energy they had invoked and extinguished the candles. Then he returned to the circle to stand with his friends.

United more deeply now in body, mind, and spirit than they had ever been, they bowed their heads and brought their hands to their hearts in the sign of *Namaste—the Light in me honors the Light in you.*

Never had that meaning been more appropriate.

Quietly, the group made their way downstairs and gathered once more in the coffee shop. When they were together, Kevin gently broke the silence.

"Tomorrow morning I'll call Sarah's brother, Brian. He's been looking to purchase a building in this area for the expansion of his computer business. We had already spoken about the possibility of relocating Fibonacci's, if he found a property large enough. I'm certain that with the guidance of the Brotherhood we can find an even better home for the Friends of Ancient Wisdom in New York."

"And perhaps Conroy's To Your Health can be part of the equation," offered Debbie. She was surprised that she could utter a word after the vision she had experienced. "My sister's lease expires in six months."

"'Tis a grand idea to have both Conroy sisters under one roof," said Lucky.

Debbie smiled gratefully, but spoke no further as the meeting concluded and the Friends all went home. However, her mind was full of thoughts as she made her way to her tiny apartment and prepared for bed.

"He must be getting closer," she said aloud, feeling a deep longing to reconnect in the physical with her soul's other half.

He is near, declared her inner voice, prompting her to focus her attention on her heart and send out a beam of love and the brilliant golden light of illumination she knew was still scintillating in her aura.

She waited, expectantly. Nothing came, no response. And then she heard him—her twin flame:

My soul is trying to reach you, my love. Wait for me. Pray for me. I am trying, my darling. Do not give up hope. Keep sending me love and light, and I will follow that ray home to your heart where I have always lived. You will know me. Help me to know you, and I will remain with you forever. I promise.

Five

Jeremy was exhausted. And it was only Monday evening. Seven o'clock to be exact, though with September days growing shorter, it could have been later.

He had stretched out his tall, lanky body on his sofa, feet on the coffee table, tie off, shirt open at the throat, sleeves rolled up, hands behind his head. A lock of dark brown hair fell across his forehead.

Chinese take-out or Italian? That was the only decision he was prepared to make at this moment. Tonight he needed somebody else to cook dinner. He sighed and closed his eyes. He just needed to rest here for a few minutes until he had the energy to dial for food.

Work had been brutal. Ever since CEO Hildy Gleeson had fired Greta Nordemann from the financial services company that Greta's husband, Karl, had started a dozen years ago, the organization had been steadily declining. Hell in a hand-basket, for sure.

What is hell in a hand-basket? Jeremy wondered darkly. He had no idea. What he did know was that his career as a financial consultant was well on its way to purgatory.

He was at a cliff edge with no easy answers. Although he'd sworn he would never do so, he was wondering if he should try to contact Elder Brother—the mystical adept who had been a gentle presence in his early life. That is, until everything had gone wrong, even with that.

No, he wasn't that desperate. Not yet. But, still, he was thinking about it.

There had been little that was gentle in Jeremy's early life. Not that his parents and older sister were actually physically abusive. But they were not gentle and they were not kind.

The problem was, he was different. And in the way of family tribes, he had been made to feel his difference as an irreparable flaw, almost from the cradle. How they could have sensed in an infant that he was not like them was unfathomable. Yet they did.

Perhaps they suspected that, even as a toddler, he would be able to sense their negative inner thoughts and feelings that were reflected in their auras. And that the muddy colors and jagged, bestial images he saw there would frighten him.

If his mother, Maeve, had bothered to nurse him, he would have tasted bitterness from her breast. Instead, he'd been fed a store-bought formula that upset his delicate system. It made him colicky, which made him cry, which made him even more disagreeable to the other three, who simply looked askance at this creature who had invaded their tidy world.

Theirs was a landscape of studied material perfection built on rigid minds that prided themselves and their sullen daughter on a brittle conventionality that left no room for questions or alternate thought. Nothing ruffled the surface calm of the Madden household. Except Jeremy.

Very early in life he began to catch the drift of how things were going to go with this family. He tried to conform, to be what his mother called peaceful—what he would later call comatose. But he just couldn't seem to manage. Especially when he so easily drifted into the realm of the unseen.

By any other family's measure, he would have been considered a very imaginative and active little boy who was not unlike other gifted little boys. He was graced with a quick mind. Or, he would decide later that his quick mind was a grace. He had learned to read early. He knew his numbers and how to tell time before most kids were in preschool. That was the only thing his father approved of—his intelligence.

"The boy could amount to something if he wasn't such a terror," was the only semi-positive comment Josiah Madden ever made about his son. Never to his son. Only in reference to him as if he wasn't standing in the same room with the other two Maddens scowling at him.

Jeremy knew he wasn't a terror. But when he'd learned to talk, he'd made the mistake of assuming that everybody could see the spirit beings who came to play with him. He had excitedly told his sister who told his parents. That revelation had earned him the back of his mother's hand and his father's everlasting disdain.

By the time he was old enough to attend public school, he had accumulated a long list of offenses against the placid front the elder Maddens were determined to maintain.

Since his very presence—and perhaps his insatiable curiosity and persistence in taking apart things like toasters and land-line telephones to find out how they worked—sent Maeve into the rage she claimed she didn't have, he spent a lot of time alone in his bedroom.

That's where he'd first met Elder Brother.

One day, when Jeremy was seven years old, an unexpected visitor appeared in his room. The lad had been engrossed in a book on pyramids—one of his favorite subjects—so he hadn't heard this person enter.

"Hello, Jeremy," said the man simply. His voice was soft, his smile warm as a sunbeam, his demeanor comforting. The boy felt immediately at ease.

The visitor was dressed all in brown. His garment was a long robe with a hood that lay back on his shoulders. He had tied the robe at the waist with a piece of rope. His sandals were plain. The man's dark brown hair and beard were fairly long, but well-trimmed. He wore a sort of woolen beret on his head, but no adornments.

His appearance was so completely earth-toned that, to the child's creative mind, he might have risen straight out of the ground. Except for his eyes. Yes, they were also brown, a deep chocolate color. But they were in no way earthy. In fact, they were luminescent and focused on the boy with an expression of unconditional love that he had never experienced in this life. He wouldn't even have known what to call it.

Jeremy felt his heart flutter in his chest. He wanted to run into the man's arms and beg him to take him away from this family that was as alien to him as if he'd been born to people from another planet.

However, he'd had manners drilled into him, so he forced himself to remain seated on his bed with his book in his lap. Never mind that he was jumping up and down inside.

"Hello," he said at last. "Who are you?"

Jeremy knew this was no friend of his parents. Those people were all equally dour and disapproving. This man was the opposite. His very presence was a waterfall of good cheer and kindness.

If I'm dreaming, thought the little boy, I don't ever want to wake up.

"You may call me Elder Brother or simply Brother," replied the man in his melodious voice that was a blanket of comfort to the lad. "Have no fear. We have known each other of old. The time has come for us to renew that friendship."

"Won't you sit down, Brother," said Jeremy, remembering to be a good host. He indicated the straight-backed chair next to his bed. Then he took the risk of offending his visitor and asked, "Why are you here?"

"I believe you have questions," answered Elder Brother with a smile that would light the darkest room. "If you wish, I will do my best to answer them."

No one had ever offered to answer Jeremy's questions. He was always made to answer theirs, usually about his behavior and occasionally about his lessons, as he was a precocious student. But questions he had, indeed. About the stars, the planets, galaxies, solar systems. He especially wanted to know about pyramids and ancient civilizations.

He had often felt his mind reaching far back into the past or out to the future. Once, when his family had taken the only automobile trip he could remember to visit an aunt and uncle in upstate New York, he had spent an entire hour lying on his back on their lush, green lawn, looking up into the summertime sky, trying to see how far eternity went. He'd been so overwhelmed by the immensity he perceived that he had remained silent throughout an entire dinner hour, which pleased his mother to the extent that she had nearly smiled at him.

Others might have considered Jeremy's questions too deep or complex for a seven-year-old. But Elder Brother acted as if he expected the lad's curiosity—and encouraged it.

"Shall we set up a course of study?" asked the man after the boy had flooded him with inquiries into at least two dozen subjects.

"Yes, please." Jeremy answered eagerly. He'd leapt off his bed and for several minutes had been pacing around the room as questions tumbled out of his mouth, his thin child's legs carrying him back and forth in the excitement that his body could not contain.

Of course, he hadn't mentioned the burning question about why he was part of this family. However, by the end of his conversation with Elder Brother, he had a feeling the man knew not only the answers to the questions he had asked, but also the solution to the problems he had not voiced.

"Very good," said Elder Brother. "I will see you here tomorrow after school and we will begin. Be prepared for surprises, Jeremy. I am pleased to have made your acquaintance. Again."

"Thank you," said the lad. He offered a handshake as he'd been taught. When Elder Brother took the small, dry hand in his large, soft one with its long, elegant fingers, a tingle of sparkling energy ran up Jeremy's arm and lodged in his chest with such an intensity of genuine interest and appreciation of him as a person that he began to cry.

Embarrassed, he turned away and fished in his pocket for the tissue his mother had told him he must always carry. When he turned back to apologize to Elder Brother, the man was gone.

The adult Jeremy rarely napped after work, but his musings about Elder Brother had caused him to doze off. And the short rest had revived him.

Hoisting himself up to sitting, he pulled out his cell phone and pushed the speed dial number for The Won Ton Café. They knew him so well, they recognized his voice when he called and assumed he would want his usual order: egg drop soup, shrimp fried rice, and Kung Pao chicken. He had frozen rice milk in his freezer. That much he could manage on his own.

"Hello, Mr. Wong. . . . I'm fine. How are you and your family? . . . That's good to hear. . . . No, only one order tonight. No lady friend yet."

Mr. Wong always asked when Jeremy was going to find himself a girlfriend. They both laughed.

"Yeah, it's Monday night take-out. . . . That's right, usual order. . . . I'll pick up. . . . Twenty minutes? Okay, thanks, Mr. Wong."

Jeremy hoped a good meal would make him feel better. Not even the brisk, six-block walk back to his apartment from the MetLife building where Nordemann Financial had a branch office had cleared his head. Living in Queens had not been his first choice, but he had come to enjoy the area. It was certainly convenient to work. And Mr. Wong's family restaurant was only minutes away.

Of course, he would have ordered from them even if they'd been located across the East River. He felt that close to the Wongs.

How odd to think of your local Chinese restaurant as family, thought Jeremy. But he did. Mr. Wong treated every customer as a lifelong friend. And, for that reason, plus his really great food, many of them were.

Jeremy liked to count himself in that number.

As he changed into sweat pants and a warm jacket and prepared to walk the three blocks to The Won Ton Café, he found his thoughts returning to Elder Brother and the first incredible journey they had shared. As promised, it was thoroughly surprising and totally cosmic.

Six

The school day couldn't finish fast enough for Jeremy. He was so excited about receiving another visit from Elder Brother that he ruthlessly disciplined himself not to cause any disturbance at home or in class. He was determined that no unwelcome behavior on his part should deter the wonderful man from keeping their appointment.

Already a latch-key kid at age seven—nobody seemed the least concerned about his safety despite their living in a run-down urban neighborhood—he let himself into the family apartment. His sister always went to a girlfriend's home for a couple of hours, so he was alone until their parents returned at dinnertime—a respite from the general atmosphere of disapproval he otherwise endured.

Jeremy went to his room and waited. He was not very good at waiting. He sat on his bed. He got up from his bed. He walked around the room. He picked up a book to read, then set it back on his nightstand. He crossed to his single window and gazed out at the dirty grey brick buildings that were part of the apartment complex where the Maddens lived.

He was facing out when he felt a presence enter. He was so excited that he almost didn't want to turn around in case he was wrong that what he sensed was not Elder Brother. But, of course, he did turn to greet his visitor.

The sight before him was, indeed, a surprise.

Elder Brother was no longer dressed in brown. Today he was clad in an elegant Roman toga. Jeremy was familiar with togas from reading about ancient Rome. Senators and scholars wore the garment and theirs were often trimmed in deep borders of elaborate embroidery as was the one worn today by Elder Brother.

If Jeremy had not known his friend—yes, he was certain they were going to be the best of friends. If he had not known his friend by the light that glimmered out from his deep brown eyes, he might not have recognized him. Today the man's hair and beard were a dark russet color. He was slightly balding on top and his beard reached to the center of his chest.

He was holding the model of a pyramid in his hand and placed it on Jeremy's very tidy desk for the boy to examine. They went right to work on their first lesson.

"I suggest we begin with the pyramid," said Elder Brother. "But before we discuss this ancient structure, do you know whose appearance I have assumed today?"

Jeremy needed no time to reply. In one of his books on ancient history he had seen a portrait of the Greek philosopher, scientist, and spiritual teacher who had founded a school at Crotona, Italy, in the sixth century BC.

"You are Pythagoras," declared the lad. His friend nodded. Because Jeremy naturally followed an answer with another question, he asked, "Why have you appeared as the great teacher today?"

"The reason will become clear as we proceed," replied Elder Brother with a smile. "So I will answer your question with another. Why is the pyramid important?"

"The pyramids are important because they are some of the most ancient structures in the whole world," Jeremy answered confidently. "They are thought to have been tombs, but no mummies have been found in the Great Pyramid, so they may have had different purposes. Possibly even as energy transformers."

"Very good. I can see you have been reading more than children's books. But you did not answer what I asked." Elder Brother waited.

Jeremy's face fell. He was instantly crestfallen. Was he wrong? He could not bear to be wrong, and began to silently chastise himself.

"My dear boy, do not berate yourself. Your information is correct and more enlightened than many who have studied ancient Egypt for years. However, I asked why the pyramid—the shape, not the structure—is important. Can you tell me that? And, understand, there is no harm in saying you do not know."

Jeremy hesitated briefly, then said quietly, "No, Sir, I do not know." He had never dared utter those words in the presence of an authority figure. The very act had him quaking inside.

"Then I will tell you," said Elder Brother with a cheerful smile. "Bring a chair, my boy, and we will explore the metaphor behind the physical reality."

The two had been standing. Now they each pulled up a straight-backed chair alongside Jeremy's desk. Anyone watching the scene would have observed two eager faces leaning toward the model, a bright golden glow emanating from the tops of their heads.

"The pyramid is the measure of an enlightened man or woman's life," explained Elder Brother. "Here is the symbol of the path that those who would be wise must follow. You are very smart, Jeremy. Would you also be wise?"

The boy had never considered there was a difference. "Yes, I would. How do I do that, Sir?"

"First, you begin at the bottom. What is this shape?" He pointed to the base of the pyramid.

"A square."

"Exactly. Do you know what the square of the pyramid represents? No? I will tell you. Each side is an aspect of the human being and also of the environment in which we live. Four sides, four elements. Fire, air, water, earth. These four sides are also the four bodies of human-kind. You have an etheric body—spirit or fire. A mental body—which contains your mind. Emotions are what we call the water body. And finally, the physical, the most obvious, is earth. Do you understand?"

"I do," said Jeremy eagerly. "I have friends in all four elements, and when we play together I see myself change to look like them."

Elder Brother smiled at the lad and nodded his approval.

Jeremy was quite literally on fire with the man's acceptance. No one had ever believed him when he said he played with invisible beings of fire, air, water, and earth. He eagerly asked another question.

"What about the sides of the pyramid, Elder Brother? Each one is a triangle that connects to a side of the base. I know the triangle is the most stable physical shape. Are they related?"

"They are. And here the metaphor goes deeper. For each side of the triangle represents a quality, an essence that lives in you as a spirit spark. Follow me now. The qualities at the center of every positive endeavor, which the ancients crystallized in the pyramid form for future generations to perceive, are truth, beauty, and goodness—each balanced with the other and each resting on a firm foundation.

"If you learn nothing else from our time together, Jeremy, learn this. Here is your life's work in a single shape. As you perfect yourself—no, my boy, do not shudder. I do not mean perfect as in the rigidity of your family. The soul is not perfected in matter, but in spirit. Strive to attune your mind with your heart—with the triangle of essence that abides there—and you will reach the apex. Do you understand?"

"I'm not sure, Elder Brother."

"Then you already show wisdom, my boy. For understanding the pyramid is the work of a lifetime."

Jeremy looked into the face of this amazing being whom he could see was no ordinary teacher. As he gazed, three bright plumes that looked like blue, gold, and pink feathers or flames appeared at the center of his friend's chest. Just for a moment, but long enough for the boy to remember the image forever.

"Well done, Jeremy," said Elder Brother. "Your clear seeing has earned you a reward. I recall your interest in our solar system and far beyond. Would you like to explore the Milky Way?"

"Is that possible?" The boy's eyes were wide as moons.

"It is. Take my hand and close your eyes until I tell you to open them. I am placing my other hand on your brow, which will quicken the inner sight that you already possess. Hold tight, and do not be afraid. We will return safely in time for your evening meal."

Jeremy had succeeded in forgetting many things about his childhood, including the scary images he observed with his inner sight. He had even succeeded in blocking Elder Brother from returning. But he had never forgotten his voyage to the Milky Way.

He had felt his friend's hand holding his and a light touch on his brow. Mindful that he wanted to obey the man who was now his teacher, he had kept his eyes tightly shut until he heard Elder Brother's gentle voice say, "Open your eyes, Jeremy, and keep hold of my hand."

Astonished beyond questioning, he would not have dared let go of the hand that held him as he and Elder Brother glided among the stars. Galaxies upon galaxies. Star systems. Spiraling nebula. A million colors and variations of brightness. They avoided black holes and ventured deep into the orbits of unknown planets.

Jeremy had seen photos from the Hubble Space Telescope and had wondered what it would be like to be a space traveler. Now he was one.

However, what amazed him even more than the sights he expected to see was the feeling he could not have anticipated. Here was love. Love so awesome, complete, so all-encompassing, so indescribable and so personal that Jeremy had no words.

Before this, even at his tender age, he had always had words. No more. For the first time in his life, he was speechless and at peace. He was calm in the profound silence of pure majesty and pure love. He promised himself he would always remember.

True to his word, Jeremy's friend returned him to his room in time for dinner. The boy's cheeks were wet. His eyes were glistening.

"I will leave you now," said Elder Brother. "We have covered much today. You will need time to consider what you have learned and what you would like to explore next. I have some suggestions, but those will wait for another time.

"Call to me when you are ready for your next lesson, my son. You have done very well today. Guard our communion. Not everyone will understand as you do. Until we meet again, you have my blessing."

With a serene smile, Elder Brother placed his hands on Jeremy's head. The lad could feel light energy beaming into his mind. He closed his eyes briefly. When he opened them, his friend was gone.

After receiving so much instruction in such a transcendent experience, events should have gone well for Jeremy. But, of course, they didn't. Not in the Madden household.

Though he tried not to show it at dinner, the lad was giddy. He was so filled with light that he found himself snickering at his family's responses to their day's experience. His father had received a negative review of his work. His mother was irritated about something. His sister was pouting because her girlfriend had a new dress that she coveted.

And all Jeremy could do was chuckle. If he had kept his amusement to himself, he might have escaped notice. But he didn't.

When he father complained that his discovery of a new mental disorder had been claimed by a colleague, Jeremy laughed out loud. After experiencing a loving universe, he found utterly ridiculous the whole notion of dissecting natural human behaviors into scores of illnesses to be medicated away.

"Father, did you know that the universe is made of love?" The words were out of his mouth before he realized he had spoken aloud. Three Madden faces turned to him with narrowed eyes and tightly pursed lips.

"Where did you get such an idea?" demanded Josiah.

"From Elder Brother." For some reason, Jeremy found himself unable to keep silent about his lessons and about traveling through space. It was all too wonderful. Surely, if he explained to his family they would understand him at last, and they could all be happy together. That was his other mistake.

"And who is this 'elder brother'?" His mother's voice was shrill. "Have you let a stranger into the apartment while we were gone?"

"He's not a stranger, Mother. He's my friend, a wise man. He's teaching me about pyramids and star systems and all kinds of things."

Josiah Madden shot up from the table in horror. "Jeremiah! Go to your room this instant!" he shouted. "You! Do the dishes!" He stabbed a menacing finger at his daughter, who cowered in her chair at the dining table.

"Come with me!" He commanded his wife and stomped off to his den where he and Jeremy's mother put what they considered to be their very knowledgeable heads together.

Clearly, their boy had suffered a psychotic break. Given his persistently erratic behavior, such an occurrence had always been possible. Fortunately, they told themselves, with their work as psychiatric researchers, they had access to the latest pharmaceutical interventions.

When they went to Jeremy's room and found him staring intently at the pyramid model they were not aware was in his possession, they stood momentarily stunned. Then Maeve clutched her throat and Josiah seized what he thought was a gift from a sinister stranger, smashing the model with his foot.

"You are going to the doctor, young man, first thing in the morning," he declared. "Until then, I don't want to see you or hear a sound coming from this room. Don't come out unless you're called, and then do not speak. This foolishness ends now!"

That's when they'd started giving him drugs "to keep him calm," Jeremy remembered with a shudder as he opened the door to The Won Ton Café.

He had never asked Elder Brother to return. Although the medications made him feel like cardboard inside and gave him weird dreams, they'd also made it fairly easy not to think about his friend.

Until now. Why was he remembering Elder Brother now?

It had been over fifteen years since Jeremy had summoned the courage to refuse to take any more drugs. He had long since shut off his inner sight and he'd figured out how to manage his behavior, so parents and public school teachers left him alone.

Fortunately, his mind still worked. But he wasn't sure about his heart. And he had no idea if he had a soul or if his soulless parents had driven it out of him so he could survive living with them.

Seven

Sarah and Kevin MacCauley were finishing breakfast the morning after they and the other Friends of Ancient Wisdom had agreed that Lucky would accept A. B. Ryan's offer to buy Fibonacci's.

They had spoken little when they arrived home last night. The twins had been ready for their nighttime feeding and Sarah was exhausted. Now she had a question.

"Hon, there's something I've been wanting to ask, if you have time." She was sipping the nourishing tea blend Debbie had created to support her body as she nursed two hungry babies. Such loving care from her friend never failed to touch her deeply.

"For the mother of my children, I have time." Kevin's blue-green eyes sparkled as he stroked her long auburn hair and kissed her cheek.

"It occurred to me," she began, "that since Ah-Lahn and Dearbhla grew up as friends, Ah-Lahn must have known her grandmother who was Róisín. That would have made her Alana's great-grandmother."

"That's right, he did. I did. Though not well, because I was either with Uncle Óengus or deep in my studies with Old Quinn, who was *Ceann-Druí*, Chief Druid, for Cróga and his father before him. I was his replacement when Óengus chose me over Arán Bán."

Which precipitated the conflict that ended Ah-Lahn's life, Kevin thought, but did not say. There was no need. They both knew that story.

"So was Lucky embodied as Old Quinn?" Sarah continued. "When I watched him conduct that amazing service last night, I saw him as a great master druid, though I've never put the two together until now."

"Old Quinn was surely an adept, and so is Lucky, although our friend has a lot more humor about him this time. Isn't it interesting how a soul can manifest different personalities in different embodiments?"

Sarah agreed. "That's why I didn't recognize him, even though he's in our book about our lifetime as druids. And, by the way, the book is going to print this week."

"That's great, Hon. I'm proud of you."

"Well, you helped, especially with characters like Old Quinn."

Kevin gazed into the distance and let his mind cast back to ancient Ireland. "I think he was born old in that embodiment. He was very wise and he was also very stern. Nothing got by him in Druid Council or at any other time. As a rambunctious young student of druidic mysteries, I can assure you I received my share of reprimands."

"Do you think you're going to take over for Lucky at some point?"

"I believe that is the plan." What Kevin didn't say was, "If I live long enough." He was not going to give power to that thought by speaking it aloud, but after his run-ins with Arán Bán, it was always there in the back of his mind.

Sarah noticed a look of concern on her husband's face. She never wanted to see him burdened, so she changed the subject. "Weren't you going to call Brian?"

"I texted him first thing this morning. I'm just waiting for him to call me back. He said he has some news and would be in touch later today. Gotta run now, Hon. What do you have planned for today?"

"The twins and the fur kids and I are spending the day at home. The house needs straightening after our busy weekend, and I may write a bit. I think my muse has her nose out of joint from my lack of attention. Today feels like a day for communing."

They chuckled together at the image of her muse feeling neglected, and Kevin kissed her warmly. Leaving his family, even to go to work, was always a poignant moment for him that he carried in his heart all day.

"Good idea. Will you write something for me?"

Sarah spent the morning doing housework. Unlike her novel-writing days, when domestic chores were a burden that wrenched her out of the story she was trying to capture on paper, today she recalled the first days of her marriage when she'd discovered the joy of creating a home for her and Kevin.

She cherished that gift all over again, only with deeper and wiser gratitude. She sang as she vacuumed. She recited poems to her babies as she dressed them in the outfits her mother had sent.

She talked to Hero the wolfhound and Sprite the mini-panther as she gave them each a good brushing. She explained to the twins what she was doing and told them that one day soon they would be big enough to help take care of their pets.

The morning flew by and suddenly everybody was hungry again. She knew Kevin would eat at Fibonacci's. As she nursed her babies and ate her own lunch, she listened. And she began to hear cadences of a poem.

Her muse was at work, percolating an inspiration in the back of her mind, leading it into her heart where it could flow out through her pen. The urgency of words that would not be denied was demanding her attention, lest they be lost in that flash of inspiration that can disappear like quicksilver.

She tucked Gareth and Naimh in for their nap and curled up in the upholstered easy chair in their bedroom with Hero at her feet and Sprite squeezed in between her hips and the chair's soft rolled arm.

She closed her eyes and let her breath deepen. Her body relaxed.

Gareth and Naimh. She said their names. And in her mind's eye she saw her son as a youth dressed in Elizabethan doublet and hose in shades of teal, dark green, and purple. His slouch hat sported an enormous ostrich feather. His shoes were of fine leather with buckles polished to a bright sheen.

Naimh was also elegantly clothed in a long brocade dress in the same teals and greens and purples. Her red-gold hair was caught up in a net of silver mesh. Her slippers were delicately embroidered.

"Why the elaborate costumes?" Sarah asked.

"We come finely arrayed to honor our parents," said her daughter with profound deference. "Today my brother speaks to our father. On another day I will speak to you. I've written a poem I know you'll like."

She stepped back and Gareth came forward. He looked directly at Sarah as if to remind her to write down what he was saying.

She quickly took up pen and paper.

> Ah-Lahn, my father, I begged to be your son
> To follow in your footsteps
> To learn once more from your wise heart
> To share in the love you give so freely
> To tie my soul to yours for fellowship's sake
> To stay with you and share your trials
> To walk the pilgrim's path as compatriots and friends.
> You were always the example I carried in my heart.
> Let me learn to be like you, my father,
> And I will count myself the most fortunate of sons.

Sarah's cheeks were wet when the image faded. She closed her hazel-green eyes and gave herself up to sleep until the babies awoke.

"Hello, my loves," she said when she heard them making little noises at each other and starting to whimper for her attention. "Who wants to be changed first? Gareth? Yes, *mo chroí*. Let's get you and your sister ready to greet your father when he comes home."

Their violet eyes were bright with recognition that here was their mother. They delighted her with genuine smiles while she changed them and returned their happy cooing. This was a first. She couldn't wait to tell Kevin.

Once the babies were changed and fed, she put them in their stroller in the kitchen where she could talk to them as she made an early supper.

"I have news!" called Kevin, almost before he got all the way in the door.

Hero scrambled up from the floor by the stroller where he'd been watching the twins. Already the relationship between the big dog and his tiny humans was developing. The twins were beginning to notice him when he put his head close to them or gave them a gentle "Woof!"

Kevin scratched his dog on the head and kissed Sarah deeply as she stirred soup on the stove. Then he pulled up a chair in front of the babies' stroller.

"Hello, my little ones," he said happily as he gently tickled them under their tiny chins. His blue-green eyes danced when each baby grasped a finger and held on tight. Kevin was a man in the bliss of a hundred thousand welcomes. "They recognize me, don't they?"

"They do," said Sarah cheerfully. "I have news, too, but yours first."

"I finally spoke with Brian late this afternoon. Your brother moves fast when he has a mission in mind."

"He does that. What he did he move on today?"

"He and Ivy made an offer on the house two doors down the street from us. He said the deal looks good to go through. They'll know in a couple of days if their offer has been accepted."

"Oh, that's great. Ivy told me about it last Saturday at the *céilí*. She said her twins had their lives all planned out to move here. It was only a matter of time. Determined souls, aren't they?"

"Runs in the family," said Kevin with a wink. "Brian and I talked about Fibonacci's and A. B.'s letter. He's working with a top real estate attorney here on Long Island. He'll find out all he can about A. B.'s offer."

"Good, I really hope you can stay out of that whole situation."

"Me, too. Meanwhile, your brother thinks he may have found a building to buy. You know the Carlton Block?"

"That great old white elephant on the corner of Main and Franklin? The owners have been trying to sell it for over a year. I wonder if Saint Germain has been saving it for us."

"Could be. The price has recently been lowered because the place needs work. But Brian says the bones are solid, the layout is workable for his needs, and the retail space is nearly perfect for us to relocate Fibonacci's. There's even a storefront for Debbie's sister if she wants to join us."

"That is fantastic."

"So, what's your news?"

Sarah set the soup on simmer. She pulled another chair over next to her husband and took Naimh on her lap, as the little one seemed to be uncomfortable.

Kevin picked up Gareth and was rewarded with a tiny smile.

"Did he just grin at me?"

"He did, and that's part of my news. They both started smiling today and I think there's a reason."

Before Sarah handed her husband the paper with Gareth's poem, she told him what she had seen and what their children had communicated to her. "Now you may read what your boy wants you to know."

Kevin read and re-read the lines from the soul of his son. He was silent as his eyes filled and words failed him. He set down the paper and held the infant away from him, gazing lovingly into Gareth's tiny face. The baby burbled at him and smiled again. He clasped his son to his chest and held him there until he could compose himself.

"My baby boy," he said quietly. "What a gift you are to me. As Ah-Lahn I longed for this relationship with my son, Tadhgan. As Kevin I was never close to my father.

"Now you have told me what fathers and sons are meant to be to each other. You were Ah-Lahn's aide, my boy, and a more loyal, reliable lad there never was. Our love will only grow stronger. We will learn from each other. I promise not to let you down."

Sarah softly brushed the top of her baby's head and kissed her husband on his cheek. "I remember that Gareth grieved deeply when Ah-Lahn was murdered. Have you been together since then?"

"Not that I know of. Perhaps our souls waited until we could make the most of our connection."

"And young Naimh was Gareth's sister who was apprenticed to Dearbhla. A little firecracker, as I recall. I wonder what gifts she is bringing with her this time. She promised me a poem in the future and other surprises which she wouldn't reveal."

Kevin looked into the distance and felt the quickening of his inner sight. The presence of his druid self, Ah-Lahn, came into his awareness as he spoke prophetically: "A golden future lies before us, *a ghrá*. Come what may, I feel the gift of these children portends mighty blessings ahead."

Eight

The first Friday in October dawned as one of those gloriously bright mornings that made a body want to be outside in the sunshine. Autumn colors were painting Long Island's thick stands of sycamore, oak, maple, and ash trees with the spectacular display that Debbie wished she could spend all morning absorbing.

However, she, Róisín, and Sarah had agreed to meet Glenna in the ballroom at Fibonacci's to discuss the upcoming *Samhain* costume ball. Exactly four weeks remained until the end of October, and many tasks were yet to be accomplished.

The women were pleased to support Glenna's organizational efforts, and they were eager to hear about her plans. She was learning fast, but there were details about Fibonacci's she was probably not aware of. Her success meant a lot to all of them.

Debbie had arrived early so she could sit by herself for a few minutes at the large round table that had been set up for their meeting. She was contemplative these days and needed a bit of time alone in this space that was to her profoundly sacred.

She'd always found it inspiring to walk into the vast room when no service or special event was about to take place. Even with the curtain drawn that protected the altar and the great golden sun disc above it, Debbie was aware of the radiation that remained in the room after one of the services led by Lucky, and occasionally by F. M. himself.

To her inner sight, which was growing increasingly acute, the ballroom was never really empty, and it was never quite the same from one visit to the next. On any given day, she might find herself in the company of a group of angels or other spirit beings who were holding conference or who were simply present, anchoring their light energy and etheric consciousness on behalf of a world in peril.

At exactly 10:00 a.m., she heard the laughing voices of the friends she thought of as family. She relished their time together in a way that often caused her light green eyes to mist in gratitude.

Róisín entered carrying a tray with mugs and a pot of tea to go with the cranberry muffins Debbie had brought upstairs when she arrived. Glenna held a large plastic file box in one hand and was opening the ballroom door for Sarah, who was pushing the stroller where seven-week-old Gareth and Naimh were tucked in after their mid-morning feeding.

"Thanks for accommodating the twins' schedule," said Sarah as she situated herself with the bags and various accouterments of motherhood that Debbie found amazing.

"It's the least we can do to make sure you can join us," she said. "You're becoming very agile with all of your gear."

"I have to be unless I want to stay home for the next six years," laughed Sarah. "I'm just grateful the bookstore has that tiny elevator so we can meet up here. I love being able to bring the twins into the ballroom's atmosphere, even when it's empty."

She looked over at Debbie, who nodded in agreement. They both turned to Glenna. "Are you ready for us?"

"I am. If you'd all like to be seated around the table, I can show you where we are and where we're going."

"You weren't kidding about being organized," said Debbie. Her eyes were wide in admiration of the lists and charts Glenna had laid out.

The young woman smiled playfully. "I've done some stage managing in my time in the theatre. Every production is a bit like a military campaign. You wouldn't believe the detail that goes into putting on even a simple show. Helping to create a seamless event really is a thrill."

"We're glad you're here to manage this one, *a chara*," said Róisín sincerely. "Show us what you've got and let us know how we can help."

The four women leaned in together as Glenna spread out her lists of the Friends of Ancient Wisdom along with the types of costumes she had been able to secure from her colleagues at a couple of costume rental shops in Manhattan.

"Fortunately, none of us are portraying devils, witches, vampires, gladiators, courtesans, or cavemen," joked Glenna. "Those costumes were all reserved weeks ago. I wasn't sure I could find enough togas for all of the Pythagoreans, but a small theatre in Westchester has their own stock which they said we could use *gratis*.

"I've got a decent assortment of wings for angels and fairies, so we're set there. I'm not sure how many crowns we'll need. My sense is that most members don't consider their royal embodiments as their most advanced."

"I know I don't," Sarah murmured as she comforted a fussy Gareth so he wouldn't wake his sister.

Glenna studied her friend with interest. She could feel Sarah's contentment in motherhood and wondered if she could ever be satisfied in that role. She realized she had gone silent when the other women stared at her.

"Glenna, do you have more for us?" Debbie prompted her gently.

"Sorry. Yes. I found the costumes Craig requested, though he swore me to secrecy about his choice. I haven't been able to find any gold torcs for the druids, but I'm still looking."

"This is grand," Róisín commented. "And remember, we've had *Samhain* balls in the past. None this large. We were a much smaller group then. But some of our longtime members will have their own costumes from before. Our folks are very resourceful and they love to dress up."

"Yes, I've discovered that when I've phoned people to invite them. Did you know that one of our members is a retired costume designer? When I told him about the ball, he started pumping me for details. He asked for a list of requests from other members and promised to fill as many as he could manage, which may be quite a few, considering he used to create costumes for an entire Broadway musical in the same number of weeks. From what he hinted he might be able to accomplish, the man is a genius and quite possibly a magician."

She turned back to the list of names and pointed to the ones that hadn't been checked off.

"These are the folks I haven't been able to reach. If any of you are aware of how to contact them, that would be great. I know F. M. wants everybody possible to attend. I don't want to miss a single soul."

"Róisín and I can help you with these," confirmed Debbie. "Between us we'll gather in the stragglers."

"Wonderful. That will leave me free to work on decorations."

"You know Fibonacci's has enough twinkle lights for the millennium," joked Sarah. "And we have a very willing crew of decorators to put them up."

"Super," said Glenna. "That gives me even more time to work on the bit of theatre I want to include in the festivities. We have enough singers and musicians among the Friends to start our own performing troupe. I'd like to take advantage of their talent to make this event more than a dance. I asked Lucky and he said F. M. was hoping I'd come up with something. I'm still working on the details, but I've already got a group pulled together. This is going to be so much fun!"

"Wow, I can see why audiences loved you on stage," observed Sarah.

"I agree," said Debbie. "Glenna, you're a bundle of charisma when your creative juices kick in."

"Oh, you're going to make me cry. I love you all so much and I'm just so glad to be here with you."

"Darlin', Fibonacci's wouldn't be the same without you," said Róisín. She handed Glenna a tissue and put her arm around the young woman. "Now, how else can we help you?"

"Well, let's see." Glenna dried her eyes and looked down her task lists. "Do you each have your costumes?"

"I do," answered Sarah and Debbie together. Their characters from their first-century Irish incarnation were the ones that called to them.

"What about you, Róisín?" asked Glenna. "Who are you coming as?"

"Guess," she said with mischief in her bright green eyes.

"Brigid!" The three women declared in unison.

"Aye, but the goddess or the saint who was a bishop?" Róisín challenged them.

"It must be quite a responsibility to be a bishop, much less a saint," said Glenna. "I'd rather be a goddess."

They all laughed.

"As would I," agreed Róisín. "I've been a bishop and 'tis no fun at all." She shook her head.

"Were you Saint Brigid, then?" asked Sarah.

"Oh, no, darlin'. That honor went to one of my more formidable sister nuns. And a force of spiritual fire she was, too. Imagine running a dual monastery for men and women and keeping them focused on their spiritual duties instead of each other.

"Of course, that was sixth-century Ireland before the old Roman celibates kicked out the women priests and forbade the men to marry, so things weren't as strict as they became later.

"But I can tell you, Brigid earned her sainthood in the sheer ferocity of her love for the monks and nuns. We were often terrified of her, but we loved her profoundly. We gladly did anything she asked, which was a lot, I can assure you.

"Her sermons were unforgettable. 'I'll not leave you as ignorant lambs to the slaughter!' she would cry in her ecstatic preaching. 'You must learn the wiles of the serpents, my children. Discern their crafty egos and walk the path of *An Síoraí*, the Eternal One. Tend the flame in your heart as we tend the physical flame here in Kildare. That is the way through the traps the fallen angels will set for you.' "

"Fallen angels? Really?" Glenna was incredulous. "Do you believe in such creatures?"

Róisín fixed the lass with an expression that was both direct and compassionate.

"After your run-in with Arán Bán, my girl, I am surprised you would ask that question. But yes, I do believe in such creatures. Consider what you and Rory experienced at Clonmacnoise, and then tell me if Saint Brigid wasn't right."

Debbie put her arm around Glenna as the young woman's blue eyes grew wide and her hand went to her mouth. She was silent as she remembered the ordeal. "I see," she said at last, very quietly. "I had no idea that's what was meant."

"So now you are wiser, darlin', and that wisdom cannot be taken from you," stated Róisín firmly. "It will be tried and tested, but you cannot lose that insight unless you willingly give it up."

Nine

Jeremy was stumped, and he didn't like being stumped. His quick mind could usually solve any problem he put to it. Except about himself, of course. Then he could twist that mind into a Gordian Knot of mental confusion to the point he could barely remember how to tie his shoes. When that happened, his only recourse was a trip to the library or a bookstore.

He figured today was as good as any for a mental health day. He'd finished all of his month-end reports for September. And since this was the first Friday of October, many of his fellow employees were taking the day off. With Hildy Gleeson at the helm of Nordemann Financial, mental health days were becoming a trend that Jeremy did not find surprising.

Today he chose his favorite bookstore at Union Square. Four floors of books ought to be sufficient for his needs, he chuckled to himself as he planned his expedition.

He would take the train into Grand Central and transfer from there. He'd walk a bit in the early October sun that shimmered on trees putting on their golden autumn light show. Then he'd treat himself to lunch at the café across the street from the bookstore before indulging in two or three hours of biblio-therapy. Perfect.

His usual ritual was to peruse a half-dozen titles on different topics until one sparked his particular interest. That book would often go home with him.

Today's assortment included a thick biography of Pythagoras, a fully illustrated volume on warfare in ancient Greece, a lush coffee table book on gardens of Ireland, a thin volume on the care of African violets, and one random pick: *You and Your Mini-Panther.*

He was about an hour into his ritual when he heard someone speaking to him.

"That is a fascinating collection of titles," commented an impeccably dressed man whom Jeremy had not heard approach. A quick appraisal of the stranger showed his outfit of navy blue wool trousers, tan shirt, matching tie, and herringbone sports coat to have been expertly tailored. He wore the garments with an air of casual elegance that was at once remarkable to the setting and perfectly natural to the man.

His light brown hair, beard, and mustache were neatly trimmed. His smile was both enigmatic and striking. His extraordinary violet eyes hinted at unfathomable mystery.

"Forgive the intrusion," said the man in the smooth vocal tones that spoke of a cultured background. "I am always fascinated by what others are reading. I must say, your selection is more varied than most. May I join you?"

"Please do," replied Jeremy, surprised at his uncharacteristic willingness to be interrupted.

"Thank you," said the man as he took a seat in the wingback armchair covered in burgundy fabric next to the matching one Jeremy occupied. "Allow me to introduce myself. F. M. Bellamarre, at your service."

He handed Jeremy a business card printed on expensive ivory stock with a deep purple *fleur-de-lys* embossed on the front. Following his name were the initials A., M. C.

"Jeremiah Madden." He offered his own card and extended his hand. When F. M. Bellamarre accepted the greeting, the young man was more than a little startled that a small jolt of energy traveled up his arm and continued vibrating in his chest, even after the two men separated hands.

"I don't recognize the initials after your name, Sir," said Jeremy after he collected himself. "Are you connected with one of the universities or colleges in the city? There are so many, it's hard to keep them straight."

Actually, Jeremy knew the names and locations of nearly every academic body in the New York metro area. He was making small talk while he tried to place this man who had seemed to materialize in the alcove he had chosen for its privacy.

"From time to time I have been attached to several institutions of higher learning," replied the man. "Please call me F. M."

"Jeremy is fine for me. Only my parents call me Jeremiah, and that's usually when they're disapproving of me. Which is nearly always. In fact, I don't remember them ever calling me Jeremy." And why am I telling this to a complete stranger? he wondered. "About those letters . . ."

"Ah, yes, forgive me. These days I am Alchemist, Master of Consciousness."

"That's quite a credential," remarked Jeremy. "Where did you study, if you don't mind my asking."

"Mostly abroad. London, Leipzig, Paris, Dublin, and a very fine academy in Italy. Mine has been an eclectic education. I have many interests, as I see you do, as well. May I ask a question in return?"

"Of course." Jeremy was finding this man intriguing. There was something puzzlingly familiar about him. But how could that be?

"Are you conscious, Jeremy?"

"An unusual question, but, yes, I believe so. I am certainly awake and have been since six o'clock this morning."

"Many would say the same. But are you truly awake to your outer world and, more importantly, to your inner world?"

"Actually, I am a keen observer of life," said Jeremy, mildly annoyed. "For example, I detect the hint of a British accent in your voice. Your shoes are undoubtedly Italian leather. The chairs where we are sitting have been recently re-upholstered. The leg on this coffee table is in need of repair. From the smear on the face of that little boy over there, I would guess the cookie he's eating is chocolate chip.

"His mother appears burdened. Her dress probably fit her once, but now it hangs on her thin frame. The man in the third aisle is about to steal the book he's been reading. The book covers on the shelves to our left are predominantly red and black. The couple who just walked by are wearing identical shirts under their jackets. Shall I go on?"

"No, indeed," said F. M. with an amused smile. "As you say, you are a man keenly observant of his surroundings. What can you tell me about your inner landscape?"

"Such as?"

"What details do you detect in the world of your mind and heart? What are your thoughts and feelings in this moment?"

Jeremy did not hesitate. The world of thought was the place to which he homed.

"I'm wondering if there is a purpose to this interrogation. I'm thinking that I'm ready for my afternoon cup of coffee. I wish I had picked up the book on architecture I saw earlier. I really do like your shoes." Jeremy laughed at himself. "I have many thoughts about many topics. I doubt that you want me to fill the remainder of your afternoon with them."

F. M. nodded. "No, indeed, although I observe that these thoughts are all somewhat superficial. I am wondering if perhaps there is a door to deeper awareness that you do not care to open."

Jeremy did hesitate now, suddenly wary.

"There are elements of consciousness I do not wish to explore," he said flatly. He felt irritation rising and fought to check it. He saw no reason to be rude, even if his partner in conversation was urging him into the personal depths he assiduously avoided. He changed the subject, steering the focus from himself to what he hoped was another direction.

"Do I know you, Sir? F. M., that is. I feel that we have met, though I can't think of when or how."

"We have met, Jeremy, behind that closed door you are so reluctant to open. Many years ago. You were quite young. You were in the midst of some rather remarkable space travel with a good friend of mine. He introduced us at a location far from here. I found you to be a very polite and exceptionally bright young man."

F. M. paused ever so briefly, considering. He felt the confirmation of *An Síoraí* in his heart and proceeded. "'Tis a pity your family tried to squelch your spirit. But you persevered admirably, my son, and freed yourself in the only way you knew."

Jeremy shivered and his breath hitched. He could feel the color rising in his cheeks. He clenched his hands into fists and bit his lips together in an attempt to quell the mixture of anger and fear that suddenly churned in his belly.

"Now you must free yourself again, my son," F. M. continued. "This time from the prison of your own making."

Jeremy stood abruptly and ran his hands through his hair. He knew his face was flushed. His insides were shaking. He wondered that he was able to stand, and then he wasn't. His knees buckled and he sat down hard, facing the man who was calmly turning his world inside out. He looked at F. M. with panic in his eyes. "How can you say such things to me? You don't know me. You can't know what I've told no one."

"My son, I regret the need to shock you. With defenses as firmly in place as yours, sometimes the use of what undoubtedly feels like a cosmic sledge hammer is required. Please be assured that Elder Brother and I have only your best interests at heart."

Jeremy could feel those defenses crumbling. No, they were melting. The mental barriers he had erected years ago against the intrusion of otherworldly insights were dissolving like lead in the refiner's fire.

F. M. had identified himself as an alchemist. It appeared now that merely being in the man's presence was sufficient to liquefy the persona Jeremy had spent twenty-three of his thirty years constructing, brick by determined brick.

The name Elder Brother had flipped a switch in his brain. Not that he hadn't remembered the name himself only the other day. But F. M.'s speaking it aloud echoed in the deep chambers of Jeremy's being that he had kept firmly locked up since the fateful day when his wonderful friend had taken him flying among the stars.

He slumped in his chair with his head in his hands and tried to choke back a sob. He would have been massively embarrassed, except that he and F. M. seemed to be alone, as if this strange person had drawn an invisible curtain around the alcove where they sat.

"Did you know that tears are one of transmutation's surest signs and one of its most critical elements?" F. M. was watching Jeremy as a father might hold a space of tender care for a son who is trying to maintain his dignity amid a flood of emotion.

"When we weep at times such as what you are experiencing, we dissolve old patterns that have burdened our souls. Tell me now, my son, do you not notice the sensation of being purged, perhaps even cleansed of a weight you have carried for a very long time?"

Jeremy sat up slowly and pulled a tissue from his pants pocket. He dried his eyes and was still for a moment, carefully perusing the inner territory into which he had not ventured for two decades.

At last he spoke. "I must admit that I do feel somewhat lighter."

"Excellent. And can you tell me, what is the status of that door you had so securely fastened shut?"

"I think it may be cracking open a bit." Jeremy smiled wanly. Then he had to ask, "F. M., does Elder Brother exist or was he the figment of a desperate child's imagination?"

"He was and is as real as you and I. He wants you to know that he understands why you never invited him to return and why you fiercely closed off your inner sight. However, he has never stopped watching over you and inspiring your many interests. If you should one day desire to regain your ability to see into other realms of consciousness, he is available to help you. You need only ask."

Jeremy's eyes filled again. All he could do was gaze into the vibrant and incredibly kind violet eyes of F. M. Bellamarre. Any words he might have spoken were lodged in his throat. His heart was so full of emotion he felt he would break down completely if he tried to speak.

"And now, my son, I see the hour is advancing. Before we part, I would like to invite you to a very special costume ball being held at the end of this month to celebrate the Celtic New Year's festival of *Samhain*. Are you familiar with the Irish corner holidays?"

"I am." Jeremy found he could answer a simple question. "Believe it or not, my family is Irish. You wouldn't know it from their behavior, but that's the gene pool."

"I have your card. With your permission, I will ask one of my friends to contact you with details. As a matter of fact, I believe we are mutually acquainted with Kevin MacCauley. He will be pleased to act as your host and to introduce you to a very special group known as the Friends of Ancient Wisdom."

"Yes, I know Kevin. Not well. We worked at different branches of Nordemann Financial. People were really disappointed when he was laid off. He was a balancing presence in the company, which is long gone. I'm thinking of leaving myself."

F. M. beamed a smile that warmed Jeremy to the core of his being.

"Speak with Kevin. He may have some ideas for you. And do come to our celebration."

"Thank you, F. M. I will." The younger man looked down and took a deep breath. "I'm sorry that I snarled at you."

"No offense taken, my son. I pushed you very hard. You have passed an important initiation today. Should you continue in this wise, a rich and meaningful life can be yours for the living."

The two men stood and shook hands. Jeremy meant to follow F. M.'s departure, but then he thought to check the time on his wrist watch. When he looked up, the man was gone. The aisles through which he could have passed were empty, except for a few patrons who obviously were not the alchemist who had effectively rearranged the younger man's molecules—body, mind, heart, and soul.

Jeremy was a man of his word. In fact, he considered integrity to be one of his better qualities. If he made a promise, he kept it. Especially when that promise was made to a person like F. M. Bellamarre. When Kevin phoned the next day, he answered his cell on the first ring.

"I realize we're tossing you into the deep end by inviting you to a costume ball," said Kevin with a chuckle after they had exchanged greetings. "But I think you'll enjoy yourself. Many of these folks are Irish and they know how to have a good time. The music alone will be worth your making the trip out to Long Island."

"I told F. M. I would be there, so I will," said Jeremy with only a hint of hesitation in his voice. "Only two problems. I don't have a costume and I don't have a car."

"The car's not a problem. If you don't mind a couple of transfers on the train, I can pick you up in Oyster Bay. We're not far from there. Just text me when you get close."

"Easily done, thanks."

"As far as a costume, I can have our organizer Glenna call you to toss around some ideas. She's a Broadway actress who seems to know everybody in costuming in Manhattan. I don't suppose you'd wear a toga?"

"I might, why?"

"Apparently, Glenna has enough togas for the entire cast of Julius Caesar and there's no fitting involved. We have a study group—mostly college students, though I'm hoping to start adding some adults. They've decided to call themselves 'The Pythagoreans' because we're going deep into the philosophy he taught at his school in Crotona, Italy. Anyway, they're all wearing togas for the ball."

Jeremy was quiet for long enough that Kevin wondered if the call had dropped.

"Are you there, Jeremy?"

"Oh, yeah, sorry. I was thinking about life's coincidences. I happen to be very interested in Pythagoras."

"Really? That is a coincidence. Or maybe not. With Fibonacci's and F. M. Bellamarre, I'm not sure there is such a thing as a coincidence."

"I'm beginning to see that. Can I ask you a question?"

"Sure, go ahead." Kevin's intuition sparked and he heard his inner voice: *Pay attention. This conversation is important.*

"Have you ever felt like you've lived before?"

Kevin was tempted to remark about how many lifetimes he knew he had lived, but he caught himself and responded simply.

"I have, yes. Have you?"

"Not that I recall. But just now when you mentioned Pythagoras and Crotona, a scene flashed in my mind."

"Did that bother you?" He was quite sure that it did.

"Yeah, a bit. I've read about past lives, but I'm not prepared to believe in them."

"Well, just so you know," said Kevin carefully, "reincarnation is a popular topic at Fibonacci's, but we don't push it on anybody. Especially not on our guests. I think you'll enjoy the Pythagoreans. They're philosophy students, and so far we haven't discussed past lives in that group. I'm confident you'll have some people to talk to at the party."

"That's a relief. Not knowing anybody and meeting a big crowd all at once isn't exactly my thing."

"Mine either, trust me." Kevin agreed with a congenial laugh. He was grateful to feel Jeremy relax on the other end of the line. "If you want to come out for coffee sometime before *Samhain*, I can show you around and introduce you to the owners and whoever is working that day."

"That's okay. I'm going to be busy between now and then. Possibly job hunting. Let's just say that Nordemann Financial isn't what it was when you worked there. By the time I see you at *Samhain*, I may be ready for a complete change."

"Is that a fact? Send me your résumé. I may have an idea for you."

"F. M. said you might. I'd appreciate any consideration."

"Glad to help. We're going through changes ourselves that are likely to open up some opportunities. Your meeting F. M. may turn out to be advantageous for all of us."

"That would be great."

"There is one thing—if you don't mind, I'll need to pick you up early on the day of the party. That way you can get your costume from Glenna and I can introduce you to a few people before the big crowd arrives."

"No problem." Jeremy was pleased that Kevin was so easy to talk to and more than a little surprised that he was feeling his heart open in a way he usually didn't with people he barely knew.

"And, listen," Kevin offered, "if you find that you're uncomfortable, I'll understand. Fibonacci's is located only five minutes from the Oyster Bay station. I can always run you back over there if you decide you want to leave early. There's no pressure for you to stay longer than you want."

"Thanks, Kevin, I'm grateful."

"You're welcome, Jeremy. Text me if you have any questions."

Ten

With only two weeks remaining before the big *Samhain* celebration, Debbie and Róisín were going over details for the costume ball with Glenna. As she had claimed, the lass was proving herself to be an expert event organizer. She mainly needed moral support, which her friends were pleased to provide.

They had spent the last hour upstairs in the ballroom and were now ready for a break in the coffee shop. The lunch rush was over, so they took advantage of a lull in business to claim the back booth where they could enjoy a private conversation.

"What do you remember about growing up in Ireland?" Debbie asked Róisín. "I find myself thinking about the Emerald Isle nearly every day now. Some mornings I wake up feeling as if I've been there in the night."

Róisín looked into the distance for a minute, then said, "Many little things come to mind. You'll laugh, but one of my persistent memories is of having a red neck."

"You're kidding."

"Not at all. The wool could be coarse, you see, and we all wore jumpers, that's pull-over sweaters, made by our grannies. We were the original red necks." She laughed. "Not from the sun. There wasn't much of that. But from the itch of the wool."

"That's not a very romantic image," said Glenna.

"Well, *a chara*, life in Ireland has never been as romantic as we like to think of it. Not with the English doing their best to wipe us off the face of the earth."

Róisín's color rose in a combination of grief and righteous anger over the treatment of her people which she rarely let slip into her conversation. She quickly brushed her hand across her face as if to banish the thought, and softened her tone.

"Life has never been easy for the Irish, my loves. But that's not to say it hasn't always been liminal. For there's life in the soil and magic in the stones. And the people who worked the land, like my own grandparents, carried the belief and the connection in their bodies and their souls. Shall I tell you about them?"

"Yes, do," said Debbie. "I have some time before I need to be back at work. A story would be wonderful."

"Very well, then. Once upon a time . . . and it was once upon a time, my girls, for this way of life has all but vanished. Our young people, even my own parents, have left the old ways behind. And they've lost the intelligence of Nature that the Irish kept for generations in the rural communities. Especially in the Gaeltacht where the language itself carries the sounds and rhythms of the land and the seasons."

"Did you grow up speaking Irish?" asked Glenna. "After spending time with Rory's relatives who are mostly native speakers, I really want to learn more of the language. But it's not something you easily pick up."

"That it's not," agreed Róisín. "For that reason alone, I'm glad I learned Irish from the cradle. I like to think that hearing and speaking our native tongue gave me a link to my own soul and spirit that even living here in the States for nearly thirty years hasn't weakened."

"I know what you mean," said Glenna. "There's a lilt and a grounding that carries you along and embraces you at the same time."

"And like any language, the vibration depends on who's speaking it," said Róisín warmly. "For you, a chara, Irish is a language of love spoken to you by your man and his family who adore you."

They all looked up to see Sarah walking through the curtain that separated the coffee shop from the kitchen and upstairs offices.

"May I join you? I've left the babies upstairs with Kevin and Lucky. I'd love to sit with you for a few minutes."

"Of course," said Debbie, scooting over to make room for Sarah beside her in the booth.

"When I came in you were talking about the Irish language. I heard bits of it during my writing retreat in Ireland's Ancient East near Dublin, where there's not much spoken. What I did hear took me to a place my soul knew instantly."

"It's the longing," said Debbie dreamily. Her eyes misted as she contemplated a scene that Glenna and Sarah did not see. Róisín noticed a quickening in the soul of her fellow seer.

"It's the music in the ballads and the love songs, for sure," Debbie continued. "But even the jigs and reels go straight to the heart. When I hear a bodhrán drum, my soul stirs and my entire body tingles."

"'Tis true," Róisín agreed. "And once you acknowledge the longing and your soul's yearning for Home, you never get over it. In fact, when you let your soul speak, as it will through your body, perhaps even more clearly than through your heart or your mind, the longing gets stronger."

"I feel that," said Debbie. Her light green eyes were intense as she looked into Róisín's deeper green ones. "I have such a yearning in my soul these days. And the more you work with me on my intuition, the stronger the yearning grows in my heart, my mind, *and* my soul."

"I'm pleased to hear it," acknowledged Róisín. "And I would say to each of you—pay attention to what you hear and feel in the depths of your being. Discern the vibration and choose the highest way. What Debbie is describing is what I think of as the intuitive faculty of the heart—because that's where the soul lives when it's in tune with the wise inner voice of your True Self."

"I believe that's what the Master is trying to teach us," said Sarah.

"I know it's what I need to learn," offered Glenna thoughtfully.

"We all do, darlin'," added Róisín. "As long as we're living in time and space, we will always have elements of our human consciousness to overcome."

"And I have to say that the support I feel between the four of us is a gift beyond price," said Glenna with profound sincerity.

The women spontaneously reached across the table to each other and held their hands together in the bond of spiritual sisterhood that was becoming more precious to each of them every day.

"I'm sorry that I have to go back to work soon," said Debbie reluctantly looking at her watch. "Róisín, is there any chance you could tell us about your grandparents before I need to leave?"

"Of course." Róisín eased back in the booth and lifted her eyes for a moment, remembering.

When I was a little girl I cherished every opportunity to visit my mother's parents, Granny and Grandda Nélan, on their farm in the fertile area called the Golden Vale. My parents had moved me and my siblings to Limerick town, but the countryside was where I preferred to be.

They say that second sight is usually passed from mother to daughter or from father to son. In my case, I could have inherited the ability to see from either grandparent.

Often my mother showed fine intuition. But I believe she remembered being a princess in a former life, which made growing up on a farm a bit of a come-down—though she did love the animals and made pets of every creature, except the pigs.

Her father, my Grandda, wouldn't let her name them or play with them because they were meant for sale or for the table. They didn't keep the dairy calves long enough for her to grow attached to them, so she focused her attention on the horses, cats, and baby chickens.

Once when she was a grown woman, I saw her set herself down in the middle of the hatching barn and scoop up a handful of baby chicks as if she were five years old again. The look on her face was pure bliss.

Granny was the one with powerful inner sight. You could never surprise her or hide anything from her where her family was concerned. She loved children, which was lucky as she had eight of her own and seemed to collect most of their friends and cousins who preferred her company to their own mothers.

Her greatest love was the land. She could grow anything and often said she'd rather be in the fields with her husband and three older sons than in the house with her three daughters and two younger boys.

She lived her whole life in a thatched cottage. Never had indoor plumbing and cooked at the hearth until her older boys added a kitchen for her with a wood stove several years after they'd left home.

Granny wasn't sophisticated in a worldly sense, but she was highly intelligent. She could tell you anything you needed to know about plants, home cures, the ways of animals, and the birthing of babies.

And, like I said, I also could have inherited the sight from my Grandda. He could forecast the weather by the feel of the air, the look of moon, or the color of the sunrise. He could also find water. He was what's called a water witch—a dowser.

Once when our family was visiting the farm, he took me and my mother with him to locate a well for a neighbor. He cut a fresh willow branch, with two stems growing out of one. He grasped the two and the single one was the pointer.

He made us stand several yards away. Then he walked out into the field and just stood there for several minutes. I knew he was communing with the nature spirits. He told me not to watch on the inner because my attention could interfere with what those spirits were telling him. If they detected me, they wouldn't know who to talk to.

So all I was allowed to see was an old man walking very slowly and purposefully across the land, following what I knew was his inner guidance and the energy he could feel pulling through the willow. Then all of a sudden, the branch began to vibrate in his hands so powerfully he could hardly hold it.

At the exact spot where his neighbor was meant to drill the well, the pointer went to ground. And sure enough, when they dug, water came flowing out like they're turned on the tap.

"That's amazing." Glenna's blue eyes were wide in wonder.

"Actually, to my grandparents' generation and those that preceded them, there was nothing amazing about it," said Róisín. "Dowsing for water was as natural to them as any other part of their daily and seasonal routines. They lived enfolded in Nature's cyclical rhythms and couldn't imagine acting as if they were separate from the landscape that was as much a part of their inner worlds as the outer.

"With all her wisdom about the life of things, the most important statement my Granny ever made to me was, 'You must find your stone.'"

"Your stone?" Debbie had never heard Róisín speak of stones.

"Yes. The one whose inner language brings you peace and a feeling of being alive at the same time. You know what I mean, don't you Sarah?"

"I do. I found mine in the remains of Uncle Óengus's grove. Those stones had been neglected and damaged. But they still held the innate structure and resonance deep within that allowed us to bring them back to life. And they brought Ah-Lahn and Alana back with them."

"Rory and I found our stone together, too," said Glenna. "Ours was the promise stone at *Inis Cealtra*. That's where I felt we first sealed our marriage vows." She snickered. "How funny. I guess I've had three wedding ceremonies."

The women all laughed together.

"Did you find your stone, Róisín?" Debbie could feel her soul beginning to vibrate with an excitement that spoke to the vision she'd had when they decided to sell Fibonacci's.

"I did, yes. There was an outcropping of carboniferous limestone on my Grandda's farm. I used to climb up and sit on one particular rock. After a short while, I'd feel myself settling into the stone, almost like I'd become part of it. Sometimes I would lie down on the rock and when I did, if I was very quiet and accepting of the peace that was available to me, I could feel the stone breathe."

"Really?" the three young women exclaimed.

"Yes, stone does breathe. Any dry stone wall builder will tell you that. When you relax and listen through your body, the rocks will share their breath with you, very slowly. And they will speak to you. Especially if you're building a wall. They're real big on placement and relationship."

Memories of stone walls came to mind for each of the young women.

"Pay attention next time you're out where there are rock formations," Róisín continued. "If you can rest in a circle of stones, that's best. They may appear to be separate, but if you observe with soft eyes and a listening heart, you'll notice that each one is in perfect relationship to its fellows.

"When you find your stone—and you will when the time is ripe—you'll come to ground in a way that cannot be taken from you because your stone will hold your yearning for as long as you live and perhaps for much longer."

"Is that why the ancients built their stone circles?" asked Debbie. "To hold their longing for the Home that lies beyond this earthly plane and for the generations who would follow them?"

"That is one reason, my daughter," said F. M. He was standing by their booth with an expression of deep knowing in his violet eyes. Of course, they had not heard him enter.

"Please, join us," said Róisín.

"Yes, do," agreed the others. They were always delighted to see their Master.

He pulled up a chair and continued his explanation. "The ancients understood the power of the circle as a ring of protection. By creating that ring in stone, they anchored in the earth a sealing action for the sustaining of oneness, especially of twin flames who would face many challenges to their union. Often those challenges would erupt into the physical shortly after the two experienced a powerful soul reconnection when they discovered their stone."

Sarah and Glenna looked at each other, their eyes wide with recognition of their own experiences.

"That's exactly what happened to Kevin and me," said Sarah. "Arán Bán attacked us outside of the grove immediately after our incredible bonding with our stones and merging with our druid selves, Alana and Ah-Lahn."

"He waited until Rory and I were at Clonmacnoise," said Glenna, "and then he tried to separate us from each other and from our own souls."

F. M. nodded. "So now you observe the pattern. Twin flames must always be aware of the opposition to their union that the brothers of the shadow continue to plot. That oneness is often in greatest peril after a dramatic bonding has taken place."

"Then I have a question," said Debbie tentatively.

"Yes, my dear?"

"What if I find my stone, but not my twin flame? How will this pattern apply to me if I'm never bonded with my soul's other half?"

"Remember, Debbie," said F. M., "that bonding may take place on the inner, if not on the outer. Finding your stone could be the impetus for a strictly spiritual reunion."

"I never thought of that. Then none of us should ever let down our guard."

"That is correct. Watch and pray, my friends, and take no blessing for granted."

Debbie checked her watch and sighed. The Master nodded.

"Yes, my dear, I understand. You are expected at your sister's store and, Sarah, your babies are missing you. Róisín, I have a matter to discuss with you shortly if you do not mind first allowing me a few minutes with our master event planner."

F. M.'s smile was particularly infectious today.

The women quickly excused themselves, and he gracefully slid into the booth seat across from Glenna.

"Will you show me your plans for *Samhain*? I confess to being eager for our celebration. We will be gathering new Friends of Ancient Wisdom at this event. I want to be certain our guests are heartily invited. "

Eleven

Glenna was having the time of her life. Today was October 31, *Samhain* Eve, and she was rushed off her feet with final preparations for the costume ball. She was grinning from ear to ear. Her smile was so wide that Debbie couldn't help being caught up in her enthusiasm for the event that would be happening in a matter of hours.

"I don't think any of us knew how important this community is to us until we realized we could lose it," Debbie remarked as they finished skirting long tables that would soon be laden with food and the urns of elixir punch that Lucky was mixing in the kitchen downstairs.

"If I put my attention on that, I'll cry. Tonight I refuse to be sad or think of a future that none of us can predict," said Glenna resolutely.

"I agree," said Debbie, looking appreciatively at the arrangements in the ballroom. "You've done a fantastic job, Glenna." She gave her friend a big hug.

"Thanks to you and the community. I think every single member of the Friends of Ancient Wisdom has contributed, and we've been promised mountains of food for tonight. The Pythagoreans did all of the decorating. I'm glad F. M. invited them to be a part of the community, at least for *Samhain*. I only had to show them a diagram of how I thought the room should look and they did the rest. They would make a terrific theatre stage crew."

Glenna picked up the clipboard that had been her constant companion for the past month (Rory had sworn to Kevin that she slept with it) and began ticking off a few last-minute items.

"The musicians will be here in an hour to finish setting up. Rory and I had the final rehearsal with the performers this morning. Most everyone has their costume and those who don't will meet me in the coffee shop next to the changing tents we've set up. It's been cold, so people who plan to wear thin or short costumes can dress here. Two couples who are longtime members will be greeters in the bookstore. And I think that's about it."

When she looked up from her lists, she realized that Debbie had gone silent. The expression on her friend's face troubled Glenna.

"What is it? You've been staring into space most of the day. Is something wrong? You're beginning to resemble Róisín in the way she grows very still when she's sensing things the rest of us may not see. Your eyes are really intense right now."

"What? Oh, sorry. You're right, I keep drifting away. Ever since our decision ritual, I've been feeling a presence or a pressure that I can't quite identify."

Of course, she knew that a big part of that pressure was the presence of her twin flame who had come to her in a vision during the ritual. But that was not all. Something intense was coming upon them.

"I'll think I know what I'm feeling and then I don't. I'm dreaming a lot at night, but when I wake up in the morning the images evaporate. As if they don't want to be remembered, or more like some force doesn't want me to remember. It's probably nothing more than the veil between worlds thinning like it does every year at *Samhain*. If F. M. were here I could ask him about it, but he hasn't been around since we talked to him a couple of weeks ago."

"I imagine he's working on his surprise," said Glenna with sparkling eyes. "And no, I don't know what it is. Only that he said he had to get permission from his Chief. Imagine, a master like F. M. having to get permission."

Debbie nodded. "That's the incredible thing about the Great White Brotherhood. Lucky says that hierarchy goes all the way to the sun at the center of our galaxy and far beyond that. Masters, angels, cosmic beings stretching to the infinity of Light."

"Hmmm," Glenna murmured thoughtfully. "Your saying that sparks a memory for me. I remember Master Druid Óengus showing me a vision of exactly that. When I was the bard Gormlaith, we used to have lovely telepathic conversations between our villages."

"I remember that," said Debbie wistfully. "The children you taught used to wonder how Gormlaith and Uncle Óengus could talk to each other when they were miles apart."

"I'm so happy when these flashes come to me," enthused Glenna. "That's another reason I love being here at Fibonacci's. Rory says it's a portal to other dimensions, and I believe it. Every time I walk in the door now I can feel my consciousness opening, my perception sharpening. And every once in a while a veil will lift, like just now."

"Then I'm not the only one going quiet and staring into space," teased Debbie. "I wonder if Saint Germain isn't picking up the pace for all of us. That may be one reason we haven't seen F. M. of late."

Glenna agreed. "I really feel that. Why do you think that is?"

"I suspect the Master is very busy with inner work. It occurs to me that he may be standing back to observe how much we'll tune in and meet him where he is. That may be the extra pressure I'm feeling. Yes, I'm sure that's it. There are things he wants me to see and I have to discern them myself."

"You're probably right," said Glenna warmly as they finished prepping the tables, "and I'm sure you'll do just that. Right now, I've got to check on Lucky and Róisín in the kitchen and then get ready myself."

Debbie picked up her coat and turned to leave. "I'll see you later then. I'll be back in time to help you with costumes or whatever. I'm dressing at home so you can put me to work as soon as I return."

"Great. Most of the jobs are covered, but I'd enjoy your company while people are coming in for their costumes. You can introduce me to Friends I've only met on the phone or by email.

He shouldn't be nervous, Jeremy told himself as his train pulled into the Oyster Bay station an hour before the *Samhain* party was set to begin. He and Kevin had texted a couple of times and spoken once by phone for a brief discussion about his résumé. All very straightforward. Nothing that should have his insides in knots.

Kevin was waiting for him on the platform. Although it was already growing dark, they recognized each other immediately and shook hands like old friends, which by now Jeremy was beginning to think they were.

"I appreciate the ride," he said as they pulled away from the parking lot. He'd already said thanks a number of times. Nerves made him repeat himself.

"No problem," said Kevin. "Feeling jumpy?"

"Yeah, a little."

"I was, too, before my first event at Fibonacci's. Don't worry. Almost nobody bites, unless you get into a discussion of Irish history with one of our Celtic warriors." Kevin grinned. "They're easy to spot, so you can steer clear of controversy, at least for tonight."

"Okay," Jeremy laughed and felt himself relax. "Good to know. And I wanted to tell you—I am convinced that my conversation with F. M. in the bookstore was not happenstance. I've felt my awareness opening since then. Nothing big, just little perceptions."

He hadn't meant to say anything about his childhood, but the words were out of his mouth before he thought to check them.

"I used to see things when I was a kid."

"Really?" Normally enthusiastic about asking questions, Kevin's intuition told him not to pry.

"Yeah, but I stopped. F. M. said I could pick up the skill again if I wanted, but I don't. Seeing auras and reading people's minds caused too much trouble. When you see the good, you also see the bad. I've had enough nightmares to last a lifetime."

"I wonder if nightmares are required," ventured Kevin. "There are a number of seers in the Friends community. My wife Sarah, for one, although she's not as accomplished as Róisín, one of the owners, who is the real expert. You might want to talk to her. Or Debbie. I'll introduce you to them and you can decide if you want to broach the subject."

"I'm okay with meeting them, but don't say anything about the seeing or my wondering about Crotona, okay?"

"No problem. Tonight's meant for fun. And here we are."

Kevin parked in front of the coffee shop so he could take Jeremy in through the front door.

"This is where the Pythagoreans meet most Fridays and where we have our informal gatherings. Tonight we're in the ballroom upstairs. We'll head back to the kitchen so you can meet Lucky and Róisín and then you can pick up your toga from Glenna.

"After you've changed, I'll take you upstairs to meet some of the students who are already there. And Rory. He's one of the team who's helping me strategize the academy we're starting. He's a former history teacher, a kindred spirit for sure."

Twelve

Jeremy felt immediately enfolded in warmth and good cheer when he shook hands with Lucky and Róisín. He was quite taken with the tall Irishman, who sported a ponytail and an amethyst stud earring, and his handsome wife, whose abundant white hair set off deep green eyes.

They were busy in the kitchen making punch and sandwiches, so he and Kevin didn't stay longer than for them to greet him and say a few words of welcome. As they were leaving the kitchen, Kevin glanced back over his shoulder in time to see Lucky give him a thumbs-up that told him F. M. would be very pleased that Jeremy had made it to the party.

The young man's reception at the costume table was another matter.

"Hi, Debbie," said Kevin cheerfully. "I expected to see Glenna handing out robes and angel wings. This is Jeremy. F. M. invited him and I've made sure we got him here. Glenna is supposed to have a toga for him."

He had never seen his friend Debbie respond like this. She was usually very gracious when meeting new people, but at the moment she was staring at Jeremy and not saying a word.

"Debbie? Toga? Do I need to find Glenna?"

She shook her head, as if coming out of a trance.

"Oh, no, sorry. I was thinking about something else. Hello, Jeremy. Yes, I've got your costume right here." She reached behind her to the table where all the remaining items were labeled with who would be wearing them.

"You can change in the men's tent over there." Debbie's tone was surprisingly direct and not particularly inviting as she pointed across the coffee shop. "You can put your street clothes in one of the bins our Glenna has placed in the tent and then just leave your toga there at the end of the evening with your name label on it."

Jeremy stood staring back at Debbie until Kevin tapped him on the shoulder and motioned him to the men's changing tent.

What's with those two? Kevin wondered. And then he remembered the first time he'd seen Sarah. I'll bet I had the same stunned look on my face, he chuckled to himself. I wonder if they recognize what just happened.

Too bad Debbie's not very friendly, thought Jeremy as he changed quickly into his toga. Guess I won't be talking to her about second sight. Really is a shame. She's gorgeous. Those misty green eyes, flaxen blonde hair. Oh, well.

"Sorry I can't give you the full tour of the bookstore," said Kevin as they said hello to the greeters and made their way upstairs to the ballroom. "After tonight, if you're interested in coming back, we can spend time in the stacks. The esoterica collection in the loft is a treasure I'm always eager to share."

"I'm already interested," said Jeremy eagerly. "Books are my world."

"Then, welcome home," laughed Kevin. He steered Jeremy to the bandstand where Glenna and Rory were putting finishing touches on the musicians' set-up. After more quick introductions, the two men crossed to the round table where most of the Pythagoreans were gathered. He noticed that Rudy wasn't among them.

"Noah, Jenny, Valerie, Finn—this is Jeremy. A fellow Pythagorean by way of interest and F. M.'s invitation. Glenna has more jobs for me, so I'm leaving him in your care for the evening."

"Welcome, Jeremy," said Jenny, offering him a seat next to her. "Kevin told us that you've read a lot about our favorite philosopher, so we're prepared to interrogate you." They all laughed.

"Okay," replied Jeremy. "I didn't bring my notes, but ask away." He didn't want to appear overly confident, but he figured he could match wits with this group. At least they were friendlier than that Debbie person. Beautiful woman, he thought again. Too bad about the attitude.

"Gosh, I'm sorry I abandoned you," apologized Glenna as she hurried to the costume table where Debbie was sitting with her head in her hands. "Did you have any trouble? I didn't mean to leave you here by yourself for such a long time. But Rory wanted to go over some music with me and then Kevin came by to introduce us to Jeremy, the new fellow that F. M. invited. Tall, dark, handsome man. Kind of stunning the way that lock of hair falls across his forehead."

Glenna was so caught up in the excitement of the party she didn't immediately notice that Debbie was not responding.

"Jenny of the Pythagoreans certainly thinks he's handsome. The girl didn't waste any time, flirting shamelessly. The whole table was already deep in conversation when I came back downstairs. Rory was on his way to join them. I'll be lucky to pry him away from ancient history long enough to sing our song."

Her smile turned to a frown when she looked at Debbie. Her friend's expression was pure bewilderment. Glenna immediately sat down at the table and put an arm around her shoulder.

"What's wrong? You've got me seriously worried now."

"It's him, Glenna."

"What? Who?"

"Jeremy. It's him."

"Debbie, tell me what you mean. You're not usually this cryptic."

"The man I've been seeing in visions, starting right after your wedding reception. I haven't said anything about what I thought I was seeing because I wasn't really sure. That lock of hair did it. I almost reached up to brush it from his forehead. I used to do that. I remembered the gesture before I recognized his face. Then I just stared at him. And I was practically rude when I handed him his costume. My heart stopped when I saw him."

Glenna was stunned. "Do you think he's your twin flame?"

Debbie nodded hopelessly.

"What are you going to do about it?" With her heart open to her dear friend, Glenna started thinking of solutions. "Should you tell Róisín or Lucky? Do you want me to say something to them? What about Kevin? I wish F. M. were here right now."

"Darling Glenna," said Debbie, taking her hand. "There's really nothing I can do at the moment. I'm sure he didn't recognize me. I can't exactly walk up to the new guy and say, 'Hi, I'm the love of your life.' "

"Well, that is sort of what Rory and I did, but then we did recognize each other right there in the mist on Mount Brandon, so that's not really the same." She grimaced. "I'm not helping, am I?"

"No, but I appreciate that you're trying to."

Glenna thought a minute. "Listen, go take a break. I'll finish up here. Get something to eat upstairs. People have already brought a lot of food. Lucky should be ready to start the program in a few minutes. Forget about twin flames and enjoy yourself. If Jeremy is who you think he is, things will work out. What is it that old song used to say?—'What will be, will be.' My grandparents liked to sing it when times were tough. Try not to worry."

"Thanks, you sweetheart." Debbie stood and rolled her shoulders. "I'll go ask Róisín if she needs any help taking sandwiches upstairs, and then I'll do just that." She gave Glenna a quick hug and walked through the curtain that separated the coffee shop from the kitchen.

What *am* I going to do about Jeremy? Debbie asked herself for the hundredth time. She was trying not to think about him, but wasn't doing very well.

At the moment, she was delivering a selection of sandwiches upstairs to the ballroom, so she'd taken the elevator. When she placed the tray at the end of the food line, she found herself face-to-face with Jenny and Jeremy, who were filling their plates as they chatted amiably on the other side of the table.

"Hi, Debbie," chirped Jenny. "Great night so far. Have you met Jeremy? He's new. F. M. invited him, so we know he's okay." She batted her eyelashes at him.

"Yes, hi again, Jeremy," said Debbie, doing her best to bring a warm tone to her voice and only moderately succeeding. She extended her hand, which he accepted, very briefly. "I'm sorry I was a bit abrupt when I gave you your costume earlier. Something had just come up."

"No worries." She really was a lovely woman standing tall and willowy in that long green dress that was only a shade or two darker than her eyes. She reminded him of something from Nature, but he couldn't quite put his finger on exactly what.

Jenny noticed his attention wandering and gave him a nudge. "I think Lucky's about ready to begin. We'd better go back to our seats."

"I see you've found your tribe, then," said Debbie, doing better with a genuine smile this time. "Welcome to the Friends of Ancient Wisdom, Jeremy. Enjoy your evening."

"Thanks, I will."

And he did. He'd been so engrossed in conversation with Rory and the Pythagoreans that he hadn't noticed the ballroom filling up until he and Jenny wended their way through the crowd to reach the food table.

When he and his eager new friend rejoined their group, he was astounded by the array of color, texture, and historical characters that had arrived while he wasn't looking.

He'd had some idea of what to expect in terms of theme. And, being a well-read person, he knew what he was seeing. Yet this variety was more than he could have imagined.

It appeared that several individuals, like the Pythagoreans, had opted for group costumes and were seated at their own tables with small, tent-card signs identifying who they were representing.

Angel bands had gathered according to their ray of specialization: blue for protection, yellow for illumination, pink for love, white for purity, green for healing, purple and gold for service, violet for transmutation. The individuals who had chosen to be archangels projected an extraordinary power that one did not need second sight to recognize.

There were fewer royals than Jeremy expected, but an abundance of monks and nuns from a variety of Western and Eastern religious traditions, including several men and women in saffron who identified themselves as Brothers and Sisters of the Golden Robe.

One of the more interesting groups, whose name card said they were Francis Bacon's Good Pens—a title unfamiliar to Jeremy—were clothed in stunning Elizabethan fashion. He would have to learn more about them, he promised himself.

The teenaged female baristas were flower fairies in a dozen shades of chiffon with wings that looked real. They were obviously relishing their youthful beauty, flitting around, waving their fairy wands while minding the food and beverage table.

Many parents had brought their children, who were dressed as elves, fairies, gnomes, and a couple of undines in watery blues and greens. One little boy was aptly attired as a many-hued fire elemental. His gleeful personality and abundant energy perfectly fit the role.

When Craig made an entrance with the Celtic warriors, the other guests exclaimed then applauded. The men had agreed that their most masterful embodiment had been as the highly disciplined troops of the Spartan King Leonidas. Glenna had outdone herself, finding scarlet cloaks and boar-bristle-topped helmets for six complete outfits. They were an impressive sight that had several of the baristas swooning.

Jeremy assumed that the woman standing with Kevin was his wife, Sarah. They were both dressed as druids. Circlets of oak leaves graced their heads. Their white robes were made of very fine linen that had been woven with arcane cabalistic and Celtic symbols, and they were wearing magnificent gold medallions that flashed when they moved.

Glenna and Rory were dressed in rich bardic blue, as were most of the musicians who were sitting or standing at the bandstand.

Fibonacci's owners, Lucky and Róisín, made an impressive couple as they stood together at the front of the ballroom where they prepared to officially open the festivities.

He was dressed as a master druid, his white robe belted and bordered with embroidery of gold and silk thread in rainbow hues. His torc was made of real gold and he carried a crosier, which Jeremy knew from his reading that some of the most powerful druids did use.

Róisín was a vision. Her character was the Goddess Brigid who had brought the rainbow light and a torch of illumination to Éire in ages past. Her long gown appeared to have been created from ethereal substance. Layer upon layer of gossamer-fine fabric floated and swirled as she moved.

Thin bands of silk in every color encircled her gown and trailed behind her. She carried a wand that flowed with streamers of golden silk.

She was like a living rainbow, exuding love and blessings to the entire room. Jeremy was not ashamed to admit he was in awe.

"Welcome Friends of Ancient Wisdom and guests," declared Lucky when the room had hushed for his introduction. "We are delighted that so many of you have joined us this evening for a very special celebration. As you know, *Samhain* is the traditional beginning of the Celtic New Year when the veil between this world and the next is said to be thinnest."

Róisín stepped forward to speak.

"Since we are not able to build an actual bonfire in the center of our ballroom, we ask you to kindle the flame of love in your hearts tonight, for our community and the world at large. To aid in the anchoring of that light, we're going to begin the dance with lively waltzes and polkas. And for you wild Celts, I know our band has plenty of jigs and reels planned." She laughed as they cheered and stomped their feet.

"We are grateful that many of our earliest members are here tonight along with newer members and guests," she said. "I'd like to encourage you to dance and visit with as many people you don't know as possible. Our community is growing and we want everyone to feel part of our mission to bring Divine Light and Love to the world."

"Thank you, darlin'," said Lucky as he concluded their introduction. "In about an hour we'll give you a rest from dancing so you can enjoy the entertainment that our performing troupe has prepared for us. And after that, Master F. M. Bellamarre has promised a visit and a surprise.

"Now, to set our intention for the evening, I would like to offer an invocation. Then have a grand time, everyone."

As Lucky prayed, his melodious tenor voice resonated throughout the ballroom, powerfully setting the tone of cosmic purpose so particular to the Friends of Ancient Wisdom.

O Spirits of East and West, South and North, give ear, we pray, to our sup-plications. Angels of our world and the next, bless this assembly with your protection and inspiration.

Beloved An Síoraí, may the words of our mouths and the deeds of our hands bring health and abundance to all our people and safety to

our homes, our leaders, and those we love both near and far, here with
us and in gracious Tír na n'Óg, Land of the Ever-Living.

Where had he heard that prayer before? Jeremy wondered as the band struck up the first notes of a beautiful melody in three-quarter time. When Lucky and Róisín immediately swept into a waltz worthy of a televised competition, he obliged Jenny by asking her to dance.

He wasn't bashful about being one of the first couples to follow the owners' lead. He knew he was a good dancer, thanks to a college roommate who had insisted that taking ballroom lessons was a good way to meet women (which he had quickly decided against).

Soon the dance floor was filled with other couples who were beaming wide smiles as they swirled around the room. Almost instantly, Jeremy felt himself enfolded in a kaleidoscope of sound and color and the exhilarating energy of this unique community that radiated love and light as they moved in time to the uplifting rhythm of the waltz.

He was grateful that Róisín had asked the company to dance with as many different partners as possible. Jenny was becoming a bit too friendly for his taste, especially since he was twelve years her senior. If he was going to be a part of the Pythagoreans, he would have to nip that behavior in the bud, he decided.

But not tonight. He was having too much fun. He had quickly picked up the pattern the longtime members had established for regularly changing partners. They had obviously done this before and had developed a routine for spinning from one partner to another in the middle of a dance and then staying with that partner for half of the next.

The process was a delightful game that kept everyone literally on their toes. When Debbie and Jeremy spun into each other's arms, he discovered that he was pleased and slightly amused when she blushed.

"Are you having a good time?" she asked as he guided her expertly around the floor. She noticed how naturally they fit together and wondered if he did as well.

"I am," he responded. "I've never been to an event like this."

He pulled her closer to avoid another couple that was spinning rather too exuberantly toward them, then found himself disinclined to relax his hold when the couple passed them. Debbie made no move to pull away.

"This is only the warm-up," she said cheerfully. "Just wait until you see what Glenna and her troupe have planned. I've watched a couple of their rehearsals. They're quite good."

"Kevin told me that you're a seer." Jeremy had not meant to bring up that fact. He hadn't wanted to talk to Debbie about his childhood visions. But now that he was holding her, he couldn't think of any good reason not to. The dance would be over soon and he wouldn't have to pursue a longer conversation.

However, the look in Debbie's eyes surprised him—as if she wasn't sure she wanted to talk about the abilities which Kevin had so casually claimed that she possessed.

Jeremy felt her body tense slightly and quickly released her when the first dance concluded and they waited for the next to begin.

"I don't have Róisín's skill," she said somewhat hesitantly as they stood face-to-face. Downplaying her abilities seemed like a good idea. "I know I was a master seer in a past embodiment. Róisín was my teacher then, and we've resumed the relationship."

She didn't want Jeremy to guess that she had recognized him, but she couldn't help asking, "Are you interested in clairvoyance?"

He gulped, not sure how he wanted to answer that question. Fortunately, the music began for the next waltz and he knew he'd be out of danger in a couple of minutes.

"Only theoretically," he lied, parrying the topic. "I've read a lot of esoterica, which is one reason why I appreciate F. M.'s invitation. I can't wait to spend a day exploring the bookstore."

"I'm sure you'll find lots to interest you," said Debbie rather flatly when the other couples began separating for the next exchange. "Thanks for the dance."

As Jeremy watched her being claimed by one of the Spartan soldiers and somewhat reluctantly accepted Jenny's twirling back into his own arms, he couldn't help wondering why Debbie's misty green eyes had drooped with what looked like disappointment. Or was it regret?

Thirteen

Entertainment time!" called out Lucky when the band stopped playing after the promised hour. Dozens of couples retired to their tables, now with occupants from different groups laughing and sharing conversations with friends new and old.

Glenna took her place in front of the bandstand, and in her best stage voice announced the presentation that she and seven others, including Rory, had put together. She had changed from her long blue bard's gown to a calico dress in the style of the late 1800s in the American Midwest. A curious alteration, thought many in the audience.

"Good evening, ladies and gentlemen. My name is Glenna O'Donnell. My husband, Rory, and I are grateful to be new members of the Friends of Ancient Wisdom.

"Some of you may know that I've been a singer and actress on Broadway. When I learned about the *Samhain* celebration, I asked Lucky if we might include some musical theatre as part of the evening's entertainment—because I quickly discovered that there is a lot of theatrical talent in this community. So, with Lucky's encouragement and F. M.'s gracious approval, here we are, the Fibonacci Players."

Several cheers went up amidst a round of enthusiastic applause.

"Thank you. Just briefly, I'd like to tell you what you're going to see and hear. The Players and I had some serious discussion about what would be appropriate for our maiden presentation. There are so many great musicals to choose from that we finally decided to offer you some songs from the first modern American musical, *Oklahoma!* which was produced in 1943 when our nation was still engaged in World War II.

"Recently a friend of mine wrote a lovely reflection that I'd like to share with you, by way of explaining why we felt this musical was the best choice to begin a new cycle in the Celtic year. Here's what she said:

We think of America as a place, a single country, when it's really an ideal that has lived in our hearts for eons. Every person of Light contains the spark of freedom that inspired our founders and that draws people here from all over the world. Free civilizations have existed in other places and other times. We remember how it felt to be part of them. So we're all together again. And we know that our hearts are joined with others who share the spark that's meant to light a world.

"As we send our love and light out to the world, the Players felt that the timeless songs of Rodgers and Hammerstein were one of the best ways to celebrate that spirit of freedom that lives in the heart of every member of the Friends of Ancient Wisdom—in this world and the next."

The audience applauded and Glenna stepped back as a handsome young man in a cowboy hat, plaid shirt, jeans, and chaps strode out to sing "Oh, What a Beautiful Morning." Because this was an evening to celebrate community, he was soon joined by seven other singers in the heartfelt opening number.

Two chairs were quickly put into place, where a different tenor and an actress to whom he was soon to be married in real life were seated side by side for "The Surrey with the Fringe on Top."

Glenna and Rory then took center stage for their charming rendition of "People Will Say We're in Love," which left no doubt in the audience's mind that these newlyweds were deeply in love.

"The Farmer and the Cowman Should Be Friends," which starts with an altercation between two groups of landowners, struck a chord of the perennial necessity for people with different views to get along.

A young woman with a lilting soprano voice enchanted the audience with "Out of My Dreams," and all of the Players led the crowd in a rousing, sing-along version of "Oklahoma!" to conclude the presentation.

The ballroom erupted into wild applause, cheers, whistles, and stomps, as the Fibonacci Players took a bow. When they were about to exit the stage, F. M. Bellamarre entered and stood in the center of the performers, between Glenna and Rory.

This evening he was costumed in the eighteenth-century fashion that had been worn by the renowned Wonderman of Europe. His breeches were dark purple velvet, his waistcoat lavender brocade, his coat a lighter shade of violet, also brocade, embroidered with subtle designs that, on close inspection, revealed themselves to be cabalistic symbols familiar to students of alchemy. Delicate lace fell at his wrists covering his hands to the knuckles. His neck stock was of finest linen.

"Well done, Fibonacci Players," he declared with a radiant smile. "I believe we will all be humming these tunes for many days to come. And rest assured the Friends of Ancient Wisdom will welcome more theatrical presentations at our future celebrations.

"Glenna, I must echo your friend's reflection on America residing in the heart, not in an earthly place. The same can be said for Fibonacci's, for I must announce to you this evening that the physical location of our gathering place may disappear for a while in the future, possibly in a few months or sooner."

Cries of "Oh, no!" "Surely not." "We can't lose Fibonacci's," rippled through the crowd.

"Never fear, dear ones," said F. M. raising his hands. "The Brotherhood needs Fibonacci's as much as you do, perhaps more. Any dislocation will be temporary until a new home is found—and I prophesy that a new location will prove to be an even better home.

"I am telling you this so you will not be surprised when circumstances change, as they must. And so you may begin this Celtic New Year with the resolve to keep the flame of Fibonacci's in your hearts, wherever you are.

"We are entering a difficult time, dear ones. There is much turmoil in the world and more uncertainty ahead. Yet I have faith that all of us together will weather the coming storm with fortitude and grace, and that we will emerge stronger, more resilient, and more committed than ever to the purposes of soul freedom for which we were born.

"Let not your hearts be troubled and do not despair, for greater is he that is in you than he that is in the world. Do you believe me?"

"Yes!" cried the crowd in a single voice.

"Remember your reply, my dears. And remind each other, should any of you begin to falter in days to come."

F. M. stood quietly for a moment, gazing out at these precious souls whom he had gathered to his heart as Friends of Ancient Wisdom. Then his expression and his tone brightened.

"Now then, I believe you were promised a pleasant surprise, not a shock, and your Wonderman is pleased to deliver the former to erase any concern you may have over the latter."

A murmur of relief flowed through the crowd and an audible sigh could be heard from many voices.

"Please be seated, my dear friends, for a short explanation of the experiment in elevated awareness I would share with you. Many of you know, or have suspected, that Fibonacci's coffee shop and bookstore functions as a portal to realms of higher consciousness, for you have had experiences here that cannot be explained otherwise.

"But have you ever wondered how that is so? Yes, the Brotherhood has anchored a great deal of Light in this location, but these physical atoms are not capable of containing the magnificent radiance necessary for a portal to exist.

"Your hearts are the real portal, my dears, and your continued striving to elevate your consciousness keeps it open. Tonight I would show you the divine structure of which our businesses here are but a replica and an approximation. This is one of the Temples of Light to which you travel at night in your soul bodies. And this is the etheric structure that makes this physical manifestation a possibility."

F. M. looked out at the faces which had grown more cheerful during his explanation. The hearts of his Friends of Ancient Wisdom and the guests he had personally chosen to attend this celebration were ready for the vision he was eager to share with them.

"We are going to form a circle now with gentlemen on my right and ladies on my left. Lucky and Róisín will stand opposite me, marking the center line. Parents and friends, please gather the children so we have women and girls on my left, men and boys on my right. Anyone who needs to remain seated may do so. If necessary, please form several rings, keeping the center line congruent with Lucky and Róisín."

F. M. indicated that Kevin and Sarah, each holding one of their twins, should stand next to him, with Glenna and Rory by their sides. Debbie was positioned next to Glenna. On a very strong prompting from his inner guidance, Rory motioned for Jeremy to stand with him.

Well-primed for another game, the community members moved quickly into place and faced F. M. to receive his next instruction.

"Well done, my responsive friends," he said with an approving smile. "Follow me now as we begin. Open your minds and hearts to the tremendous Light that has already been gathered in this room as we sound the OM together.

"Visualize the Divine Love of *An Síoraí* flooding your aura, this room, and extending out to bless our city, state, nation, the entire planet. Please continue the chant until I signal for the next part of our ritual."

OMMMMM.

F. M.'s powerful voice sounded the sacred tone on a high note and soon the ballroom was filled with the resonance of harmonies according to each participant's vocal range. Very soon the forcefield of accelerating light that he desired was established.

As he folded his hands at his chest for the chant to conclude, the figure of F. M. Bellamarre dissolved into the resplendent, white-robed presence of the Ascended Master Saint Germain who began to address the gathering.

As he spoke, his violet eyes sparkled and he poured out waves of love from his heart that glowed with vibrant plumes of royal blue, gold, and ruby light rays.

My beloved sons and daughters, I bring to you in this hour of celebration a revelation of the advent of a great Light that is coming upon our earth. My word to you in this hour is that all Friends of Ancient Wisdom must accelerate in consciousness to meet this influx of radiant energy.

With increased Light comes a sifting, dear ones. Not all of you may wish to remain with our community. That is your free will. However, my prayer is that the best part of you will overcome any residual patterns of weakness or fear of change. For the greatest joy is within reach—if you will but open your hearts and receive what is so lovingly offered to you from the Brotherhood.

We would see you victorious, beloved ones. Souls free from the burden of karma and the condemnation that dark forces heap upon you every day, so continuously that you have become accustomed to a layer of astral soot that, despite your devotion and your good deeds, is never quite cleared away.

I am here tonight to offer you a clearance, to sweep your chakras clean for a period of time. How long a time depends upon your ability to hold the Light that comes to you through my address and our meditation.

Let us begin with deep concentration.

Visualize now a milky white radiance beginning to form in the center of our circle. This is the visible manifestation of the Light you have been invoking all evening.

Notice how the radiance increases and yet does not grow dense. It merely intensifies until hundreds and then thousands of light points begin to coalesce in the center of the circle.

Let your concentration deepen as the lights begin to spin and swirl around the room, now moving to encompass the circle in a spherical network of golden threads that connect the most concentrated points, creating an antahkarana, a sacred symbol of spiritual community.

Rest for a moment in this luminous network, allowing your physical, emotional, mental, and etheric bodies to become accustomed to the delicate, yet powerful, radiation that surrounds us.

Hold the vision of our antahkarana that has always existed between us in spirit and that must become more physical for our future work. As you maintain the felt sense of the enormous tensile strength of this matrix, simultaneously bring your attention to the center of our circle.

Soften and widen your gaze to perceive yourself and your physical Friends of Ancient Wisdom being joined by vast numbers of the Great White Brotherhood in spirit, and let your awareness accept their gift this *Samhain* eve for your blessing in the New Year.

My dear friends, your devoted concentration makes possible this evening a vision of what has been in the etheric and what is meant to be in the physical. May I introduce my brother, Master K. H., who carries in his hand the matrix of Fibonacci's past, present, and future.

A statuesque man in a robe the color of pure gold stepped into the center of the circle and bowed to Saint Germain. His long dark hair and well-trimmed beard were not remarkable in this gathering. Several other men were similarly styled.

However, the light emanating from him clearly marked him as an adept, a master of considerable attainment.

Kevin and the other men moved to the side so this visitor could stand next to Saint Germain, who continued his discourse.

Master K. H., or Elder Brother, as you may wish to address him, has received a dispensation to walk and talk among you as did F. M., who will retire from your midst for a while.

I, Saint Germain, will always answer your calls to me in times of need. And let it be known that my brother K. H. is able and willing to act as teacher, guide, and support while we engage in the changes that are quickly coming to pass.

Be wise, dear ones. Be observant. Discern the spirits you encounter. And love each other in support of wise choices. I cannot tell you the future. But I can say, 'tis time to trim your sails and be prepared to ride the waves of change.

May the blessing of *An Síoraí*, the Eternal One, be with you this night and throughout the New Year as the Celts count the seasons of our Mother Earth.

So saying, Saint Germain's figured dissolved from sight. However, the antahkarana matrix remained visible, as did the figure of Master K. H., who stood at the apex of the circle holding aloft a model of Fibonacci's that shimmered as if it were formed of etheric substance. The reaction of those gathered was as varied as their costumes. Some were excited, others dismayed. All were amazed by the ritual in which they had participated and by Saint Germain's announcement of a new guide for their spiritual studies.

Many of the Friends and quite a few of their guests found the structure familiar, as if they had visited it in their finer bodies during sleep. Others viewed it as extraordinary. And all agreed that here was a spacious home of Light—with a grand tower and a great many rooms.

After a few minutes, the glistening antahkarana began to fade, as did the model of Fibonacci's. However, Master K. H. remained and addressed the gathering in conversational tones of great kindliness.

"Good evening, friends, for so I hope to count you in anticipation of many hours of enlightening communion in days to come. As the hour has advanced and many of you and your children are more than ready to be put to bed, may I wish you all the most pleasant of good evenings. If anyone wishes to stay longer for more dancing, to assist our hosts with clean up, or to speak with me, the ballroom will remain open for another couple of hours. *Namaste.*"

He bowed deeply to the company and many, including Lucky and Róisín, Glenna and Rory, Debbie, the Pythagoreans, and the entire group of Brothers and Sisters of the Golden Robe, gathered around to welcome this new Wonderman to their community.

Kevin and Sarah had wanted to stay to greet Master K. H., but the hour was past their babies' bedtime. And it was obvious from the wide-eyed look on Jeremy's face that he was ready to leave.

The only sound in the MacCauleys' car as they drove their guest to the Oyster Bay train station was the slight fussing of the twins, Gareth and Naimh, who were now wide awake and ready for a nighttime feeding. Otherwise, the adults kept their counsel for another day.

Fourteen

On any other Sunday morning after a big party the night before, Fibonacci's coffee shop would have been as quiet as a churchyard. This morning, however, every available seat at the long library tables was filled. Extra patrons were squeezing into booths, and it was standing room only at the coffee bar.

Apparently, the entire community of Friends of Ancient Wisdom and their guests had returned this morning, especially those who had not had an opportunity to speak with Master K. H. at the *Samhain* celebration.

Róisín's young baristas, who usually opened the coffee shop for her on Sunday mornings, had called her in a panic when dozens of customers were waiting at the door before 7:00 a.m. By 8:00 a.m. they had served nearly all of their pastries, and the bakers had been summoned from their beds to please come in and make more muffins!

Lucky was laughing and talking while he ground coffee beans, made lattes and Americanos, and refreshed the big urns of regular and decaf coffee that were being emptied almost as soon as he could fill them.

Debbie had hurried over from her apartment two blocks away and was helping Róisín serve specialty teas. She had called her sister Cyndi, who readily volunteered to keep the condiments stocked while she and Glenna wiped down tables and bussed plates and cups to and from the dishwasher as fast as they could manage.

The coffee shop was buzzing with conversation as individuals and groups shared their experiences about last night and their questions about the future. Glenna was thoroughly enjoying catching snippets of those conversations as she moved around the room.

"Did you get to meet K. H.?" an elderly lady—one of the original

Friends—asked a much younger acquaintance who was seated with her and her husband at a table with new friends they had met last night.

"I did, and he was very kind. Did you meet him?"

"We both did. He made a point of seeing some of us older folks before we went home. I thought that was very sweet of him."

"Is F. M. going away?" One of the Friends who had been dressed in Elizabethan costume with the Good Pens of Francis Bacon was anxiously questioning his pal. "I didn't understand what Saint Germain meant."

"I know we can pray to the Master for his help."

"But I've never spoken directly to Saint Germain. Only to F. M. How do you address an ascended master? That's what he is, right?"

"Yes. Just say, 'Beloved Saint Germain' and tell him your situation."

A young lady whom Glenna recognized as the mother of the exuberant little boy who had been dressed as a fiery nature spirit was speaking to a table of other young mothers. "I'd like to meet K. H., but I don't know what I'd say. Do you think he'll come around very often? F. M. wasn't always with us."

Glenna was pleased to allay at least one customer's concerns.

"Master K. H. is next door in the bookstore. Lots of people had to go home early last night, so he's come back today. Lucky said that the Master wants to meet as many of the Friends and their guests as possible this morning. Kevin and my husband, Rory, are making sure everybody has a turn. They're seating groups of seven, so you can wait here until they get to you. It shouldn't be long."

Next door, the two men were facilitating the flow of community members as they gathered around K. H. in the lounge.

As Glenna had described, they were inviting seven people to visit with the Master at the same time. He appeared to be enjoying himself. Today he was dressed as a Franciscan friar and was dispensing wisdom, good cheer, and blessings in equal measure.

"I would like to know your names and something about you," he said in greeting each group, "And feel free to ask a question. If you do not have any questions, I will ask you one in our brief interview. And never fear, dear ones, we will have many opportunities for conversation in the days and weeks to come."

Kevin and Rory considered themselves mightily blessed to witness these small group sessions. The Master's dark brown eyes were alight with compassion and genuine interest in the eager community members arrayed around him. He listened intently to how they described themselves, even though the men suspected that he already knew more about each individual than they did about themselves.

He answered their questions with generous patience and was particularly taken with their responses to his question of what they considered the most important reason for a community such as theirs.

Enfolded in the Master's aura, the entire proceeding took on a timeless quality that left everyone satisfied that they had been seen and heard by K. H. Those waiting their turn in the coffee shop were at peace and either chatted amiably with their friends or sat patiently in silence.

By noon, all but one table of community members had been seen and the crowd had dispersed to a trickle of the normal Sunday morning customers, which the regular baristas were handling on their own.

Róisín was returning from the kitchen with the last tray of muffins she estimated they would need for the day. Debbie had wanted to speak with her all morning, but things had been too busy. Now she was hoping for a few moments with her mentor when her cell phone rang.

"Debbie, it's Sarah. Are things calming down? The twins had sniffles or I would have been there to help. I hear you've had quite a morning."

"That's an understatement. Mysteries are unfolding with F. M. gone and Master K. H. in his place. I think he met and counseled every member of our community who was here today. Are you and the babies okay?"

"We're fine. It's you I'm calling about. Kevin sent me a message that you looked awfully tired. He said I should check on you. Are *you* okay?"

"Actually, I'm not. I hardly slept last night. I was just now going to speak with Róisín, but I really need support from all of my spiritual sisters. Cyndi has left to open the health food store. I'm wondering if you and I and Glenna and Róisín could get together in a little while. Maybe at your house, if you don't want to go out? I can tell the others."

"Of course. Come over as soon as you can. I'll ask Kevin to stay at Fibonacci's and help Lucky so Róisín can join us. Actually, I think he and Rory are getting some suggestions from Master K. H. about how to organize their academy, so I know he won't mind."

Less than an hour later, the four women were gathered around Sarah's kitchen table. She had heated cups of soup and Róisín had brought some fresh muffins, since none of them had eaten more than a morsel here and there during the morning rush at the coffee shop.

As soon as they were settled, Debbie told them the full story of the visions she'd been having and of her startling meeting with the man she was certain was her twin flame. Glenna knew more of the story than the others, but even she hadn't heard about Debbie's experience while dancing with Jeremy.

"When he was holding me as we danced, it was like we just *fit*," she said at last. "Do you know what I mean?"

"Completely," replied Sarah and Glenna.

"The first night I met Kevin in the library of this gorgeous old house at a party neither of us had wanted to attend, I could almost hear our souls locking together like fine gears." Sarah interlaced the fingers on both hands to show what she meant.

"And when Rory was carrying me piggy-back off of Mount Brandon with my injured ankle, I could honestly feel myself meshing with him," said Glenna. "Like our two beings were sort of melting into each other." She closed her eyes and smiled sweetly as she remembered.

"And now that you've had this experience, Debbie, what do you want to do about it, and how can we help you?" asked Róisín tenderly.

"Even now, as I told Glenna the other night, I don't think there is anything I *can* do. I just needed to tell you all and ask you to pray for me."

"Debbie, you know we will, and gladly," exclaimed Sarah.

"Absolutely!" declared the others. With their hearts joined as one, the women stood together and enfolded Debbie in an embrace of sisterhood they knew was more ancient than time itself.

Fifteen

On Monday morning November's damp, cold weather blew into New York with a fury. Those with experience in such matters called it a reaction from dark forces to the extraordinary light released on Saturday, and they prayed to dissolve it so others weren't burdened.

A. B. Ryan's foul mood matched the weather's meanness with anger to spare. He was furious, and it was doing him no good. Anger used to accomplish things. It made other people ask how high when he said, "Jump!" Now they just let him stew in his own perversity.

He'd offered Lucky more money and more time to seal the deal on Fibonacci's because he wanted that damn building. He'd long since forgotten exactly why he wanted it, only that he had something to prove and he wouldn't rest until he got it.

Actually, he'd figured that by adopting a conciliatory tone in his offer he and his slick lawyer could trick Lucky into giving away more than he intended. But the lawyer Lucky had hired was slicker and had out-maneuvered A. B.'s man, which meant he was stuck keeping his promise to pay more and not take possession of the property until the spring.

He'd been surprised and half-way disappointed when Lucky said he'd sell. A. B. had wanted to crush him, but there'd been no battle, no refusal. Only polite and extremely adept negotiation and even a grateful handshake because Fibonacci's wouldn't have to close immediately. They appreciated the extra time to relocate. Blah-blah-blah.

A. B. had nearly choked on the solicitude. Who did these people think they were anyway, slinking away from a fight? That's what A. B. really wanted. At the moment he needed to punch somebody, but he was alone.

He'd driven everybody away, except for his assistant, Tony, who stayed because of the unspoken, mutually assured destruction pact that had been their relationship for twenty years.

His fiancée, Ursula, had left him. His private investigator had located her in Majorca, but she claimed she wasn't coming back unless A. B. apologized.

To hell with her, he grumbled and poured himself another shot of Scotch. He owed her nothing. Certainly not an apology. She was the one who should be apologizing to him, he scowled into his glass. She was the one who should be sorry.

Her no-talent insistence on starring in the Broadway show he was financing had ruined it before it got off the ground. She'd stolen thousands of dollars from him, and apparently was counting on him begging or bribing her to come back to him.

She liked Majorca, she'd told the P. I., and she had enough money to stay there quite comfortably for several months. A. B. could go whistle up a tree for all she cared.

Well, two could play at that game, he decided. If she stayed away, maybe he could convince Newhouse to revive their Broadway show with real talent. There was still time.

"Tony!" he yelled through his open office door. "Get Newhouse on the phone. And what happened to that kid Rudy? He was supposed to give me a report on the big party they had at Fibonacci's. What gives?"

"He didn't go," said Tony. "His mom was sick and needed him to stay home."

What Tony didn't say was that his nephew knew A. B. would pump him for details. If he didn't go to the ball, he wouldn't have to lie. Rudy hadn't admitted as much, but it was pretty clear to his uncle that he was growing fond of the people at Fibonacci's.

Meanwhile, A. B. was fuming. "You tell that kid he'd better figure out his priorities or I'm going to stop supporting his mother. Worthless woman. I'm tired of people bleeding me dry, living off my good nature. You tell him. I mean it!"

"Okay, A. B.," said Tony. Keeping what there was of his fractured family together was getting harder and harder. "Your call's on line one."

"Got it." The boss growled, then quickly sweetened his tone.

"Roland? A. B. here. How's the theatre business? . . . Good to hear. Listen, I'm sorry about that blow-up with Ursula. . . . Yeah, well, she's out of the picture. I've still got some cash to invest. Any chance we could revive the show? . . . What about that actress you wanted to hire before? Glenna something. Would she do it? . . . Yeah, call her if you think we could get her. Let me know. I liked the songs I heard. Too bad Ursula butchered them."

He hung up, laughing sardonically. He was satisfied with the call and was perfectly willing to throw his former paramour under the bus. And he'd played dumb about not remembering Glenna's name. He knew exactly who she was.

She and her husband had slipped through his fingers a few months back, but they ought to know better than to think he'd give up so easily. He wasn't entirely sure what he would do if he got her under his control again, but he was determined not to be defeated by these people.

If anyone had asked him why he hated them so much, he probably couldn't have said. But hate them, he did. And that was all that mattered to him these days.

Personally, Jeremy hadn't noticed the negative energy that was swirling around. He'd been so blown away by the arrival of Elder Brother, whom F. M. had introduced as Master K. H., and by the appearance of Saint Germain, an actual ascended master who looked like F. M., that he'd gone mentally and emotionally blank all day Sunday.

The only emotion that had slipped into his awareness was confusion. Why had Rory waved him over to stand with him for the circle meditation? Why had they put him in the same position on the men's half of the circle as where Debbie was standing with the women? And why hadn't Kevin said anything about it?

Was this some kind of set-up? A cosmic blind date? When Jeremy considered what he knew about Kevin and Rory, he found he couldn't ascribe devious motives to either of them.

Probably just a coincidence and nothing more.

Besides, he mused as he got ready for work on Monday morning, he'd only spoken with Debbie during their one dance, and he didn't suppose they had much to discuss in the future. Which was a shame. He had to admit that he did find her very attractive.

The angry energy that others had been feeling erupted in Jeremy's world when he got to work.

When he walked into Nordemann Financial at exactly 8:00 a.m. a full-blown argument was going on in the branch manager's office. Herb's door was open and he was making no attempt to keep the altercation from his staff. He'd been their manager for fifteen years. His people were like family and he was determined to defend them.

"What do you mean you're letting everybody go? Today? You can't just waltz in here and shut down an entire branch office! We have client meetings scheduled, reports to file, services promised! A dozen detailed processes that you've never bothered to learn about!"

Herb was shouting at CEO Hildy Gleeson. She didn't visit the branch office very often, but whenever she did, there was trouble.

"I told the Board your office isn't earning its keep." Hildy was standing smugly in her four-inch heels and short black designer skirt, hands on her hips.

"You know that's a lie," challenged Herb.

"They agreed we need to economize, and I told them that Queens is the obvious choice for elimination. We're transferring your functions to the main office.

"You've got till Friday to transfer everything to Wendell and Sheila in Manhattan. Tell your people to call their clients and move them today. I see no reason to delay. The company is bleeding money and I'm not closing the main office, so deal with it.

"Pick three people to do the transfers. Everybody else is considered non-essential as of close of business today. The Board approved standard severance packages and reference letters. Tell people to apply for unemployment. That's what it's for."

She held up her hand when Herb tried to speak. "Not another word, or I'll decide you're non-essential, too." She turned on her high heels, whipped into the lobby, impatiently punched the elevator call button, and flew away from the carnage she'd just inflicted on innocent people.

The staff had been party to the entire confrontation. They now clustered around Herb, asking questions that he was too stunned to answer about who was staying and who should start packing up their office.

There were tears and anger and mutual commiseration, but no way out of the situation.

Jeremy hadn't bothered asking about his job. He knew he was out and honestly couldn't say he was sorry. He'd never done much to personalize his office, so handing off his files and emptying his desk was easily done. He was on his way back to his apartment by lunchtime.

Guess I'd better call Kevin about that job, he said to himself as he walked the six short blocks away from the MetLife building where the branch office of the company that Karl Nordemann had nurtured and built with heart and common sense would soon be vacant.

And he'd better start looking for some place cheaper to live. His financial consultant salary had been more than adequate to cover his three-thousand-dollar-a-month rent in the fancy high-rise that had been home for the past couple of years. But unemployment wasn't going to cover that plus his other expenses.

Boy, F. M. hadn't been kidding when he talked about major changes ahead, Jeremy thought to himself as he rode the elevator to his apartment on the fourteenth floor. At least he had a few weeks to make other arrangements. Life was going to get very interesting.

Master K. H. watched with compassion as abrupt change came to the life of Jeremy Madden. He remembered all too well what it was like to live through the complexities of human incarnation. The young man had no idea exactly how interesting his life was about to become.

Sixteen

Hero was a very happy dog. He'd been that way since the man, Kevin, had picked him out of the cage and brought him home with the woman, Sarah, and her kitten. They'd been a family ever since.

He hadn't been happy at the shelter. He didn't understand why he was there. In those early days there was a lot he didn't understand, but even a puppy knows when it's not wanted. Too many times, he'd heard the words "bad mix" applied to him and his litter mates. He didn't know what had happened to them. He guessed they'd wandered away from where they'd been left by the side of the road. Or maybe he did.

A lady who had called him to her with food had brought him to the shelter. She'd smiled and patted him on the head, but she didn't want him. Dogs in the other pens didn't say much. They were mostly just sad and silent.

Hero had tried not to be either of those things, but after a few days of watching people look at his big paws and turn away shaking their heads, he was beginning to feel depressed.

Then he and Kevin had shared the look he would always remember. Without waiting, the man had scooped him up and carried him out of the cage area and was showing him to Sarah, who was holding a kitten. They were laughing and nodding and, just like that, Hero and Sprite had a home.

Now that there were two little humans for Hero to watch, he was very content. Every dog needs a job, and he liked getting the babies to make cooing noises, which they did more frequently now that they were getting a little older.

Actually, he and Sprite shared baby-care responsibilities. Sometimes a purring cat worked better than his soft woof or antics that caught the little ones' attention so they would forget to cry.

Besides his home duties, every Tuesday and Thursday afternoon (and, yes, he did know which days were his work days) Sarah would brush him till his wiry grey and white coat was fluffy and then she would take him to the bookstore for his "Paws to Read" sessions with some of the local children.

It was hard to tell who enjoyed their reading more—the kids or the canine. Hero continued to gain composure and attentiveness, and the young readers gained confidence and proficiency.

He couldn't quite remember the incident that had happened with the young man named Rudy. It was a long time ago, and if an event wasn't happening right now or very soon, the dog didn't worry about it.

He did have a faint recollection of something snapping in him when Rudy tried to hit Sarah. All he knew was that in his doggie being was the instinct to protect and the strength to overcome an adversary.

Although he had been praised and cuddled for his bravery, he was glad not to be a defender very often. His ancestors had been trained to kill wolves and intruders, but Hero was a gentle dog at heart.

He liked his normally peaceful life. Cashiers and customers all loved this very large dog who now stood thirty-two inches at the shoulder and was living up to the wolfhound's nickname of "Gentle Giant."

Today was Tuesday, and Sarah had brought Hero to the bookstore earlier than usual so she could run some errands. He had been napping in the upstairs alcove when he heard Kevin's voice coming from the coffee shop. He was walking in with another man—a very tall one—with dark hair that fell across his brow.

"I think the book we're looking for is upstairs," Kevin was saying. "Hi, Buddy." He stopped to scratch Hero behind the ears when the dog ambled over to greet him and began vigorously wagging his whip of a tail.

"This is Hero. He's mostly wolfhound, which is why he's so big. And why he's a marshmallow inside. Aren't you, Buddy?" Dog and man continued their affectionate exchange, and then Jeremy and Hero got a good look at each other.

Jeremy stopped in his tracks and stared at Kevin's big dog. Hero stopped wagging his tail and fixed his attention on the stranger. But this was no stranger. Something far back in the dog's memory clicked. This was Madwyn, his friend from long, long ago.

Before Kevin could grab his collar, Hero rushed over to Jeremy, crying and whining and wagging his entire body. He lifted up to his full height and put his paws on the tall man's shoulders, the way they used to play together when they both lived in ancient Ireland. His name had been Hero then, too. *Laoch* in Irish.

Dogs who have been extraordinarily loved do reincarnate with the people who have loved them. That's why Hero was living with the Mac-Cauleys. And it was why now, in this instant, he remembered the young man who had cared for him when Alana and Ah-Lahn were away.

Despite Jeremy's determination to keep the door of his mind tightly closed to memories of past embodiments that he didn't quite believe in, the spontaneous affection of this gentle giant blew the latch off a lifetime of control. In an instant, his mind flashed back to first-century Ireland, to an incarnation he had cherished.

"Laoch!" he exclaimed and began speaking endearments to the dog in Gaelic. "You remember me, don't you? Of course, you do. Come, talk to me."

They hurried into the alcove where Jeremy sat on an easy chair. Hero followed, rolling over on his back for a belly rub, then springing up, dancing around, and finally flopping down with his head in his old friend's lap.

Still speaking Gaelic, Jeremy turned to Kevin, who appeared to him as a druid. They weren't in the bookstore, they were in Dearbhla's garden where Madwyn had been her assistant.

"*Go raibh míle maith agat* for bringing Laoch to visit, Ah-Lahn. I've missed him and I think he's missed me."

"Yes, he has," said Kevin. Although he was deeply concerned about the scene that had erupted around him, he was speaking evenly. He looked on as Jeremy continued petting Hero. The dog was sighing contentedly with his head in the man's lap, but his current owner was worried about what to do next.

Jeremy was experiencing a sudden breakthrough of past-life memories, intense enough to bring the old language with them. Now what? Certain that the man and dog should not be left alone, Kevin was grateful when Róisín appeared at the alcove doorway.

With a motherly smile, she pulled up a chair at Jeremy's side and laid her hand on his shoulder. "*A chara*, what have we here? Have you done a bit of time traveling, lad? Do you know what's happening?"

"Hello, Róisín. Yes, Laoch and I are having a grand reunion."

"I can see that. Can you tell me where you are, seated in this nice comfortable chair with your good friend?"

She gently turned Jeremy toward her where they could look at each other face-to-face. She focused her deep green eyes on his brown ones and opened her heart to him.

After *Samhain*, Kevin had mentioned to her Jeremy's comment that he used to see things as a child, so she was being very careful in how she approached bringing him back to the present.

"I was wondering what would open the door for you, *a chara*," she said, not forcing him to say more than was comfortable. "It happens here at Fibonacci's. Sooner or later, we start remembering."

At first Jeremy looked at her with dazed eyes. But as she spoke, his expression began to clear, and his gaze became less distant. Róisín simply kept her eyes focused on him until he scrubbed his hands over his face and stopped petting Hero, who raised his head to ask why.

The young man spoke haltingly. He was coming back to the present with memories of the past he wasn't sure he wanted to recall.

"I know—I'm Jeremy. Not Madwyn. But I don't want to remember. I've spent my whole life making sure I don't see things like I did as a child. Now this, from a dog. And not just any dog. Laoch, Hero, my pal. I used to take care of him for Alana. That's your wife, Sarah, right?" He looked up at the man he had spoken to as Ah-Lahn only moments before.

"That's right." Kevin breathed a sigh of relief. "We're willing to share Hero whenever you're both around."

"Actually, I'm more of a cat person these days," said Jeremy, "though I think I've just changed my mind."

"We have one of those, too." Kevin was smiling now. "A black mini-panther named Sprite."

"You're kidding." More coincidences, like that silly book he had picked up the day he met F. M.

"No, that's what she is. Much easier than buying Sarah a full-size panther that would scare the neighbors. We don't usually bring Sprite to the store, but you never know."

"How are you feeling, Jeremy?" asked Róisín.

"Like I've been blown open."

"Come downstairs with me, lad. You need a sandwich and one of our special brews. And we'll talk. Or you talk, and I'll listen. This is a tender time for you now, and you're safe here, Jeremy. You can see or not see. Remember or not remember. No pressure and no judgment.

"Here at Fibonacci's it's not unusual to have one foot in two worlds. Those of us who do are always glad for company on the bridge."

Jeremy was fully aware that he was sitting in a comfortable booth at the rear of the coffee shop, eating a delicious sandwich, and drinking a cup of tea that had amazing restorative properties. He felt like a thirsty plant standing in a soft Irish rain, being watered with a mother's love for the first time in his life.

He had never been offered—or allowed himself to receive—the kind of nurturing that Róisín was extending to him, merely through the openness of her presence as she sat across from him while he ate.

"I was speaking Gaelic, wasn't I?" he ventured. "And I called you Róisín."

"That's right, *a chara*, and I've been Róisín since my soul was born."

"Have you always been a seer?"

"Always is a very long time, but I've been a seer for many lifetimes."

"A little while ago, in my mind, when you sat by me, I remembered you. I knew you before, didn't I?"

"Yes, darlin', we've known each other, but I'm not going to tell you more than that. The remembering is for you to do when you're ready."

"I understand and I'm grateful." Jeremy finished his sandwich and took a large swallow of tea to wet his throat. "Are you frightened when you see things?"

"I have been in the past, and I can't say that sometimes disturbing images won't come to me as a warning or even a prophecy. But if you're meaning random, nasty scenes or creatures, I've not been troubled by them since my Granny taught me to pray to Archangel Michael to protect my inner sight."

"Who's Archangel Michael?"

"Oh, lad, were you never taught about the archangels and their bands? No wonder you were frightened of what you saw. A lamb to the wolves, you'd have been."

"That's what I felt like. My family didn't go to church, didn't believe in God, and certainly never talked about angels. They were materialists to the core, and our home—which was no home to me—was infested with the jaggedness of their irritation and meanness.

"The only brightness that ever came into my childhood was when Elder Brother appeared to me. But I was too stupid to keep my mouth shut, and my parents drugged me for daring to share my experience that the universe is made of love.

"I forced myself to stop seeing anything years ago, and I'm terrified it's all going to come flooding back at me like a tsunami. If all I got from opening up again was darkness, I think I'd kill myself."

He pushed his plate away and held his head in his hands. Róisín reached across the table and took his hand.

"Jeremy, look at me. Seeing does not have to be an astral journey, but you do need protection. We're not going to leave you vulnerable when you're in this transitional state.

"Lucky and I have a guest room in our home that's not being used at the moment. I want you to come stay with us in our forcefield of Light. We'll teach you how to protect yourself so that, if your inner sight decides to open, you'll be like a flower blooming. No one is going to force you and you'll not force yourself—either to see or not see."

"You would do that for me? You and Lucky? You hardly know me."

"A chara, I know you very well. I have loved you like a grandson and I'll not let you come to harm, I promise."

"I don't know what to say."

"Say, 'thank you, Róisín,' and come with me. We'll speak with Lucky and he'll make the arrangements. Don't you need to give up that expensive apartment you can no longer afford?"

Jeremy looked into her sparkling green eyes.

"You're right, I do. And I don't own much except books, some clothes, a bicycle, and a few pieces of furniture, so packing up won't be difficult."

"Then come along. We have a truck, and Kevin will help with his big SUV. With two vehicles we'll have you moved in no time. There's a shed behind Fibonacci's where you can store anything you don't need right away. This is urgent, *a chara*, so don't drag your feet."

She squeezed his hand in a way that let him know she meant business and did not expect her hospitality to be refused.

Seventeen

Early the next morning Debbie was sitting in the back booth at the coffee shop awash in emotion. With Róisín's permission, Sarah had called her last night to explain that, thanks to Hero—of all the unexpected triggers—Jeremy had experienced a sudden recollection of his embodiment as Madwyn.

No, there was nothing that Debbie needed to do right now, Sarah had insisted. Róisín only wanted her to be aware of what was going on. She and Lucky had immediately moved Jeremy to their guest room and were making sure that the opening of his inner sight, which was taking place, was gradual and not traumatic.

Now Debbie was waiting for Róisín, who had sent her a very short text saying that she needed to speak with her right away about an urgent matter than concerned Debbie personally. She couldn't help feeling a bit like a naughty schoolgirl who'd been called to the principal's office.

"Did I do something wrong?" she asked as soon as her mentor slid into the seat across from her. "Your text was so cryptic, I thought Mother Superior was going to discipline me for an infraction I wasn't aware I had committed." She grimaced. "Sorry, old Catholic school guilt raising it's head."

"Oh, no, darlin'," said Róisín. She reached over and patted Debbie's hand. "As Sarah told you, we've been rushed with a sudden change of events, bringing Jeremy to stay with us for a while."

"That's incredibly generous of you and Lucky. I felt bad that I couldn't help, but I knew you were handling things. Can you tell me, what is his state of mind?"

"He's doing fine. He is, after all, a grown man who happens to be very intelligent. He also knows a lot about his own mind because he's been controlling it for most of his life. However, he has some deep childhood scars around his clairvoyant abilities, and we need to help him heal."

"I wondered why he said he wasn't interested in clairvoyance," said Debbie. "Is there anything I can do? I feel like a race horse that's not allowed to run."

"That's why I asked you to come over in a rush this morning." Róisín focused her loving and very direct gaze on Debbie exactly as she had looked Jeremy in the eye yesterday. "I believe I have hit upon the perfect solution for both of you, at least for the next couple of weeks."

"Róisín, that's fabulous! Thank you."

"Well, darlin', you may not thank me once you hear my idea. I want you to stay away from Jeremy and Fibonacci's until Thanksgiving."

"But why? Now that he's finally remembering?"

"Especially now. I'm asking you to trust me in this."

"You know I trust you, Róisín."

"I do, which is why I know I can trust you to do as I ask. Remind me, now. You said that Jeremy didn't recognize you at *Samhain*."

"Not that I could tell. I was terribly awkward because I recognized him, so even if he had remembered me, I don't think he would have wanted to actually get to know me."

"Good. I want to keep it that way for a while. I know this will be difficult for you, darlin', but when he does begin to remember you, I want the experience to be positive for both of you."

Debbie closed her eyes and hugged herself as if she was cold. "I had no idea I was going to feel such pain."

"I know. Being so close and yet not able to reach him tears at your soul. But if we're easy now, the time will be less. I'm sure of it."

"If *you're* sure, then I'll try to be, too."

Róisín thought a minute. "If we weren't in the middle of November, I'd send you to Ireland for a holiday. But this isn't the best time to visit."

"That's true." Debbie looked across the coffee shop at the customers coming in bundled against the cold. "Whenever I do go to Ireland, I want to visit gardens, collect herbs and healing recipes."

"As you should," agreed Róisín. "So, for now, why don't you spend more time with your sister. You could babysit for Sarah. Explore your creativity. Write poetry. Meditate."

"I could, but you do think my remaining in the neighborhood is a good idea? Our health food store and my apartment are only two blocks away. Jeremy and I might still run into each other."

"That is a danger. If we were already into spring, I'd set Jeremy to digging and planting in my garden instead of letting him come here. But Kevin is putting him to work sorting, cataloging, and packing books. The man needs to do physical work so his mind can relax. If his clair-voyance comes back, we don't want him experiencing any more jolts."

"I understand." Debbie closed her eyes, considering. "Perhaps I could go on a retreat somewhere. Not too far away, but far enough that maybe I'll stop thinking about him. I was hoping to spend more time with Master K. H., but I suppose that can come later."

"Good lass. We'll hope for the best and create an atmosphere for Jeremy where the best is what will emerge for him and from him. With any luck and by the grace of *An Síoraí*, we'll all enjoy a big celebration feast at Thanksgiving."

Róisín's expression brightened with inspiration. "Debbie, what has Saint Germain taught us about attracting our twin flame?"

"He said to meditate on what is most real about ourselves, our True Self, and to become more of that. Because what's real in us is also real in our soul's other half."

"Exactly. I believe K. H. can help you there. He knows Jeremy very well. Even if you're on retreat, you can tune into the Master's presence and ask him to help you accelerate your own consciousness so you can support Jeremy spiritually. The lad must come to you of his own free will. And you must not do any probing or trying to contact him on the inner. No willing or wishing."

"You know I wouldn't do that, Róisín. No matter how tempting, that borders on witchcraft."

"I know, darlin'. I'm just making sure we are agreed. Go deep within your True Self for the sake of your own soul and aim straight up to *An Síoraí*. Nothing is more attractive than authenticity. Find your Self, and your other half will awaken. He still may choose not to come to you. Free will is supreme. But the only way your reunion can be lasting is if you both bring your wholeness to the meeting."

"Thank you," was all Debbie could say. Her eyes were moist and so were Róisín's. They both rose from their seats and embraced warmly.

"The men will be arriving soon to work on packing books, so you'd best be running along now, my dear adopted daughter."

"I will, my dear adopted mother. I promise to be perfectly invisible until you say otherwise. I'll let Sarah and Glenna know."

Later that afternoon, Jeremy, Kevin, and Rory were taking a break from packing books in the alcove that had served as a study room and private meeting area adjacent to the esoterica collection in the bookstore's up-stairs loft.

Hero was snoozing peacefully amidst the partially filled boxes that were being carefully packed and labeled for whenever they would be able to display these most valuable volumes.

Kevin and Rory were relieved to see that Jeremy seemed to be hold-ing steady after his big upset yesterday. Nothing like physical work and Róisín's healing teas to calm a man's mind and body.

"I wish these books weren't the first to be packed," said Jeremy wistfully, remembering that, as of last night, his own books were also packed up. "I would like to have spent some time reading them, not wrapping them up."

"I know what you mean," said Rory, and Kevin nodded. It was a wonder they were actually making progress on packing. Any one of the three men would have happily spent the day immersed in the ancient books, many of them written well over one hundred fifty years ago.

Instead, they had begun to develop a rhythm that allowed them to make careful note of which book was going into which box, wrapping them against dust or damp, and labeling all four sides of each box so any-one with a list could find a particular title when it came time to unpack.

Jeremy had been staring into his mug of coffee for several minutes as Kevin and Rory discussed which shelf should be next for packing. When they came to a pause in their conversation, he took a deep breath and asked the question that had been on his mind since *Samhain*.

"How did you meet your wives? You both seem well matched with the women you married. I'm wondering how it all happened."

"Blood, sweat, tears, and divine intervention," joked Kevin, shaking his head. "Sarah and I have gone through some really rough patches. If it weren't for Saint Germain, I don't think we would have made it to where we are now. I know we wouldn't have twin babies or a profound understanding of ourselves as twin flames."

His gaze went deep and distant.

"We've known we belonged together since the first night we met in a library in a grand old house on the Upper West Side. We decided to take turns reading a short piece we each had written, and the veil parted. She recognized my voice and I remembered another auburn-haired beauty from hundreds of years in the past. After that we just knew.

"I'm quite sure neither of us had any idea what we were really seeing in that first blush of recognition. Only that we had been together many times and were meant to be together in this life. Even in the roughest times, underneath disagreements and misunderstandings, that experience of knowing never completely left either of us."

All three men were silent for a while. Hero stretched and wandered over to Kevin and put his head in his master's lap.

"What about you, Rory?" Jeremy asked.

"Glenna and I both started dreaming about each other. Not full-blown story dreams. More like snippets of events or impressions. But with definite images of the people we had been in past lives.

"I know what Kevin means about the veil parting, except for us it was a very thick mist on the slopes of Mount Brandon in County Kerry, Ireland. We were both out hiking with friends. I thought I heard a woman singing, and then it was a woman crying for help—which turned out to be Glenna. She'd become separated from her companions and twisted her ankle. We took one look at each other and that was it.

"Of course, we've had our problems and one very harrowing escape from an evil Viking on the astral plane—thanks to Kevin and Sarah in their druid forms as Ah-Lahn and Alana. But we've known since that first day that we were supposed to be together."

"Why the questions, Jeremy? Do you have a woman on your mind?" Kevin had an idea who that might be, but he knew better than to voice his intuition.

"No, there's never been anybody. I've spent my whole life pretty much in my thoughts and my books. I don't think I *could* fall in love, or would know love if it knocked me on the head."

"Do you want to fall in love?" Rory was genuinely curious. "I fought it. Didn't think I was supposed to sacrifice my vocation as a monk to be with Glenna, even though I was powerfully drawn to her.

"I don't remember when we figured out that we were twin flames— you know, two souls who started out as one eons ago. But that knowledge did help me understand why doubts and fears couldn't negate the feelings I had. We were then and still are unalterably attracted."

"Have you ever felt deep affection for another being? Other than for my dog?" laughed Kevin. Hero had ambled over to put his head in Jeremy's lap. The man was gently scratching the dog behind his ears.

"Well, this may sound wild, but when I was a kid, a being I knew only as Elder Brother—who I guess must have been K. H.—visited me and took me flying around the Milky Way and far out into the Universe. That's where I met Saint Germain for the first time, although I didn't remember until F. M. reminded me.

"But when we were out in space, at one point I felt this all-encompassing sensation that somehow I knew was love. It was personal, yet impersonal. Beyond human and yet human in that I felt known by this force, like it was in me and I was in it. Does that make sense?"

"Perfectly," said Rory. His gaze had gone deep within. "I often feel that in my meditations and sometimes with Glenna. Not always, but there are moments when I know I am love, that we are love. No separation. It's a state to strive for—to be that complete."

"How do you get there?" asked Jeremy. "I honestly can't imagine."

"You have to let the other person be who they really are," said Kevin. "And I think you can only do that when you let yourself be authentic. No self-condemnation or trying to be what you're not—acting from some kind of persona the world has projected on you."

"Or trying *not* to be what you are," added Rory. "That's been my big test—denying my calling to teach, for example. I never entirely stopped being a teacher, but I also never fully embraced what it means to share what I know and then learn from others. I'm hoping that being part of the Friends of Ancient Wisdom and working with Kevin on the academy will give me the opportunity to fulfill my *dharma*—my sacred labor—as a teacher."

"And as a husband and father," said Kevin. "I'm just now beginning to understand the sacredness of those roles. Of knowing that I would lay down my life for my family. The instant those babies were born, I think I grew up. I know I am a much better partner to Sarah than I was before because there's so much more at stake now than even our being each one's other half."

Jeremy crossed his arms over his chest and leaned back in his chair. He blew out a sigh. "This is big."

"It is," agreed Kevin. "And you get there step by step. Every once in a while life challenges you to come up higher. When that has happened to me, many of the revelations have appeared like another door opening or somebody pulling back the curtains to let in the sunshine. And every time I find more of my True Self that's probably been there all the time if I'd only had the courage to look outside the prison bars I'd erected myself."

"Yeah, the self-created prison." Jeremy nodded and looked away, pondering. "I've spent my whole life denying what I was, what I was told I shouldn't be. That's how I survived as a kid. But when I met F. M. he told me it was time to break out of the prison I'd created."

"We've all been very clever at building prisons that are so much a part of who we believe ourselves to be that we don't see them," said Kevin. "I think that's one of the brilliant things about our community. We can help each other detect the bars that we're blind to."

"Just spending last night with Lucky and Róisín and listening to them talk about the community and their love for the Friends of Ancient Wisdom, I began to get an idea of how you all support each other," said Jeremy with genuine appreciation in his voice.

Kevin had an idea.

"You might want to talk to Master K. H. about how you've survived and how you can move on. You already know him as Elder Brother. Lucky says he knows a lot about psychology. And he's coming to our next meeting of the Pythagoreans. We're skipping this week because the students have tests. So, two weeks from now, I was hoping you'd join us. Could you handle that?"

Jeremy considered the idea for a minute and felt a shiver go through his whole body.

"Yeah, I think I could. And I'd like to, except that girl Jenny was coming on to me pretty strong. I'm not used to that."

"A guy with your looks?" teased Rory. "I thought you'd have women after you all the time."

"I've managed to avoid them," Jeremy said simply. He hoped he wasn't blushing in front of these two men he was beginning to like a lot.

"No worries about Jenny," chuckled Kevin. "Noah set her straight right after *Samhain*. He told her you were too old for her and stuck in your ways. He painted a very unattractive picture of your personality."

Jeremy winced. "Good old Noah."

"You'll be fine. Besides, we need your input for the academy." Kevin was trying to encourage, but not push. He wanted to tell Jeremy they were thinking of calling it Crotona Academy, but he decided not to say that word just yet.

"And you don't have to worry about Valerie," added Rory with a grin. "I understand that she and Finn have been together for a couple of years. Besides, she studies like mad and thinks rings around most of us. You can match wits with her and Rudy. He's another sharp one."

"Okay, I'm in," agreed Jeremy. "Thanks for answering my questions. Elder Brother did when I was a kid. And Róisín and Lucky have been great. Now to know I can talk to you guys—well, let's just say I'm more grateful than you can imagine."

"That's a kind of love, you know," said Rory.

"It is," agreed Kevin. "And so is packing books." They all laughed.

Eighteen

Róisín was right about this not being a good time for overseas travel, Debbie admitted while she worked in what she liked to think of as her own alchemist's lab in the back room of Conroy's To Your Health.

If this had not been the darkest time of year, she would have been on a plane to Ireland in a heartbeat so she could roam green fields, collect unique plants, commune with fairies and devas, and find her stone.

However, that excursion would have to wait. And that was probably a good thing. She looked up at the clever rack she and Cyndi had hung from the ceiling to dry herbs and flowers for teas, tinctures, and spices. Róisín's garden had produced a bumper crop of powerful healing plants that were dried and ready for Debbie to work her alchemical magic.

Today she was filling dropper bottles with the echinacea tincture that was now ready for use and sale. With flu season in full swing, their customers had been asking for more of her alcohol-free remedies to boost their immune systems, and she was behind in getting this product on the shelves.

She needed grounding she decided as she labeled the last bottle and cleaned up her work table. It was time she settled into her heart and got out of her head. Maybe she'd put away the recollections of past lives that were flooding her consciousness because Jeremy was near, but not aware of her. Was there a message in this?

He might not be remembering very much, but she was recalling enough ancient events for a book—many chapters of which she knew ought to be transmuted. Meanwhile, she told herself, she could pay more attention to this job of creating remedies, which used to bring her peace, and to her sister.

"Do you remember how we used to love taking the train to the Bronx Zoo and then to the Botanical Garden?" she reminded Cyndi as they were closing the store for the day.

"I do. We were always torn between spending more time with the plants or the animals. We would be so thoroughly entertained by the monkeys and elephants and lions and giraffes . . ."

"Don't forget the pandas," chimed in Debbie.

"And those gorgeous tigers." A faraway look came to Cyndi's sea-green eyes. A true strawberry-blonde with more freckles than she thought any nose should have to tolerate, her face always gave clear expression of her emotions. "I think I liked the tigers best."

"They were stunning," Debbie agreed with a wink. "Such rich colors. Same as your freckles."

"Very funny." Cyndi wrinkled her nose. "And then we'd go into bliss walking through the long enclosures lined with trees and shrubs on our way into the Conservatory, and then we'd stroll along the river if we had time. It was all so magical."

"It was," Debbie said dreamily. She smiled at this sister, closest to her in age and the one most likely to understand what she was going through. At least she hoped that would be true.

"Are you thinking of taking a field trip?" asked Cyndi. "Most of the flowers will be gone for the season, but you would still see some color in the fall foliage. And of course, there's always something beautiful in the palm dome and the greenhouses. I'd go with you, but there's so much to do here. Which is something I need to talk to you about."

Cyndi's expression grew serious. She pressed her lips together and took a deep breath. "Will you come back to the office with me?"

Oh, boy, thought Debbie. Here comes a difficult conversation. Both sisters walked silently to the corner of her workroom that served as their office.

A desk with a computer and printer, two chairs, and a cupboard for office supplies were tucked in amongst tall shelves that held extra stock and the bottles, bags, and other containers for the products that were Debbie's primary responsibility to formulate.

"What's going on with you, Sis?" Cyndi asked straight-out. "I'm trying not to be annoyed with you, but you're not really much help to me right now. I thought you were excited about the store being a family venture, but you seem to feel closer to the people at Fibonacci's than you do to me. If you were a regular employee, I would be asking for your resignation."

"I know," admitted Debbie. "I'm sorry that I've been slacking off."

"More like AWOL," retorted her sister. "Even when you're here physically working with the herbs and essential oils, your mind is elsewhere. You're not focused on the practical aspects of making this business a success. If you need a break, take one.

"Of course you can stay in your apartment, but I'm going to ask Stacey to increase her hours while you decide if you can contribute more than a few remedies to our enterprise."

"That's probably a good idea." Debbie looked up at the ceiling and sighed. "I do honestly regret that you're right—at least for now. I should have told you what's going on with me, but I haven't been sure myself. I can explain now, if you want to hear."

"Will I understand? Or is this one of your visions?" Cyndi's tone softened and a smile played around her eyes.

"It's been a vision and now it's a reality. I won't burden you with lots of detail, except—you know how I've told you that each of us has a twin soul or twin flame?"

"Uh-huh." Cyndi frowned. "I've always thought that was an excuse some people use for bouncing from one relationship to the next, shopping for their perfect mate."

Debbie nodded. "I know that does happen. In my case, though, over the past few weeks I've been having dreams and visions of past lives when I was with my soul's twin. I might not have put much attention on those images, except that my teacher . . ."

"The one you call F. M. Bellamarre?"

"That's right. He told me that my twin flame is approaching in the physical. The other night, at the big costume ball we had at Fibonacci's, the very man showed up. I immediately knew he was the one."

"That's so romantic." Cyndi gushed, instantly forgetting that she'd been upset with Debbie. "So, are you getting married? Can I be your maid of honor? How did he propose?"

"No, my darling sister, he didn't propose. Jeremy—that's his name—didn't even recognize me. In fact, I was so awkward around him that I'm sure he's far from interested. And in the meantime, my friend Róisín wants me to stay away from Fibonacci's for a couple of weeks until she and some of the others have an opportunity to work with him.

"Jeremy used to be a seer and now he isn't and . . ." Debbie threw up her hands and blew out an exasperated sigh. "It's all too complicated. And painful."

Cyndi's eyes were wide. "Wow, I can see why you need to get away."

"Exactly. He may never recognize me, which makes me feel like I'm in mourning for the loss of a relationship that may never begin. Róisín said I've got some deep inner work to do before Jeremy and I can possibly have a future together. I need to connect with the real me, and to do that, I think I need to go on a retreat for at least a week."

"Then go find you. And maybe this man who has you so upset will wake up, sweep you off your feet, and put us both out of our misery." Cyndi laid a gentle hand on her sister's shoulder. "Do you know where you want to go?"

"I do. There's this amazing retreat center in the Catskills, close to Woodstock. I'm too late to sign up for a program, but their website says I can just hang out and participate in their drop-in yoga and meditation sessions if I want to. There are trees everywhere and it's totally secluded and serene. I promise I'll be better when I get back."

"Don't make promises you can't keep," said Cyndi firmly. "Just figure out what you want and where you fit. We'll go from there."

"I love you, Sis," said Debbie.

"Good. I love you, too. Now go pack and get out of here as fast as you can." Cyndi grinned and the two sisters hugged like they used to do when they were little girls.

Early the next morning Debbie was in her car heading north. She had texted Róisín, Sarah, and Glenna to let them know what she was doing, and to say that if traffic wasn't too heavy, she would arrive at the retreat center well before lunch time.

When she'd called the center yesterday, the very helpful concierge she spoke with said there were a number of opportunities for her to create her own get-away retreat. And, yes, they did have a private room available for ten nights, as one of their regular visitors had canceled her reservation earlier that day.

A ten-day retreat would take a serious bite out of Debbie's finances. But she knew she needed an extended length of time to penetrate as deeply into her consciousness as she felt she must, in order to pass this initiation that she only partially understood.

What she did understand was that she needed to physically relax and create a peaceful internal climate that would invite insight. She scheduled a spa treatment for the afternoon and planned to sleep for hours after that.

Would she dream at this site that had been sacred to native peoples for centuries? Or would her nighttime visions be silent for a while? Only being on the land would answer that question.

Traffic was unusually light this Friday morning. The sun was out, the sky was amazingly clear for November, and the other cars on the road were all moving as if guided by unseen hands. Was today a holiday of some sort? Debbie wondered. Or were angels clearing a path for her?

As she sailed over the Throgs Neck Bridge, skirted the Bronx, passed Mount Vernon, and entered the scenic Taconic State Parkway, she began to feel herself taking deep breaths. Leaving the pressure of urban population and pollution made a difference. She also had a feeling that she was not alone in her car.

Róisín had said she should tune into the presence of Master K. H. for help in understanding her psychology. She had spoken only briefly with the Master on the outer, but she was certain they were well-acquainted on the inner. When he'd appeared at the *Samhain* celebration, her heart had nearly leapt from her chest—so thrilled was she to see him in person.

"If you're here, Master K. H., I welcome your companionship," she said aloud. "Please help me discover what I must in these few days. I know there are insights that escaped me when I was Dearbhla, that I must realize now for the sake of my path, my friends, and for Jeremy— whether or not we are ever together."

Instantly the atmosphere in the car shimmered and she heard the reassuring voice of K. H. answer, "I will."

A remarkable feeling of peace came over her and her mind stilled. The thousand thoughts and questions that had recently troubled her sleep quieted. As she drove along the open road, she slipped into a sense of timelessness, simply enjoying the sensation of movement, relishing the reds and golds and greens that painted Nature's lush forest canvas in glorious shades of autumn beauty.

The quieting of mind and heart she experienced driving through the mountains reminded her of the discipline of maintaining silence for five years that Pythagoras had insisted upon for his advanced initiates in their community of Crotona, Italy, during the sixth century BC.

Surely I can be quiet for five days, she thought.

As soon as she was settled in her pristine accommodations, she fashioned a little name tag that stated *I am in silence.* Here was a place where others would honor that discipline. Knowing she could maintain a peaceful cocoon around herself, she felt another wave of relaxation.

With some time remaining before lunch was served, she had planned to walk around the perimeter of the main retreat property to familiarize herself with the location of the various buildings. But as soon as she finished unpacking, she strode out of her cabin, across the central lawn, and down a slope into a stand of tall white birch trees whose delicate gold and crimson leaves flashed in the sun like a holy fire.

As if guided to the spot, she flung her arms around the largest tree, closed her eyes, and leaned her cheek against the paper-thin bark that glowed in the warmth of the midday sun.

Here was a vibration and a presence Debbie recognized deep within her bones. In times of stress or crisis, Dearbhla had frequently walked into the forest surrounding the *túath* of *Tearmann* to do the same thing— to fill her soul with the revitalizing energy of trees and to experience the comforting touch of the mighty devas who ensouled them.

Debbie's heart was full to bursting with love and the joy of communion she always felt when in the presence of the unseen. "I knew I would find you here!" she silently exclaimed to the devas she could feel all around her.

"Yes, daughter," she heard them answer her heart's greeting. "We knew that one day you would come to this holy place. There is much for you to absorb here. Remember how to learn through your pores, for we are not separate from you. Gain your wisdom through proximity to us. Breathe us in as Dearbhla practiced and all will be well."

Debbie stepped back from the tree and felt her chin lifted as if by a loving mother. She raised her eyes and beheld a group of magnificent tree devas, whose tall, ethereal forms shimmered in a hundred shades of green and gold that flickered in the sunlight as it danced through leaves rustling in the soft mountain breeze.

"The earth will hold you and oneness will expand as you allow."

Debbie felt the devas' promise in the secret chamber of her heart and then beheld the welcoming smiles of these luminous beings. Their radiation enfolded her, filling her with confidence and a sense of knowing the truth of her oneness with every tree in this part of the forest.

As hunger drew her attention to the dining hall for lunch, she was grateful to be wearing her little sign of silence. She could not have spoken a word to the other guests, who greeted her warmly with palms together in the gesture of *Namaste*.

Nineteen

Debbie's personal retreat flowed like Spirit's gentle river, carrying her where she needed to be when she needed to be there. She attended some inspiring meditation sessions, did yoga and T'ai Chi alone or with small groups, and walked and walked.

Because of the lateness of the season, the retreat center was not crowded, so she was able to wander the grounds and rest in some of the more popular meditation spots without being disturbed. She always took her camera and journal with her because she was well aware of Nature's power to inspire a beautiful photo or a poem.

Dearbhla had been a lover of the Word whose language had often been expressed in prophecy. As Debbie gave herself up to listening and watching the play of Life in its vastness of form, she wondered if the future would make itself known to her.

She knew not to probe and so focused on the present. When she did, a few lines of verse often came to her, not only as expressions of her experience, but also with a hint of instruction and comfort.

> Trust the silence
> And feel the sound of immensity
> Stir in your deepest heart
> Where you have never dared to venture.

Tuck these words away for safekeeping, came the prompting from her inner wisdom. *They are for a purpose which you soon shall know.*

Five days of silence could have been five minutes or five weeks, so completely was Debbie immersed in the timelessness of Spirit's flow through Nature. She followed inspiration where it led her into depths of presence she had not experienced in this life.

In the absence of outer speech, inner wisdom often spoke in images or glyphs. The music of Nature became clearer. The warbling of birdsong, the splashing of waterfall, the gurgling of stream, or the crunch of fallen leaves underfoot became a symphony of profound meaning that said to Debbie, *Here is Life and the Love intrinsic in all of creation.*

On the night of her fifth day of silence a husband and wife presented a concert played on hang drum and traditional Tibetan singing bowls. The event was conducted in the largest hall where listeners could be seated or were welcome to invite deeper meditation by lying on yoga mats with a blanket for warmth.

Debbie was grateful that she chosen the reclining meditation, for she easily lifted out of her body in an experience of cosmic unity that went far beyond the vast acreage of the retreat's pristine forest. Here was a true mountain-top experience, as the whole world lay before her and she was one with it.

Again, time stood still until the very end of the concert when the softer, ringing tone of crystal bowls brought everyone back to earth. In that moment, Debbie was aware of the presence of Master K. H. He nodded to her and silently conveyed a single word: "Tomorrow."

The next morning Debbie rose early. After a simple breakfast she walked with inner purpose to the secluded pond where she liked to sit and contemplate the serenity and myriad sounds of Nature one hears only when still and patient.

The prompting to arrive was so strong that she was not surprised to see Master K. H. seated by the clear, reflective waters.

Dressed as a Franciscan friar, he was deeply engaged in speaking to the chickadee perched on his shoulder, the red-tailed hawk sitting majestically on a nearby branch, and the collection of rabbits, squirrels, and foxes who were gathered at his feet.

Debbie also noted a couple of owls paying close attention from a hole in a large tree to the Master's left. And she had a feeling that at least one shy mountain lion was hunkered down behind a rock outcropping where it could attend the Master's discourse without being seen.

She had instinctively slowed her pace as she approached the pond. So as not to disturb the scene before her, she stilled her being and brought to mind the feeling of unity consciousness she had experienced the night before.

After a few minutes, the Master's gentle voice brought her out of her reverie. All of the animals had departed, and he was motioning for her to join him on the bench.

"Silence and bliss are excellent partners, are they not?"

"They are, yes," Debbie answered. She spoke softly and somewhat hesitantly, as she had not uttered a word in five days. She would look back on this moment in realization that she had indeed tuned into the Master's vibration when she added, "For silence allows bliss to emerge unfettered, and bliss silences all unlike itself."

K. H. nodded his approval.

"You have done well, my daughter. The way is now prepared for our conversation. I am interested in hearing about your retreat experiences. Since your arrival, what have you learned while in communion with our stately devas and with your higher faculties of awareness?"

Debbie looked into the warm brown eyes of this extraordinary master. His vibration was uniquely his own, as she knew each member of the Great White Brotherhood emanated the radiance of their own adeptship. Yet she was also aware of the oneness that K. H. shared with her dear F. M.

Surely, all masters are one, she thought to herself as she began to unfold for him what had been transpiring in, through, and around her. She turned and gazed across the pond, remembering.

"On my first full day of silence I was standing amidst this extraordinary group of birch trees, looking up, up, up into their tallest branches. As I did, I felt my consciousness reaching, exceeding their height, touching the sky, and then going far beyond the clouds.

"I let my awareness continue extending, all the while listening to the sound of wind in the trees, as if the devas were whispering to each other and then to me, words of blessing and encouragement.

"And then the whisperings became a sort of silent song which prompted a poem. May I share it with you?"

"Of course, my dear. I believe that poetry is one of the most direct ways of accessing the wisdom of our soul and our True Self. The verses we compose are always first for our individual learning. The important thing is that we gain insight into what Spirit is trying to say to us. That is the most vital conversation. All else is extra. Please, proceed."

Debbie opened her journal and began to read: "I call the poem *Crann Taca*, which means tower of strength in Irish."

> Remember me in silence.
> You will always find me
> in the soundless sound
> of your heartbeat.
>
> I am your Tree of Life
> planted in the ground
> of your soul.
>
> Never doubt that I hold you
> complete in the garden
> where we live as one,
> as you stretch your branches
> higher and higher toward
> the Sun of all Being
> where I AM.

"What do these lines mean to you?" asked the Master.

"The Sun of all Being reminds me of the sun disc that hangs over our altar at Fibonacci's. As I was reading to you, I could see the face of *An Síoraí* in the center, now surrounded by a huge, circular rainbow light."

K. H. was watching her closely. "Go on, my dear."

"I have spent many hours looking up to the heavens, as if the devas were literally pulling me from where I've been to where I need to go.

"On the second day of my silence, I was out walking and came upon a stand of trees that still had nearly all of their leaves. They were pure gold. I don't remember ever being in the midst of such vibrant radiance emanating from a physical form.

"I stood for a long time, feeling this glorious color being absorbed into every pore of my body, my mind, my heart, my soul. And when I felt that I couldn't take in one more atom of golden light, I whooshed up into a city of Light. I've had that experience before in one of the meditations at Fibonacci's. I believe this is an actual place, perhaps an etheric retreat. Could that be so? Do you know this place, Master?"

"I do," he affirmed.

"Is this where you and I have met, perhaps where I have studied with you?"

"It is one of our connections, my daughter. And I am pleased that your memories of our long association are becoming so clear to you. What else did you detect from this vision?"

Debbie closed her eyes, recollecting the sublime experience of being surrounded in what she felt was the flame of Wisdom itself.

"Jeremy was there with us. I believe he is there, often. If that is so, why doesn't he remember?"

"Is it not true that you are only now gaining full access to these inner experiences, my dear? And you are not burdened by the negativity he was subjected to as a child in this life. He will remember when his soul is ready. What does this tell you?"

"That in patience I will possess my own soul," laughed Debbie. "And that the more I learn about my own True Self, the more connection I gain to the True Self of Jeremy, which can only help him."

"That is correct. And, if I intuit correctly, I believe you have another poem for me that has to do with your discovery. Am I right?" Debbie smiled broadly at his inquiry.

"Of course, you know what a strong affinity I have to Ireland and its legends. I was reflecting upon Saint Brendan's voyage, which is called his *Navigatio* in Latin. He and his monks are said to have sailed for years without trying to steer their open boat or presuppose with their minds where Spirit desired them to go.

"This poem feels like a strong admonition for me not to try to figure out the future. Dearbhla was never told her prophecies in advance. I know I need to have more trust and not be afraid of what may come."

Let go your oars
Release all expectations
Welcome the currents of wisdom greater
Than what you have imagined till today.

A soft breeze is blowing
Across the waves of possibility,
Ready to enfold you
In the Divine Mother's loving care.
You are already home
In the ground of here and now.

This journey is unlike all others;
For having reached the labyrinth's center,
The only way up to Truth
Is out to greet the thirsty souls
Who await your coming.

You cannot disappoint
As long as you remember:
You must become the boat.
Sail on!

Debbie could see that K. H. was listening intently, now with his eyes closed. He said nothing, so she continued.

"The night before the third day of my silent retreat it snowed. Not a heavy blanket, only a dusting that caused the trees to drop most of their leaves. It also clung to each tiny branch and blade of grass so the entire landscape appeared to have been laced in crystalline white.

"I bundled up and walked around, marveling at the beauty of each scene. I was simply overcome by Nature's delicate artistry. When I sat by the pond to gaze at the reflection of such exquisite detail, this poem emerged."

> Beauty floats on the breeze
> Of Holy Spirit's Presence.
> She flies up on angel wings
> Spreading dew drops of perfection
> To quicken the hearts of all
> Who will receive her gifts with gladness.
>
> She bonds her place
> And all who live
> With stories of the past,
> Giving courage for today
> And for tomorrow.
>
> The telling is her treasure.
> Ears feel Beauty as her sound
> Tickles their inward parts,
> As bodies rest easy in the fragrant grass
> Where Beauty's delicate bare feet
> Have cleared a path,
> And fairies hold up firefly lanterns
> To light the way.

Debbie was so immersed in her recollections, she forgot that Master K. H. was seated next to her.

"The fourth day of silence was deeply serene. I went on a long hike and found myself paying very close attention to how I placed my feet on the earth and how I moved along the path. When I came to a small clearing that was surrounded by enormous pine trees whose devas emanated a vibration of profound nobility and honor, I stopped and stood in their presence until I could again sense that spirit of oneness this land seems to foster.

"Here I perceived the truth that there is no competition in Nature, that *An Síoraí's* power is as gentle as it is strong, and that to realize my destiny, I must walk softly into what is next."

Soft the ground
that graciously holds me
standing easily—*with* the earth, not on it

softly folded in a warm breeze
that lightly carries
delicate bird song

as a soft brown bunny
of cotton-tailed fluffiness
scampers noiselessly
through soft grey shadows

while wisps of tall, thin grasses
wave their fine, ripe tops

a community of elegant greeting
and gratitude for my soft gaze
that receives their hospitality
and shares their gentle encouragement
for being soft with where I am.

Debbie felt the Master's attention upon her now and turned to him. His eyes were open, but he was not looking at her. Instead, his gaze was focused in the distance, as if he were listening to his own inner wisdom. At last he spoke in a solemn tone.

"This is well done, my daughter. I am pleased. Because you have surrendered to the holiness of these sacred hills instead of entertaining your curiosity about the past or the future, I am given permission to offer you the insight your heart has yearned to receive regarding you and your twin flame. Are you prepared to have the akashic records opened to you? If so, I will tell you a story."

Debbie shuddered as a feeling of trepidation rippled through her body. Now that the revelation she had sought was offered, she actually did not want to hear it.

K. H. noted her reticence. His eyes met hers with an expression of profound loving-kindness as he waited for her response.

She closed her eyes and settled her consciousness in her heart. Here was the eye of the needle she knew she must pass through. A moment of no return. An opportunity she knew her soul had requested and which she must accept in her outer awareness.

She opened her eyes, which had become very clear and direct. "Yes, Master, I will receive the gift you so graciously offer."

Twenty

"Because Sarah has let you read parts of her book, you already know some of this story," Master K. H. began. "However, not all akashic records were opened to her, as she was commissioned to write only those events that pertained directly to the path of twin flames that she and Kevin yet walk.

"You and Sarah know that you were together in ancient Egypt and in first-century Ireland. You and she were also sister priestesses on the Atlantean island of Poseid in the Temple of the One Light overseen by Lady Nhada-lihn, as she was known in those days.

"You were of great support to your friend as you both escaped from Atlantis before the devastating flood. You sailed together to Egypt and, because of your unselfish devotion to each other, you both incarnated in that land several times—including as granddaughter and Queen Mother during the 18th Dynasty.

"In the Atlantean embodiment, Kevin and Jeremy were fellow priests in Lady Nhada-lihn's temple, but their association became complicated and did not end well."

Debbie clutched her heart and felt her body stiffen.

"Do not be afraid, dear one," said K. H. "You are safe and will not be harmed by the scenes you are about to witness.

"You are familiar with the life reviews we conduct on inner planes. In this holy place, we are sealed in my aura. The pond will act as our projection screen. Fix your attention on the still waters and when images appear, step into them as you have done in other times and locations."

Debbie did feel safe and enfolded in the soft golden cloud of the Master's presence. She closed her eyes and let herself sink into the life review process, as she knew K. H. was accelerating her consciousness.

When the vibrations reached the familiar level of intensity, she opened her eyes. Where the pond had been, a scene of ancient Atlantis lay before her, exactly as Sarah had described it in her book.

Debbie and her friend, known as Víahlah and Treylah, were on a ship that was anchored at a small quay and ready to depart. They were waiting for Kevin, known as Khieranan, and several of his fellow priests. One of them was Jeremy, who in those days was called Wyn.

However, a terrible battle was taking place at dockside.

The ship's captain was ready to cast off, but Khieranan had not yet boarded. When he turned to join the others, a troop of temple police marched onto the quay, carrying torches to light their way, and pushing before them his best friend who was bruised and bloodied.

The High Priest was decked out in full regalia as if he were conducting a sacred ceremony. While Treylah and Víahlah watched in horror, the High Priest thrust out his right arm and directed a terrible, laser-like ray at Khieranan's friend.

The man writhed in pain as another bolt and then another struck with wicked force. Finally the tortured man slumped, his body shattered by the withering energy of the crystal rays that once had been used only for healing. As murder weapons, they were viciously effective.

"Stop!" demanded Khieranan, raising his arms to deflect the rays of deadly energy the High Priest now turned on him.

"Take off!" he yelled back to the ship's captain, who, with his terrified passengers, was standing transfixed by the dreadful sight unfolding before them.

The captain jumped at the command and sprang into action. He immediately launched his vessel, which powered away from the harbor with the speed of a gale-force blast of wind.

With a lightning-fast sweep of his arm, Khieranan threw off his traveling cloak, revealing himself clothed in the vestments of Lady Nhada-lihn's followers. He appeared to grow in stature as his aura shimmered with fiery blue light.

"No, Khieranan, no!" cried Treylah in a panic. She would have leapt off the ship had Víahlah not restrained her.

Khieranan appeared not to hear her. Instead, he planted his feet and raised his arms to the heavens. Then he began to chant the sacred words that had not been spoken outside of the Temple of the One Light since Lady Nhada-lihn had mysteriously disappeared more than two years earlier.

Sensing the power the lone priest was invoking, the High Priest and his soldiers escalated their assault, howling in rage against the shield of Khieranan's blazing blue aura that temporarily repelled their murderous energy back upon them.

Nevertheless, Khieranan realized he could not survive the brutal attack. Even with the abilities Lady Nhada-lihn had imparted to him, he had only minutes before his strength gave out. He would not allow himself to be captured and tortured to reveal the names of his compatriots. He had only one clear choice.

Abruptly, he lowered his arms and smiled at the High Priest. This move so surprised his assailant that for an instant the aggressor forgot his insane hatred of this honest man who represented everything the High Priest despised.

Taking advantage of the momentary reprieve, Khieranan summoned every erg of his remaining strength and connection with the One Light. Raising his arms again, he cried aloud, "Now!"

Instantly, a shaft of dazzling rainbow light descended from the ethers and landed between him and his attackers. Hovering above them was the luminous image of Lady Nhada-lihn herself.

Stretching forth her hands, she shot out a ray of pure white light to link with Khieranan's upraised arms, creating a figure-eight flow of scintillating energy between their figures.

Khieranan became perfectly calm. He quickly glanced back over his shoulder to ensure that the ship was safely out of danger. Then, with an expression of sad disbelief, he looked once more at the malignant crowd gathered on the quay.

He held absolutely still for a few seconds and then raised

his eyes to Lady Nhada-lihn. She nodded to him and, in a flash, a blinding ruby light blazed out in rings upon rings of fire across the harbor, causing the attackers to collapse, sightless and senseless. In that instant, Khieranan vanished from sight.

Víahlah was doing her best to comfort Treylah, who was beside herself with horror and grief. At the same time, she felt herself quaking at her own terrible realization that Wyn, her husband, had not appeared on the quay. He was supposed to accompany them on the ship, but he had not boarded.

Where was he?

In those days, Víahlah was gifted with extraordinary powers of clairvoyance, especially where her loved ones were concerned. As she cradled Treylah in her arms and felt her friend fall into an exhausted sleep, she cast her own vision back onto the island of Poseid, where they had all lived and served the One Light.

It did not take her long to find Wyn. He was rushing along a dark alleyway, carrying a bag with some of her belongings that she had not asked him to bring, but that he knew were precious to her. His intuition had told him to leave them behind, that he needed to hurry to join his wife. But being certain that he had plenty of time, he had ignored the prompting.

He was nearing the final passageway that would bring him to the quay when the High Priestess, who had usurped Lady Nhada-lihn's position, stepped out of the shadows and blocked his path.

She was clothed in a rich, black cloak that seemed to billow around her as if it had a life of its own. She fixed Wyn with an intense stare and threw back her hood to reveal long, ebony hair that spilled down her shoulders, framing her full bosom that was barely covered by the tight bodice of her crimson satin gown that rustled as she moved toward him.

"Where are you going, Wyn?" she purred and placed a firm hand on his shoulder with a power that made it impossible for him to move. "Surely not to join that silly woman you call your wife. She's long gone. Left without you. When my lover, the High Priest, attacked your supposed friend, Khieranan, they scattered like frightened mice. But not before they rendered that stupid man inert.

"Now I have no one to look after me," she said pitifully. "How fortunate that I found you, my big strong Wyn. You're exactly the kind of man I've been looking for. Come with me and we'll talk about how we can take care of each other."

"No," Wyn insisted. "You're lying. Víahlah is pregnant with our child. She wouldn't leave without me."

"Oh, but she did." The words oozed out of the High Priestess's mouth as she leered at Wyn. She kept her left hand on his shoulder and made a sweeping gesture with her right arm that conjured the very scene she was describing.

Wyn could see all too well that the ship carrying his wife was making great speed away from Poseid. He was furious. How could Víahlah abandon him like that? Such a betrayal was unforgivable.

"Don't be angry, Wyn," cooed the High Priestess. "I'll take good care of you. And besides, your parents will be delighted to know that I have prevented you from leaving us. Those very useful scientists have been helping us reign in misguided priests like you and Khieranan. He escaped, but you will not."

The scene faded from view and Debbie found herself once more seated on the bench overlooking the pond. Master K. H. was beside her, holding her hands between both of his. When he saw that she had come back to herself, he released her hands and offered her a cup of cool water.

"You need not witness more," he said gently. "However, there is more to this story. Shall I tell you the rest?"

"If the story is important," said Debbie faintly. Her body was shaking. "Although that last scene left little to the imagination of what happened to Wyn. He should have listened to his intuition."

"That is true," said K. H. "Unfortunately, that realization came to him too late, and he berated himself for the error."

"Surely with his own inner sight he could have figured out that Víahlah didn't betray him," insisted Debbie. She could feel a troubling emotional intensity vibrating in her solar plexus.

"One would hope so," said the Master, observing her closely as he continued with the story. "However, they both misperceived the situation, to the great sorrow of their souls."

Events did not unfold exactly as you might think or as the High Priestess obviously desired. Wyn was a large man and strong of mind and body. Despite the woman's wiles and considerable occult power, he was able to resist her seduction.

However, because he emphatically declined her attention, she was furious with him and turned him over to his parents. Those individuals were part of a conspiracy to undermine the freedoms which the people of Atlantis had worked hard to establish, but which were being gradually taken from them through deception and their own failure to stand for the principles earlier generations had fought to preserve.

Wyn attempted to counteract his family's maliciousness, but he was one man, isolated from his friends. Although he was still upset with Víahlah, he did try to contact her on the inner.

However, she was so angry at him for what she perceived as his betrayal with the High Priestess that she prevented him from finding her or witnessing the birth of their son in Egypt. And because he knew that she had blocked his vision, he soon stopped trying to locate her.

Not long after that, the volcanic eruptions that destroyed the last vestiges of the great Atlantean civilization began, and Wyn was caught in one of the first lava flows that swept through the capital. Both he and Víahlah died angry, never knowing the fate of the one who was their soul's true partner.

Contacting this record was like a knife in Debbie's heart, but she urged K. H. to finish the story. "I know there is purpose to this disclosure, Master. May I know what it is?"

"Yes, my daughter, and by asking you show the courage of which I know you are capable.

Wyn's soul was devastated by the events he had seemed powerless to avoid. As soon as he was able to petition the Great Karmic Lords for new opportunity, he begged to reembody with Víahlah and their friends so they might once again take a stand for the freedoms they knew to be their right and their duty to defend.

That is the main reason he was born as Meke's loving protector, Jarahnaten in ancient Egypt. Sadly, on the way to Ireland he valiantly put himself in danger to save others and was lost at sea. However, his devotion to Meke earned him the lifetime as Madwyn in the first century AD.

Those two incarnations resulted in much good karma. They were a dispensation for both of you to forge a stronger bond in anticipation of this very hour, because the karma of Atlantis is now coming due.

As you may have guessed, the parents of Wyn are Jeremy's parents in this lifetime. His karma with them is complex. For a long time he did not understand the repressive activities they were conducting on Atlantis. In fact, some of his actions actually assisted them until his friend Khieranan enlightened him as to their true intent. He never forgave them for ensnaring him in their diabolical schemes, which kept them karmically tied.

In this life, he saw through these individuals when he was still a child. However, he was once more alone and angry at them. Thus they overcame him with drugs until he was old enough to successfully resist.

There remain others he must face and conquer in this life. I cannot tell you who they are or when he will meet them, but your prayers will be of great assistance to his soul and to the union of your twin flames.

The Master could see that Debbie was in need of rest. However, there was one more point to their conversation.

"I have one final question for you, my dear. What insight came to mind about the concert you attended last night?"

Debbie breathed deeply and thought for a minute. Recalling that elevating event began to ease the pain in her heart.

"I was impressed with the power of sound. We do a lot of chanting with the Friends of Ancient Wisdom."

"And what does that tell you?"

"That while creation surely began as a thought in the Divine Mind, 'Let there be Light!' was the fiat that brought that idea into form. I'm ready to start invoking light again." Debbie breathed a sigh.

"And so you must, my daughter. Sound produced with harmonious tones and balanced rhythms brings heaven to earth and opens a corridor of light which the soul travels from earth to heaven.

"Never leave off your strong visualizations, yet couple them with your focused chants and mantras. Then you will surely perceive what miracles *An Síoraí*, the Eternal One, can perform."

"I will do that, I promise," said Debbie firmly, her fervor restored.

"Of that I am certain," K. H. affirmed. "Only remember, you can pray for your twin flame, but you each must pass your individual initiations if you are to be together and remain united.

"I must leave you now and I encourage you to take some rest. A delightful surprise is on the horizon, which will bring much joy to the remainder of your retreat."

"Thank you so much," said Debbie with her whole heart. She could feel her perceptions of the past and expectations for the future shifting within her.

"Remember, my daughter, illumination is often the greatest compassion we can offer a soul, especially one who is striving, as you are. I will see you at Fibonacci's when the time is right. Be strong and hold fast to what you have received. Many challenges lie ahead for you and your beloved. You are now more able to meet them than you have been in a very long time. Please stand now, so I may give you my blessing."

Debbie and the Master rose from the bench where they had been seated undisturbed. She closed her eyes as he placed his hand on her crown chakra. Beams of restorative radiance flowed into her mind and through her body like a waterfall of golden liquid light.

"And now, my daughter, is there anything you would like to ask me before we part?"

Debbie looked into his compassionate face and ventured the question that had been simmering in the back of her mind since the second day of her retreat.

"There is," she said. "My five days of silence unfolded like a familiar discipline, and the insights that came to me felt as if I were remembering them, not experiencing them for the first time. Is it possible that I was one of your students at Crotona? And was Jeremy there as well?'

The Master's deep brown eyes became noticeably luminous. "What does your heart tell you?"

"My heart says, yes," said Debbie softly.

Answering her with a serene smile, Master K. H. folded his hands together in the gesture of *Namaste*. He remained in that attitude as they held each other's loving attention in the profound communion that is known only to masters and their sincere students.

Then he raised his right hand in silent benediction, turned, and walked into the forest, leaving his friend of ancient wisdom feeling amazed, enlivened, and deeply moved by all that she had witnessed.

Twenty-One

Debbie took the Master's advice and returned to her room to rest. Not surprisingly, she slept through lunch and woke as the sun was setting. Groggy from her very long nap, she realized that dinner would probably be served soon. She definitely needed to nourish her body after her astonishing conversation with K. H.

On her way to the dining hall, she removed her little *I am in silence* tag and readied herself to actually speak with other retreat-goers. She opened the main door and was instantly met by two familiar faces.

Maggie O'Toole's cheery voice greeted her first. "Debbie, *a chara*, there you are! Róisín told us we'd find you here. We asked at the reception desk, but they said you were keeping silence. We didn't want to disturb you."

"So we thought we'd ambush you here at dinner time instead," laughed her husband, Tim. "We'd nearly given up, but Maggie said you were on your way."

"My goodness!" exclaimed Debbie as she took each of their hands in hers. "How wonderful to see you both. Did Róisín send you to check up on me?"

"Oh, no, darlin'," Maggie assured her. "We come here when we can't get home to Ireland. Now's not a good time to visit, but we needed some time in a thin place, which this certainly is. We happened to mention to Róisín that we wouldn't be at the service they're having on Saturday night and she said we might see you. And, truth be told, she did ask us to make sure you were all right."

"Yes, I am," said Debbie honestly. She was more than all right. After her rest, she was feeling wonderful. And hungry. "Let's get our food and have a good visit. We've seen each other for years at Fibonacci's, but we've never had a long conversation. I think we should correct that while we eat."

She wasn't ready to share much about her retreat experiences, but she was quite curious about this couple. Were they the delightful surprise K. H. had predicted?

They looked like twins, each dressed in olive green khaki pants and waxed cotton jackets worn over heavy Irish fisherman knit sweaters with matching tweed newsboy caps that perched on full heads of very dark brown hair. Their crystalline blue eyes appeared not to miss a thing about their surroundings, even as they radiated a vibration of joy and love that was truly infectious.

"I noticed you were part of the Brothers and Sisters of the Golden Robe group at *Samhain*," Debbie began. "Since Master K. H. appeared in that same apparel, I'm wondering if you've known him before?"

"We have, yes," said Tim. "We met him many years ago in another spiritual activity. When Saint Germain began gathering the Friends of Ancient Wisdom, K. H. said we should join."

"'Twas a grand decision," beamed Maggie. "Such lovely people and so many wild Celts, like my Tim, here. We felt right at home. Now, like you, we're practically old-timers, with all the new folks coming in."

"So, are you swimming in akashic records up here in the forest with nature spirits all around?" Tim's bright blue eyes twinkled at Debbie. She gaped at his very direct question.

"Tim, you weren't supposed to bring up such things before the lass has had a chance to eat her dinner."

"But look at her, Maggie. She's practically glowing in the dark, she's got so much light in her aura. We've only been given a couple of days with her. I want to know how we're supposed to help her."

"Well, now that the man has let the cat out of the bag, I may as well tell you the whole story," confessed Maggie as she playfully rolled her eyes at her husband. "I would have waited until after dinner to tell you that K. H. sent us. 'Tis true that we come to this retreat when we need a break from the density of the city, but we also go on missions for the Master when he needs us."

"We are blessed to have been associated with K. H. for a *very* long time," said Tim with emphasis.

"Ours is a mutual relationship of undying loyalty, love, and service," explained Maggie. "We will do anything to support his mission, and we know he will do anything to further the progress of our souls. We are unencumbered by the usual obligations of employment or family, so K. H. is able to take advantage of our flexibility when one of his friends, like you, needs a boost."

"That is so gracious of him and of you." Debbie's voice caught with emotion, and Maggie reached over to pat her hand.

"So, lass," Tim continued eagerly, "are the old records Atlantean, Egyptian, or some other flavor of antiquity? Those are the ones that are coming up for lots of our friends these days. Those and intergalactic problems. But from the look of you, I'd say Atlantean."

"You're right," Debbie admitted.

"Ha! I knew it," Tim exclaimed, slapping his knee. "Atlantis is my specialty. Those records can be hard to navigate because most folks don't believe there ever was such a place."

"I know there was," said Debbie softly.

"And don't forget the black magic in Egypt and Ireland," added Maggie. "If you've dealt with one, you've probably dealt with both." She turned to Tim. "So what's our plan, *a ghrá*?"

"Fresh air, vigorous hikes, and lots of seventh-ray violet flame chants. Saint Germain's gift of transmutation will dissolve the energy patterns of those records that K. H. has shown you, *a chara*. Your chakras will be spinning like tops by the time you go home. On Monday, is it?"

Debbie could only nod and smile at these two delightful people who had swept into her life and were obviously prepared to transform it.

The next day was Friday. The couple met her for breakfast and explained their strategy for the next few days. Tim had planned the routes and Maggie had arranged for the packed lunches they would take with them.

"Today we start with the easiest hike, tomorrow the medium challenge, and then Sunday we'll drive off the property where we can go all the way up the mountain," said Tim enthusiastically.

"We'll do plenty of chanting on the way," added Maggie. "One of the advantages of this retreat is that everybody chants, so we can give lots of mantras to the violet flame. That's the key for you now, *a chara*."

"That's perfect," said Debbie. "And while we're together I'd like to hear everything you can tell me about Ireland. I really do want to go back. My sister and I visited the Golden Vale area several years ago. That's where she got the idea of opening a health food store."

"'Tis a lovely part of the country, to be sure," said Maggie. "If you want a different view, spend time in Southwest Kerry near Kenmare. We lived there several years back. There are some grand sights and many that have kept their vibration from the old days."

And so Debbie and her companions set off. Tim set a brisk pace which Maggie was obviously accustomed to matching. Debbie was surprised that she could keep up. There was something about being with these two that buoyed her body as well as her spirits.

It must be the violet flame, she thought—remembering how the masters encouraged their students to regularly invoke the high vibration of the seventh ray which Saint Germain had revealed in the twentieth century. Ever since those early days he had emphasized this ancient practice as essential for individual and group transformation.

Debbie was well aware of the violet flame's effectiveness in transmuting records of the past, but she was beginning to think she hadn't invoked it enough.

Clearly, Maggie and Tim O'Toole had mastered using the seventh ray. They were the most consistently jovial people she'd ever met. Nothing seemed to bother them, yet they were very grounded, not silly or dismissive of the challenges she laid before them. Obviously, there was no reason not to tell them everything about her experiences with K. H. and the akashic records he had opened to her.

On their first break she gave them all the details, which somehow didn't appear to surprise them.

"We've a new mantra that will help you, lass," Tim offered without hesitation—almost as if he'd been expecting her story.

"When you give it, think of those old records the Master showed you or new ones that come up in your dreams, as they're sure to do. Picture the image surrounded in violet light. Use both sound and visualization and you'll see those ancient patterns dissolve, literally burning up in the holy flames of *An Síoraí*, the Eternal One."

"Thanks for the reminder," sighed Debbie. "These records are so heavy that, even with the blessing Master K. H. gave me, I feel a strange resistance to praying. As if there's a force that's holding these patterns together, and it doesn't want me to transmute them."

"We'll work on that, *a chara*. With the three of us chanting together, we'll make grand progress," Maggie assured her.

"We've no time to lose, lass," said Tim. "I'll start us with a little prayer to the violet-ray beings, and you'll see."

In the name of An Síoraí, the Eternal One, the Presence of the I AM within my heart, beloved Saint Germain and all angels and great beings who embody the violet flame, I ask you to send forth your mighty light rays to transmute all records of darkness, and charge me with your pure Light radiance as I pray:

Violet flame is near.
Violet flame is here.
Violet flame will cheer
My soul all the year.

Violet flame is the ray.
Violet flame is the way.
Violet flame is here to stay
When I speak it every day.

All that day and throughout the weekend, they chanted this mantra and others while hiking up hills, through valleys, around boulders, over fallen trees, across streams.

Walking, standing, sitting, and or lying down on beds of brightly colored leaves while looking up at the sky, they chanted and marveled at how their pace and rhythm and pitch naturally accelerated. A few times the mantras were going so fast they were practically running.

By the end of Sunday afternoon, Debbie was convinced that she would never worry again, at least as long as she continued to chant this simple mantra that sounded like a nursery rhyme, but that held the power to transmute the darkest energies of the past or the present.

"We'll see you at Fibonacci's, darlin'," promised Maggie as the three of them stood together next to Debbie's car on Monday morning. She was packed and ready to drive home—and feeling a serious twinge of trepidation about what might await her when she arrived.

"Be very careful on the highway, lass." Tim warned her. "You've been in a rarefied atmosphere for ten days. Going back into the city can be a difficult adjustment, but don't worry. Keep your wits about you and be gentle with yourself for a few days. The Master has his eye on you. Keep your heart set on his and you'll be fine. May Archangel Michael protect you and seal you in the arms of *An Síoraí*, the Eternal One."

Maggie and Tim each gave Debbie an enormous hug. Immediately she sensed a protective power flowing into her being from the auras of these extraordinary people who must surely be adepts as well as associates of Master K. H.

"Thank you for everything," she said, and did not try to stop the tears that filled her eyes. "I am so glad we'll be together again soon."

And with that, Debbie was on her way down the mountain.

Twenty-Two

"This is a perfect picture," observed Sarah as she and Debbie stood side by side in the O'Donnells' new apartment. They were admiring the unobstructed view of the Long Island Sound from the large bow window—the only window—in the living area of the third-floor studio apartment that Rory and Glenna had found not far from Fibonacci's.

A single bright ray of morning sun pierced through a bank of low clouds, casting a golden shaft of illumination on the Connecticut shoreline that lay to the west across the Sound.

"It is, yes," agreed Glenna. "I love to just sit here and watch the light change or the mists roll in and out with the tides. You know, when I first met F. M. Bellamarre at the Guggenheim Museum, we were admiring Monet's genius for painting the mist. Now I have my own ever-changing view of Nature's artwork."

"Are you glad you and Rory decided to rent in this neighborhood?" Debbie asked. The three women were clipping rings onto the curtain panels that would slide onto the wrought iron rod Glenna had chosen to frame the window.

"I am," she said. "I could have reclaimed the apartment in Brooklyn that I sublet before I went to Ireland, but Rory and I agreed we should be closer to his work and to all of you. I appreciate you both coming over this morning to help me since Kevin and Jeremy needed him at the bookstore. You, and the babies of course, are welcome any time."

The women glanced over at the little ones who were three months old today and were making wonderful progress on their motor skills. At the moment they were enjoying "tummy time" in their playpen, pushing themselves up on their arms and raising their heads.

Ever since they were barely a month old they had surprised everyone by managing to scoot next to each other in their crib, even while swaddled, where they would make little cooing noises and put their foreheads together.

Sarah was always pleased to take her babies on an outing. She also wanted to stay in close contact with Glenna. She suspected that her friend would be at loose ends after the excitement of the Fibonacci Players' performance at *Samhain*.

Also, she and Glenna were making a point of supporting Debbie while she continued to stay away from Fibonacci's.

"I thought you might be dejected from not being able to go to the coffee shop, but you're glowing," observed Sarah.

Debbie's face was a study in serenity.

"Róisín was very wise in giving me this time to not worry that I might run into Jeremy and what would happen to us if I did. Some day I hope I can share with you the incredible experiences I had on retreat. So much of it was beyond words. However, I can tell you that K. H. was watching over me the whole time, and one day we spent several hours in conversation."

She noticed the look of relief on her friends' faces. "You've been praying for me, too, haven't you?"

"Of course," said Glenna happily. "We promised that we would. We understand the challenge of twin flames trying to reunite. Sarah and I both have been through plenty of trials with our beloveds. The feeling that you know you're meant to be together but the not knowing if you will ever get through the obstacles is a trying time."

"Thank you for understanding. My heart is so full. I hope you can feel how much I love you both."

"The feeling is mutual," said Sarah, and Glenna agreed.

Ready to change the subject for now, Debbie turned to Glenna. "Have you decided against going to any auditions?"

"I have. My agent, Mel, offered me a list of shows that were casting, but I simply couldn't bring myself to try out. Even for a couple of directors I know and who were interested in me. After everything we've been through, I couldn't imagine Glenna O'Donnell following in Glenna Morrissey's tap-dancing footsteps."

"Is it hard for you, since you're sort of in the middle of nowhere right now as far as a career?" asked Sarah.

"Not really, which is rather surprising. I'm enjoying making a home for Rory and me. Fortunately, I was able to retrieve my furniture from Brooklyn, and this apartment came with a Murphy bed, so we didn't have to buy a new one or share my single." Glenna giggled at the idea.

"My folks have been very generous. My dad decided to buy a new car that was easier for my mom to get in and out of. He sold us his used one for less than blue book value. So we're good."

Sarah and Debbie held the long curtain rod while Glenna slipped the rings and panels in place. They each grabbed an end and lifted the rod as she guided them to the brackets she had expertly drilled and screwed onto the wall.

"Set-building experience," she grinned and playfully flexed her arm muscles. All three stepped back to admire their handiwork and noticed that the babies were falling asleep after their exercise.

"Are they okay there?" asked Glenna. Sarah nodded and put a light blanket over each twin. "Then let's take a break. I'm ready for a snack and some tea."

"Me, too." Sarah followed her and Debbie into the compact kitchen and sat at the small dining table where she could watch her little ones nap in their playpen. "I'm always hungry and thirsty these days. Nursing two babies requires a lot of fuel."

Glenna put on the kettle for tea and sliced the zucchini bread Róisín had sent home with Rory last night. "Why do you think F. M. is retiring?" Her voice was wistful. "I'm going to miss him, although I'm sure Master K. H. will be a wonderful friend and adviser."

"He is beyond wonderful." Debbie assured her. "I hope you get to know him as I did during my retreat. When you think about it, F. M. never promised that he could maintain his physical form forever. It takes a lot of energy to do so, even for an ascended master."

"That never occurred to me," said Glenna, as she measured loose tea from one of Debbie's nourishing blends into the prepared pot and poured in hot water.

"Of course, ascended masters have access to universal substance, but they also have many obligations," explained Sarah. "World conditions are such that I think Saint Germain needs to focus on them, especially on our country. I'm remembering that beautiful quote you read to us before the Players' performance."

"That makes sense," agreed Glenna. "I forget that there are laws the masters must abide by."

Sarah looked into the distance. "There are. I remember hearing Lucky explain that dispensations are never permanent. Our hope is for the opportunities given to be fulfilled so that new ones can be earned. I have the sense that Saint Germain is not allowed to do more for us than he has already accomplished as the Wonderman F. M. Bellamarre."

"And we'll have different lessons and opportunities with K. H," added Debbie. She could feel her heart burning with love for her Master. "His being with us is a new dispensation. He is profoundly loving and strong, like the antahkarana that formed during our decision service."

Sarah helped herself to a generous slice of zucchini bread and accepted a cup of aromatic tea from Glenna. "I believe our job right now is to prove what we've learned from F. M."

"I can see Róisín and Lucky doing that," Glenna said thoughtfully. "Lucky is very powerful, especially when he leads services. Even when he's being humorous, underneath is this amazing, balanced strength. And Róisín has become really masterful in daily life. Rory told me how she has a way of showing up at the exact moment you're thinking you need to call her."

"And don't you feel their mastery pulling all of us up?" commented Debbie. "To me, that's the idea of hierarchy—everybody continuing to move up, accelerating consciousness, lending a hand to those behind, and aspiring to become like those above. 'A continually rising tide raising all boats,' as I've heard Lucky describe the process."

"Yes, I see that," agreed Glenna. "The pupil assimilates the teacher and the teaching so the teacher can move on, and the teaching is shared with more and more willing pupils. That's the purpose of Fibonacci's and all of us being drawn together, isn't it?"

"I'm sure of it," said Sarah. She sipped her tea and smiled at her friends. "I do believe we are all coming up higher."

After helping Sarah bundle up her twins to go home for lunch, Debbie returned to work at Conroy's To Your Health, and Glenna cleaned up her kitchen. She was relaxing on the love seat that served as a sofa in the living room when her cell phone rang.

"Hello?"

"Is this Glenna Morrissey?" inquired a vaguely familiar voice on the other end of the line.

"Glenna O'Donnell, yes. Who is speaking?"

"Roland Newhouse, here, Glenna. And may I offer my sincere congratulations on your marriage."

"Thank you, Mr. Newhouse. What can I do for you? I'm surprised that you would be calling me."

"Yes, well, I'll come right to the point, my dear. We had our little difficulties, Mr. Ryan and I. But we're back on track and so is our show. I'm calling to find out when you can start rehearsals."

This was the last phone call Glenna expected to receive. She sucked in a startled breath and forgot to exhale until she managed to answer.

"I'm really not interested, Mr. Newhouse."

"My dear, you can't mean that. Not when your career can take off as never before. Your notices from Dublin were spectacular. I regret that prior engagements prevented my seeing you in person. Imagine the press for your starring role. Audiences will be falling at your feet and so will the critics."

Glenna could see the headlines in her mind's eye as he declared:

Tony Award Nominee Glenna Morrissey Returns to Broadway
After Smash Success in Dublin

"You can't tell me that you're not itching to get back on stage. Lights, costumes, smell of the greasepaint, roar of the crowd, and all that. It's in your blood, Glenna. Once an actress, always an actress. Surely you don't want to come as close to a Tony Award as you did last season and then

give up before taking home the prize you've worked for your entire life."
It all came flooding back. Newhouse was right, the clever salesman.
He knew her love of performing and was playing on that desire. Anyone
who'd watched her on stage knew how she glowed in front of an audience. She'd never lost the professional actress's thrill of being on the
boards or the pull to get back there when you're not.

Glenna had told herself that being married to Rory was enough, that
it would be enough, that she didn't need to be singing or dancing or
acting. But she did.

She'd had a career and she wanted it to continue. If it didn't, she was
suddenly afraid she would start blaming Rory for taking her away from
her dearest love. Though he hadn't. He'd said she should keep acting.
And wasn't *he* her dearest love?

She felt like she was being torn in two. Glenna closed her eyes and
breathed a prayer to *An Síoraí*, the Eternal One. And in that moment she
knew what she must do for the sake of her soul, her marriage, and her
twin flame.

"Your offer is very tempting, Mr. Newhouse."

"No pressure, my talented Miss Glenna," he interrupted her. "Of
course, I'll need an answer by next Monday." Sure of her agreement, he
cackled at his joke like a fisherman who'd hooked a prize catch, which
meant he was shocked speechless by her response.

"As I was saying, your offer is very tempting, Mr. Newhouse, but the
answer is no. Good bye."

Glenna hung up the phone, sank to the floor, and burst into tears.

That's where Rory found her when he came home. He'd had a feeling
that something wasn't right with her and decided to bring her some
lunch from Fibonacci's. He mentioned it to Kevin on his way out.

"Take the afternoon if you need it," his friend had encouraged him.

Rory walked in the door of their tiny apartment and rushed to his
wife. She was sitting in the middle of the floor by the love seat, sobbing.

"*A ghrá*, what's wrong? Is it your mother? Did something happen to
your family?" He sat next to her and gathered her into his arms where
she buried her face against his shoulder. She was crying so hard, he could

hardly understand what she was saying.

"I thought I didn't need it," she wailed.

"Need what, darlin'?"

"Acting, singing, dancing. Being in shows. On stage with the lights and the audiences and the glamour. I love you, Rory. I truly do. But I'm an actress. That's all I've ever wanted to be. It's all I've known. And now that I'm not that, I don't know what I am."

"You're Mrs. Rory O'Donnell, my wife," he said softly, more than a little hurt.

"Exactly. And I'm thrilled about that. But who is Glenna?"

"What brought this on, *mo mhuirnín*? When I left you this morning you were shining like the sun at the prospect of putting up curtains with your girlfriends. What happened to change you so?"

"Roland Newhouse called. His big show is on again, with A. B. Ryan financing. He wanted to know when I could start rehearsals."

"Would you consider that? With all we've gone through?" Rory shuddered to think how narrowly they had escaped having their very souls destroyed by Arán Bán. He couldn't imagine Glenna going anywhere near A. B. Ryan.

"No, I told Newhouse I wasn't interested. But I was! Rory, my love, I was so tempted." She sighed and sank further into his arms. "What am I going to do?"

Desperate to help her, he prayed for inspiration and tried to think of a solution.

"Could you and the Fibonacci Players put on some shows?"

"Perhaps, but everybody else has a regular job. And besides, with the bookstore and coffee shop closing, where would we perform and for what purpose?"

"Maybe your friends at the Aeon Theatre in Dublin would ask you back once in a while as a guest artist."

"You wouldn't mind? I'd be gone for two or three months."

"Glenna, darlin', I saw how much they loved you and you them. Why would I mind? I might even beg a job from them as a stage hand and go with you, depending on what's doing at Fibonacci's."

"That's very sweet, *mo chroí*, but not very practical."

"What about teaching at Kevin's academy? He's thinking of offering classes for all ages. Have you ever thought of teaching acting, stage presence, even short plays for children? You could create a whole program."

A memory suddenly came to him. "Glenna, remember your embodiment as Gormlaith. You were wonderful with children when you were the head bard. You could be again. I know it."

An image flashed in her mind of the little redheaded girl she had witnessed singing her heart out on the strand in Dingle Town, County Kerry. The child had looked at her, almost with a deep knowing that, even then, had sparked her memory of how Gormlaith had worked with the *túath* children in *Tearmann* so many centuries ago. This was the inspiration she was looking for.

"Oh, you wonderful man, thank you!" she exclaimed. They were still sitting on the floor with Rory cradling her in his lap. She threw her arms around his neck and bowled him over.

The long braid she had plaited into her dark blonde hair that morning had come undone. He brushed stray wisps from her face and kissed her deeply. He focused his light blue eyes on hers that were shining with the color of cornflowers.

"Why don't you come with me to the Pythagoreans on Friday afternoon? K. H. is supposed to be there. Kevin says the Master loves music and has quite a lot to say about Pythagoras and his theory of the music of the spheres. I know you would contribute, and we need more women in the study group. We're a bit male-heavy at the moment."

Glenna pushed away from him, feeling rather miffed. "So you want me to participate because of my gender?"

"No, I want you to participate because you're brilliant and you have years of experience with music. I also happen to be madly in the love with you. And you have no idea how much other people love and respect you, no matter what it is that you are or are not doing."

"You've convinced me, my darling husband. Now, can I persuade you to pull down that Murphy bed and spend the afternoon with me?"

Rory grinned at her. "My thought exactly, my Lady of the Glen. No convincing necessary."

Twenty-Three

Debbie was right about the wonderful quality of K. H.'s presence, thought Glenna to herself as the Pythagoreans and the Master were getting acquainted. The light that emanated from him was like a golden filigree. He radiated such illumination that Glenna could feel her own crown chakra tingling in response.

She was also aware of an opening occurring within her consciousness, such as she had not felt in this life. She was beginning to believe that she had known a similar openness in at least one previous lifetime.

Ever since Rory had reminded her of how Gormlaith had taught children in the bardic arts of poetry, song, and chant, she'd been dreaming of how she might bring those gifts to life here at Fibonacci's.

While she wasn't as interested in philosophy as her husband, she was hopeful that K. H. might offer her insight, or perhaps some spiritual practices, that would further unlock her teaching abilities.

This morning the study group was seated around a large round table in the coffee shop. Jenny and Valerie immediately welcomed Glenna and invited her to sit with them so the women were together.

Jeremy was seated between Rory and Kevin at an angle where he didn't have to look directly at Jenny. The Master was next to Kevin and heading the discussion.

Kevin was doing his best not to be annoyed that Rudy was late. He would speak to the lad later. For now, he was determined to focus on the present, as he was intensely interested in what K. H. would bring to his first formal interaction with the Pythagoreans.

"Thank you for your generous welcome," said the Master. "I enjoyed meeting many of our Friends at the *Samhain* celebration and I have particularly looked forward to gathering with a group of Pythagoreans."

The warmth of his smile filled the room and everyone felt their hearts open in anticipation of hearing what K. H. would say.

"By way of introducing our first discussion, I would like to ask you a question: What does it mean to be a Friend of Ancient Wisdom?"

For a minute, no one had a ready answer. Then Noah ventured, "We are friends of old, bound together by an ancient wisdom that goes back to the very beginning of time."

"Do you all agree?" asked the Master.

The others nodded affirmatively. "That's what Kevin and Rory have told us about being part of this community," said Jenny.

"And, since we've been meeting here, I've felt the truth of it," added Finn. "I didn't used to think about past lives, but every once in a while now I get a sort of shivery feeling that I've been with these people before. I especially feel like I've known you, Sir."

Finn knew he was blushing and wished there was something he could do about that tendency of his face to turn as red as his hair.

"So do I," said Valerie. She squeezed Finn's hand and did not blush.

"Yes, I believe our association is quite ancient," agreed the Master with an expression of acceptance that warmed their hearts. "Now I would ask you a slightly different question: Are you, as individual members of this community, friends to that ancient Wisdom?"

"I hadn't thought of Wisdom as needing our friendship." Kevin voiced what the others were thinking. "Would you explain?"

"I will. Because you asked and because this is a key to the success of our mission together."

Everyone at the table settled themselves to receive the Master's discourse. There was something about his gentle, yet very precise voice that quickened their perception.

We must each ask ourselves: Can Wisdom depend upon me to uphold her, to champion her, to unselfishly and accurately share her with those trapped in ignorance?

If we would be true 'philo-sophias'—which means lovers of Wisdom, who is called Sophia—we must treat her with respect and honor her precepts.

We must be trustworthy and dependable in her service and not given to flights of fancy or negative emotions.

Wisdom urges us to gain mastery over all human tendencies that are neither wise nor loving. For if we allow our energy to fall below the level of the heart, we are in danger of compromising even the mastery we may previously have gained.

Wisdom aims high and urges us to strive for the excellent, the beautiful, the true, and the good in ourselves and in our fellow travelers on the mystical path. For then does Wisdom nurture each one according to his or her capacity and need.

Like the most tender and attentive of mothers, Wisdom understands our differences. She gives of herself most ardently to see that those varied gifts are maximized. Her desire is for the soul to reach not only its potential in daily life, but also its union with the Spirit that inspires its highest aspirations.

Learning, knowledge, experience, trials, and triumphs are all part of growing in Wisdom, which is nothing short of Love in action. For Wisdom is not a thing, but a quality that is demonstrated in our behavior.

We have no idea if a person is wise until we observe that one in action—until we can assess their words, until we feel ourselves transformed by their presence, until what they naturally impart lifts us up in heart and mind and soul.

Then we know we are in the presence of true Wisdom—and we are inspired to do and be likewise.

The aura of Wisdom is transformational. That is how we can be certain of what we have perceived.

We become true philosophers because the Divine Love inherent in Wisdom touches us with the liberating power of Truth that frees our souls to be who we were born to be.

As the Master was speaking, Róisín looked lovingly across the coffee shop at the students and their mentors. Most of them had their eyes closed, a look of sheer bliss on their faces.

K. H. returned her gaze with an easy smile that spoke volumes.

Róisín could feel his pleasure and read in his expression his gratitude to Saint Germain for asking him to fill in for F. M. Bellamarre while that master was away. "Here are souls of high quality," he silently communicated to her. And she agreed.

The Pythagoreans were beginning to shift out of their meditative state when Rudy suddenly dashed in and plopped down in the chair they had left vacant for him between Rory and Jenny. His intrusion shattered the forcefield of peace and illumination the Master had created. The entire group shuddered.

"Sorry, I'm late, guys," said Rudy breathlessly and looked beseechingly at Kevin. "I really do have a good reason."

"That's fine." Kevin was trying to still his heart that was pounding from the sudden shift in energy. "We'll talk later. For now, I'd like you to meet Master K. H. He's going to be with us while F. M. is engaged elsewhere."

Rudy surprised everyone by standing, reaching across the table to accept the Master's extended handshake, and sincerely expressing his regret for being late. "I do apologize, Sir. I didn't know you were going to be here."

"Rudy missed the announcement at *Samhain*," explained Kevin.

"Your apology is accepted, Rudy," said the Master. His gentle voice carried the vibration of a healing balm. "I know you did your best to arrive on time with your friends. Perhaps one day soon you and I may speak of the obligations of friendship."

"I'd be grateful," said Rudy with uncharacteristic deference.

Indicating Jeremy, who was sitting to his left, Kevin began, "Rudy, I'd also like you to meet . . ."

As if someone had flipped a switch in the young man's brain, he took one look at Jeremy and bolted from his seat. Hurrying around the table, he clapped the man on the shoulder, grabbed his hand, and pumped it vigorously, pulling him out of his chair.

"Hey, Madwyn, how are you? Long time, no see."

Kevin shot Rudy a reproving glance, which only provoked him.

"What? Aren't we all about picking up where we left off in past lives? Madwyn and I knew each other." Rudy looked Jeremy in the eye, challenging him to respond. "You remember me, don't you, Madwyn?" Jeremy stared at Rudy. Kevin and Rory stared at Jeremy. Jenny, Noah, Valerie, Finn, and Glenna looked back and forth between Rudy, their mentors, and K. H. And everyone held their breath.

This was not supposed to be happening. The first rule of decorum among the Friends of Ancient Wisdom was that no one was to force a past-life recognition onto another person.

"I do remember you, Tadhgan," said Jeremy. His voice was flat, bordering on anger. "You were older than I in those days. Now I'm older and wiser . . ."

That was as much as Jeremy was able to articulate. As he had always feared, a tsunami of dark images suddenly flooded his mind's eye. He saw it all—the horror that Tadhgan had unleashed when he accidentally summoned the monstrous energy that caused his death.

And in that opening to the astral plane, all of the murderous energies and jagged images that had haunted Jeremy's childhood came rushing at him like a landslide.

"I don't want this!" he cried and lost consciousness.

When he awoke some minutes later, he was in the bookstore lounge with Kevin, Rory, and Master K. H. gathered around him. He was too tall to stretch out on the sofa, so they had made him a pallet of cushions where he was lying on the floor.

Róisín was kneeling beside him, bathing his forehead with a cool cloth. As soon as his eyes flickered open, she raised his head and encouraged him to take a few sips of a sparkling beverage that partially revived him. "Here, *a chara*, drink this. It will steady you."

As soon as the healing elixir had taken effect, Róisín moved to Jeremy's feet and Master K. H. took her place where he and the young man he had watched since childhood could look into each other's eyes.

"My son, can you tell me what you are seeing?"

Jeremy's voice was faint, more moan than real words. "Monsters, black bird-like thing that killed Tadhgan. My parents, sister, angry, threatening. Ugly images, foul energy." His face contorted and his body shuddered. "I don't want this!" he cried again, like a child. "Make it stop! Elder Brother, make it stop." He shuddered and once more lost consciousness.

The Master was perfectly calm as he replaced the cloth on Jeremy's forehead with his right hand. He placed his left hand over his own heart chakra and began intoning ancient mantras that Kevin recognized from the days of his Atlantean priesthood. Apparently, so did Rory and Róisín.

Sensing their recognition, the Master nodded ever so slightly and, as if they had rehearsed this event on the inner, they joined in the chants and shifted positions, all kneeling by Jeremy's body.

K. H. moved around to the top of the man's head, which he now held with both of his hands. Róisín held Jeremy's feet while Kevin took his left hand and Rory his right.

How long they remained in this position, none of them could have said. The light they were invoking on behalf of their friend and brother sustained them as well. They simply maintained their vigil until they felt the darkness clear from Jeremy's chakras and his aura.

They had not been alone in their service, for their partners had been participating throughout this healing ritual that was reintegrating parts of Jeremy's soul with his inner and outer awareness.

Róisín had witnessed him being carried to the bookstore lounge and had called Lucky to reassure the study group—minus Rudy, who had fled as soon as Jeremy collapsed—while she joined the Master, Kevin, and Rory.

Glenna had sprung into action, first calling Sarah to alert her that prayers were needed. "I knew something had happened," her friend said as soon as she answered the phone. "I've already joined my consciousness with Kevin's and you should do the same with Rory's. Find a quiet place and concentrate on invoking as much light as you can."

"Should I call Debbie?" asked Glenna. "I don't want to upset her, but I think she needs to know that they're trying to help Jeremy."

"Yes, you're right. She needs to know, even if it upsets her. Regardless of outer circumstances, she and Jeremy are linked soul to soul. Call her and tell her exactly what happened. Whatever he's going through needs all of our prayers."

As soon as Glenna had relayed what she knew about Jeremy's condition, Debbie had rushed upstairs to her apartment. Now she was trying to calm herself enough to pray for her beloved twin flame. And she was calling to the master who had said he would always be available in time of great need. This was one of those times.

"Saint Germain, it wasn't supposed to be like this! I have done as Róisín instructed me. I have meditated on *An Síoraí*, the Eternal One. I have prayed for union with my Higher Self. I have invoked the violet flame to clear my consciousness of negative energy and karmic patterns. I have begun to feel more like my True Self than ever in this life.

"I thought that would be enough to bring Jeremy to me. What have I not done? Where have I been remiss?"

She fell to her knees and wept as she prayed.

"My dear Master, show me how to help Jeremy. Even if he never comes to me, I will be content to know that he does not suffer. I have been alone until now. I can continue alone, as long as his soul is not in torment.

"If I need to leave Fibonacci's so that Jeremy can remain, I will not hesitate. I can go to Ireland. I have always wanted to go back. There are Friends of Ancient Wisdom in Éire. I can find my place with them and be whatever you need me to be. Only let me know your will, and that I will do." She sank to the floor in complete surrender and simply waited.

Ever so gradually, she felt a sense of calm come to her heart. After a few minutes, her body, mind, and soul finally arrived at a place of inner peace.

Then, and only then, did she hear the voice of comfort from the master who had first contacted her as she sat by the Bronx River communing with her devas. The master who had brought her into the Friends of Ancient Wisdom. The master whom she adored with her whole heart.

"My precious daughter." His voice filled her with such unspeakable love that the tears filling her eyes were now tears of joy.

Standing before her in all his resplendent glory was Saint Germain. He took her two hands in his and raised her to her feet. Speaking in tones of clear, vibrant energy, he lifted her awareness to the level of his ascended master Presence.

My precious daughter, you have passed this most difficult test that I have set before you—to be separated from our forcefield of Light and left in the dark, as was the practice of old when training seers to deepen their sight.

You have done well, my Debbie. My Dearbhla. My Meke. Your surrender has freed Jeremy to make his own decision, which he is doing, even now. I cannot tell you what he will decide. Our Elder Brother K. H. is tending that alchemy.

However, I can say that your soul will be at peace, as will your beloved's. Your inner reunion is at hand, regardless of what transpires on the outer. That is the Brotherhood's goal, which will assure your being together in a future embodiment, should one become necessary.

Have faith, my daughter, and all will be well. Now, focus your attention on *An Síoraí*, the Eternal One, and abide in peace in anticipation of the future that must be lived to be known.

Twenty-Four

Jeremy was sitting on the sofa now with K. H. on his right and Róisín on his left. Kevin and Rory were seated on chairs in front of him, though not so close that their knees would touch. The Master was speaking softly to the man.

"My son, I do not want you to open your eyes until I give permission. Your inner sight is coming to life, but in this moment I want you to tell me what you are feeling and only that."

Everyone was silent, waiting. When Jeremy spoke, it was in the same soft, careful tone with which K. H. had addressed him.

"Love. I feel love. And family. I feel myself surrounded by people who love me and want the best for me."

"That is true, my son. Now you may very gradually allow your inner sight to open slightly. Can you tell me where you are?"

"My soul family and I are in a temple. It's so beautiful. Glistening white marble that shines like sunlight on snow. There are fountains and flowers and colorful birds and music and the chanting of prayers that I know. I am chanting, too. The sound lifts me up and we are one in spirit, all of us together."

"Yes, my son. We are all here."

"Do things change, Master?" Jeremy began to frown.

"They do, as they always must. But you need not worry and, for now, you need not see or feel anything less than the love of your true family. We will change the setting now. Are you ready to move with me?"

"Yes, will you show me another beautiful scene?"

"I will. Your friends are here with us. Let us all intone the OM as we travel together, surrounded in a sphere of purest light."

OMMMMM. Kevin and Rory and Róisín joined the chant.

"Keep your eyes closed, my son. You may begin to see more images. However, there is no need for you to force any response to my questions. Can you tell me where you are now?"

"I see pyramids, great temples and statues. Enormous pylons and buildings that shimmer in the desert sun. There are different people here and many of the same. My family. My loved ones. And one special young woman. I am older than she, but we are very close. She loves me as no other and I am devoted to her.

"The scene is changing, and we are no longer on land, in Egypt. We are on a ship, sailing far, far to the west. To a land of mists and green meadows and valleys and mountains. But something happens. She is on the ship, but I am in the sea." He was beginning to get anxious. "Must I know why? I do not wish to see what happened."

"Be at peace, my son," said K. H. "There is no need for troubling images. Remember only what you wish. What else are you able to notice?"

"The sea is kind and does not trouble me. I am not afraid. The water is a womb and I am a child again. I will be born once more on that green island. On Éire. And I will see my Meke again."

"That is true, my son. You are doing very well. Can you let yourself be born on the Emerald Isle?"

"I can. And it is wonderful. Though not quite at first. My mother is gone, but I can see all kinds of marvelous beings. Fairies, elves, gnomes. And the beautiful woman who takes me in because I have second sight like she does. She recognizes me and treats me with great kindness. She teaches me to enhance my gifts as a seer.

"I grow up in her glorious garden with her other students, and when I'm older, I become her assistant. I care for her and, oh, she grows old—this woman, Dearbhla, who looks like a deva with her white-blonde hair streaming down her back. I find her one day in the garden, unable to rise. I cradle her in my arms, and she reaches up to brush my hair from my eyes. Her strength fails and I hold her hand until I feel her spirit lift off to higher realms.

" 'We will meet again, Madwyn,' " she tells me as she departs, and I know that is true. "Is today when we will meet, Master?"

"It is, my son. You may open your eyes now, and see your friends, your true family who have loved you since the days of ancient Atlantis and before. In Egypt, at Crotona, in Ireland, and here at Fibonacci's."

When Jeremy opened his eyes, he saw not only Master K. H., Kevin, Rory, and Róisín, but also Sarah with her babies, Glenna, and Lucky. They were smiling at him as if he were returning from a very long voyage.

"Welcome back, brother," said Kevin. He did not say how worried they had been that they might lose him.

Jeremy gazed from face to face, actually allowing himself to feel the radiation of true friendship beaming out at him. If this was a dream, he never wanted to wake up. But something was missing. Or someone.

A puzzled look furrowed his brow. "Where is she?" he asked. "I thought you said my family was all here, but I don't see her. I feel that I have met her, but she is absent. Why is that?"

"Whom do you seek, my son?" asked K. H. "You have met her and recently. Do you know her name?"

Jeremy closed his eyes, searching his memory. After a moment his eyes opened wide. "I see." He drew out the words. "Her name is Debbie. Of course. The one I'm missing has been here all along. But where is she? I need to see her and tell her that I understand. That I know who she is."

"Your beloved has undergone a rigorous test these past several weeks," explained K. H. "Saint Germain and I deemed it best for her to pursue her own acceleration of consciousness, which she has done. This was for the good of her soul and yours. She is waiting for you at the health food store in this neighborhood. There you may meet at last in full awareness of yourselves as twin flames."

"Then I must go to her," said Jeremy urgently. He attempted to stand up too quickly and a wave of nausea and dizziness sent him sitting back down on the sofa, holding his head.

"*A chara*, you're not going anywhere until you've had something to eat and another restorative tea," said Róisín with motherly firmness. "Debbie can wait for you a while longer, as she has been doing for quite some time."

Debbie had come downstairs to the store and was busying herself dusting shelves, straightening the greeting card spinner, sweeping the floor. Anything to keep her hands occupied and her mind off of simply waiting—for what she hardly dared to believe could be true.

Upstairs in her apartment she had felt the shift in energy and knew at once that her prayers had been answered. She was grateful that weeks ago she had apprised her sister of at least some of what was going on, so her behavior, while a bit strange to her sister's way of thinking, was at least not cause for the woman to be alarmed.

And now Debbie felt Jeremy coming to her. She knew when he turned the corner from Fibonacci's and when he walked the two blocks to the store where she waited.

Her heart was pounding and she feared it would leap out of her chest when the little bell that announced the opening of the front door sounded the end of her life as she'd known it and the beginning of the life she'd dreamed of.

She had thought she might meet him half way across the store. But when the tall, handsome man with dark brown hair crossed the threshold, she could not stir. She could only lean against the counter, gripping its edge for support. A living statue, the only movement of her body was the flow of tears that spilled out of her misty green eyes and trickled down her cheeks.

Jeremy closed the distance between them and took her hand, lifting it to his lips as he gazed at her. When she looked into his eyes and reached up to brush a lock of hair from his forehead, any remaining doubts flew from his mind.

Speaking with the assurance Debbie had been longing to hear, he asked, "Where can we speak in private?"

She pointed to the stairway that went to her apartment.

"Then come with me. We have a lot of catching up to do."

With the surety of Jarahnaten leading Meke out of Egypt, he led her to the second floor where they would pick up as they had left off many centuries in the past.

Twenty-Five

Would you like some tea?" offered Debbie when she and Jeremy had entered her apartment and closed the door behind them. Somehow they each recognized in that simple gesture the conclusion of all previous chapters of this incarnation and the beginning of perhaps the most important one they had ever lived.

"I'd like that," said Jeremy. "May I sit here at your table so I can watch you make it? Will that bother you?"

Debbie was quiet for a moment as she put the kettle on to boil. "No, I don't mind. Then we can try to comprehend this threshold we've just crossed."

"Hmm," Jeremy considered. "And after that we can stare at each other for, I don't know, the next century or so."

They both laughed.

While he watched, she got out her best china tea pot and cups. She plated some lavender shortbread cookies and set the table for their refreshment. She was spooning loose tea into the prepared teapot when Jeremy chuckled.

"What is it?" She realized that she did feel a bit shy with his attention on her.

"The setting is different, but the activity is the same. Dearbhla was always mixing up her latest herbal elixir. What's this one for?"

"Calming emotions and mental clarity," she said with a wry smile.

"Excellent choice." He paused. "Have you been in a forest recently?"

"Yes. I spent ten days in the Catskills in a wonderful retreat center. I'll tell you about it one of these days. What do you see?"

"I see you walking among tall trees with their leaves blazing in fall colors." He paused again, observing. "There they are."

"Who?"

"Your deva friends. Now I know for sure that you're my Dearbhla."

Debbie's breath hitched and she turned quickly to face the stove to compose herself. Here was the moment she had dreamed of. Her beloved knew her. She was so nearly overcome with emotion that she had to will her hands not to shake as she poured hot water into the teapot.

When she carried it to the table, Jeremy could see that her light green eyes were sparkling with tears. He stood and took the teapot from her. Placing it on the table, he took her in his arms and tenderly stroked her hair.

"I didn't mean to make you cry. I thought you'd want to know what I was seeing."

"I do. I think I'd better sit down and drink some of this tea." Jeremy pulled out a chair for her. She picked up the teapot and poured them each a cup. "I guess part of me didn't believe we would ever be sitting here in my kitchen. What else do you notice?"

"Your aura is full of this amazing violet light."

"I'm glad you can see it. I've been feeling it strongly ever since I met these extraordinary people at the retreat center who taught me a new mantra for invoking the violet flame. Actually, they're members of the Friends and they've known K. H.—maybe forever. Oh, Jeremy, there is so much to say. So much to share. I don't know where to start."

He put down his cup and gazed into her eyes. "I do." He reached across the table and took her hands in his.

"I wasn't kidding about staring at each other," he said with a wink. "Will you look at me as I look at you and see where we go?"

"Sounds interesting, but first I think we should . . ."

"Right. Róisín's prayer to Archangel Michael. She's been teaching me how to protect my inner sight so I don't get lost or overtaken with astral images. It's a funny little ditty, but it works."

"She originally wrote it for the children of some of the Friends," explained Debbie, returning his gaze.

"The kiddos were having nightmares. Wolves under the bed, that kind of thing. She taught it to a group of them who loved it so much they insisted that their parents say the prayer with them at bedtime. Now it's a community staple. Shall we give it together?"

"I think we'd better. Will you give the prayer to start? I'm not quite up on how to do that."

"Of course. It's like talking to friends you've known forever."

In the name of An Síoraí, the Eternal One, all great beings and powers of Light and Archangel Michael, we invoke your Presence with us, as we pray:

> Beloved Michael, archangel bright,
> Seal me in your blue-flame light
> So nothing astral, nothing false
> Can enter in my feelings or thoughts.
>
> Keep me focused on the Good
> Of the Great White Brotherhood.
> Banish darkness by your might
> And help me see and do what's right.

They found themselves naturally repeating the prayer over and over like a mantra until Debbie's apartment was bathed in a brilliant royal blue light. They both felt the presence of Michael and his angels.

"Thank you." She squeezed Jeremy's hands and graced him with the radiant smile he'd been hoping to see. "I'm ready for our experiment now. And I think I know where we should go first, although I'm not sure that staring at each other is the way to get there."

He sheepishly rolled his eyes. "You're right, of course. Back to the garden. And we follow the light to get there."

"Exactly. Kevin and Sarah do this all the time when they're on a mission for one of the masters. Still your mind and focus on the light that's surrounding us. I can already feel it increasing, can you?"

"I can. Where in the garden shall we visualize?"

"With all of this blue light, let's head for the bluebells. That wonderful patch in the woods that was like a carpet of flowers, exactly this color. I think there's something we're supposed to do or see there. Please, keep holding my hands, Jeremy."

"I'll never let you go, Debbie. I promise."

Neither of them mentioned what stage of their relationship in ancient Ireland they wanted to revisit, but they each said a silent prayer to Archangel Michael that it would be when Madwyn was older and serving as Dearbhla's assistant.

As they felt themselves lifting out of their physical bodies and into the bright blue orb that enfolded them, they instinctively closed their eyes and focused their inner sight on remaining within the orb until they reached their destination.

When they knew they had arrived, they opened their eyes, but were surprised to discover that they were not in a field of flowers. Instead, they were standing in a luminous chamber whose walls and furnishings were saturated with shades of blue even deeper than the orb they had traveled in.

Standing before them was a magnificent angel who must have been seven feet tall and whose aura flashed with an almost blinding radiance.

"Welcome to Archangel Michael's retreat," said the angel. "I am called Sylvanus, one of his lieutenants, although in consciousness we are all Archangel Michael. You have invoked our presence and we have guided you to where you needed to go, not where you, in your human consciousness, thought you should be."

Debbie and Jeremy were still holding hands. They turned and looked at each other with chagrin on their faces.

"We meant no disrespect," said Jeremy.

"We understand and we forgive your enthusiasm, but you must be careful, dear ones. You were wise to call for our protection, for by that exercise of free will you allowed us to help you. If you will be seated, there are matters we would bring to your attention."

Sylvanus indicated two straight-backed chairs upholstered in rich blue silk with Celtic symbols woven in gold. The couple sat as they were directed and waited for further instruction. Clearly the angel was in charge. He raised his hand and beakers of sparkling elixir appeared

before them and then disappeared as soon as they had drunk the invigorating liquid.

"Please place your attention on the screen you see before you. You
will feel yourselves drawn into the scenes. This is perfectly natural and
safe. Debbie was correct that there is something for you to see and you
will, indeed, find yourselves in the midst of bluebells. Your error was in
skipping the important step of coming here first. Fear not, dear ones. I
will be guarding you during this experience."

With that, the angel activated what appeared as a movie screen at
the front of the chamber. Images came immediately into view.

Sixty-year-old Dearbhla and thirty-year-old Madwyn had been gathering bluebells for a healing remedy they had often prepared together
throughout the twenty-plus years that he'd worked with her as appren-
tice and then as her indispensable assistant.

They had been at work for about an hour and were resting on a fallen
log, for the bluebells grew deep in the forest. Madwyn was looking into
the distance and Dearbhla was watching him.

"What do you see?" she asked, as she did at least once a day. This
question had been the staple of his training as a seer. Now it was simply a
ritual they shared as her acknowledgment that he was at least as accomplished a clairvoyant as she.

Most often his inner sight would reveal a member of their *túath* who
needed a remedy or encouragement or sometimes a suggestion for how
to resolve a difficult situation.

On other occasions he would gain an insight into his own character or he might have an idea for how Dearbhla could take better care of
herself. He worried that she was always available to others and rarely
rested. Today his inner gaze deepened and brought a furrow to his brow.

"What do you see, Madwyn?" Dearbhla repeated. "Is this a troubling image?"

"It is, and I would not speak it, except that it might be prevented."

I see great calamity for our people. Wave upon wave of invaders,
century after century, until it seems there are hardly any people

of the Light remaining here in Éire.

We embody again and again to fight the same fight against the same forces. Light against dark. Good against evil.

I would despair of our ever being victorious, except I see a glimmer of hope far in the future. There is the possibility of a turning. Where there was ignorance, illumination begins to dawn and people start seeing that the brothers of the shadow have sown their seeds of hatred and discord in every part of life.

Madwyn shook his head and scrubbed his hands over his face as if to banish the dark images from his mind's eye. Dearbhla placed her hand on his forehead and said a clearing prayer that her friend, *Ceann-Druí* Ah-Lahn had taught her.

"I am all right now," said Madwyn. "But what shall we do, Dearbhla? I feel so helpless against these forces that are determined to wipe us not only from our land, our planet, but from the very universe. They desire nothing but ultimate control. How do we stop them?"

"We must continue the fight, my dear. No matter what, we must trust that *An Síoraí*, the Eternal One, remains more powerful than the darkest foe."

"Then why does he allow such evil to continue?"

Dearbhla's gaze deepened and her voice grew serious as she took up the young man's vision and spoke a prophecy.

Free will, Madwyn. The people themselves must rise up and overthrow their oppressors. But first they must be enlightened or they will attack the very ones who would save them from destruction.

For they will have been taught by misguided parents and teachers to see the world through jaded eyes. Many will believe that good is evil, while evil will have perfected the black art of cloaking itself in the semblance of good.

We will continue to return, you and I and others, to be teachers of the people. You have many years yet to live to enlighten our people, while I have only a few.

But we will be together again. And we will fight the good fight. We will make a difference where we are, many times in many centuries to come.

For a few minutes Dearbhla and Madwyn remained silent, allowing the wonder and profound appreciation they always felt after a prophecy came to them. When Dearbhla stood at last, she was outwardly subdued, yet inwardly buoyant for she knew that prophecy was meant to bring hope that even dire predictions could be reversed.

"Come, my dear. Let us take our bluebells back to the workroom. Their essence is best when they are fresh, and Biddy Goodwin is in need of a treatment."

The images on the screen faded, and Debbie and Jeremy were once more surrounded in an orb of blue light. As they felt themselves traveling back through the ethers, they heard the voice of Sylvanus speaking a passionate request from the heart of Archangel Michael:

We serve with you to illumine the people and vanquish darkness, but we must receive your free-will command to intervene. Do not fail to pray to Archangel Michael and his legions of Light. We stand ready to assist you, but you must give us permission. Put us to work! Victory can be ours if you will invoke it!

Debbie and Jeremy opened their eyes and looked at each other in amazement. They were seated in her kitchen, still holding hands across the table. Yet they had been changed and they knew it, for ringing in their hearts was the plea from a mighty angel, *Pray to us and we will tell them!*

Twenty-Six

"Wow." Jeremy drew out the word as he released Debbie's hands. He sat back in his chair and checked his watch. "That entire adventure took less than five minutes."

He picked up his tea and took a sip. He looked into the half-full cup and set it back on its saucer. "My tea's not even cold."

Debbie followed suit. "Neither is mine. I guess we won't forget that lesson for a while."

"No kidding," he rolled his eyes as Debbie freshened their cups of tea. She held out the plate of cookies and he took two.

Not quite sure of what to say next, they sat thoughtfully drinking tea and eating lavender shortbread until Jeremy broke the silence.

"I have a question."

"Okay."

"Has Róisín told you anything about me?"

"Not really. Only that life hasn't been easy for you. She's been very protective of you. In fact, she sent me away so we wouldn't cross paths until her intuition told her the time was right. While I was on retreat, Master K. H. gave me some insight into an embodiment we shared on Atlantis. Not something I can discuss right now, but soon."

"Okay." Jeremy helped himself to another cookie.

"Has Róisín told you anything about me?" asked Debbie.

"Nothing. Except it is obvious that she loves you dearly and is very protective of you."

"She was Dearbhla's grandmother and we're very close now."

"Then Madwyn must have known her, at least briefly. That's why she told me she'd loved me like a grandson. A few puzzle pieces are falling into place. Have you been in her garden room?"

"Yes, incredible, isn't it?"

"And healing. I've spent a fair amount of time in there since I've been staying with her and Lucky. Just sitting. Enjoying the colors of the bird-of-paradise and the orchids. And the fragrances."

"Especially the gardenias," enthused Debbie. "When they're in bloom the atmosphere is heavenly."

"They're budding now."

"Will you let me know when they blossom?"

"I will."

Debbie surveyed the empty cookie plate. "Would you like something else to eat? I could fix us a quick bite."

"No, that's okay. I think my system is too stunned to eat a meal and too full of shortbread. Do you know what I'd really like to do?"

Debbie raised her eyebrows and felt her color rise.

"No, not *that*," said Jeremy with a grin. "Well, yes, *that*. But not yet. Not until we've actually learned who we are in this life. Right now the past feels clearer to me than the present."

"I know," said Debbie. She smiled back at him. "So what is it that you would like to do?"

"Even though it's November, I'd like to roam around the Botanical Gardens while we tell each other our stories. I don't think I can just sit here and rehearse my childhood—or my lack of a childhood. But I have a feeling the support of the nature spirits will ease the discomfort."

"That's a wonderful idea. And just so we don't completely overwhelm ourselves with serious memories, why don't we go to the Holiday Train Show while we're there."

"Really? I've never been."

"Then we have to go. You'll love it. There are loads of decorated Christmas trees interspersed with the plants. The trains are fun, but the real attraction is the displays of famous New York landmark buildings. They hire a company who creates them in miniature using only natural materials like acorns, bark, leaves, moss, nuts, and seeds. It's like walking into a garden version of the city's architectural past."

"That sounds fantastic. Could we go tomorrow?"

"Tomorrow is Saturday, so it will be busy, but late afternoons are less crowded. I was thinking I could pick you up, but would you mind if we met at Fibonacci's? I haven't been there for over two weeks and I miss the place. Plus, I haven't seen Róisín or Lucky in all that time."

"Because of me?"

"Because of both of us and of what Master K. H. and Róisín knew we both needed to go through to get to where we are now."

Jeremy was beaming. "Then I'll meet you there for a leisurely breakfast so neither of us has to get up too early tomorrow."

"Perfect. We can wander in the gardens and then we'll be on time for our admission. They make sure that visitors can actually get a clear view the exhibits rather than the backs of other visitors."

Jeremy looked at his watch again and said with obvious reluctance, "Guess I should be going. I don't think I can handle any more intensity this evening."

"Neither can I. Do you want me to drive you to Róisín's and Lucky's?"

"No, they're still at Fibonacci's. I'll walk back and report in. I can feel them getting a bit anxious about me—about us."

"Give them my love, won't you? And tell them we're fine. We *are* fine, aren't we?"

"More than fine. Good night, Debbie. I can't believe I actually found you." He took her hand and brought it to his lips. "I'll see you in the morning." And won't it be amazing to say that every night for the rest of our lives? he thought as she walked him down the stairs and out the front door of Conroy's To Your Health.

Jeremy was correct about Róisín and Lucky still being at Fibonacci's. They did their best to appear nonchalant, but they both let out an audible sigh when he walked in the front door. They had been sitting at a table where they could see the coffee shop entrance. They rose as soon as he crossed the threshold.

"Waiting up for me, were you?" He grinned at these two incredible people who already felt to him like surrogate parents.

"Technically, it's too early to be called 'waiting up'," joked Lucky, "but we are relieved to see you, lad."

Róisín took both his hands in hers. She didn't say anything, only looked at him, her eyes deep and penetrating. Satisfied with what she perceived in his aura, she patted him on the cheek. "Good. Now let's get you something to eat, darlin', and we'll all go home for a good night's rest. It's been more than a full day."

When Debbie walked into Fibonacci's the next morning, Jeremy waved to her from the back booth. He was enjoying a warm scone and one of Lucky's special brews from the "Coffee Alchemist's" secret menu.

As soon as Róisín saw Debbie come in, she hurried from behind the bar and warmly embraced the young woman she loved like a daughter. The two women stood hugging with misty eyes and overflowing hearts.

"You did well, darlin'," said Róisín. "I could see that K. H. was pleased by the way he nodded when I inquired about you. Of course, he left the telling of your adventures to you, if and when you want."

"There's so much to share," said Debbie with deep feeling. "I can hardly believe all the gifts of inspiration and profound lessons I gained in ten short days. All I can say right now is thank you for sending me away."

Róisín took Debbie's two hands in hers.

"I've sorely missed you, darlin'. I had no idea that your discipline would also be one for me. I was sorely tempted to contact you while you were on retreat. I knew not to, but I had to discipline myself not to send you a message."

"I felt your love and I knew you were holding me in your heart. And those lovely people, Tim and Maggie, did convey your concern. That was enough. I had to pass this test. I understand that now even more clearly than I did at the time. I never felt your consciousness intruding on mine, so I think you passed your test as well." She hugged her beloved mentor one more time.

Róisín kissed Debbie on the cheek. "You go sit with your man, then, and I'll be back to join you in minute. A mighty angel told me you have something to share with me."

Jeremy stood up as Debbie approached. Watching her walk toward him was like a vision he hadn't realized he'd been seeing for a long time.

He guessed he'd been blocking it from his outer mind. No longer, he told himself. He took her hand and guided her to sit next to him so he could put his arm around her.

She noticed that he had a scone and a pot of tea waiting for her.

"Thanks for breakfast," she said and poured herself a cup. "Yum, my favorite. Did you tune in to what I like?"

"No," he admitted. "Lucky told me."

"Well, you get points for having it waiting for me." She kissed him on the cheek and they smiled into each other's eyes.

Jeremy broke their gaze first and squeezed her shoulder. "Róisín said she wants to speak with us before we leave for the Bronx."

"I know. Apparently Sylvanus wants us to tell her what happened yesterday at Archangel Michael's retreat."

"I hear that confession is good for the soul."

"The whole experience was humbling, to say the least," admitted Jeremy when he and Debbie had related their story. "Sylvanus was kind, but he was also very firm about our needing protection for our spiritual work. As I was trying to go to sleep last night, it occurred to me that just because we can see into other realms doesn't mean we should. Or at least we shouldn't be deciding for ourselves what we're meant to see."

Debbie agreed. "I never thought much about the old adage, 'Pride goeth before the fall,' but that seems to be one point Sylvanus wanted us to understand."

"'Tis very true," said Róisín, "and I'm grateful you've had this lesson brought home to you both as you begin your journey together in this life. Pride is a perpetual challenge on the spiritual path. Especially as you advance in your adeptship as seers."

"That's pretty clear now," said Jeremy.

Róisín continued. "When *An Síoraí*, the Eternal One, grants us insight and gives us additional responsibility, it becomes more and more important to remember that we are not the doer. I say 'we' because all of us in the Friends of Ancient Wisdom are challenged to hold ourselves accountable as servants, not as lords over others. The true masters are always the most humble.

"I recall one of my teachers telling the story of his being with a very advanced cosmic being, if you can imagine such a blessing. My teacher said he came away from the experience overwhelmed with the humility that radiated from that being's Presence."

Jeremy's eyes were wide open, spiritually as well as physically.

"There's something else we should tell you," said Debbie. "This is not easy to explain because I'm not entirely sure what it means."

"Go ahead, darlin'," said Róisín. "I'll follow you."

"The scene that Sylvanus showed us in the life review chamber was of a prophecy that Madwyn and Dearbhla shared of extreme ignorance befalling our people in future times. I believe that time is now. Especially because Sylvanus said that the angels stand with us to illumine those I could sense are our brothers and sisters of the Light."

"He was begging us to pray to the angels so they can help us as they want to," Jeremy added. "He said we must 'tell them.' Do you know what he was talking about?"

Róisín grew silent and closed her eyes. When she opened them again, they glistened with the compassionate intensity Debbie had come to recognize as the expression her mentor bore when she was receiving instruction from one of the masters.

"I did not know this revelation would be given to you so soon," she said in the crystal-clear tone of her own adeptship. "However, the Master says you must be illumined for your own protection and for the integrity of the mission to which you are called."

Jeremy and Debbie took each other's hand and gave their dear friend their full attention.

"As I believe Saint Germain explained to you, Debbie, the union of twin flames is one of the most powerful forces in the Universe. It is also one of the most opposed. That knowledge alone should be sufficient warning to you of the need to invoke protection around yourselves at all times.

"In addition, the bringing together of many pairs of twin flames in a community, such as the Friends of Ancient Wisdom, is a victory which the Great White Brotherhood has not achieved in many ages. If you have not already, you will soon recognize that many in our community are twin souls—as married couples, family members, devoted friends, or siblings."

"Like Sarah and Kevin's twins," Debbie suggested.

"Exactly. The community as a whole comprises a mandala—a group of souls who have served the cause of Light together in many incarnations. Within that larger network, there are smaller mandalas who embody within the community for a unique purpose."

Jeremy was beginning to see the pattern. Hadn't he been drawn into a strong friendship with Kevin and Rory, whose wives were like sisters to Debbie?

"Am I the missing link?" he asked Róisín.

"Indeed, you are, Jeremy. And because you and Debbie have passed some mighty initiations that cleared the way for you to be sitting where you are, I can tell you that you two complete a powerful mandala with the MacCauleys and the O'Donnells.

"When and how your mandala will join in a particular mission remains to be revealed. Saint Germain reminds us that the future must be lived to be known. However, he urges me to warn you that the path up the mountain is strewn with boulders and slippery inclines.

"This fact is not cause for fear or a sense of struggle. In fact, the masters are very keen that their students not enter into struggle. Stay humbly in the flow, my dears, and all will be well."

The three Friends of Ancient Wisdom sat quietly, each of them absorbing the profound insights they had received. They might have remained there for the morning, had not Lucky quietly approached and gently place his hand on his wife's shoulder.

"Róisín, *a ghrá*, we've a need for your skills in the bakery," he said tenderly. From the aura of golden light that surrounded the three sitting in the coffee shop's back booth where amazing revelations often took place, he could see that another such event had transpired.

"Thanks, darlin'." Róisín reached back and lovingly patted his hand. "I'll be right there." She turned to Jeremy and Debbie. "And you two had best be on your way if you're going to arrive at the Train Show on time."

She and the two she loved as if they were her own children slid from their seats and joined in a mutual hug that included Lucky. He found his own eyes misting in gratitude for these extraordinary people gathered here in his coffee shop.

The plan that Saint Germain had revealed to him years ago was coming to fruition at last.

Twenty-Seven

As Debbie steered her SUV around the first curving approach to the graceful Throgs Neck Bridge, she could not help being amazed that only a fortnight ago she had driven this same sweeping span over the East River on her way to the great unknown that awaited her in the Catskills. Today she was on her way to the New York Botanical Gardens, one of her favorite places in all the five boroughs, with her soul's twin, Jeremy, seated next to her. What a miracle!

"I'd like to tell you a bit about myself before we get to the train show," said Jeremy. He'd been considering how to begin this difficult story. There was something about the intimacy of riding in the car with Debbie driving that inspired him to take the plunge.

"If you're ready, I'd like that," she said.

"Okay then, here goes. My parents are atheists, materialistic scientists who basically didn't like me, almost from the moment I was born. They objected to everything about me, except my intellect, which thankfully they did support by giving me a good education. Though nothing else. Certainly not love and not even an allowance like most kids my age received.

"I had been discouraged from forming any close friendships, so I didn't learn about spending money until I was about ten. Through the kindness of an elderly man in our apartment building, I was able to earn a few dollars here and there by doing errands for him.

"My parents didn't know, or if they did, they didn't care. As long as I stayed out of their way, they were content. My being out of the apartment as much as possible became a sort of unspoken contract between us. We lived in Manhattan, so there was no end of neighborhoods and famous sights I could explore.

"Sometimes I would ride the subway, but mostly I just walked. That's one of the things I love about New York. You can walk anywhere. Anyway, I walked so I could save my pennies to pay for museum admission every couple of weeks.

"I laugh now to think how lucky I was that my feet were growing. My parents never questioned my frequent need for new shoes, which I wore out at regular intervals from all the walking.

"I haunted bookstores and libraries and galleries and parks, almost always by myself. I didn't really fit in with other kids. I guess because I was smarter and liked to learn and didn't do drugs. I knew what they did to you because my parents put me on drugs when I was young."

"That's horrible," Debbie interjected.

"It was, until I figured out how to fake swallowing the pills and flushing them down the toilet. I learned very quickly not to say anything about the spirit beings I was seeing and after a while forced myself to stop seeing anything beyond the veil.

"I think all the walking helped keep me balanced. It certainly fed my curiosity, and in the process I fell totally in love with our city. I studied Manhattan and learned everything I could absorb. I never left the island, but I got to know it from north to south and east to west. Or at least as much of the island as it was safe for a kid to explore on his own."

"Weren't you frightened? That seems like a risky way for a young boy to live." She reached over and touched his hand.

"There were a few times I wandered into areas where I shouldn't have been. But I think I must have had a serious guardian angel, because I never found myself in a situation I couldn't get out of. I guess you could say I became street smart. I was big for my age and I knew how to keep my head down. 'Don't make eye contact. Don't look like a victim. Be ready to run if you have to.' That sort of thing.

"Anyway, I'm excited to see the exhibits today. It sounds like the people who create these miniatures must love the landmarks as much as I still do."

"I'm sure you're right. We're getting close to our destination, but I'd like to return the favor and give you the first chapter of the life of Debbie." She grinned as she turned onto the Bronx River Parkway.

"I'm the youngest of five siblings. I have three older sisters and one brother, the eldest of the tribe. My sister Cyndi, who owns the health food store, is closest to me in age. We're different in many ways, except for our interest in plants and herbs—growing things. But we've always done a lot together, like visiting the Botanical Garden and the Bronx Zoo.

"Our other sisters are married and both live in Western Massachusetts. After our parents died suddenly in a car accident when I was eighteen, our brother moved to the Yukon. As the first born and only boy, he was really close to them. We girls naturally banded together, and I know he felt left out. These days he monitors wildlife in wilderness areas. Every once in a while we get an email photo of a lynx or a wolf, but that's about all we hear from him.

"So Fibonacci's has really become my family, Róisín and Lucky in particular, which is difficult for Cyndi. I'm trying harder to include her in my life in other ways. In fact, if Fibonacci's moves, I'm hoping our store can be part of the complex."

"I'm sorry you lost your parents," said Jeremy tenderly. "Were you a close family before that happened?"

"We were. All very unique individuals who somehow managed not to let those differences get in the way. At least not too much. Both of my parents were fairly intuitive, which meant that none of us could get away with any misbehavior.

"When they discovered that I could see into other realms, they were accepting and also encouraged me to guard my gift. 'Don't intrude on other people's minds or lives,' my father admonished me. 'Let them come to their own realizations.' He was very wise that way."

"You must miss them a lot."

"I do. Yet finding the Friends of Ancient Wisdom has helped me feel that they're not really so far away. And my father's suggestion has served me well at Fibonacci's because we're not supposed to tell each other what we see unless the revelation is mutual. Like we're doing now." She glanced over at him before pulling into a parking space.

"So I guess you learned to keep your head down, too, didn't you?" Jeremy suggested as they got out of the car.

"That's right, I did. Nice insight. I like that. Something you and I did the same that probably helped get us here." She paused to lock the car. "Thanks for helping me understand what happened to you, Jeremy. I know that wasn't easy to share."

She hooked her arm in his. "I want to take you to the old growth forest first. Are you ready to be amazed? "

"I am." He folded his hand over hers and together they crossed the threshold into another garden.

The centuries-old forest was awash with fall colors that mirrored the golden glow filling the auras of Debbie and Jeremy.

As they wended their way along the paved walking trails that wound through a fairyland of Nature's glorious autumn palette, they were beginning to experience a fullness of joy that neither of them could have imagined would be the result of their miraculous reunion.

Finally, they were together. Two hearts, two minds, two souls determined to never be separated again. Not in this life. Not ever.

When they entered the magical setting of the Holiday Train Show, Jeremy's eyes lit up. He was transformed into a very tall little boy who was completely captivated by the miniature New York City of bygone days.

Debbie was tempted to point out some of her favorite models, like the golden recreation of the Enid A. Haupt Conservatory. However, she decided to let Jeremy lead the way to what he found of greatest interest.

She had thought he might want to wander in silence, but she soon discovered that he was a walking encyclopedia of New York City history, especially about its architecture. And he wanted to share what he knew.

"Have you ever climbed to the top of the Statue of Liberty?"

"I have. And I've been to the top of the Empire State Building."

"So has half the world." He bent down and kissed her. "Did you know the original plan was for dirigibles to dock on the spire at the top? One tried but failed after circling twenty-five times in forty-five mile-per-hour winds."

"Nothing like empirical evidence to demonstrate a faulty idea," joked Debbie as they turned a corner in the exhibit.

"Oh, boy!" exclaimed Jeremy. "The Elephantine Colossus at Coney Island! Seven stories, twenty-one windows, served as a hotel and eventually a brothel. Burned down in 1896. For two years before the Statue of Liberty was erected, the elephant was the first artificial structure immigrants would see upon arriving in America."

"My goodness," laughed Debbie. "Can you imagine? I might have wanted to turn back."

"At least Ellis Island was an attractive building," Jeremy observed, "although the experience of getting processed as an immigrant must have been dehumanizing. But look at the detail in the model. Amazing. All that with twigs and seeds."

"Living in New York during the Gilded Age must have been quite an experience. A luxurious one if you were a Vanderbilt," remarked Debbie as she admired the model of the former Fifth Avenue mansion.

"The wealth of these people was astronomical," said Jeremy. "Many of them were robber barons, but I would like to have met old Cornelius Vanderbilt. I read an article about him just recently. Supposedly he built his empire without ever going into debt. He made his money in steamboats and railroads, and invested millions in building Grand Central Station. He lent money to other businessmen and lived a healthy lifestyle."

"I'd love to have toured this place. Too bad it was demolished."

"In 1926 to make way for the Bergdorf Goodman department store." Jeremy grimaced. "What's really astounding is how many of these gorgeous buildings have been razed for commercial purposes. Here's the real tragedy." The original Penn Station was in front of them.

"One of the most beautiful examples of Beaux-Arts architecture anywhere in the world. A few pieces were salvaged, but most were destroyed. In fact, many of the columns and marble sculptures were simply dumped in the New Jersey Meadowlands. I'll show you the photos from the interior sometime. It will break your heart. Guess what sits on top of the modern Penn Station?"

"I should know, but I don't remember."

"Madison Square Garden. Big money maker and completely artless. The only good thing about the Penn Station demolition is that it sparked the Landmarks Preservation Act which saved Grand Central from the same fate." The concerned look on Debbie's face stopped him. "Sorry. Materialism's soulless vandalism still upsets me."

She rested her hand on his shoulder. "Let's check out the Central Park display. Many of the old structures there have been preserved and restored."

"Good idea."

And it was. The models of Bethesda Terrace, the Belvedere Castle, the Dairy, and several lovely bridges were all of extant structures. There was a waterfall created from an actual tree and lots of greenery. Even lawns made of moss. Debbie was grateful to see Jeremy relax and enjoy the park-like setting. He was also paying more attention to the trains and admiring the bridges. Especially the Brooklyn Bridge.

"Did you know it took several months for the caisson on the Brooklyn side to sink down to bedrock so they could build a tower on top of it? Incredible engineering feat for the 1870s."

They were on their way out of the show when one exhibit caught Jeremy's eye. Making his way through a group of parents and small children who were watching trains, he pulled Debbie with him until they were standing in front of the New York Public Library.

"I don't know how I could have missed this one." His voice was thick with emotion. "This building saved my life. I spent many Saturdays here, mostly reading or wandering around, looking at the architecture and the murals. Sometimes I would find a place to sit and meditate on the atmosphere of knowledge and the history of human learning.

"And if things were really tough at home, I would sit next to one of the marble lions that flank the steps and ask them to lend me their strength. Mayor LaGuardia dubbed them 'Patience' and 'Fortitude' during the Great Depression. I have to say that in many ways my childhood was a great depression, although I tried not to fall into despair. As long as I could visit the library, I knew I'd make it."

Debbie's heart reached out to him. "I promise you'll never be alone again." She linked her arm through his and pulled him close. He wrapped both of his arms around her and they stood that way until the visitors walking behind them reminded them that they were not alone.

As they walked toward the exit, Debbie had an idea. "Before we leave the gardens, I'd like to go to the rain forest room where we can climb up into the canopy. Are you up for one more stop?"

"I'll go anywhere with you, my love. Lead the way."

Debbie felt certain that the warm, moist atmosphere of the rain forest would bathe her and Jeremy in a very special kind of serenity. The open metal stairway was easy to climb and in minutes they were standing in the midst of gigantic ferns and palms and other tropical plants like those that Róisín grew in her garden room, but in enormously larger sizes.

After enjoying the view from several different observation platforms, they agreed that they were ready for a meal. They were walking down the steps, which were not steep but were a bit slippery from the moisture. Debbie was holding the handrail with Jeremy beside her.

Suddenly, he whipped around and pressed her against the railing with his back to her as two men that she had not seen on the stairway passed by them. They paused briefly and glared at Jeremy before quickly descending the steps.

"Nice save," one of them sneered back over his shoulder. "You may not be so lucky next time."

"Jeremy, what's going on?" said Debbie breathlessly.

"Shhh," he hushed her and moved around to her side so he could hold her. "I want to make sure they're gone."

"Who?" she whispered, matching his tone.

"The two men who were just about to attack you. I felt them behind us. I don't think they were armed. Most likely muggers looking to grab your purse and run. But their energy was bad. Are you okay?"

"Yes, but I can't believe I didn't feel that attack coming."

"I hope I didn't hurt you. All I could think to do was block them from getting to you."

"And you did. Thank you. Will you hang onto me as we leave? I'm feeling kind of shaky."

"I'm right here, Debbie. I'm not letting anything happen to you."

He walked with his arm around her shoulder and insisted that they sit next to each other at the restaurant. As they shared a salad and a burger, Debbie began to believe that this time the one she loved with all her heart was actually here to stay.

Like two sun systems, each with their own depth and immensity, they were drawing irresistibly together—by the gravity of their memories of past separations, by identity, and by the indomitable magnet of Love's mystery.

For the next several days, that's how things were for Jeremy and Debbie. Whenever they were together, which was most of the time during the week before Thanksgiving, he enfolded her in his strength, keeping her next to him, holding her hand, making sure they were seated together in a booth if they were dining out.

Each day they learned more about each other and gradually grew closer, ever mindful now of the warnings they had received about the opposition to their union.

On the following Wednesday morning, the day before Thanksgiving, Jeremy was sitting in Róisín's garden room with Lucky and Master K. H. He couldn't help being nervous as he was about to ask a very important question.

"Do I have your permission to propose to her? And if I do, is she ready to say yes?"

As these gracious friends were the closest Debbie had to living parents, he felt it only right to ask their permission to marry this woman he now had no doubt was his soul's other half and whom he was growing to love more each day.

Master K. H. looked at the would-be groom with an expression of keen interest. "The question, Jeremy, is if you are ready to say yes to the relationship of many lifetimes, knowing it will be the most important and difficult adventure you've ever undertaken."

"We know you're in the clouds now that you have awakened to who you and Debbie are to each other," observed Róisín. "But are you ready to face the opposition from the brothers of the shadow who, apparently, have already mounted a campaign against your union?"

Her expression was firm like the loving grandmother figure she had been to him for a short time in ancient Ireland.

She was determined to keep the lad safe and not let him rush into marriage too soon. But, of course, he wasn't a lad, she had to remind herself. He was a thirty-year-old man, grown and old enough to make his own decision.

Jeremy watched these thoughts flow across Róisín's brow, for his inner sight was becoming much clearer. He reached over to squeeze her hand.

"I know you're looking out for me, Róisín, and I hope you won't ever stop. My answer, Master K. H., is yes. I'm ready to say yes to it all. I have no future without Debbie. No life. No reason to take up space on this planet unless we are one, and working for the Light side by side. I've seen that, and I know she has, too."

K. H. turned to Róisín and Lucky, who had his arm around his wife. Their faces were bright with affirmation.

"Well then, you have our blessing to marry our daughter Debbie," said the Master. "See that you remain her champion as you have been in the past, and as you have shown yourself to be even in these last few days. The tests are fierce in these difficult times, my son. And because of that, I believe you and our daughter will be much safer united in marriage than you are now living separately."

"Where *will* you live?" asked Lucky with a touch of humor. "Róisín and I are content to have you stay with us, but I don't imagine our guest room is exactly a couple's ideal accommodation."

Jeremy grinned in agreement.

"For now, I can move in with Debbie. But what I have not told any of you or her is that I am actually a wealthy guy. I've been very successful in my own investing and I received a decent pay-out from being laid off at Nordemann Financial. So I can afford to rent a nice apartment or maybe even buy a house. Whatever Debbie wants."

"May I suggest that you postpone any firm decisions?" offered K. H. "Events are yet unfolding that may inform your plans."

"Good advice, Elder Brother," said Jeremy with the broadest of smiles. "Thank you all so much. You have no idea what your love and support mean to me."

"And you'll always have it, son," said Lucky.

He shook Jeremy's hand with the same enthusiastic encouragement he was certain Debbie's own father would have done, had he been alive to honor this young man's request. "Welcome to the family."

Twenty-Eight

The many joys of family and friends filled the air at Fibonacci's coffee shop on this bright Thanksgiving morning. The giggles of Kerry and Kaitlyn Callahan carried over the voices of the adults as the now six-year-old twins entertained their baby cousins, Gareth and Naimh.

Their mothers were discussing how to arrange shared baby-sitting duties now that Ivy and Brian had moved from New Bedford, Massachusetts, to the house down the street from where Kevin and Sarah lived.

Sarah's parents, Eileen and Patrick Callahan, had driven up from the Boston area and were staying with their daughter and son-in-law so Ivy and Brian could continue getting settled in their new house.

Patrick had taken one look at his wife's face when she'd realized that both of her children, their spouses, and her four grandchildren were now living on Long Island. He had immediately sought out his son to get the name of Brian's real estate agent. Clearly, the Callahan tribe needed to be living in the same neighborhood.

Mouth-watering aromas were wafting from the kitchen where Eileen was whipping up mashed potatoes while Róisín put the finishing touches on her famous gravy. They were both chatting with Glenna's mother, Noreen, who was arranging relish trays and cutting up salad ingredients, which she could easily manage from her wheel chair at a low counter. Her husband, Dennis, was doing an excellent job of carving the turkey for easy serving on the buffet.

The Morrisseys had so enjoyed themselves at Glenna and Rory's wedding and reception that they had eagerly accepted the invitation from Lucky and Róisín to drive over from New Jersey and join in the festivities and abundance of delicious food.

Glenna, Debbie, and Cyndi were setting the tables, which the men had arranged in a square so that no one was seated very far apart. This way there was room for booster seats for Ivy's twins. Sarah's babies would enjoy the feast from their stroller.

Rory and Jeremy were making a great show of helping the ladies, although Cyndi observed that more flirting than table setting was taking place. Meanwhile, Kevin, Brian, Lucky, and Patrick were huddled in a corner, speaking to each other with quiet intensity and an occasional burst of male laughter.

Their conversation would have continued, but it was time for the serving dishes to be arranged on the long buffet table. Róisín had suggested that Eileen round up the helpers so the food wouldn't get cold.

"All right, everybody," she said like a general commanding her troops, "we need chairs at the tables and we've got bowls and platters ready to come out from the kitchen. Róisín and Noreen will hand them to you and I'll show you where to place them."

"Yes, *a ghrá*," said Patrick. He put his arm around her waist and spun her into a spontaneous dance. "We know the order. 'Plates at the start, desserts at the end; turkey in the middle, and not round the bend'."

He laughed at the silly rhyme that he'd been using for thirty years whenever his wife got a little too bossy at holiday time. As usual, it worked. Eileen grinned at him and kissed him on the cheek. She went back to supervising the buffet table, but in a more relaxed manner.

When the food was arranged and everyone had found their place at the table, Lucky suggested, "Let's all gather here for a moment. I'll offer a prayer and then we can fill our plates."

Beloved An Síoraí, the Eternal One, thank you for the blessings of love, of friendship, of family, of hope, and for your Presence with us. May we each one strive to bring our best gifts to fruition, and may we always be as grateful as we are today.

If the sure sign of a delicious meal is initial silence around the table, this was one of the best Thanksgiving dinners anyone had ever sampled. Eventually conversation did resume, but then halted again whenever the diners went back for more helpings, which was often.

At last, dessert was served and Róisín had a suggestion.

"Shall we take turns saying a word of thanks?"

Everyone agreed.

"I'll go first,"she said. "My heart is so full today, I simply have to speak my gratitude into the room. I am so grateful to Saint Germain for gathering you all together. He told me that you'd come, but somehow I couldn't quite imagine how he would bring to pass the vision he showed Lucky and me. Actually a vision of us all sitting around a table like this."

She brought her hand to her lips as her voice caught in her throat and her eyes brimmed with tears. "That's all."

"I'll go next," offered Dennis Morrissey. "Noreen and I are very grateful to be included in the company of such fine people. Glenna, my girl, you've chosen well and we're delighted to be here for this beautiful gathering." He wiped a tear from his cheek.

"I'll second that sentiment," said Cyndi. "I could never quite see why Debbie wanted to spend so much time here, but I'm beginning to understand. Just being with you all makes me teary, too."

"And I'm grateful that you're here, my sweet sister." Debbie put her arm around this sibling who was becoming more and more dear to her. "With our brother and older sisters living elsewhere and our parents somewhere beyond the veil, our being together is a gift more precious to me than you can imagine." The last few words were faint as emotion got the better of her.

Patrick raised his hand to go next. "Before I find myself unable to speak through all the weeping . . ." Everybody laughed. "I would like to say I'm grateful that my son, Brian, knows a good Realtor so his mother and I can move to the neighborhood. I'd hate for us to be left out of these celebrations."

"Really?" exclaimed Eileen, throwing her arms around him. "You wonderful husband! I've been married to this man for thirty years and he still surprises me. I am a very grateful woman."

"I'll go next," said Kevin, "but I'm not going to try to speak my gratitude. Just look at these precious souls. My wife, my children, my friends of the ages. I am overwhelmed."

"Me! Me!" Kerry called out clearly. "I'm grateful for Mommy and Daddy and Gramma and Grampa." Both twins could say 'Rs' now.

"And Aunt Sarah and Uncle Kevin and their babies," added Kaitlyn.

"And pie!" said Kerry as he spooned up a big bite of dessert.

"It's hard to top pie," said Sarah with a grin, "so I won't try. But I do have something truly wonderful to share with you all. Hon, would you bring the box?" Kevin got up from his seat and returned with the banker's box he had stashed under the food table.

"As you all know, I've been working on a book for more than a year, and I am over the moon because it's finished! *A Tapestry of Love Through Time* is finally born. I've signed copies for each of you with love from Kevin and me." She held up the book and everyone cheered.

"My darling husband, I am so grateful for your love, your patience, your insight, and your forbearance as I often struggled to tell our story. Will you read the dedication?"

Kevin opened to the page and read. "To Ah-Lahn from Alana. Come what may, I am yours forever."

"*A ghrá,*" was all he could say. He kissed Sarah to a round of applause, and Lucky helped hand out the books. The table was silent as everyone read what Sarah had written to them. More tears were shed and many thanks expressed for this remarkable achievement.

"Congratulations, Sis," said Brian. "This really is a day for gratitude. I've got the most remarkable family a man could ask for. Kerry and Kaitlyn, Daddy loves you more than you know. And you know a lot."

He turned to his wife, beaming. "Ivy, you're the best life partner I could ever have wished for, and I don't say that enough. You amaze me, you inspire me. And you're a great mother to these two incredible children. Thank you for my family."

He paused to gather himself and cleared his throat.

"And now I have an announcement that I know is going to make you all even more grateful than you are already. A few of you have been aware of my intention to purchase the old Carlton Building for my business and as a place to house a new edition of Fibonacci's. Well, yesterday my offer was accepted. There are lots of details to work out, but we've all got a new home."

"Hurray! Well done, Brian!" shouted everybody at the table.

Lucky chimed in. "We'll have a meeting soon to explain the timetable for moving that Kevin and Brian and I have worked out, with valuable input from Patrick. Meanwhile . . . Jeremy? We haven't heard from you." He winked at the young man who had remained silent while the others expressed their thanks.

"'Tis time, lad."

Debbie gave Lucky a puzzled look, then turned to Jeremy when he began to speak.

"I have to stand," he said, taking an enormous breath. "Thank you all for getting me here, for saving me, for loving me, and for bringing me to the point where I could do this."

He took Debbie's hands and raised her from her chair to face him.

"My darling Debbie, we've been through a lot over the last twelve thousand years or so. We undoubtedly have more mountains to climb and oceans to cross, but I'd prefer that we make those journeys as husband and wife, as one forever. Will you marry me, my love? And soon?"

Everybody held their breath as Debbie gazed into Jeremy's eyes, her expression enigmatic. In that moment, she saw a vision of their many lifetimes pass before the screen of her consciousness. Yes, she thought. This is right. This is what she'd always wanted.

"Yes," she said at last. "I will marry you, Jeremy, with all my heart. I have never belonged to anyone but you."

The room went up in cheers as he swept her into his arms and kissed her. The suddenness of this proposal thrilled everybody. Kevin, Sarah, Rory, and Glenna bolted from their seats and enfolded their friends with hugs and best wishes and a few more tears.

"How long have you been dating?" Noreen Morrissey asked when their exclamations had died down.

"Five days," said Debbie sheepishly. "I know, that's kind of quick, but . . ."

"When you know, you know!" declared the two couples who had also married very soon after meeting again in this life.

"You two win the prize for the shortest time between recognition and engagement," laughed Sarah. "Well done!"

"A toast to Debbie and Jeremy!" cried Kevin lifting his coffee cup.

"To Debbie and Jeremy!" echoed their friends.

"When's the wedding?" Lucky wanted to know.

"Christmas," replied Róisín without hesitation. "It must be soon or we'll have too much of Fibonacci's packed for moving. The altar will stay up in the ballroom until the last minute. We can still manage a reception in December. After that we'll have to start shutting down operations."

"No point in waiting," Jeremy grinned and hugged Debbie again. They sat down and pulled their chairs close together so she could rest her head on his shoulder.

"Technically, we have until May to vacate the building." Lucky brought them all back to the realities of moving. "But Saint Germain told me we should be out by February 1, Saint Brigid's Day."

"There's a fair amount of remodeling to do in the Carlton Building," explained Brian, "but I've got a crew lined up to start immediately on Monday. We'll prioritize what has to open first. And Cyndi, there's a retail space for your store if you want it. We should have it ready by the time your lease runs out."

"Then are we all agreed?" asked Lucky. "All shoulders to the plow between now and the first of February, and we'll plan to open the new Fibonacci's mid-May."

"Yes!" they all exclaimed together.

"Now I think you'd best take your babies home," said Róisín to Ivy and Sarah. Kerry and Kaitlyn had their heads on the table and the infants had begun to cry for any number of reasons, as their mother knew.

While Debbie and Eileen helped Sarah and Ivy bundle up their children for the ride home, Brian pulled Jeremy aside and handed him his business card.

"Will you call my cell tomorrow? I'm prepared to offer you a job as CFO for the new business block, if you're interested."

"That would be great."

"I've got to get the family home, but I want you to think about what you'd need for a salary. We can talk details tomorrow. Also, if you and Debbie haven't decided on a place to live, I'd like to take you over to the building. There is a good-size apartment on the top floor. I'd like to have somebody living on site, if you'd consider that. Again, let's talk tomorrow. The building holds lots of opportunity and I welcome your input."

"Fantastic," said Jeremy. "And just so you know, I'm able to pay for the apartment remodel. I have some money to invest and this seems like a good place to start."

As Jeremy walked Debbie back to her apartment, a light snow began to fall around them like fairy dust in the golden light of a full moon. Amazing, he thought. K. H. had said miracles were in the offing. He'd just witnessed several of them, and he wasn't even married yet.

"Are you happy? Not feeling rushed?" He stopped walking and turned his fiancée to face him.

"Beyond happy," she answered without hesitation. "And grateful that we are of one mind and heart on the timing of this adventure. I was beginning to fear that we would miss the cycle of being together in this life. Just in time is good enough for me."

"Then allow me to seal our commitment with another kiss." Jeremy folded Debbie into his arms and kissed her with a depth of heart that he did not know he could feel.

In that moment, she felt the communion of their souls sail back in time on a beam of light, connecting past with present and on into a future of love she now wondered how she ever could have doubted.

Twenty-Nine

The Friends of Ancient Wisdom could not remember ever working as hard or on such long days as they did during the next several weeks. Lucky and Kevin had organized teams and were supervising their packing up the bookstore following the precise matrix they created.

They had made the decision that, although it meant handling all of the boxes twice, the only way to ensure the safety of the books was to move them to a climate-controlled storage facility until the new building was ready to receive them.

At the same time, Róisín was working with her baristas and other volunteers to prioritize what of the coffee shop's stock of teas and coffees could be stored for future use. Equipment that was not necessary for the reduced daily operations they had implemented was cleaned and packed.

They had all agreed on the importance of keeping the coffee shop open as a gathering place for the workers and to maintain the flow of positive energy in the daily communion and conversation that Fibonacci's clientele had come to rely on over the past two years.

Master K. H. had also let Kevin and Rory know that he considered the weekly meetings of the Pythagoreans to be a priority. "We do not allow our minds to become flabby when our bodies are taking precedence," he quipped, quoting one of his fellow adepts.

Jeremy attended those meetings, as he felt a particular loyalty to the master he would always think of as Elder Brother. He was grateful for the philosophical discussions that gave his mind a break from the detailed financial matters he and Brian spent hours on each day.

He was also involved in the hundreds of decisions necessary for the remodel of the large Tower Room apartment that he and Debbie would occupy sometime in the spring.

They were learning a lot about each other as they made adjustments in her apartment to accommodate his moving in once they were married. And they rather dramatically discovered where their preferences did and did not match during trips to the design center to select paint colors, flooring, appliances, and finishes for the new apartment.

"I'm glad we're not trying to build an entire house," remarked Debbie one afternoon following a particularly challenging discussion of the comparative merits of oil-brushed bronze versus chrome kitchen and bathroom fixtures.

"I'm not disagreeing with you," said Jeremy with an exasperated sigh. "I'm only saying that we should consider the various options before we make a decision. Intuition is fine, and I respect yours. I'm only trying to be logical."

"My intuition *is* logical," retorted Debbie as she sank down at a table across from kitchen hardware. "We don't have time to spend hours quibbling about faucets. We're getting married in two weeks and I don't have a dress yet." She surprised both of them by dissolving into tears.

Jeremy pulled up a chair and put his arm around her shoulder. He had no idea what to say. Never having been in a serious romantic relationship, he was genuinely flummoxed by tears over clothing. He and the men in the wedding party had rented their tuxes at the local menswear shop in less than thirty minutes.

"I thought your older sister was shipping your mother's wedding dress."

"She did, but it doesn't fit," Debbie sniffled. "I'm sorry to get all emotional. There's just so much going on and I'm realizing that you and I hardly know each other."

"Only in outer details," said Jeremy quietly. He was surprised how her comment hurt him. "Do you want to postpone the wedding until we finish this move?" He turned her to face him, a plea in his voice. "Please say no. We'll get through this. And I promise not to quibble over faucets." The twinkle in his eyes made Debbie stop crying.

"No, I don't want to postpone. It would break my heart. And honestly, I don't think the masters would approve. I can actually feel them pressing in on us to seal our union. I'm not entirely sure why, but I know that time is of the essence."

"Then let's move on with . . . oil-brushed bronze?" Debbie had to laugh now. "And why don't you go check in with your sister. Brian's waiting for me at the construction site. I'll probably be there past dinner, so I'll see you in the morning. Okay?"

"Okay. And thanks for being so understanding. I'll drop you off and head over to Cyndi's. I can feel her needing to talk to me."

Just then her cell phone rang. "Hi, Sis. . . . Yes, I was just about to come see you. . . . Really? That's fabulous. I'll be right there. And tell Glenna thanks a million." Debbie's face was glowing as she hung up her phone. "It's a miracle!" she exclaimed and gave Jeremy an enormous hug that eased his mind considerably.

"What is?"

"Glenna has asked her costume designer friend to come to the store to do a fitting for my dress. He's the one who created all the fairy costumes for *Samhain*. He's bringing fabric samples to add some tasteful blue touches to the gown so I'll have a real Irish wedding dress. I can't believe it."

To Jeremy's sincere consternation, she began to cry again.

"Clearly, I'm out of my depth here." He kissed her cheek. "Let's go. Brian is wondering where I am. I'll make up a list of other remodeling decisions we need to make right away and what can wait so you can spend the time you need with Glenna and your sister."

As Jeremy climbed the stairs to the site of their new apartment, he realized that in the eyes of his bride a wedding gown was much more than a dress. An afternoon spent dealing with straight-forward construction details and financial spreadsheets was sounding really good right now.

When Debbie walked into the store, Cyndi's assistant, Stacey, was ably handling the stream of customers who were shopping for healthy holiday gift items. She found Glenna and her sister in the back room talking excitedly and marking pages in a bridal magazine.

"Oh, good, Debbie, you're here," said Cyndi looking up. "Come see these gorgeous floral arrangements Glenna found. She says we can have them done for half the going rate if we use her friend in Manhattan. Honestly, Glenna, I don't know what we would have done without you."

"I'm thrilled to do what I can."

Debbie could tell that Glenna was becoming a good friend to Cyndi. It made sense. The two young women were much alike in the way they organized their thoughts and actions. It helped that they were both Irish and understood the importance of creating an atmosphere of genuine hospitality in the event they were planning.

Although Cyndi was handling most of the maid-of-honor duties, between them, the women had agreed that Sarah should fill that role during the ceremony because of the ancient family connection she shared with Debbie. Glenna and Cyndi would be bridesmaids. Róisín was mother-of-the-bride, and Lucky would walk Debbie down the aisle as father-of-the-bride.

Kevin would be Jeremy's best man, and Rory was a groomsman, along with their fellow Pythagorean, Noah, who was becoming a good friend to Jeremy. They were all delighted to hear that K. H. had asked if he might serve as father-of-the-groom.

Nothing had been said about Jeremy's parents not being invited or included in the wedding. There was no need.

"Rico will be here in about fifteen minutes," said Glenna, "and then he's agreed to go with us to the bridal shop to pick out our bridesmaids and mother-of-the-bride dresses. I've already asked them to set aside what they have in the greens you like. We're fortunate that this year's Christmas brides have all gone with red, so we'll have some nice choices.

"Róisín and Sarah will meet us there. Gareth has a cold, so she's staying home until we need her for decisions and fitting. And Sarah said to tell you that Ivy has found perfect outfits for Kerry and Kaitlyn to wear as ring bearer and flower girl. She said the twins are already practicing walking down the aisle because, as they declared to their mother, 'We're the leaders of the bride and leaders are the most important.' "

"That's the twins," snickered Debbie. "I'm glad I don't have the responsibility of being most important. Takes the pressure off."

They all had a good laugh.

"Are you fine with Christmas colors for flowers?" asked Cyndi.

"Mostly white," said Debbie. "And actually I'd like gold instead of red to go with the white and green."

"Done," said Glenna. "White and gold with green accents. Got it." She checked off an item on her long list of decisions and tasks to be accomplished in two weeks. "I'll place the order while we wait for Rico."

While Glenna was on the phone, Cyndi put her arm around Debbie. "How are you doing, Sis? You look kind of frazzled."

"I'm better now, just knowing that you and Glenna are handling the planning so all I have to do is say yes or no. I can't tell you how much this means to me."

"And I have to say again how grateful I am for Glenna. The woman is a whirlwind in all the best ways. Does she remind you a little of Mom? All that enthusiasm for life?"

"That had occurred to me," said Debbie wistfully. "I miss her so much sometimes. I wish she were here now."

"Me, too. Though I'm sure she's looking down on us and smiling."

"That's something I would say to you."

Cyndi blushed. "Guess I picked it up from Glenna. She's been sharing some stories about her own wedding, and I've asked her a few things about your friends at Fibonacci's. I'm beginning to feel like I've picked up another sister."

"That makes me so happy," said Debbie as a movement in the doorway caught her eye. "Looks like Rico is here."

A slightly built man with an elfin countenance entered the back room. He was carrying several bags of blue trim and fabric samples and a satchel with the tools of a costume designer's trade.

Glenna concluded her phone call and hurried over to make the introductions.

"Rico, thank you so much for coming all the way to Long Island. We'll buy you dinner after we're finished shopping. This is my friend Cyndi." He shook hands with great cordiality. "And this is her sister, Debbie, our bride."

"Beautiful, beautiful," remarked Rico as he took Debbie's hand. His designer's eye admired her tall, willowy figure and long, flaxen blonde hair. "Do you have the dress?"

"Yes, I've set up a little changing area in the corner," said Glenna.

"I'll help you, Sis," volunteered Cyndi. She and Debbie ducked behind the screen and giggled and shed a few tears as she buttoned her younger sister into their mother's classic satin wedding gown.

On the Friday a week before Christmas, the Pythagoreans were discussing the concept of the music of the spheres.

Glenna had tried to beg off attending this meeting because she was so busy with wedding preparations. However, Rory had insisted, reminding her of how much she enjoyed interacting with all of the students, especially Jenny and Valerie.

"Besides, K. H. has declared this music week. We need your input."

She was glad she'd agreed. Everybody was contributing spontaneously and appeared to be comfortable with sharing insights.

Rudy was back with the group and Finn was taking the lead in today's discussion, which K. H. had encouraged, saying that he would like to hear what their research had revealed.

"Pythagoras postulated that each planet gives off a unique sound or frequency as it travels through space," Finn began. "That tone depends on the sphere's size, density, distance from the sun and other planets, its speed of movement. He called this the harmony of the spheres. And just as the planetary spheres create a harmony, so does the entire universe. He expressed all of this in numbers, because that's how he explained the workings of creation."

"What I find fascinating about his theory of universal harmony is that he also applied it to the soul," added Valerie. "He said that each soul has its number and its harmony, or tone, which is imperishable."

"I know we can't get away from numbers with Pythagoras," said Noah. "I'm resigning myself to that, even though it makes my head hurt." Everybody laughed. "But did Pythagoras just figure this out mathematically, or could he hear the tones he said the planets emanate?"

"He could hear them," Rudy interjected. "I'm sure of it. Judging from reports of how the Pythagoreans revered him as a divine being, he must have had a connection to higher realms of consciousness. To him, numbers were an expression of the Divine Mind and the way that Mind orders its creation. He was trying to spark that understanding in his disciples, so he used every method available, including teaching in symbols, aphorisms, and metaphors that were poetical."

"Thanks, Rudy, that helps," said Noah.

Jenny chimed in. "I think the way of life that Pythagoras taught his disciples had to do with helping them find their inner harmony. In fact, he used music, dance, and the recitation of Homer's verse to remove dissonance, to heal troubled minds and volatile emotions."

Finn agreed. "That's right. There's a story about him preventing a death by calming the would-be murderer with music and verse. Pythagoreans used songs played on the lute to calm their minds for sleep and then different melodies to awaken them for action in the morning."

"And those melodies were chosen based on how they fit in with the mathematical system of harmonics that Pythagoras discovered and then included in many of this theories," said Rudy.

"Glenna, did you have something you wanted to add?" asked Kevin. He could see her enthusiasm bubbling.

"Does it show?" she laughed. "Well, as you're talking, I'm getting a picture of how the classes I'd like to develop will fit into your academy. Especially for children, who are bombarded by so much dissonance, helping them find their inner harmony with elevating music, dance, and verse, like Shakespeare, is what I'm feeling called to do."

"And Pythagoras would thank you," said K. H. with a knowing smile.

As the study group was winding down their discussion of how music and numbers are part of the same cosmic unity, Jeremy made an announcement. "I hope you all will come to our wedding next Saturday. It's going to be a great day. Debbie and I really want you to join us."

"As do I," said Master K. H. "The Brotherhood has asked me to encourage all members of the community to be there. In fact, I would consider it a favor if the group of you would sit with me for the event.

That is, if you have no family holiday plans that day."

He looked directly as Rudy when he extended this invitation.

Rudy was surprised that K. H. would include him—considering his outburst only a month earlier that had shocked Jeremy into a sudden past-life recall. Yet he detected only genuine acceptance from this master who conveyed nothing but an unspoken assumption that the lad was doing his best.

He felt his heart swell—an unusual experience. His chest often felt tight and constricted, as if anger and resentment had built a fortress around his heart. But in the presence of K. H., he relaxed. His habit of sarcasm faded into the background and he found himself wanting to do what the Master asked of him.

"Will you accept my invitation, Rudy?" K. H. spoke quietly to the young man as they were leaving for the afternoon.

"That's very kind of you, Sir. Yes, I'll be there."

And Rudy knew he would—on time, with his hair combed, clean clothes, and polished shoes. He figured his mother would make a snide remark about him going on a date, but he didn't care. For the first time in his life, he felt a resonance in his being that, had he ever experienced the feeling before, he would have known to call it hope.

Of course, with my luck, this feeling won't last, he said to himself as he rode the bus home to the shabby little saltbox house he shared with his mother. He knew it would be only a matter of time before he had to report to A. B. Ryan.

The man frightened him and Rudy hated him for the fear he instilled in the lad's mind. And for the control the man held over him and his mother. He'd never known why they were so beholden to this tyrant. More than once he'd asked his Uncle Tony and his other uncle, Rudolfo, his namesake. But they would either change the subject or flat-out tell him he was better off not knowing.

All he did know was that he was powerless to refuse to tell A. B. what he wanted to know about the goings on at Fibonacci's. The man was obsessed with the place and the people Rudy was beginning to feel more kindly toward than he'd ever considered possible.

Thirty

December 25 was a wonderful day of celebration with family for all members of tomorrow's wedding party.

Sarah's parents had returned to Long Island to be with their children and grandchildren. Glenna and Rory had driven to New Jersey to spend the day with her parents. Debbie, Cyndi, and Jeremy had attended midnight mass with Róisín and Lucky the night before and then joined them for a quiet meal on Christmas Day.

Everyone had gone to bed that evening feeling at peace and excited about the ceremony that would take place at half-past eleven the following morning. All of the preparations had been made and all was right with the world. Once more, love was triumphant.

Earlier than she expected the next morning, Cyndi cheerfully answered her cell phone on the first ring. "Good morning, Sis. What a glorious day this is! Are you ready to become Mrs. Jeremy Madden in a few hours?"

"Cyndi, can you come over here?" Debbie's voice was weak. She sounded frightened.

"What's wrong? I can hardly hear you."

"I can't get out of bed. I'm so exhausted, I can't move. Help me, please. Call Róisín. I need Róisín." Debbie's phone went dead.

Cyndi threw on some clothes. She dialed Róisín's number while she dressed, but the call went to voicemail. She left a frantic message and jumped into her car. Although she lived closer to Debbie's apartment than their friend, Róisín was waiting for her in the parking lot behind the health food store when she pulled up.

"I knew something was wrong this morning. I woke up early and was prompted to check on our groom. I knocked on Jeremy's door and at first heard nothing, then a groan and a faint call for help. The lad was paralyzed in his bed."

"Must be the same with my sister." The two women dashed up the stairs to Debbie's apartment. They found her still in bed, pale as death. She had managed to pull herself up to sitting, but that was all.

"Thank God, you're here," she gasped. "I don't know what's wrong."

"You're under psychic attack, darlin'," Róisín surmised. "So is your man, but Lucky's with him and we've got the prayer team going. With all of us praying, we'll clear this energy. But you've got to summon your will, my girl, and shout."

"Shout?" asked Cyndi. "Shout at what?"

"All the forces of black magic and witchcraft that don't want your sister to get married today," said Róisín. "I know this may seem strange to you, *a chara*, and a lot for you to absorb all at once. But there are nasty forces at work here that will do anything in their evil power to prevent this wedding and the good that will come of it."

"That's terrible," declared Cyndi. "Who are they?"

"We call them the brothers of the shadow because they work in the dark. They sometimes know better than we do the potential of our missions. So they try to preempt our work for the Brotherhood of Light by focusing their rays of dark energy that make us sick or depressed, angry or sleepy. With seers like Debbie and Jeremy, they'll send a black-out ray that blanks your mind."

"You're right," Debbie moaned. "I can't see a thing."

Róisín pulled up a chair beside her bed. "You sit right there, darlin'. We're going to shout into the teeth of this darkness. Sarah and Kevin and your Friends of Ancient Wisdom are all doing the same thing right now. And Lucky's with Jeremy, so don't you worry."

She turned to Cyndi. "*A chara*, you may want to go to another room, as we are going to be loud. We'll just be saying prayers, but in situations like this the more energy we use with our calls to the angels and the masters, the more they can do for us."

"Could I join you? Ever since we got here I've started feeling sick. I guess these nasty forces don't like me either."

Róisín gave her a big smile. "Of course, darlin'. Pull up a chair beside me. Debbie, where are your prayer sheets?"

"Night stand."

Róisín handed Cyndi a few typed pages. "Here you are, lass. Follow along as you're able. These are simple prayers. Like little rhymes. We're going to start with the one to Archangel Michael."

"I already pray to him," said Cyndi, her face alight.

"Wonderful. Then you'll be right at home. Imagine rings of his bright blue angels surrounding us and then when we say 'Light! Light! Light' over and over, visualize pure white light flooding in, through, and around this room, your sister, Jeremy, everybody in the wedding party, and all those who will be gathering at Fibonacci's."

"The bad guys don't have a chance, do they?" said Cyndi confidently.

"No, darlin', they don't."

Considering how weak she'd felt upon waking this morning, Debbie never could have imagined that she would be dressed in her Irish wedding gown, holding Lucky's arm, and waiting for the string quartet that Glenna had pulled together from some of the musicians in their community of Friends to begin playing Mendelssohn's "Wedding March."

At a signal from Cyndi, the music began and the bridesmaids made their way down the aisle. Debbie was thrilled with how radiant they all looked. At the last minute they had agreed that dresses in a light gold were the best choice. Róisín looked like a rich golden flame in her silk dress that set off her white hair and deep green eyes.

"You look bootiful, Aunt Debbie," said little Kaitlyn as she waited her turn. Her bright blue eyes were as wide as moons as she looked up at Aunt Sarah's friend in her snowy gown trimmed in blue lace. To the little girl, the bride was as magical as her spirit friend, the Rose Lady.

"So do you, my Kaitlyn, in your blue velvet dress," said Debbie with sweet sincerity. "And Kerry, you are very handsome in your blue suit."

"I know," he said proudly. "When you lead the bride, you have to be handsome."

"Okay, you two," said Ivy. "Here you go. Kerry, stay with your sister.

Follow Aunt Sarah and walk all the way down to the altar."

"We will, Mommy," said Kaitlyn. "Bye!" She waved and started toss-ing rose petals from her basket immediately upon entering the ballroom.

When Debbie appeared at the back of the ballroom on Lucky's arm, Jeremy was awestruck. So stunned that he wondered for a minute if he had been paralyzed again at this most important moment of his life. But he knew that wasn't true. He was simply overwhelmed by his bride's beauty and the scintillating white light that glimmered in her aura.

Here was a dream come true, except he couldn't remember ever having dreamed a sight so glorious. Although he could have easily lifted right out of his body into pure bliss, he willed himself to stay conscious so he might remember every detail of his wedding.

At last he and his bride were standing before Tim O'Toole, Debbie's friend from her retreat. He had been a priest in his youth and was still licensed to perform weddings. All those in the packed ballroom were touched by the love and light in the room, the fragrance of gardenias from Debbie's bouquet, and the tenderness of Tim's delivery. It was clear that the bride and groom held a special place in his heart.

As soon as he enthusiastically pronounced Jeremy and Debbie man and wife, he quickly stepped aside as Saint Germain's ascended-master figure appeared before them. The golden disc over the altar shown with the brilliance of a sun as the Master began to speak.

My sons and daughters, I am come to you this day to bless the union of Debbie and Jeremy and also to proclaim to you a vic-tory that is an important part of our mission focused here at Fibonacci's.

Kevin and Sarah, please stand to the left of the bride and groom. Glenna and Rory, take your place on their right. Lucky and Róisín, to the right of Rory.

Let it be known to all Friends of Ancient Wisdom, that with the completion of this mandala of twin flames and soul mates devoted to the cause of Light, a new era has begun.

Legions of the Great White Brotherhood are on the march,

and you are all commissioned to come up higher in consciousness. I, Saint Germain, am also accelerating, as is my brother in your midst, Master K. H., who stands with you now as guide, guardian, and friend.

K. H. made his way from the front row and stood beside his friend and brother. Saint Germain continued his remarks.

Friends, we have much to accomplish in the coming year. May each of you see to your own house and set all in good order. For mighty challenges are coming upon us and we must be prepared to stand, face, and conquer the forces that are sure to assail even our best servants.

Will the four couples kneel now to receive our blessing as I place my hands on your crown chakras. Please remain kneeling until all have been blessed.

Kevin and Sarah, courageous druids Ah-Lahn and Alana, I make known to you that your gift to this mandala is one of power and protection. May you use it carefully and always with the intention of service to each other, your family, and friends.

Debbie and Jeremy, brilliant seers Dearbhla and Madwyn, I make known to you that yours is a gift of illumination. May you remember that knowledge is weak unless it be wise, for wisdom is the keystone in the arch, the pivot point of our mission.

Glenna and Rory, joyous bards Gormlaith and Riordan, I make known to you that yours is the gift of love. May you remain in the flow of a balanced heart and be a beacon of compassion to all you meet.

Lúcháir and Róisín, faithful friends, you have unflinchingly held the vision of twin flames so that these six could be called. Yours is the gift of selfless service to which we commend all of our community members to aspire.

The gratitude of the Great White Brotherhood goes with each of you. I depart this day for higher octaves of service, though I am ever-present with you. As we are one in Spirit and

in Love, I assure you that Master K. H. is united with me in consciousness, for all ascended masters are eternally one.

Great rays of light blazed out from the sun disc, and Saint Germain's
figure dissolved from view, leaving Master K. H. standing before the
company. He raised his hands in benediction and said, "Will everyone
please stand now as I offer the final blessing."

*In the name of my brother Saint Germain and by the power, wisdom,
and love of An Síoraí, the Eternal One, I bless you each one in the Light
of the Christ Mass and the joy that is born in our hearts this day.*

Showers of golden light emanated from the Master's hands, bathing
the congregation in an extraordinary peace and crystal clarity of thought
and feeling that remained with them for many days.

When K. H. lowered his hands, his luminous brown eyes shone
with a touch of humor as he declared, "And now, Jeremy, you may kiss
your bride."

Cheers went up from the assembly as Jeremy raised Debbie's veil
and they melted into their first kiss as a married couple.

Lucky then stepped forward. "If I may, Master K. H. and Friends—
our plan is to hold the reception here in the ballroom. I believe our volunteers are ready to move into action to transform our sanctuary into a
reception hall. The bridal party may retire to the bookstore lounge and
we will reconvene shortly."

Indeed, many hands made light work. In thirty minutes tables and
chairs were set up, trays of food were brought from the coffee shop,
more musicians joined the string quartet, and a glorious reception began
to the delight of all.

The twinkle lights that decorated the ballroom had never sparkled
so brightly. And as many couples waltzed in the joy of Christmas, soft
snowflakes began to fall outside, catching the illumination of street
lamps like so many stars blinking their joy from heaven.

Thirty-One

Rudy wasn't surprised when his phone rang early on the Monday morning after Christmas.

"Hi Rudy, it's your Uncle Tony."

"A. B. wants to see me, doesn't he?"

"Yeah, he does. He's in his Manhattan office and says to be there by noon. Sorry, kid. I'm just the messenger. Nothing I can do."

"I know. I knew you'd call sooner or later."

What Tony didn't say and what he always tried to soft-pedal was the menacing tone A. B. used whenever he referred to Rudy. Usually it was, "that good-for-nothing kid" or "that stupid kid."

Tony knew that Rudy was anything but stupid, and he tried to help his nephew when he could, but they were all under A. B.'s powerful thumb. Unless the man died or was abducted by aliens (Tony suspected even they wouldn't have him), all they could do was the man's bidding.

"Sit down and tell me what you know," snarled A. B. when Rudy walked into his office. He hated sitting in the chair opposite the man because the "guest" seat was at least three inches lower than the boss's.

Rudy had already decided to minimize what he would disclose, but A. B. had a nose for lies. Probably because he was such a skilled liar himself. So Rudy would have to be careful.

"They're working really hard to be out by February 1."

He began with basic information about the status of the buildings Ryan Investments had purchased. The fact that A. B. had given Lucky six months to vacate the property stuck in his craw because his supposedly slick lawyer had been outfoxed by Brian Callahan's even slicker lawyer.

So now A. B. wanted to know everything that was happening at his property without having to go there himself. That would be humiliating, and he'd had enough humiliation at the hands of these people.

"What else?"

"People are working around the clock packing, and every few days they take a truckload of boxes to a secret storage place."

"Find out where it is."

"They don't talk about it, A. B. I think only Lucky and Kevin actually know where it is."

"Follow them."

"I don't have a car."

"Then find out their next run and I'll have them followed."

"Okay, I'll try." What Rudy didn't say was that a couple of new members of the Friends had tried to follow Lucky and Kevin, but the truck had disappeared into a mist that they couldn't penetrate.

"What else? There was a wedding, right?"

Rudy didn't want to reveal anything about the wedding, and especially not about the big blessing. He would say the least he could. But, in trying to match A. B.'s cynical tone, he slipped up.

"Yeah, it was no great shakes. A bunch of people getting mushy about some mandala being complete and a new era dawning." When the man's cobalt eyes turned dark with sinister interest, Rudy realized his mistake.

"A new era, you say? What does that mean?" A. B. said more to himself than to the young man sitting in front of him. He gazed into the distance, then shook his head and turned his attention back to Rudy.

"Listen, kid. You keep going there. And when you find out what this mandala is and when they're expecting a new era, you let me know."

"Okay, A. B., but it doesn't make any sense to me," Rudy lied.

"Then figure it out. You tell me what I want to know or you and that worthless mother of yours are off the dole. Get it?"

"I get it."

"Good. Now scram. I'm busy and I'm tired."

That's interesting, thought Rudy as he rode the bus home. He didn't remember A. B. being anything but full of vicious energy. Had something happened to deplete the boss, or was he just getting old? Rudy would be watching for other signs of change that might free him and his family from the man's oppressive influence.

Alone in his penthouse office, Arán Bán (as A. B. Ryan thought of himself these days) scrubbed his hands over his face and ran a hand through his thick grey hair. He needed to think. His brow was furrowed, his eyes dark as midnight as he contemplated his next move.

He hated to admit that he had a problem he hadn't foreseen.

For as long as he could remember, he'd considered Ah-Lahn to be his worst enemy. Throughout the centuries, the man had represented everything Arán Bán despised, and still continued to be a thorn in his side as Kevin MacCauley.

But now, even more aggravating, he also had Lucky O'Connor to deal with. This he could not tolerate. Once and for all, there had to be a way to get rid of both these men and their annoying friends.

The brothers of the shadow agreed and assured him they were not out of options. He should be patient and bide his time. There were many more hands to be played before this game was over.

The other people who were biding their time—though for entirely different reasons—were Mr. and Mrs. Jeremy Madden. They had been patient about him not moving into her apartment until they were married. But now Master K. H. was encouraging them to delay traveling for a honeymoon.

Considering the near-attack they had experienced at the Botanical Gardens and the debilitating energy that had swamped them on their wedding day, they agreed that his counsel was wise.

"Strengthen your bond," he had suggested. "Pray together, talk about every subject that interests you. Learn each other's hopes and dreams. Practice mental telepathy, as we are encouraging all of our twin flame couples to do.

"Kevin and Sarah are very adept at connecting their minds and hearts. Rory and Glenna are developing some proficiency. You should be experts by the end of the year," he teased the two seers.

"Seriously, your ability to connect with each other across time and space will be extremely important to you and others in the near future. Do not take my words lightly."

"I guess we'll just stay here and play house," Jeremy said with a grin as they added some of his books to Debbie's library. "There are worse things than having to spend all of my time with you, my love."

She circled her arms around his waist and rested her cheek on his chest. He held her tight and kissed her on the top of her head, so she couldn't see the amusement playing about his mouth.

"I know another reason for us to become skilled at linking our minds telepathically."

"Really? What's that?"

"It's bound to help us at the design center. We still have to decide on flooring and counter tops."

Debbie looked up and rolled her eyes at him. Then she took his face in her hands and touched her lips to his. As she passionately kissed her husband, she sighed in grateful wonderment at the mystery of living as modern-day mystics. She would always remember these as some of the happiest days of her life.

Thirty-Two

The month of January—in the opinion of many, the longest, dullest, and bleakest month of the entire year—took on the excitement of a marathon race for the Friends of Ancient Wisdom.

By the time the sun moved from the astrological sign of Capricorn into Aquarius on January 21, the bookstore was completely packed and stored. Only the altar and sun disc remained in the ballroom. The coffee shop was as bare as possible while still maintaining minimum hours and service.

On January 29, Róisín baked her last batch of blueberry muffins, and Lucky ground his final pound of coffee. They invited all of the staff and volunteers to a meeting and a long-awaited announcement.

"*A chairde,* I'm pleased to tell you that we will meet our timeline of vacating Fibonacci's by February 1," Lucky declared to cheers from the group who were beginning to think of themselves as war veterans.

"Your heroic efforts mean that we can finish packing the coffee shop over the next two days. On Monday, which is Saint Brigid's feast day— *Imbolc* to you Celts—we'll gather in the ballroom for our final service.

"The purpose of this service is to say thanks to the angels, masters, and elemental spirits who've helped sustain our presence here, and to ask them to transfer their presence to our new location. Many of them have already been watching over our remodeling crews as they transform a tired old structure into a resurrected one.

"Our final prayer on *Imbolc* will be to the Builders of Form to withdraw the Light we've anchored here back into the realms of Spirit where it can never be misqualified."

"Does that mean the Light is lost?" asked one of the volunteers.

"Not at all," replied Lucky, "nor was it invoked in vain. It accrues to each of you who've worked so hard to see us through this transition. According to your service, Light will be stored in your causal body."

He winked at the puzzled faces of a few newer students. "That's like a spiritual bank account," he explained. "So you're all permanently blessed by your contribution. Enjoy your break, *a chairde*. Then we'll give one more grand old push on to the finish."

Applause erupted in the room.

Lucky and his staff had decided to hold their final service early on the evening of February 1. Due to the nature of the event, this was to be an adults-only gathering. Several parents had organized childcare in their homes, so more people could attend the service.

Sarah and Kevin had dropped off six-month-old Gareth and Naimh at the home of their Aunt Ivy, who was delighted to let these little ones keep Kerry and Kaitlyn occupied with entertaining them for the evening.

"What's wrong, Kevin?" asked Sarah as they drove the short distance to Fibonacci's. "I thought you'd be feeling buoyant after reaching this milestone."

"I thought so, too, but I keep sensing a warning. Nothing specific. Only that I won't rest easy until we've held this service and then transferred the mantle of Fibonacci's to the new location. We're starting early enough this evening that we should be able to do both tonight."

"I'm surprised I haven't felt anything," said Sarah. "I'll pay more attention this evening. Anyway, I'm very proud of you. You and Lucky showed true leadership. A number of people have commented to me about how much they appreciate your organized system and clear instructions. Your encouragement made a huge difference when everyone was so tired they were ready to give up."

"Thanks. It was a team effort, and everybody did more that I could have hoped for.

"Have you seen Rudy?" asked Rory when he and Glenna greeted Kevin and Sarah outside the entrance to the ballroom. "I was hoping he would be here so I could thank him. He worked as hard as anybody. I have to say I've changed my mind about the lad. I think the presence of K. H. has made a difference in his behavior in a way that none of us could ever have accomplished."

"I agree and I'm grateful," said Kevin.

"Wow!" he exclaimed as they entered the ballroom, which was filled to more than capacity. It was standing room only—partially because all of the chairs had been packed away and because every member of the Friends of Ancient Wisdom who could possibly attend had arrived for this very poignant ceremony.

Many eyes were already glistening with tears. Lots of hugs were being exchanged with expressions of love and gratitude flowing between friends new and old, young and not so young.

At the appointed hour, Lucky entered and solemnly lit the candles on the spiral candelabra that stood man-high on either side of the altar table. He turned to the congregation and began the service in the formal tone that reflected his deep connection with the Brotherhood.

"Dear friends of the great Light of Love, Wisdom, and Power that is the source of our being and the goal of our souls' striving, thank you for your presence here and for the mighty service you have rendered, which has miraculously brought us to this hour.

"We all owe deep gratitude to Kevin MacCauley for his leadership and staying power. Every time I showed up, he was on the job. Thank you, Kevin, for keeping us on track."

Applause and cheers made him blush and urge Lucky to continue.

"Before we speak the prayer for the withdrawal of the Light that has been anchored here, I would like to extend to each of you my personal thanks and that of Saint Germain. When the call went forth from the Great White Brotherhood to establish a community of Light that would stand as a bulwark against the growing encroachment of darkness upon our city, our nation, and our planet, you answered.

"You have exceeded my imagination of what was possible, though not the Master's expectation. He is wonderfully pleased that the vision he conveyed to me several years before I bought this building has come to this point of manifestation. He says he knew you could do it.

"So please give yourselves a round of applause for responding to Saint Germain's heart and rewarding his efforts by your presence."

The ballroom echoed with cheers and applause and expressions of love for the Master who had touched each one's soul very personally.

"Now, let us sound the OM together one more time and I will make the call."

OMMMMM!

Those gathered thought their chanting had never been so resonant, so heartfelt, so profoundly uttered as it was this night. Hearts were moved as memories of wonderful events came to mind.

Kevin stopped chanting briefly. He thought he heard a noise downstairs. But when it did not repeat, he decided it was probably the wind. He would investigate once Lucky had concluded the service. For now he would place his full attention on his friend's prayer.

Beloved An Síoraí, the Eternal One, in deepest gratitude for the countless opportunities and blessings we have received through this place called Fibonacci's, we call to you in this hour to send forth angels and Builders of Form to take up the Light that has been anchored here. Place it in the causal bodies of all who have served. Seal us each one in your Love and Light, and let us learn and grow and serve ever more faithfully in years to come in our new location.

Lucky paused momentarily. He had intended to ceremoniously extinguish the candles one by one. But before he could do so, a rush of wind began swirling from the back of the ballroom, moving around each person until it reached the altar.

As the congregation watched in amazement, each candle winked out separately, the sun disc ceased to glow, and the whirlwind whooshed up through the ceiling, causing the room to grow dim. Clearly, Spirit had accomplished the task of withdrawing the Light.

Lucky was preparing to dismiss the congregation and invite as many as would like to join in a second ritual to adjourn to the new site for the short dedication ceremony. He opened his mouth to speak when the building was suddenly rocked by a loud crash coming from downstairs and the smell of smoke began to fill the air.

Lucky, Kevin, Rory, and Jeremy had been standing with their wives at the front of the room. After spending the past several months studying with Master K. H. who had been embodied as Pythagoras, they knew in an instant what the noise and smoke meant.

All eight exchanged one horrified look and exclaimed a single word: *CROTONA!*

Thirty-Three

In a glance, they all knew what they were up against. They were in the midst of a repeat of the horrific crime committed against Pythagoras and his followers in the sixth century BC. Those individuals had been trapped in a building that was set aflame by a vengeful person who had been denied entry into the academy. All but two of that ancient community had perished in the murderous blaze.

"The bookstore's on fire!" One of the reembodied Celtic warriors shouted from the back of the ballroom. Four of these burly men immediately grabbed the fire extinguishers that had been left hanging by the ballroom entrance and dashed down the stairway.

"Doorway!" Lucky and Kevin declared together.

Only last week they had been prompted to unblock a small door that connected the front of the ballroom behind the altar with an old fire escape on the far side of the coffee shop. It would deposit people onto a side street, away from the front of the building where they had heard the crash, which Kevin thought sounded like someone had thrown an incendiary device through the bookstore display windows.

The big Celt reappeared at the back of the ballroom and shouted to Lucky and Kevin so everyone could hear, "The sprinklers are on and the fire extinguishers are working so people can use the stairs, but there's another fire in the coffee shop." He bolted back out the door to help his comrades downstairs.

"Listen, everybody!" shouted Lucky in a voice of calm authority. "We've two ways out. Anyone who is able-bodied, come this way. The fire escape is a bit rickety, but it works. We tested it last week.

"Rory and Glenna, head down now and help people on the stairs. Róisín and I will stand here and guide you folks along. Everyone, keep moving and get as far away from the building as you can as soon as you reach the street."

Kevin picked up his thought and shouted more directions.

"Anybody who requires assistance, follow me to the stairs. Jeremy and you other strong men, don't be afraid to carry your friends who need extra help. Sarah and Debbie, make sure all the older folks get out and bundle them up as best you can as soon as they reach the street."

The two women were moving swiftly to help some senior citizens who appeared stunned by the situation when Sarah saw her husband making for the stairs ahead of the crowd. He had a very determined look on his face. She grabbed his arm to stop him. "Where are you going? Kevin, don't be foolish."

"I'm not, but I've got to get to the coffee shop. I heard something earlier and I have a strong feeling I know what or who it was."

He hurried across the loft where only weeks before their precious esoterica collection had been on display. Pushing through the crowd, he reached the first floor and quickly surveyed the situation.

Immediately he noticed that some of the sprinklers in older parts of the bookstore were not putting out enough water to dowse the flames. That included the lounge under the loft. Although the warrior Celts had made some headway with the fire extinguishers, they needed the fire department—and soon.

"Jeremy, keep people moving," shouted Kevin. "You need to clear the stairs before the loft collapses."

"We're on it!" his friend shouted back as he and another man helped Debbie and Sarah usher a group of older ladies outside.

"Stay out of the kitchen, Kevin!" yelled one of the Celts who was carrying a disabled man out the front door. "The gas could blow any minute!"

"I know!" he shouted back, "but there's a lad in there! I have to get him out!" Sprinting to the back of the bookstore, Kevin managed to duck through the doorway that led to the coffee shop before the timbers that supported the loft started to sizzle and crack.

His inner sight was now fully open. In his mind's eye he saw Rudy lying on the kitchen floor, unconscious. He didn't bother calling the lad's name. He knew Rudy wouldn't hear him over the roar of flames and the din of sirens as the fire department came on scene. The smoke was getting thicker and Kevin began to worry for his own safety.

"Saint Germain, help me!" he prayed aloud, remembering similar scenarios from ages past. "Help me save my son once and for all!" He reached Rudy's prone body and shouted this time, "Wake up, lad!"

"What?" Rudy said faintly. "My hands, they're burned. Ah-Lahn, help me! Dad, get me out of here. I didn't want to do it. He made me set the fires with gasoline. I got too close."

"Come on, Tadhgan," said Kevin. He realized the boy had flipped into his former identity as had happened when he tried to attack Sarah over a year ago. "I've got you. Out the back now. Hurry!"

Half carrying, half dragging the young man who had been his best friend on Atlantis, a fellow Pythagorean at Crotona, and his son in ancient Ireland, Kevin reached the back entrance of the coffee shop just before a smoldering timber fell on the stove, instantly igniting the gas, and blowing up the entire kitchen with enormous force.

The energy of the blast tossed Kevin and Rudy across the parking lot where they landed and now lay unconsciousness from the impact, bruised and bleeding, and in Rudy's case, badly burned.

"My husband is in there!" cried Sarah frantically to the firemen who were urging people further away from the building when they heard the terrifying explosion in the coffee shop.

"We can't go in there, ma'am," said the fire captain. He was firmly holding her back from trying to do exactly that. "We'll check the perimeter. If he got out, we'll find him. Go with your friends."

Debbie and Jeremy put their arms around Sarah and led her away from the building to where an emergency shelter had been hastily set up. Glenna and Rory soon joined them. At the back of the shelter they could see Lucky and Róisín speaking with the EMTs who were taking care of anyone who was injured. Neighbors were showing up with blankets and coffee. The Friends of Ancient Wisdom appeared to have survived intact. If only they could find Kevin.

"Can you see him?" demanded Sarah. Debbie and Jeremy were

searching intensely for Kevin with their inner sight. Rory was standing behind Sarah with his hands on her shoulders and Glenna was holding her hand. She was trying to be calm, but the idea of losing her husband was more than she could bear. Surely they wouldn't have to go through another tragic separation.

Finally Debbie's face brightened. "I see him. The EMTs are loading Kevin and Rudy into an ambulance. Jeremy, will you go find out which hospital they're being taken to? Don't worry, Sarah. We'll get you there as fast as we can."

Kevin woke up in the hospital with a pounding headache. His mouth tasted like he'd been eating cinders. His lungs burned and his tightly bandaged arm hurt like the dickens. But he was alive. Thank God, he was alive.

"Sarah," he said faintly and coughed. He reached out to his wife who was sitting next to his bed. "Did they all get out?"

"Everyone, my love. Everybody made it. Only a few bumps and scrapes from climbing down that rickety old fire escape. And some of those who went through the front door breathed a lot of smoke."

"The building?"

"It's a total loss. But it's not our loss, is it? Ownership had already been transferred to Ryan Investments, hadn't it?" She couldn't bring herself to say the name of the man she had a feeling was behind this terrible event.

"You're right. Not our loss." Then Kevin remembered. "Rudy? What about the lad? I got him out before the explosion. Is he okay?"

"He'll live, but he's under police guard. They're charging him with arson and possibly attempted murder. He could go to jail for years."

Kevin tried to sit up, groaned, and sank back on the pillows behind him. "I need to talk to him. We've got to hire him a lawyer right away. He told me that he'd been forced to set the fire and got too close."

"You're not doing anything tonight. You're staying here until you're better. I'm not sure Rudy is even conscious yet. But you are, and we've all been waiting for you to wake up."

Kevin looked past his wife and saw Debbie and Jeremy, Glenna and Rory, Róisín and Lucky standing in the doorway to his room. They were all completely disheveled. Sooty as chimney-sweeps, they were smiling and pouring out their love to him. He was genuinely touched.

"Thanks for coming. You didn't have to, but it's really great to see you. All of you. Sarah says everybody's safe."

"Looks like you got the worst of it," observed Rory.

"Yeah, well . . . " Kevin didn't know what to say.

"They salvaged the sun disc," Jeremy told him. "Most of the building collapsed, but it was as if the disc and the altar just sank gracefully to the ground. The firemen were able to pull it, the candelabra, and the big crystals from the rubble. The only thing that broke was the chalice and then the bowl only came loose from the base. It can be repaired."

"We're going to take everything to the new building first thing tomorrow morning to anchor the Light there," said Lucky. "Róisín and I have to go retrieve all the pieces from the fire department, but we wanted to make sure you were okay first. We'll see you soon."

"I'm sorry you'll have to make do with hospital food for now," said Róisín with regret. "I'll bring you something better tomorrow."

"That's okay. Seeing your face is healing enough." Kevin croaked and coughed hard.

"What can we do for you tonight?" asked Debbie.

"Will you check on Rudy for me? There's something behind his actions. More likely, somebody, and I think we can all guess who that is. I feel responsible for him. Do you know he called me 'Ah-Lahn' and 'Dad'. A soul is at stake here. I couldn't save him on Atlantis, at Crotona, or in Ireland. I've got to try now."

Kevin coughed again and clenched his teeth in pain.

Sarah looked at their friends, a plea on her face.

"We'll take care of it, Kevin," said Jeremy. "Rory and I will go to his room. Debbie, will you and Glenna stay with Sarah?"

"No, something tells me I should go with you. Glenna, will you stay?"

"Of course. Someone needs to be with Kevin and Sarah tonight. I'm happy to be the one."

When the three friends found Rudy's room, the officer on duty wouldn't let them enter. "He's heavily sedated because of the burns," he explained. "Family only. His uncle is with him. I can ask him to step out if you want."

"We'd really appreciate it," said Debbie. "We're all friends."

The officer went into the room and soon Tony came out. Debbie had never seen him so dejected, so without affect. He had obviously been crying and his eyes filled again when he recognized her.

"Debbie, sweetheart, it's so good to see a friendly face."

She held out her arms to him. "Come here, Tony, let me give you a hug. How is he?"

Tony briefly laid his head on her shoulder and took a deep breath. Debbie held him for a moment until he could pull himself together.

"He's in bad shape, but the docs say he'll make it. Poor kid. He doesn't deserve this. I should have done more to protect him, but A. B. had a noose around my neck."

"I think you'd better tell us what you know," said a very serious Jeremy.

"Tony, this is my husband," explained Debbie. "I agree with him. We know there's more going on here than appearances would suggest. Sarah's husband, Kevin, is down the hall. He was injured saving Rudy and he needs to be told what I can see very clearly that you know. It's the only way we can help your nephew and our friend. Otherwise, Rudy's looking at prison. You know he wouldn't survive."

"Come on, Tony," said Jeremy taking the man by the arm and leading him toward Kevin's room. "Time to confess, and maybe that noose won't feel so tight."

"Or it may get tighter," grimaced Tony. "Either way, there's no going back now."

Thirty-Four

Kevin was wide awake. His friends were arrayed around him, standing or seated on the few chairs that would fit in his hospital room. Tony was sitting on a chair facing all of them.

"What I'm about to tell you could get Rudy killed, or me. I guess if anybody deserves to pay the price for this mess, it's me. The kid has been a pawn since he was born. It's time that stopped so he has a chance for a decent life. I imagine many of you know parts of Rudy's story. What you don't know is that he is A. B. Ryan's illegitimate son."

Kevin and Sarah looked at each other, stunned. Not again. The soul of Arán Bán owed this young man life because he had taken that life as the High Priest on Atlantis. In Ireland he had seduced Ah-Lahn's wife who had given birth to Tadhgan. Here again in the twenty-first century, A. B. Ryan had given Rudy life, and then manipulated him to potentially lose it.

They all turned their attention to Tony. The man took a long sip of the water Debbie handed him and began the story of his nephew's unfortunate history:

Rudy lives with his mother, my sister Rita, in a run-down neighborhood. If you think he's volatile, you should meet his mom. She's a piece of work. Always has been, ever since she was young. A real hell-raiser and emotionally fragile.

I can't tell you the number of times I've had to bail her out of jail or get her into rehab. But that's not where the story begins.

Twenty years ago she worked as a campaign volunteer for A. B. Ryan. He was extremely handsome in those days and made a habit of seducing sweet young things who were enthralled with politics, but mostly with him. He wasn't married and no doubt a number of those young ladies hoped to be the future Mrs. Ryan. He was already rich and powerful. A real catch, as they say.

He hadn't meant to seduce Rita, or so he claimed. As a matter of fact, she went after him and got pregnant on purpose, thinking she could force him to marry her. He refused because she was so unstable.

The Argenti family—my family, I'm sorry to say—have big-time connections with organized crime. Supposedly, that's why A. B. was first interested in Rita. He wanted a part of that action. When our older brothers found out that he'd gotten her pregnant, they beat him up badly. Almost killed him.

But he was already building his network of bribery and extortion of state and local officials. He promised the family big favors. Over the years he's kept that promise, so they've tolerated him.

A. B. paid for Rudy's upbringing as long as nobody disclosed who he was. But the family held a sword over his head. Unfortunately, he's had one over mine, too. It's part of our mutually assured destruction pact that keeps us tied to each other.

I used to be part of the family business, although I always had a weak stomach for some of their more creative crimes. Anyway, my involvement led to an argument with a really good friend. He hadn't known about my line of work until one night we got to talking in my apartment and it all came out. He was furious and said he was going to turn me in to the authorities. I couldn't let him do that, so I hit him and we fought.

It was summer and the living room door was open. I still don't know exactly how it happened, but my friend went over the balcony and fell fifteen stories. It really was an accident, but nobody believed me.

The family fixed the situation. They have a way of making bodies disappear. But they also decided I was a liability, so they sent me to work for A. B. Turns out I'm a good writer, so the job itself has been rewarding—except for the anxiety of being A. B.'s minion, which Debbie and Sarah understand.

The two women rolled their eyes. "All too well," said Sarah.

Glenna looked down at her hands which she had unconsciously clutched together. Rory noticed the gesture of self-protection and touched her shoulder. She reached up and grasped his hand. Better than many in the room, they understood the vicious nature of the man in his druidic form.

Tony continued:

> So, back to Rudy. Rita hated the little guy because he was a constant reminder of her trying to manipulate a master manip-ulator and losing everything. She'd get drunk and hit the kid. The family finally sent him to live with our brother Rudolfo, who isn't in the business.
>
> He did his best for the kid, but eventually Rudy got to be too much for him. So he sent him back to Rita and told me to take care of both of them. That's what we've been doing for the past ten years.
>
> I got Rudy into college and he's smart, so he's done well, in spite of his tough-guy attitude. He does some work for me when I get swamped with A. B.'s demands. That's why he's on the payroll.
>
> Rudy and I have been able to make this work. But if what you say is true—that A. B. forced him to set fire to Fibonacci's— the situation has really deteriorated.
>
> If I tell the family, I'm sure they'll decide that A. B. is no longer useful. But that won't help Rudy if the DA is ready to charge him.

"Tony, you've got to go to the authorities with this," said Sarah.

He shook his head. "Do you know how many of them A. B. has in his pocket?"

"What about the DA?" asked Debbie.

"Depends on the jurisdiction."

"What about here on Long Island?" asked Rory.

"She's probably okay."

"Good," said Kevin. He could feel his strength returning. "We'll hire one of Sarah's brother's high-powered legal firms. They may decide to contact the insurance company that A. B. used to prove coverage for the purchase of Fibonacci's. I imagine they'll be very interested to know that the current owner of the building forced a person in his employ to destroy his own property."

"That may be a tough case to prove," said Jeremy. "It will be Rudy's word against A. B.'s."

"You're right," Tony agreed. "But I think in this case the family will do everything they can to protect their nephew. If they turn on A. B., the feds can get him on enough other charges that the DA may actually believe Rudy."

"Then we'll hope for that," said Kevin. "Thanks, Tony. We'll keep this confidential and make sure the attorneys don't tip off A. B. about your involvement. They will have to speak with you, but maybe that can happen at the new Fibonacci's."

"That could work." Tony's face brightened. "With Rudy unable to spy on you for A. B., he may decide I should do the job. He knows that Sarah and Debbie and I are well-acquainted, so that gives me a legitimate reason to visit once in a while. We'll see what happens. The main thing is for Rudy to get better."

It was a small and very somber group that gathered at Fibonacci's new location on the following morning. Kevin was being released from the hospital later that day, but he wasn't well enough to participate in the ceremony. They didn't want to delay anchoring the light for the building's final resurrection, so they moved forward with the ritual.

In addition to the third floor Tower Room apartment where Debbie and Jeremy were going to live, the building had a large space on the same level that could have been a ballroom at one time. This is where they set up a make-shift altar. They couldn't install the sun disc yet, but they could light candles in the free-standing candelabra.

As Lucky lit the tapers, Glenna, Rory, Debbie, Jeremy, and Róisín chanted the OM. He joined them and the six continued the chant for several minutes until they felt a definite resonance building in the room.

Lucky was preparing to offer a prayer, when Master K. H. entered.

"Greetings, friends," he said in his wonderfully soothing voice that always evoked a vibration of peace and encouragement.

"You have been through quite an ordeal. After living through the record of the tragedy at Crotona, perhaps you are feeling rather war weary. Would you allow me to make the calls for you, to set Fibonacci's on its trajectory of success?"

"We would be very grateful," said Róisín. "I believe our auras are a bit ragged after yesterday's dramatic events."

"Then we must do something to repair them," said the Master with a loving smile. "Let us proceed. Please arrange yourselves according to the matrix I am holding in my mind."

The six friends looked at him for a brief moment, and then without discussion or question, created a circle with K. H. at the head in front of the candelabra, men to his right and women to his left. Lucky and Róisín stood next to each other across from him.

They left a space on either side of the Master. Jeremy and Debbie were next, then Glenna and Rory so they were in the order of the blessing Saint Germain had given them at the Maddens' wedding.

"Excellent," said K. H. "Now please close your eyes and keep them closed until I say to open them. Place your full attention on your hearts. We will chant the OM together again and then we shall see what blessing *An Síoraí*, the Eternal One, has for us."

OMMMMM. The six friends chanted with their Master. The sound built quickly, as did the radiation they could feel increasing in and around them. Time ceased to be and physical sensation became one of extreme lightness in their bodies until each of them experienced lifting out of their physical forms.

"You may open your eyes, dear ones," said K. H. gently. Yet was this K. H. who stood before them? He had never before appeared to them in such glory. *Yes!* they heard the voice of inner wisdom declare.

For here was the Ascended Master Kuthumi in his spiritual office as World Teacher, radiantly clothed in the garment of the Brothers and Sisters of the Golden Robe. His aura glowed with colors of golden-pink that illumined the ballroom, whose proportions had quadrupled in size.

As the six friends looked around the circle at their companions, they saw that each one wore a white robe with a beautiful stole in the colors of their blessing rays. White for the O'Connors, ruby for the O'Donnells, yellow gold for the Maddens, and lapis blue for the MacCauleys. Kevin and Sarah had joined them in their finer bodies.

Somehow these appearances did not surprise them. What did cause their hearts to catch in awe and their eyes to grow wide was the sight of rings upon rings of other souls of Light who were gathering with angels and elementals on all the rays. Surrounding them was a mighty conflagration of masters and cosmic beings.

All were facing into the circle with their full attention focused on Master Kuthumi. He took the hands of Kevin and Sarah, bidding the other six to complete the circle as he began to pray.

In the name of the entire Spirit of the Great White Brotherhood and by the authority of An Síoraí, the Eternal One, I welcome each one to this new home of Fibonacci's, which we dedicate this day to the work of the Divine Light that does not fail.

Great hosts of Truth, Goodness, and Beauty, we ask you to anchor your Presence in these hearts you see before you and within these walls so that all who enter here may prosper in their souls and transcend the former self as each one is given to do.

Bless this company of initiates in all their strivings in the loving service each one now pledges. (As a single voice, the eight declared, "I pledge my loving service.")

I AM Kuthumi. This day I also pledge my commitment to Divine Purpose as envisioned by Saint Germain and those who sponsor him. We are one in Mind. We are one in Heart. We are one in Spirit. So shall we remain by the grace of An Síoraí, the Eternal One.

As the eight mystics watched in amazement, an enormous golden sphere appeared suspended above the Master. It shone like an actual sun, casting rays of pure white light in all directions. At the same time, the unspeakably beautiful sound of angelic choirs could be heard singing paeans of praise while each one of the assembled spirit beings raised their palms, projecting beams of light toward the center of the circle.

The walls, ceiling, and floor of the expansive ballroom glowed with light, and each one gathered for the ritual felt their individual consciousness quickened to new heights of awareness and capability.

Eventually, the golden sphere dissolved. The rings of spirit beings and the songs of angels began to fade. When all had disappeared, Master Kuthumi indicated that the group should drop hands. He brought his palms down in a graceful gesture that caused them to close their eyes.

When they opened them a moment later, they were once more in their physical bodies, standing in a circle in the unfinished ballroom. Kevin and Sarah were not with them.

K. H. was present, clothed in his usual habit of a Franciscan friar. He was gazing at the six friends with an expression of profound compassion and gratitude for the initiation each one had passed.

"Dear hearts," he said, "you are truly a bonded mandala. In coming weeks and months, you will find yourselves acting as instruments of illumination and miracles. I am honored to serve as your guide through these difficult times. May you love each other as I love you, and all will be well."

He brought his hands together at his heart in the gesture of *Namaste* and vanished from their sight.

Thirty-Five

When the Friends of Ancient Wisdom looked back on the six weeks between *Imbolc* and Saint Patrick's Day, they would remember three things: A. B. Ryan's arrest on multiple charges of fraud, extortion, and racketeering; Rudy's miraculous healing; and round-the-clock construction work at Fibonacci's.

Tony had been correct about his crime family turning on A. B. Without their influence as a shield, he was powerless to avoid his karma that would no doubt send him to prison, unless the family decided to silence him lest he turn State's Evidence against them. Either way, he was about to lose the very dangerous game he had been playing for thirty years.

Rudy's injuries turned out to be little more than skin irritations, which the doctors could not explain. They were reluctant to admit that the young man had been healed by the congenial Franciscan friar who had come to visit him.

When the burn specialist had examined the patient that morning, he was still under heavy sedation. The multiple third-degree burns were going to require skin grafts and probably several surgeries to return the young man's hands to full functioning.

After the friar departed, Rudy was sitting up, asking for food and some cream for his hands which were red, but showed no signs of their earlier serious condition. In less than a day, he was released into the care and safety of Lucky and Róisín's guest room.

Until the DA could review the case as it was being brilliantly argued by Rudy's attorneys, the lad was placed under house arrest, which was a divine solution. Here he was safe from any who might wish him harm, and he was receiving the best possible treatment of body, mind, and soul under Lucky and Róisín's watchful ministrations.

In less than two weeks, the DA dropped most charges against Rudy. He still faced federal penalty for setting off an incendiary device, but his attorneys were working hard to get him a minimum sentence, given what had been revealed about A. B. Ryan.

To everyone's amazement, the man had confessed to forcing his employee to set fire to the building he owned. No one could explain this sudden turn-around, other than to perhaps attribute it to the visit of a Franciscan friar who said he had come to the jail to minister to the prisoner's soul.

Was A. B. trying to buy some good karma to offset his many ill deeds after hundreds of centuries? That was one mystery the Friends never solved.

Meanwhile, remodeling of the third floor at Fibonacci's was being fast-tracked. The team had all agreed that the new ballroom and altar took priority so they could start holding full services rather than the small-group gatherings that were taking place in people's homes.

Lucky knew he was pushing Brian to complete a lot of work in a very short time, but it couldn't be helped. "We're making do as best we can, but we'd like to come together as a community, possibly as soon as March 17. Can you handle that?"

"Don't worry, Lucky, we'll make it work," Brian said confidently.

Sarah had thought her brother might disagree with Lucky's assertion. Instead, he hired an additional crew to work solely on the third floor. He wanted Debbie and Jeremy to start living in the Tower Room space as soon as possible. And since Jeremy was paying for construction of their apartment, the ballroom was a small expense compared to the other sections of the building.

Brian's call center and extensive computer facilities required more complex work, which made building out the bookstore and coffee shop look relatively easy. Conroy's health food store would be the final project, but completion was still anticipated by the time Cyndi's lease expired at the end of May.

Time truly did fly, and before they knew it, a sunny March 17 arrived. It was an especially joyful day at the O'Donnell apartment.

"Happy Saint Paddy's Day, *mo mhuirnín*," Rory greeted Glenna with an affectionate kiss, a cheerful grin, and a cup of Irish tea made just the way she liked it with a dash of milk.

Go raibh maith agat, mo chroí, she responded with an equally cheerful smile. "Why are you so jolly this morning? Except that today is your favorite holiday, of course."

"You won't believe who just texted me that he's coming for a visit."

"Did your brother get booted out of Ireland by Aunt Finn?"

"Not likely. In fact, I think there's other news brewing there. His last e-mail had a touch of mystery and no jokes, which is unlike Craig. Do you remember how quickly he answered our aunt's call to come help her? I'm pretty sure that he and Cousin Mary are getting married."

"Then who is our visitor and what will we do with him?"

"F. M.'s assistant Phelan is the man, and his plane will be landing in a couple of hours. He apologized for the lack of notice—said he'll explain when he gets here. I thought I'd asked Debbie's sister Cyndi if he could stay in the apartment over her store now that the Maddens have moved into their new apartment.

"Jeremy told me they were leaving Cyndi's place furnished. He bought all new furniture for the Tower Room. Something about not pouring old wine into new wine skins."

"That's a grand idea," said Glenna. "I know Cyndi likes having somebody living on site. Even if Phelan is here for only a short visit, that should work well. Nobody else really has room for him right now."

"*Go hálainn,*" said Rory enthusiastically. "I told Phelan I'd pick him up at JFK. Do you want to come with me?"

"No, I need to get over to Fibonacci's. I've got last-minute To-Do's on my list for the celebration. I'll phone Cyndi for you. I'm sure she'll be willing to accommodate our friend. Especially when I remind her that Phelan helped you get me off of Mount Brandon the day we met in the mist. She's become quite the romantic."

"Thanks, darlin'," said Rory, kissing his wife once more. "I'll be off, then. I'll get Phelan settled and we'll both see you later at the party."

"It's a good thing we opted for a large kitchen." Debbie laughed as she and Jeremy surveyed their granite counter tops, which were covered with platters of baked goods that were the main refreshment items for today's Saint Patrick's Day celebration.

The coffee shop downstairs was far from ready to provide food or beverages, so Róisín and company were using the Maddens' spacious new kitchen as the serving station.

Debbie had a feeling this wouldn't be the last time her apartment was commandeered to support a party in the ballroom. And that pleased her. The community was coming back together at last. She was delighted that she and Jeremy could help make that happen.

"Róisín and Lucky will be here any minute. With them away from home, should you join the Pythagoreans in their garden room while the students keep Rudy company?"

"No, they're fine. Noah has some notes for a discussion and Jenny will keep everybody in line." Jeremy smiled to think how that young lady had flirted with him at *Samhain*. Now they were friends and he no longer felt like he had to avoid her. He was glad of that. He was enjoying being part of the community.

"Besides," he said, "I'd like to be here to play host. Since this is our actual home, I want to make our guests feel welcome."

"That's quite a change from the man who used to not have any friends and said he liked it that way." Debbie was enjoying the humor that percolated through their conversations.

"Well, I guess I was just waiting for the right friends. And you." He wrapped his arms around her and drew her close. Could a man be any happier? Jeremy thought not.

Thirty-Six

"Have you seen F. M. recently?" asked Phelan as soon as he and Rory greeted each other at the airport and collected his luggage.

"I haven't, no. From what we can tell, Saint Germain's dispensation to appear as a Wonderman is over for now. We don't know if that's permanent or not. The last time we saw him was *Samhain*, when he introduced Master K. H., who's taken F. M.'s place. Have you met him?"

"I haven't and that's one reason I'm here. F. M. didn't really tell us anything in Ireland. I get the feeling that he didn't know he was going away and was over here in America when his Chief informed him. This is all assumption on my part, but I have spent a lot of time with F. M. in the last couple of years, so I figure my guess is as good as anyone's."

"Makes sense," said Rory as he maneuvered his car onto the freeway. Afternoon traffic was picking up, so he had to be mindful of other drivers on the road while discussing such an important issue as the location of their Master.

"I know a couple of people who've been able to contact Saint Germain in prayer. But that's all. No sign of F. M. Bellamarre."

"Interesting," said Phelan thoughtfully. "And not very comforting for the students in Ireland."

"My wife, Glenna, and her friends believe it takes a lot of energy for an ascended master to maintain a physical presence and that there are other issues the Brotherhood needs Saint Germain to concentrate on."

"That's what's come to me in my meditations," agreed Phelan.

"I've given this a good deal of thought," continued Rory. "With F. M. gone we've all had to step up our vibration and improve our intuition. My sense is that Saint Germain was given a certain amount of time and energy to establish a nucleus of souls of Light in community—specifically our mandala of twin flames, though I know there are other mandalas within the community. Once we came together, I think his Chief instructed F. M. to withdraw. Seems to me that he had to work fast."

"I believe that," said Phelan. "When we first met, I asked F. M. about his interest in you. All he would say is, 'Time is short. He must be ready.' I guess that has applied to all of us."

Rory nodded as he moved into the far right lane of traffic. "Fair play to that. Glenna and I still feel like we have cosmic timetables that we must stay attuned to meet. Nothing we can point to. Just a feeling."

"I've had the same feeling. I know several other students would agree. Merlin Wolffe, the director at the Aeon Theatre in Dublin, has stepped up to lead that group. He's been encouraging them to put into practice the instruction they've received from F. M. over the years."

"I can see how he would be a good leader."

"He is, yes. And, of course, Merlin was the beneficiary of more time with the Master than most, so he's in a position to help the others. They started getting along better once they realized each one has to paddle his own canoe, so to speak."

"We're all learning that lesson." Rory smoothly exited off the interstate onto a side road so he could show Phelan more scenery and less freeway.

"But F. M.'s absence has been hard on the students in Dingle," his friend continued. "They never had as much contact with him as I did. They're newer students on the path, so they have less experience with the Master to fall back on."

Rory nodded. "Makes sense. I know I can tell a difference between my own experience and some of the senior members of our community."

"'Tis interesting how much you pick up over time," said Phelan thoughtfully. He looked out the car window and admired the landscape that was becoming more rural. "So, lad, have you settled into living around millions of people?"

Rory chuckled. "A bit, I suppose. But all the rush and hustle still overwhelms me sometimes. If I start feeling crowded, I go sit by the water. We've got some nice shoreline and a beach close to us and we've a grand view of the Long Island Sound from our apartment. You'll have to come for a visit. So, what else about the group in Dingle?"

"I've tried to help them as best I can. We were making some prog-ress, but then I got the powerful intuition that I was supposed to come over here. So I've left them, too. I have to trust that all is proceeding according to some greater plan than what I can perceive right now."

"A plan is quickly unfolding now that Master K. H. is with us," agreed Rory. "I know you'll like him. He might be at the party tonight, and I expect him to meet with our philosophy study group called the Pythagoreans."

"A study group?" Phelan's face lit up. "That's grand. Could I sit in some time? Remember, I was reading philosophy before I became F. M.'s assistant."

"You'll be very welcome. From what I've observed, a big part of K. H.'s philosophy focuses on helping us master our psychology. Like the next step of self-mastery, even adeptship. Several times I've heard him use the phrase: 'Transcend your former self.' "

"I'm lucky to be here for that," said Phelan.

"So are we. We're grateful for any guidance in accelerating our consciousness and shoring up our inner defenses. My mandala of three couples has been mightily challenged by a man named A. B. Ryan—or Arán Bán, to use his old druidic name."

"F. M. did mention something about an adversary who harbors an intense hatred toward some of you."

"He does that. Pray you never meet him. I didn't quite believe in embodied evil until he tried to kill Glenna and me at Clonmacnoise. I no longer scoff at the idea of fallen angels or devils incarnate."

"Wow," exclaimed Phelan. "Things are serious here."

"They are. Probably because Fibonacci's is a major outpost of the Great White Brotherhood. That's the main reason we're working so hard to finish the remodel on our new location and establish a strong forcefield of Light."

"I'm willing to help for as long as I'm here. I hope you can put up with me for a while," grinned Phelan.

"We're excited that you're joining us. Glenna and I live in a small studio apartment, but her friend Cyndi owns a health food store with a one-bedroom upstairs that's recently been vacated. While I was waiting for your plane Glenna texted me that Cyndi is glad for you to stay there. She likes having somebody living on site. Makes her feel that the store is safer that way."

"*Go hálainn*. Great. I didn't expect my own apartment."

"We'll go there first so you can meet your landlady, and then we're expected at the party we're having this afternoon at Fibonacci's. It's not a big do, as the new building is still being remodeled. But the ballroom is finished and the whole community is likely to be there. 'Tis is our first opportunity to all be together since Debbie and Jeremy's wedding."

"*Go hálainn*," said Phelan again. "'Tis grand to see you, Rory. I was hoping my showing up would be in the flow. So far, I feel a guiding hand."

"As do I. You'll like our Friends of Ancient Wisdom and I know they'll greet you with open arms. Anybody who has worked directly with F. M. is considered a treasured source of inside information. Prepare to be affectionately interrogated," he said with a wink as he parked in front of their destination.

Rory could hardly wait to get Glenna alone at the party so he could describe to her the scene he'd witnessed when he and Phelan entered Conroy's To Your Health. From the expression on his face, Glenna knew she was in for a good story.

> You should have been there, darlin'. When Phelan and I walked into Cyndi's store, she was waiting for us so she could lock up and come on over to the party.
>
> 'Cyndi, meet our friend Phelan,' I said. I expected them to shake hands and then she'd show him the apartment. Instead, they just stood there like statues, their eyes wide as moons. I think she was holding her heart. He dropped his bag and said not a word.
>
> They might still be standing there, staring at each other, except I cleared my throat and that brought them out of their

trance. 'Cyndi, do you want to show Phelan the apartment?' I suggested.

'Oh, yes,' she answered. She seemed to click back into the efficient lass we know, but she still walked a bit unsteadily up the stairs and her hands were shaking when she opened the door to the apartment.

'Here you are,' she said. 'My sister and her husband have left everything very clean. I've put fresh linens on the bed and towels in the bathroom. There's not really any food in the kitchen, but we can figure that out tomorrow.'

'Do you want me to wait while you unpack?' I asked Phelan.

'There's no need for you to hang around,' Cyndi volunteered. 'I have some chores to finish up here. I'll bring Phelan over to the party with me. You can run along now, Rory.'

'Twas clear I'd been dismissed. Phelan said thanks for picking him up, then he and Cyndi went back to staring at each other. And look, there they are. Like two peas in a pod, chattering to Debbie and Jeremy. I don't know if they've been dreaming about each other like you and I did, but there's no question of them recognizing each other.

"Isn't that adorable? When you see sisters hugging like that, you know something's up." Glenna's heart was dancing.

"Some weeks ago Cyndi asked me to tell her about twin flames. She wanted to know if I thought she had one. I told her that everybody does, somewhere, and that she could support hers on the inner by sending that person love and light, even if they never met in the physical.

"I explained that she might even draw that person to her, if their reunion was the will of *An Síoraí*, the Eternal One. I guess she took my advice. Want to bet on how soon I'll be planning another wedding? Maybe I should start a business."

Husband and wife gave each other a big hug. No matter what else was happening at Fibonacci's, love was in the air on this very special Saint Patrick's Day.

"What's up, Rory?" demanded Jeremy. It was 9:00 a.m. the next morning and he had a dining room full of people. "Your text sounded urgent. Is everything all right with you and Glenna?"

Rory had sent a short message to his fellow Twin Flames of Éire, as they were beginning to call themselves, asking if they could meet first thing this morning at Fibonacci's.

Cyndi's assistant was opening the health food store for her, so she and Phelan were having breakfast with Debbie and Jeremy. They had invited everyone to gather at their apartment. Brian was there, too.

"Sorry I'm late," said Kevin as he hurried in and closed the door. "The twins are teething, so Sarah's staying home. Hope that's okay."

"Of course," said Glenna. "Rory didn't mean to alarm you. We should have explained more in the text, but we're so thrilled about the news we have to share that we wanted to tell you all at the same time."

"You're pregnant!" exclaimed Debbie.

"No, not me. Rory's distant cousin Mary, Aunt Finn's lady-in-waiting. Apparently, she didn't—wait that is. She and Craig are expecting, so the wedding they were planning for the summer has been moved up to *Bealtaine*."

"They want us to be in the ceremony," said Rory. "Since I'm Craig's only brother, I'm to be best man."

"Cousin Mary has plenty of sisters and cousins to be bridesmaids, but Aunt Finn insisted that I be there, too." Glenna was flushed with excitement.

"How does she feel about the coming attraction?" asked Debbie.

Glenna smiled at her friend's use of a theatrical term. Wasn't it heartening to observe how their mandala of twin flames was bonding so that they naturally picked up each other's expressions.

Rory explained. "I called my mother as soon as I got word from Craig. She said that Aunt Finn was none too pleased at first. But now she's collecting baby clothes and figuring out how to build an addition onto her house. Craig and Mary were meant to live with our aunt to keep her safe in her home as she ages. The need for family space would have occurred sooner or later. It just happens to be sooner."

Glenna chimed in. "So, the reason we asked you all to meet us is that, if we went to Ireland for the wedding, we'd be gone for at least ten days at the end of April and early May. We know the grand opening for Fibonacci's is tentatively set for May 16, the feast day of Saint Brendan, the Navigator. We're concerned that our being gone will cause a problem with our tight timelines. Rory's supervising the bookstore set-up and I'm doing most of the event planning. What do you think?"

The group was silent as everyone considered the ramifications of their proposal. Having two valuable team members absent in the final days before grand opening could present a serious challenge. Brian spoke first.

"This is an interesting development," he began. "Normally, I would be tempted to say we can't spare you. But the more time I spend with all of you, the more open I am to change. So here's an idea:

"It has occurred to me in the last couple of days that we may be pushing our timelines too hard. What if we delayed the opening to Memorial Day weekend? That would give us two more weeks to go through final construction punch lists and work out the bugs in our systems."

"That would be grand," said Rory. "We really do want to attend the wedding, and *Bealtaine* is an excellent time to visit Ireland. Not too many tourists, the big fire festival, rhododendron in bloom."

"I can fill in for Rory at the bookstore," offered Phelan.

"And I can pick up event planning tasks for Glenna," Cyndi put in. "We did well together organizing Debbie and Jeremy's wedding."

"Speaking of weddings," interjected Jeremy. "Actually, speaking of honeymoons, we never had one, except for staying home and rearranging furniture for a week. I'm wondering if Debbie and I could join you in Galway for the wedding and then spend a few days traveling around?"

Debbie picked up his thought. "We would love to go to Ireland. Maybe this is the time, as long as having four of us gone wouldn't put too much strain on everybody else. And if Craig and Mary would like to invite us, of course."

"I know they'd be pleased to," Rory said, then grinned. "And Jeremy will get to meet Aunt Finn. That event alone justifies your going."

Debbie squeezed her husband's hand to let him know that meeting Aunt Finn was a good thing. She had enjoyed getting to know the great lady at Rory and Glenna's wedding in the States.

"We'd love to show you around," enthused Glenna.

"We would, yes," Rory agreed. "We'll have had enough family time during the wedding festivities. We could head south after that, driving together. Would that be all right with you two?"

"Whatever you suggest is fine by us," said Jeremy. He put his arm around Debbie and she hugged him in agreement. "I've never traveled anywhere. This sounds like a perfect plan—as long as everyone else agrees."

"I think you should make the trip," said Kevin without hesitation. "I'm already working with Lucky on Fibonacci's finances. We had previously agreed on the need for Jeremy and me to be cross-trained between our businesses and Brian's. We'll just accelerate the process."

"I agree," said Brian with a touch of humor in his usually matter-of-fact delivery. "And once our operations are humming along, I plan to take Ivy to Ireland to visit the homeland of the Callahans. So you all can return the favor when I'm away for a couple of weeks."

Kevin turned to the couple whose input was vital. "Lucky? Róisín? You haven't commented. Any thoughts? Will this work for you?"

They looked at each other and a thought passed between them.

"It will," Lucky replied. "With this much notice, we'll be fine."

"I'm actually glad for the extra two weeks," said Róisín. "Setting up the coffee shop and new kitchen is a big job. This will give me and my helpers time to work out our procedures before the big event. Thank you, my dears. I'm relaxing already." She sighed and blew out a breath.

"Are we agreed, then, Brian?" asked Lucky. The final decision was up to these two owners.

"We are. And we'd better get to work."

Everybody laughed. Although they all enjoyed lingering over coffee and conversation, today was not a day for dawdling. Time was fleeting. Fortunately, they knew how to make the most of it.

Thirty-Seven

Six weeks later, while the Maddens and the O'Donnells waited to board their flight from JFK to Shannon, Glenna told Debbie stories about her wedding at Aunt Finn's home and explained what they might expect the arrangements to be for Craig and Cousin Mary's ceremony.

Rory had been showing Jeremy their proposed sight-seeing route on a large map of Ireland, which had somehow led them into a discussion of some fine points of Pythagorean philosophy.

Now that they had boarded, the two couples were sitting with their spouses. Those who could see such things would have been quite taken by the rosy glow of true love emanating from their auras.

There was also an element of seriousness about them. None would ever forget that less than three months earlier they had survived the devastating fire that had burned the original Fibonacci's to the ground.

"May I say again how incredibly generous this is of you, Jeremy?" beamed Glenna. She was enjoying a gourmet dinner in her spacious, business-class airplane seat which would soon open out into a sleeper. The prospect of several hours of actual rest on a red-eye flight across the Atlantic had her almost giddy with delight.

"Enlightened self-interest, I assure you," responded Jeremy with a grin. He had purchased business-class seats for himself, Debbie, and the O'Donnells. "It's the least I can offer, considering Rory will be doing a lot of driving and you'll both be acting as our private tour guides around Galway, Clare, and Kerry."

"We're so excited to share Ireland with you." Glenna was bubbling with enthusiasm. "And to have a real honeymoon of our own. There's so much to delight the senses. We'll be visiting some of our favorite places and mostly taking in sights we didn't have time for on our last adventure."

"All the more reason for us to be rested when we arrive," Jeremy replied. "Besides, grown men do not belong in seats that were designed for gnomes."

He and Rory reached across the aisle and bumped fists.

"Fair play to that, brother," agreed Rory. "Flying to the States during the daytime last September wasn't too bad. I would have been awake anyway. But I'm glad for some rest now, especially since we'll be inundated with family the minute we arrive. I hope you know what you're getting into, being part of this big event."

"I'm sure we don't," laughed Debbie, "but we greatly appreciate being included, just the same. Now, I'm going to snuggle into this comfy seat so I can wake up the minute Ireland appears out of the mist."

"You'll have a perfect view on your side of the plane," said Glenna, remembering her first glimpse of the Emerald Isle.

"I was here once before with my sister when we were younger," said Debbie. "But this trip is so much more special. Thank you, my love." She leaned over and kissed her husband. "I'll never forget this trip or your kindness to my friends."

"Like I said—enlightened self-interest. And you're more than welcome. What is it the Irish say? *A ghrá?* Yes, *a ghrá*, you're very welcome."

"Craig!" Rory called out as soon as he saw his brother waiting for them in the lobby of the hotel where the two couples would be staying. They had rented a car at Shannon Airport and, thanks to his familiarity with driving on the left, they'd made good time getting to Galway City.

"I wouldn't miss seeing my little brother." Craig teased Rory by mussing his hair. "And, truth be told, Aunt Finn sent me to make sure you were comfortably settled. At this point, any excuse to get away from wedding preparations is welcome. You remember how it was with a dozen women hovering. It's even more exciting when one of them is pregnant."

"I can imagine." Rory grinned and found himself wondering what Glenna would be like when they decided to have children. "At least you're having only one ceremony. The folks will be here so you don't have to do an encore in Donegal. Right?"

"Right. Mary and I are flying to France the day after." Craig turned his attention to his sister-in-law. "Ah, I remember this beautiful bride." He gave Glenna a warm hug. "And Debbie. Will you congratulate me, lass?"

"I will," she said, smiling as they shook hands. "And I'll introduce you to my husband, Jeremy. You were on your way to your new life here in Ireland before F. M. drew him into our circle of Friends."

The two men surveyed each other and quickly decided they liked what they saw.

"I believe we may have been acquainted before." Craig grasped Jeremy's hand and arm in the double handshake of friendship so common in the druidic community of *Tearmann* in first-century Ireland where they had, indeed, known each other.

Debbie held her breath. How would Jeremy react to Craig's enthusiastic acknowledgment of a shared past life?

For a minute, Jeremy wondered, too. But he was pleased to feel not a ripple of trepidation.

"Right you are. I was only a lad when we first met, but I recall your being a good tribal chief. That is, once Riordan tamed you a bit." Jeremy surprised them all by winking at Craig. "And as *taoiseach* you were always kind to me and Dearbhla."

The men had a good laugh and Debbie breathed a sigh of relief. She could feel her soul rejoicing that positive connections were coming full circle.

"Let's get you checked in, then," said Craig. "Aunt Finn is eager to see you. She's busy making sure all the preparations are up to her very high standards. 'See that Rory and Glenna and their friends have what they need and tell them I'm expecting to see them for lunch at half-twelve,' she said before I left to come over here."

"I told you," Glenna whispered to Debbie and Jeremy. "Aunt Finn will have everything under control. And wait till you hear how she greets Rory. It means 'brave boy' in Irish."

"You know the way, so I'll leave you to it," said Craig. He gave his brother a powerful hug. "Thanks for coming, lad. I had no idea I'd be so nervous. I'm glad you're here."

"Glad to return the favor," said Rory. "Tell Aunt Finn we've arrived safely and can't wait to see her."

"*Buachaill cróga!*" cried Aunt Finn. She'd been watching for their arrival and opened her front door before Rory could ring the bell. She pulled her nephew into her arms and then opened them to her adopted niece. "Glenna, my girl, come here and let me look at you."

She focused her sky-blue eyes on the young woman who had been quite pale at her first wedding last August in Ireland. She hadn't completely regained her color for her second wedding a few weeks later in the States. The ordeal with Arán Bán had taken a toll on both Rory and Glenna. Their aunt was encouraged to see them brimming with good health.

"I am remembering not to flood you with Irish, my dear," she winked at Glenna, "though my heart is overflowing to see you, *a pháistí*. My children," she quickly corrected herself.

"We're thrilled to see you, too, Aunt Finn. You remember our dear friend, Debbie?"

"I do. *A chara*, I'm delighted you accepted my invitation to join us."

"We're very grateful to be included, Aunt Finn," said Debbie. "May I present my husband, Jeremy Madden. Jeremy, this is Rory and Craig's Aunt Finola."

Jeremy had made sure his appearance was well-polished before they left the hotel. He wanted to make a good impression on this formidable lady. It was clear that she was greatly loved by her family, which included anyone she approved of, and he wanted to be part of that circle.

"It's a pleasure to meet you," he said with all of the grace he could muster as he felt himself being inspected.

"And you're very welcome, Jeremy. I'm sure they've told you I ask my family and good friends to call me Aunt Finn. I invite you to do the same. I can see by the way you and your bride are with each other that this is a fine match."

She looked at Jeremy again, her expression and tone serious. "See that you never waver, lad. Our Debbie is a treasure and to do her wrong would be a great mistake."

Aunt Finn held Jeremy's gaze just long enough for him to wonder what flaw she was seeing in his character that could make him stray from his soul's twin. He was about to ask when she waved her hand in front of her face and smiled warmly at her guests.

"Come in, now, and welcome. We'll go straight to lunch, as Cook is ready to serve. Craig and Mary will join us. All the others are out sight-seeing or running errands for the ceremony. Rory, rehearsal is at eleven tomorrow morning and the rehearsal dinner, the big family meal, is at half-six in the evening. Of course, that includes you, my dears," she said to Debbie and Jeremy as she glided into the dining room.

"Impressive," he whispered to his wife as they followed Rory and Glenna down a spacious hallway. "And more than a little frightening."

"I know," she whispered in return. "You did fine." She patted his arm as they were seated at the very large walnut dining table that had been laid with Irish linen tablecloth and napkins and exquisite china, crystal, and silverware.

Jeremy couldn't help feeling that he was in the company of royalty.

"Why do people cry at weddings?" Jeremy asked Debbie and Glenna two days later as they walked from the Catholic church where the ceremony had taken place to the hotel where the reception was being held. Rory had remained with the wedding party for photos and would join them as his best man duties allowed.

He was taking those responsibilities very seriously. He wanted to do right by his brother and he also had a bit of payback in mind. He doubted that he could top Craig's hilarious best man speech that had included many jokes poking fun at their brotherly shenanigans. But he did have a few recollections that might cause the groom to blush a time or two.

"I'm not judging," Jeremy continued. "I found myself tearing up during the vows and I'm not usually a weeper."

Glenna was still dabbing her eyes. "It reminded me of my own wedding at Aunt Finn's, and how completely overwhelmed with happiness I was to be marrying the love of my life. I was so grateful that day. To be alive and to know that Rory loves me as much as I love him."

"I think the word overjoyed is the key, as if our souls are being rushed upward by the experience," said Debbie thoughtfully. "I felt the same at our wedding when Jeremy and I said our vows. And then being given the extraordinary honor of having Saint Germain appear to bless us and our twin flames mandala. I was over the moon with joy."

"I've had similar experiences when a piece of music has moved me or when I've been allowed an insight into the presence of *An Síoraí*, the Eternal One," added Glenna. "It's almost like my physical body can't hold all the joy and the way it responds is to weep."

"That's a very good explanation," said Jeremy. "When we first greeted Aunt Finn yesterday, she said her heart was overflowing. I could see that her eyes were brimming."

Then he added, "As we're talking about the sensations, it occurs to me that I got teary just now because I felt something dissolving in me. Like a hardness of heart that had rejected some aspect of Love. Having that brittleness removed lifted me higher and gave me hope that I could be more loving."

He looked over at Debbie. She reached up and brushed a lock of his dark brown hair that had fallen across his forehead and gazed back at him, her face bright with love.

"Let's find your table," suggested Glenna as they entered the hotel ballroom that was set with large round tables for the sit-down reception meal. "I'll stay with you until Rory comes in, then I'll join him at the head table. I'm considered family, which I think is very sweet."

Debbie took Jeremy's hand as they walked to their assigned seats. She knew what he was thinking. Family had an entirely different meaning for him than it did for the gregarious and fun-living O'Donnells.

Even her own family wasn't as emotionally expressive these days as it had been when her parents were alive.

She and Jeremy would have to create their own family, their own traditions and circle of love that she prayed would always include their Friends of Ancient Wisdom and the Twin Flames of Éire.

Thirty-Eight

Are you ready for more O'Donnell family fun tomorrow?" asked Rory as he drove his wife and their friends back to their hotel after the reception. He was still beaming from the day's festivities, especially the success of his best man speech. Everyone agreed that he had acquitted himself well, sufficiently embarrassing his brother and adding a beautiful sincerity to his remarks about love and family.

"We've had a lot of fun already," Debbie assured him. "And we're always ready for more. You were right about being here for *Bealtaine*. My senses are quite delighted. There's so much to see in the historical part of Galway City. Thanks for making sure we explored Eyre Square on Friday while you were at the wedding rehearsal. That was a real treat."

"I could have spent an entire day at the Galway City Museum," commented Jeremy. "Fascinating exhibits."

"I loved the 3D simulation video that walks you through the medieval city," said Debbie. "And the booths and buskers in the market area. I can see why people say not to miss Galway."

"The city does *Bealtaine* right," agreed Rory. "Music and all the arts are a big deal here."

"So what's doing for Sunday?" asked Jeremy.

"We'll join the family for mass at Galway Cathedral, which I know you haven't seen. Neither has Glenna. We're on our own for lunch in town, and then my parents and family who are staying another day are expected at Aunt Finn's for what's known as 'The Noble Call'."

"What's that?" Debbie wanted to know.

"It's a sort of farewell gathering where everyone offers a party piece," explained Rory. "As you've probably guessed, Glenna has married into a family of bards. A few are professionals, though most are amateurs. The

O'Donnells love to get together to share music, poetry, or whatever is on their hearts. We've stayed bonded that way for my whole life and I'm sure for many generations before."

"Will we be expected to participate?" Jeremy gulped. He had thoroughly enjoyed his conversations with Rory's family, but performing for them was a different matter entirely.

"I'm told that no one escapes." Glenna's couldn't help teasing him. "But don't worry. The point is to join in the fun, not to be perfect. In fact, the less perfect, the more applause. Or so Rory tells me."

"I hope that's true." Jeremy furrowed his brow.

"So you've been warned," grinned Rory. "I didn't want to spring this on you, which is usually how it's done. Most Irish have at least one song or story or rhyme always ready for the sharing. As you're still learning what it means to be a Celt, Jeremy, I'm saving your reputation."

"Fair play to that, brother," he said, doing his best to sound Irish.

"Just don't sing 'Danny Boy' or ask anybody else to," warned Glenna. "It's considered a cliché that only tourists request."

Jeremy had never been to high mass at an incredible cathedral like Our Lady Assumed into Heaven and St. Nicholas, also known as Galway Cathedral.

He'd read up on the history of the building, which had been completed in 1965 to considerable controversy in the local community. Many had labeled it a monstrosity, one of the ugliest buildings ever built, a blight on the city.

But Jeremy found it remarkable. The architectural style was listed as Renaissance, although the large rounded arches, dome, and thick stone walls looked more Byzantine to his eye. He found the Fourteen Stations and other sculptures appealing in their graceful austerity. The stained-glass window images were clearly modern, almost cubist in style.

What he most appreciated was the way the light flooded through those creations and the gorgeous rose windows, bathing the sanctuary in bands of rainbow hues that relieved the precision limestone walls from a heaviness that could have been oppressive. Instead, he found their strength and the curved barrel ceiling inspiring, as if each element of the structure combined to affirm, "This edifice will not crumble under the hatred of the world."

He followed Debbie and the rest of the congregation as they stood and knelt and prayed. The ritual was new to him and he wasn't entirely sure what he thought of it. In many ways, he found their services at Fibonacci's more inspiring, more radiant, more transcendent. He wasn't judging; just noticing.

And then the organist began to play the postlude, a stirring piece called "Sortie in B Flat" by Guy Ropartz. He had read that the Galway Cathedral possessed one of the most magnificent pipe organs in Ireland. That was an understatement. He had only heard recordings of organ concerts, which he'd enjoyed. But hearing this incredible instrument live was instantly overwhelming to his senses.

No, he said to himself. This wasn't hearing. This was being played as if one's body were one of the pipes, resonating with sound that must first have been witnessed in heaven before master craftsmen found a way to translate that sound into the physical octave.

Jeremy's entire body was vibrating. He was riveted to his seat. Time and thought and distance all disappeared as he became one with the music. Later he would remember that the Ascended Master Kuthumi was said to play an organ in his etheric retreat in Shigatse, Tibet. But in this moment, Jeremy was simply one with the sublime power of this instrument that pulsated with the heart of a living being.

When they were leaving the cathedral and Debbie asked him what he'd thought of the service, he could only sigh, put his hands to his heart, and nod.

After lunch and one more walk around town, the two couples arrived back at Aunt Finn's to see that furniture had been moved around and more chairs brought into the parlor. Including babies in arms and children seated on the floor, Debbie counted at least thirty-five O'Donnells and assorted cousins with names she knew she wouldn't remember.

Almost immediately a few of the professional musicians got things going, although this was obviously a group that needed no encouragement to perform. She was particularly taken with the offerings by nearly all of the children who were old enough to talk or do a little jig to the delight of their many relations. They received sincerely warm applause from adults and other children.

"Glenna, are you sure you're not pregnant?" Debbie whispered to her friend who was holding a toddler on her lap while blissfully listening to an eight-year-old sing a beautiful ballad.

"I'm sure." She blushed as the song ended.

"But you're thinking about it, aren't you? So is he." Debbie tilted her head toward Rory who was encouraging the teenaged lad next to him to take his turn at The Noble Call.

Glenna smiled at her husband.

"He is. We both want a large family, so we guess we'd better get started if we don't want to be chasing toddlers in our fifties, unless they're our grandchildren. Maybe we'll be lucky to have at least one set of twins to save time."

Both women laughed. "Twins might reduce the number of pregnancies," said Debbie with her eyes twinkling. "But considering the work of double everything that Sarah and Ivy go through on a daily basis, that prospect is one perhaps better not wished for."

Several adults were now sharing their party pieces. There were sad songs, glad songs, love songs, rebel songs, jokes, limericks, tall tales, stirring jigs and reels played on whistle, fiddle, and flute. Several poets recited their works, which gave Debbie the courage to offer one of hers.

"I call this 'The Vivid Step'," she said by way of introduction. "I'm going to try not to get teary. You can guess who inspired these lines."

You know what this is now . . .
when your mind surrenders all its knowing
and sinks gratefully into the heart's embrace,
where they abide together,

a new faculty,
a reborn way of seeing,
that is not really seeing at all,
but simply resting in mutual resonance
that knows no difference
between self and other.

For now love is only love,
enfolding and unfolding,
giving of itself and receiving
in perpetual motion,
deepening in sweetness whose only limit
is its capacity to be hourly
more true, more good, more beautiful.

For a moment, the only sound in the room was the soft whimpering of a child. Then cheers and applause erupted as Jeremy embraced his wife and kissed her deeply, then rose from his seat.

"I guess this is my cue. Debbie, my love, you know poetry isn't my strength, though I am a lover of the spoken word. But being married to you is cause for the occasional verse. And since we're on our honeymoon, the muse of romance obliged. So here goes."

He pulled a sheet of paper from his jacket pocket and began to read:

Now is the time for love.
These days are meant for love.
Let's get caught up in the moment;
No thought about somewhere in time
When life meant or will mean more.

Let now be the moment
That steals our breath away.
And let's fill that pause with the recognition
That we are two souls sharing life.

Today. Now. We smell the roses.
Let's be that rose,
Perfect in every moment
of its existence.

Let's be more than that rose.
Let's celebrate in the awareness
Of our essence and the knowledge
That you will be part of me,
Forever.

Come, celebrate these days with me, beloved.
We have never had more cause to rejoice
Than today.

Jeremy handed Debbie a rose that Aunt Finn suspected he had picked from her garden. He was instantly forgiven.

"Well done, brother." Rory clapped his friend on the back and everyone applauded generously. Then he said mischievously, "I see that some heads are beginning to nod—and not only the babies. However, my Broadway-actress wife will not let me escape the odd performance.

"So Glenna and I would like to sing you a duet she insisted that I learn. This is called 'If I Loved You' and it's from the musical *Carousel*, which you may know."

As murmurs of approval rippled around the room, Glenna signaled the flute player they had asked to accompany them.

This song had always been remembered as one of the most beautiful of all the Rodgers and Hammerstein duets, and Glenna and Rory did it more than justice. Many hearts were stirred and eyes filled as their voices soared and the love between them radiated around the room.

"*Go raibh míle maith agat,*" said Glenna when the joyous cheers and applause quieted. "If I may be so bold as to suggest that we are saving the best for last—Aunt Finn, I'm sure everyone would love it if you would recite something for us." She turned to the family. "Am I right?"

"Yes, please! Give a speech, Aunt Finn!" called several voices at once.

"I know what I would most like to hear," said Glenna. "Would you give us Portia's most famous lines?"

Glowing with pleasure, Finola, *grande dame* of the Irish stage, rose with great dignity.

"Thank you, Glenna and everyone. It seems like only yesterday that I was privileged to speak the Bard's lines to appreciative audiences, though none so dear to me as you, my family. This is one of those timeless speeches one never forgets, as it rings even more true today than when it was written."

> The quality of mercy is not strained.
> It droppeth as the gentle rain from heaven
> Upon the place beneath. It is twice blest:
> It blesseth him that gives and him that takes.
> 'Tis mightiest in the mightiest; it becomes
> The thronèd monarch better than his crown.
> His scepter shows the force of temporal power;
> The attribute to awe and majesty
> Wherein doth sit the dread and fear of kings;
> But mercy is above this sceptered sway.
> It is enthronèd in the hearts of kings;
> It is an attribute to God Himself;
> And earthly power doth then show likest God's
> When mercy seasons justice. Therefore,
> Though justice be our plea, consider this:
> That in the course of justice none of us
> Should see salvation. We do pray for mercy,
> And that same prayer doth teach us all to render
> The deeds of mercy.

The entire room rose to its feet and applauded with cheers of "*Brava!* Aunt Finn! We love you, Aunt Finn!" Someone else had picked several of her garden flowers and handed them to a little boy and girl who presented them to the grand lady with a bow and a curtsy that neither of them had been coached to perform.

I guess I'm not the only one who considers her royalty, Jeremy thought to himself. He didn't say anything to Debbie, but he wondered if she'd noticed that Aunt Finn had delivered the last two sentences of Portia's speech directly to them.

"*Oíche mhaith, a pháistí, codladh sámh.* Good night, my children, sleep well," said Aunt Finn at last. "You have brought me more joy than you can imagine, and I thank you all a thousand times."

There were hugs all around and best wishes to those who were traveling yet this evening or in the morning as the gathering of loved ones reluctantly dispersed.

"I can't bear the thought that we might never see her again," said Glenna with great emotion as Rory drove their party back to their hotel.

"We won't let that happen, *mo mhuirnín*." Rory reached over and stroked her shoulder. "Besides, I don't think Aunt Finn is going anywhere any time soon. Not with Craig and Mary bringing a new life into her home. She has too much to live for."

Thirty-Nine

And we're off!" exclaimed Rory as he pulled the roomy SUV they had rented out of the hotel parking lot and into Galway's Monday morning traffic. "Thanks, everybody, for getting an early start. This is one of our more ambitious sight-seeing days, but fortunately distances in Ireland are relatively short, so we should be all right."

"We'll stop for tea in Ballyvaughan and then we're only thirty minutes from the Cliffs of Moher," explained Glenna. "When we were here before, Rory insisted that I experience the raw power of this place. He was right. Now I wouldn't miss it."

"Great!" said Jeremy and Debbie together.

"You'll want to hang onto your hats, literally," she went on. "The wind howls, the waves thunder, and the land shudders."

"No, darlin', that was you shuddering," teased Rory.

"Yes, it probably was," Glenna admitted. "Anyway, if you've ever wondered what inspires the wild Celtic spirit, you've only to walk the Cliffs of Moher. This is Ireland at its fiercest."

"No kidding about ferocity," Jeremy shouted to make himself heard over the roar of wind and wave as they gazed out over the wild Atlantic. He and Debbie were clutching each other for warmth and security. "For a kid raised in New York City, this is quite a change."

"One of our more dramatic offerings," laughed Rory. "The rest of our tour may seem tame by comparison, but I promise we won't short you on beauty or astonishing geography."

That they didn't. The stark, primeval limestone outcroppings of The Burren were unlike anything they had ever seen.

"We were going to stop here for some hiking," explained Rory, "but Glenna found something even better. So we'll give you this drive-through taste of one of Ireland's natural wonders and then after lunch we'll visit a place I didn't know existed."

"This is Dromore Woods Nature Preserve," Rory announced as he parked the SUV by the visitor centre. "We thought this would be a more appealing place to hike, though I know you two would have been very interested in the different kinds of plants in The Burren."

"You'll find plants from sub-arctic to Mediterranean zones all growing together," said Glenna. "I hope this little excursion will make up for not seeing them up close."

"We'll just have to come back, and I'll bring Cyndi. She would love to see that," remarked Debbie, trying not to be too disappointed.

As they were just about to turn a bend on one of several walking trails, Glenna was continuing her commentary. "The information I found online last night said that now was an especially good time to see . . . "

"Bluebells!" Debbie and Jeremy rushed forward and knelt beside a river of blue flowers that led off into the woods.

"How wonderful!" Debbie's eyes were sparkling. "Bluebells were Madwyn's favorite of all the flowers in Dearbhla's garden, weren't they, my love?" She reached up and caressed Jeremy's cheek.

"They were," he said softly. "We used to make remedies from the bulb, and a glue that was used to fix feathers on arrows. And they're just the most beautiful flower in the world."

"You're not meant to pick them," warned Glenna.

"We're not," said Debbie. "We're petting them."

"Actually, stepping on the plants is more harmful than picking the flowers," said Jeremy. "But we won't be doing either. Do you mind if we just sit here for a while? You're welcome to stay with us or walk on."

"I think we'll walk on," said Rory. "Let's meet back at the car around five o'clock. We're only twenty minutes from Ennis, where we're spending the night. We'll still have plenty of daylight, so we can explore the town before dinner if you like."

"Thank you both," said Debbie wistfully. "This is marvelous. I have no words." She and Jeremy found a bench overlooking the bluebell river. He cradled her in his arms and they sighed into some of the happiest memories they shared of their time together in ancient Ireland.

"The fourth of May." Glenna was checking her itinerary. She and Debbie were sharing the back seat of the SUV this morning so Jeremy could stretch his long legs in the front. "Today we go to the Dingle Peninsula by way of Adare."

"I've always wanted to visit there," said Debbie, delighted.

"So have I, especially to tour Adare Manor," agreed Glenna. "They have self-guided audio tours around the grounds and the Manor House and museum, so we can adopt a leisurely pace.

"We've arranged to have dinner tonight in Dingle with our friends Ciara, Saoirse, and Cormac. They're all students of F. M., so Phelan asked that we check on them. I'd love to see them anyway, but he says they've been having a rough time since F. M. left. We thought this could be a mercy mission as well as a pleasant visit."

Touring the Adare Manor was another step back in time and incredible luxury. The grounds were immaculate and filled with spring flowers. Once more, Debbie and Jeremy were in a floral paradise.

The four laughed and joked through a hearty pub lunch, and afterward the drive to Dingle went quickly. Rory was a wealth of historical information about the areas they were passing through. However, they all agreed that the fewer old ruins visited, the better.

"Too many untransmuted karmic records," was Debbie's analysis.

As soon as they pulled up to *Teach na Beannachta*, the B&B in Dingle where Glenna had stayed, she was out of the car and dashing to the entrance. She had barely knocked when the door swung open and Fiona, the owner, was embracing her like a long-lost daughter.

"*A chara!* How grand to see you. And Rory, lad. You're a far sight happier than the last time I saw you."

"I am, yes," he said and gave the matronly woman a hug. With her light red hair and soft green eyes, Debbie thought she looked like an advertisement for Ireland's ageless native beauty.

"Fiona remembers me from one of the lowest days of my life," Rory explained.

"Mine, too," added Glenna. Then she brightened. "Fiona, these are our very good friends, Debbie and Jeremy Madden. We're sharing Ireland with them for the honeymoon they never got to take after they were married last Christmas. It's our real honeymoon, too."

"Come in, my dears, and welcome," said Fiona. "I'll see you to your rooms and then will you have some tea in the dining room? The scones are fresh this morning. We're a bit early for tourist season and *Bealtaine* is over, so you're my only guests the three nights you're here. You just let me know what you'd like to eat and I'll see it done."

"I'm sure we'd love tea. Fiona's scones are the best ever," Glenna said, then explained to their hostess, "We're meeting friends for dinner tonight. After we get settled I'll show you our itinerary so you'll know when to expect us."

"That will be fine, *a chara*," said Fiona. "Oh, 'tis grand to see you both. And married. I knew nothing could keep you apart for long, but you did have me worried."

The more time the Maddens spent with the O'Donnells, the more they appreciated them. They were delightful traveling companions and very sensitive to the fact that this was their friends' honeymoon as well as their own.

Glenna and Rory had a knack for finding something else to do when Debbie and Jeremy needed time together. And then they would show up just when the Maddens were ready for the next adventure.

They also seemed to know something about maintaining harmony between them that Debbie wished she and Jeremy knew. It wasn't that she and her husband weren't harmonious. They were deeply in love. But sometimes they weren't quite in sync.

262 CHERYL LAFFERTY ECKL - THE MYSTICS AND THE MYSTERY

She promised herself that she would find out Glenna and Rory's secret while they were together. But tonight they were meant to be focused on the Friends of Ancient Wisdom in Dingle, who were clearly having a rough time.

"We thought we'd done something wrong," confessed Ciara over a fantastic gourmet dinner at the Global Village restaurant on Main Street. "First we stopped seeing or hearing from F. M. and then Phelan left suddenly. We were sure we'd been booted from the Brotherhood."

"And the old brothers of the shadow always try to convince you that you're at fault, don't they?" said Rory.

"Well, they nearly succeeded," Cormac admitted.

"We can't tell you how grateful we are that you've come to see us," added Saoirse. "Anything you can tell us will be appreciated."

"I think we should do more than tell you," offered Debbie. She could see that they needed some practices that would help them maintain the thread of contact with the Divine in themselves and in each other.

"Did F. M. or Phelan teach you any of the chants that we do in the States?" she asked.

"They did, but we haven't kept them up. Didn't seem much point if we were the terrible people we were beginning to believe we were." Cormac winced.

"We're here to tell you that you're not terrible people," said Jeremy with conviction. "And I can personally attest to the power of these prayers. I had never done any chanting until our friend Róisín taught me. My life began to change for the better almost instantly.

"I know for sure I wouldn't be married to Debbie if I hadn't learned how to invoke the light of protection and illumination, not to mention transmuting my negative karma with violet flame."

"Wow, that's quite a testimony." Cormac was impressed.

"We all have similar stories," Glenna added. "In fact, to make sure that we're protected from dark forces while we're traveling, we spend some time each morning praying to Archangel Michael. Sometimes we even chant while we're driving, just to keep the energy clear."

"Unfortunately, Ireland has a lot of dark records of black magic and witchcraft that have been practiced for centuries," explained Debbie. "If we feel like we've run into a pocket of that energy, we chant."

"I had no idea," said Ciara. "Could you give us a refresher?"

"Of course," agreed Rory. "We're planning to hike up Mount Brandon tomorrow morning. Maybe we could get together in the afternoon. Do you or your friends have an apartment or a house where we could hold a full-throated service without bothering the neighbors?"

"Saoirse and I own a house," offered Cormac. "We needed a place where we could practice our music at all hours of the day or night. We actually sound-proofed a large back room for a studio. We can chant there at full volume and nobody will hear us."

"Perfect," said Rory. "We'll come over tomorrow for a grand old chant session. If you have other friends you want to invite, feel free. The more people you have praying together, the more powerful the positive energy you invoke."

Jeremy spoke for his companions as he picked up the tab for dinner. "My treat. A confirmation from Friends of Ancient Wisdom in the U. S. to our branch in Ireland that we believe you're wonderful people who are about to get even better after some rounds of chanting.

"And, since we'll be in your studio, would you share some music with us? Glenna said you're fantastic musicians and we'd really like to hear some traditional Irish tunes."

"We'd love to play for you," said Saoirse with the widest of smiles. "You've given us more hope than we've had in months."

"Look at them go," laughed Glenna the following morning as she and Debbie watched their husbands take off well ahead of them on their hike up Mount Brandon. The men were like two little boys who'd been let out of school.

"They're quite a pair, aren't they?" Debbie grinned. "I had no idea how badly Jeremy needed to play. Things have been so intense at Fibonacci's, I think we sometimes forget to just step away once in a while. Not letting down our guard, of course. We know that can be disastrous. But remembering to become like a little child every so often.

I can see how much Jeremy is gaining from having a brother in Rory."

"Rory feels the same. They are similar, though you wouldn't think it when you first meet either of them. I think it's partly the fact that we know we were together in past lives. That sense of camaraderie seems to be in our DNA. I certainly feel like you and I are sisters, Debbie."

"I do, too. And because we're baring our souls as we hike up this mighty mountain, can I ask you about your relationship with Rory? You two are a marvel of harmony. How do you do it? Nothing seems to bother you. You're always in the flow of what's happening."

"Oh, plenty bothers us," Glenna chuckled as she guided Debbie away from a wash-out on the edge of the trail. "But we don't let disagreements stick. We talk things out—constantly. Some days it seems like all we're doing is processing feelings, thoughts, upsets, worries."

"That's a lot of work."

"It is, yes, but the result is worth the effort. After nearly dying at the hands of Arán Bán, we realized that we had to become totally dedicated to our path as twin flames and as individuals."

"A run-in with that man would certainly be a strong motivator."

"It was, and still is. Rory found this great book on conscious love that we're studying. The idea is that each partner is one hundred percent dedicated to the other partner's success on the spiritual path. To do that, you have to be one hundred percent dedicated to your own path. Otherwise, you become co-dependent or obsessive."

"We don't want that!"

"Exactly. Your love becomes selfless because you don't want to burden your partner with your psychological baggage. So when a negative pattern comes up, you name it and deal with it."

"What if you can't name it?"

"Then you wrestle with it together until you can. We've come up with some silly phrases for those patterns so we don't get caught up in a sense of struggle. That's what can make you vulnerable to the kind of projections our friends here in Dingle have been dealing with."

"What kind of phrases?"

"My favorite is 'banana peel.' You know, an old emotion or behavior you're always slipping on. You can call yourself on a banana peel or your partner can call you on it. It's such a silly image that you laugh and stay out of criticism. These patterns are just stuff. They're not who we really are. Seeing them like that makes it easier to let go and move on."

"Does it work?"

"Eventually. Although there have been days I thought we were nothing but a pile of banana peels. At a certain point you just have to laugh at the absurdity of the human condition. And pray for enlightenment."

"We need that for sure. Jeremy's never been in a long-term romantic relationship and I've never been in a truly successful one. We do great until one of us hits a snag, then we don't know how to talk to each other about it. Neither of us wants to fester, but sometimes we do."

"It helps if you can say what you want from the other person."

"What if you don't know? Having inner sight is no guarantee you'll understand yourself."

"Then say so to Jeremy. That might get the conversation going."

Debbie blew out a breath. "Okay, I'll try it. Thanks, sister Glenna. Master K. H. was right when he said we're a bonded mandala."

"I agree. And I'm grateful."

The incline was getting steeper and they had slowed their pace. Glenna halted by a flat place beside a gentle wash-out.

"Do you mind if we stop here for a breather?" she asked, then snickered. "How funny. I think this is where Rory rescued me the first day we met. The view of the Atlantic is great from here, and it's an easy walk back to the car if it gets chilly before our men show up."

"Well, step carefully," said Debbie, teasing her friend. "I can't carry you back down the mountain, no matter how much I care for you as a sister."

They laughed and sat down to enjoy the scenery.

Forty

When they joined Cormac, Saoirse, and Ciara that afternoon, the three were primed for their chanting session. In fact, they had already been practicing.

"Last night after we saw you, we got out our sheets with the words to the chants and started giving them," said Saoirse. "Ciara came over this morning and we did more together. We have about a dozen other friends who knew F. M. and they'll all be here in a few minutes. We told them what you said and they can't wait to meet you."

So the Friends of Ancient Wisdom in Dingle were off and chanting. All they needed was genuine encouragement, a bit of instruction on conducting their own services, and the promise of support for when they had doubts or ran into problems, which were inevitable in the course of living life on the spiritual path.

"Remember to be loyal and loving to each other," Debbie told them. "Divide-and-conquer is one of the most common tactics of the brothers of the shadow. You'd think we'd catch on, but our karma blinds us. This is where community is so important. Stick together and gently hold each other to higher standards than people you meet in the world."

"This is not to say that any of us thinks we're better than other people," Glenna was quick to interject. "We just happen to know that the path of soul liberation is hard work and the point is to become more and more light. Talk out your problems. Don't blame each other.

"And please, please, don't fall into criticism of each other. You wouldn't believe how much karma you make from criticism or gossip within the community."

The next afternoon the travelers were enjoying a leisurely ramble along the graceful, curving expanse of Ventry Beach after shopping in the morning and eating lunch at Saoirse and Cormac's house.

They felt good about the spiritual work they had done with their friends in Dingle and were looking forward to the hearty, family-style dinner that Fiona had promised them for that evening. The next morning they would drive to the Kenmare Bay resort where they would spend four restful nights prior to an easy, daytime flight home.

While they had encountered some challenging energy at various points in their journey, they were hopeful that they had handled the worst of it and that these final honeymoon days would be very pleasant.

"'Tis fortunate we've an easy day today," remarked Rory as he drove along the blue waters of Dingle Bay, past the broad sands of Inch Beach toward the road that would take them south to their destination.

His passengers agreed. No one had slept well the night before.

They supposed it might have been because the Light invoked by the Friends of Ancient Wisdom in Dingle had been a mighty counteraction to the brothers of the shadow. Those forces were always disturbed when the children of the Light became aware of their manipulative tactics.

But there was something sinister lurking, and they all recognized it. Before departing this Friday morning, they had given extra time to their prayers. Now that they were on the road they were once again excited to be embarking on the final leg of their journey.

Glenna was in the front seat today, acting as navigator. Rory hadn't been on this road since he was a lad and he needed her assistance.

"We're taking the popular Ring of Kerry route along the coast," she pointed out. "We can't check in at the resort until later this afternoon, so we can stop wherever we like, walk a bit, take pictures. When we get to the Kerry Cliffs, we'll have an excellent view of Skellig Michael and then we can go to the chocolate factory."

"I also want to stop in at Ballinskelligs to get our tickets for the boat ride around the islands," Rory told them. "Are we all still in agreement that we don't need to do the landing tour on Skellig Michael?"

"Too dangerous," said Debbie firmly and Jeremy agreed. "Especially with the energy we were all feeling this morning."

"I'm so glad," sighed Glenna. "I didn't want to be the only coward in the group, but I watched a video by a visitor who climbed those 640 steps. My heart was pounding out of my chest by the time he reached the top. I can't imagine doing that and then having to climb back down."

"No worries, *a ghrá*." Rory reached over and squeezed her hand. "Now let's enjoy the scenery."

"Living here, did you ever tire of this landscape?" asked Jeremy.

"Not when I could be out in it. I think that might be one reason the monastery started closing in on me. Not enough adventures on the land. There's holiness in our soil. The old Irish knew that. Although we raised feed for our cattle at the monastery, I'm not sure we remembered the connection between soul and soil as we chanted the Office each day."

Debbie noticed that Jeremy had gone strangely silent while Rory was answering his question. The couple was sitting in the back seat, holding hands. She'd felt his attention waver.

"What is it, Jeremy?" she said quietly.

"I'm not sure. Something is flickering in my mind. A record of some import. That much I can tell."

"Do we need to stop and make some calls to the angels to clear it?"

"Not yet. I don't know what we'd be clearing."

"The angels would know," said Debbie, but Jeremy shook his head. "I need to identify it first."

"You two okay back there?" asked Rory. He had also felt his friend's attention wander.

"We're fine," said Jeremy, making light of the disturbance. "Feels like a record from the past that's coming up, but I don't know what it could be. I'll let you know if I get any clues."

"The weather gods are certainly with us today," he remarked cheerfully a little while later as they meandered across the fine sand on Kells Bay Beach on the northern shore of the Iveragh Peninsula.

"They are, indeed." Debbie made a point of matching her husband's intentionally upbeat tone. "I've actually been able to take off my jacket, the sun is so warm."

The day supported a positive attitude. And yet there was something about traveling the southwest coast of Ireland that continued to spark memories of long ago. Especially at Kells Bay Gardens.

"Doesn't this feel familiar?" remarked Jeremy as they walked through a lush forest of tree ferns that dwarfed them. These enormous plants were unlike anything seen outside of Australia or Tasmania. Or Atlantis.

"I can almost see myself wandering through sub-tropical forests like this thousands of years ago. You know the Atlanteans could grow anything. They covered their islands with greenery that hid most of the buildings. I'll bet it looked like this."

"And felt this entirely unspoiled," mused Debbie, "even if their gardens were artificially created. I can feel my body merging with these plants, the way they support each other in this rich, moist atmosphere."

"My love, this mutuality of growing things is what Dearbhla and Madwyn achieved naturally in their garden," said Jeremy, remembering.

"I'm longing to feel that again," said Debbie wistfully as she welcomed her husband's arm around her shoulders.

"Next stop, Kerry Cliffs," announced Rory as he pulled into the carpark adjacent to the walkway leading up to the viewing point. He really was enjoying his role as tour guide.

"This is the first view of Skellig Michael from this direction on the Ring of Kerry. You can almost imagine the old sixth-century monks standing here and saying to each other, 'You know, Michael's Rock is the perfect place for our hermitage. No one has died for their faith here in Éire. All the druids simply became Christian abbots and priests. Let's find the most inhospitable place possible and go there to prove our faith like the desert fathers and mothers.' They probably . . . What?"

He stopped speaking when Glenna touched his arm and pointed to their friends who were walking beside them. "Look."

Debbie and Jeremy's faces had gone chalk white and their eyes were glazed. They looked like they had slipped into another dimension.

"Jeremy? Debbie? Are you with us?" Glenna spoke gently.

Jeremy blinked and looked over at her. "Not really. I think we need to just stand here for a few minutes. This is weird."

"Okay, we'll give you some space," said Rory, but he and Glenna did not move very far away from their friends.

Fortunately, the other visitors they had passed along the walkway from the carpark had all gone. The two couples were the only ones standing by the railing at the verge of the cliffs.

Jeremy took a deep breath and held Debbie close as they gazed out across the water. "I wasn't ready to face this entire record. Now I am."

As his beloved had done in ancient Ireland and many centuries before on Atlantis and in Egypt, she asked him, "What do you see?"

I see two islands and then a much smaller one. We came upon them from the southwest. We'd been skirting the mainland some called Éire, looking for a place to safely land our ship.

The islands looked so much like pyramids. We thought it was a sign from the gods that they were to be our new home. Pyramids in Egypt leading to pyramids in the land of mist that was our destination. Rocky and foreboding as they appeared, we dared not question the gods.

The islands were incredibly rugged, but we had to know. Was this the promised land where we would be safe at last from the black magic of the vicious priests of Amun?

Everyone on board our ship was excited.

'Pull in close!' ordered the captain.

But close was too near. The seas were rougher than our sailors had ever experienced. They had known how to navigate the Straits of Gibraltar because others had gone before. They were now in uncharted waters that were tossing our ship like a toy.

Suddenly, one of the masts began to crack and lean under the strain of the violent energies of wind and wave. You and others were in the way. I rushed to protect you, and I did.

But as the mast came down, it hit me in the head and

knocked me out. I was unconscious, limp as a rag. And the next pitch of the ship rolled me into the sea.

Debbie was shaking as she picked up the story.

My heart stopped when I saw you go into the water. I ran frantically to the side of the ship, yelling for someone to throw you a rope. But you weren't conscious enough to grab one, and no one was so fool-hardy as to go in after you. Part of my soul died that day and I'm not sure it has ever come back to me.

Somehow our sailors managed to maneuver the ship away from the rocks and head back east toward the mainland. We struggled along until we found calmer water where we landed by a bay called *Ceann Mar*—the head of the sea.

The two seers clung to each other as they shivered in the cold wind that blew up from the sea below. The record was clear.

"We're looking out at where Jarahnaten and Meke lost each other," said Jeremy.

A realization stunned Debbie. "And the resort where we're staying is where Meke began her new life alone in *Ceann Mar*. Kenmare."

"This is too real. I can almost feel myself drowning."

"But you're not, my love." Debbie squeezed Jeremy's hand to keep him focused on the physical. "And I am not alone. This is a new day, a new lifetime. We're together and we have the spiritual means to transmute the record of separation."

And not only the record from Egyptian times, she realized. Víahlah would have seen the skelligs when she sailed from Atlantis, bypassing Ireland for the warmer climate of Egypt. Her beloved had not been with her then either. And in that embodiment she had not forgiven him.

No more, Debbie vowed. This time she and Jeremy would overcome the records of the past. They would not be defeated by karma or the brothers of the shadow. Now was the hour of victory. She claimed it in her heart and felt beings of Light affirm her determination.

"Let's get back to the car," she called to Rory and Glenna. "We have things to tell you as soon as we get settled in our accommodations."

Forty-One

The travelers were mostly silent as they drove further around the Ring of Kerry. They did stop at the chocolate factory for some homemade candy. And since the business offered an excellent view of Skellig Michael, Debbie and Jeremy told their friends some of what they had experienced while they all warmed up with mugs of hot chocolate.

They also stopped at a food market in the little town of Sneem to purchase breakfast and lunch items for the next several days and take-out entrees for tonight's evening meal, as no one was eager to cook.

They had decided to rent one of the resort's self-catering cottages rather than stay in the more expensive single hotel rooms. This proved to be a wise choice. They were going to need time together for the prayer work that was calling them.

Never had community been so important to the two couples as they worked to clear the records of the past.

"Thank you," said Jeremy after they completed a vigorous prayer session focused on using the violet flame to transmute negative energy patterns from ancient Atlantis, Egypt, Crotona, and Ireland that pertained to all of them.

"Remember, we're in this together." Rory laid a reassuring hand on his friend's shoulder. "Don't ever forget that we are a mandala. What happens to one, happens to all."

"I was really feeling that as we chanted," remarked Glenna. "Think about it. We all remember being with Sarah and Kevin in the druid community at *Tearmann*. We know from Sarah's book that she was embodied in Egypt as Meke's grandmother. Kevin was advisor to the Dowager Queen, and Jeremy was Meke's protector, Jarahnaten.

"Rory and I both have a strong affinity for Egypt's 18th Dynasty, so I'm sure we were there, too."

"I can see myself as your fellow soldier," Rory said to Jeremy. "Perhaps even siblings. 'Tis interesting how often I find myself addressing you as 'my brother.' I feel that connection."

"I do, too."

"Do you think you were one of Meke's sisters who stayed behind with their parents?" Debbie asked Glenna.

"That's a real possibility. Whenever I think about ancient Egypt I feel a fascination with the culture and at the same time a sense of heaviness, even grief about the time period. That's probably why."

"Then there's Atlantis," Debbie continued. "Again, we know from Sarah's book that she and Kevin were there. I remember being her sister priestess who was married to Wyn, an embodiment of Jeremy's, when we lost each other again. Or maybe for the first time."

"Our mandala probably began embodying together even before the final days of Atlantis, so it's likely that Glenna and I were with you," said Rory thoughtfully.

An insight came to Debbie. "I think we should keep up our spiritual work these next few days. The fact that we're here in this place is no accident. I have a feeling that our entire trip has been leading us to this time and place for an important work for the Brotherhood."

"And for our individual souls and twin flames," Jeremy reminded her. He felt the vibration of what Debbie was sensing, and wondered what it meant. He started to ask when a rumbling in his stomach grabbed his attention. "Apparently, this soul's body would like some food."

They all laughed and went to the kitchen to discover what dinner items they had actually purchased a few hours earlier in Sneem.

Although the two couples now agreed that their primary focus was on the prayer sessions they felt called to conduct during their remaining days in Ireland, they were also determined to enjoy the beautiful resort facilities, which included a spa, excellent dining, and musical entertainment in the lounge each night of the weekend.

The people at the visitor's centre had recommended Sunday as the best day for their boat trip, so Saturday was a day for shopping and sight-seeing in the heritage town of Kenmare.

"Let's go our separate ways today," suggested Glenna. "We may end up in the same shops or pubs, but we don't have to. Then we can compare experiences when we meet up at the end of the day."

"That's a perfect idea," agreed Debbie. "I have no particular agenda except for checking out the Druid Circle. I'm still looking for my stone."

"Your stone?" asked Jeremy.

"Yes, the one whose inner language brings you peace and a feeling of being alive at the same time," explained Glenna. "Róisín told us about it. Sarah found hers with Kevin at the ancient grove of Uncle Óengus. Rory and I found ours on *Inis Cealtra*. Maybe yours is waiting in Kenmare."

"That would be quite the synchronicity, wouldn't it?" said Jeremy thoughtfully. "The place where Meke began her new life and the place where we finally break the curse that tries to keep Debbie and me apart."

They all looked at him with wide eyes.

"Wow. I never thought of this energy as a curse, but that's it, isn't it? An ancient curse against our twin flames. Now we really have our work cut out for us."

"We do." Debbie drew out the words. "And I think you've done what you insisted you must."

"What's that?"

"You've identified the core of the energy we've uncovered in the records of our losing each other. If you all don't mind, I think we should do some more inner work before venturing out."

After another hour of prayer, the two couples did head away from the carpark in different directions, and then laughed as they repeatedly found themselves in the same shops. They even walked into the same pub for lunch.

"I guess the angels don't want us straying too far from each other," joked Glenna.

"But we promise not to follow you to the Druid's Circle, if that's where you're going after we eat," Rory grinned. "We want to wander around the harbor, so we'll be well out of your way."

"That's fine," nodded Jeremy. "And, yes, that is our plan. I think we've exhausted our desire for shopping. If you've got the car keys, I'd like to stow our purchases after lunch."

"We have the same need," said Rory, shaking his head in amusement. "We'll walk to the carpark together and then, honestly, we will disappear."

The Druid's Circle was only a short walk up Market Street. The lane was lined with charming row houses whose front gardens were overflowing with an abundance of spring flowers that nearly hid narrow walkways leading to brightly painted front doors.

"Even if we don't find our stone here, I feel that I've discovered a new sense of peace and a feeling of being alive at the same time," said Debbie. She and Jeremy were walking hand-in-hand.

"You have brought me alive, *a ghrá*. See, you're even turning me into an Irishman. Never could I have imagined such joy. Such love."

He spontaneously pulled her into a strong embrace and was kissing her deeply when he suddenly raised his head. "Do you feel that?"

"I do. We must be near the Druid's Circle. Let's go see."

They walked up a gravel path to a little information hut where a plaque told a brief story of the Kenmare Stone Circle.

This is the biggest stone circle in the southwest of Ireland, where about 100 examples occur. Stone circles were built during the Bronze Age (2,200 - 500 BC) for ritual and ceremonial purposes. Some studies have indicated that they were oriented toward certain solar and lunar events, such as the position of the horizon on a solstice. The Kenmare example may be oriented on the setting sun.

In the center of the circle is a type of burial monument known as a Boulder Burial. These are rarely found outside of southwest Ireland.

Debbie and Jeremy walked to the entrance of the circle and stopped. Unlike many stone circles that are located in an open field, this one was bounded on the back by a row of enormous pine trees whose branches looked more like lacy ferns than pine boughs. They were swaying in the breeze that wafted gently around the stones.

Other visitors might have remarked on the movement of the pines. Debbie and Jeremy saw something else.

"Look," he said, "your devas are dancing."

"Oh, they are." Debbie walked up to the tall beings and caressed the branches as if she were holding the outstretched hands of her friends the devas, whom she had known so well as Dearbhla.

Jeremy smiled in loving appreciation for this special gift of hers, just as Madwyn had done in profound respect for his mentor, the one he came to know as his twin flame.

"What are they saying, my love?" He could see that she was participating in an intimate conversation.

"Many things. Messages without words. Images with deep meaning. Feelings that go beyond speech. Love beyond our human comprehension."

Her face clouded. "And a warning to pay attention to the heart. Nothing more."

As quickly as the cloud had come, it faded into a sunny smile.

"And now they're saying that we're to walk the circle and find our stone. We're to walk separately until we come to the same stone that speaks our inner name. Then we will know what to do."

"Then let's begin here," suggested Jeremy.

They faced away from each other and began to walk slowly around the circle. Nine times did their paths cross and nine times did they continue walking until they both stopped at the large stone on what would be nine o'clock if the entrance to the grove sat at six o'clock.

No words were necessary. This was their stone.

Without speaking, they moved to opposite sides of the stone so their bodies were in alignment with the rest of the circle. They placed their hands on the stone and stood there until they felt time cease to be and they entered a cosmic interval.

There in the timelessness of Spirit, they felt themselves lifting out of their bodies into a realm of Light and Love that was beyond human thought or feeling. There was no longer a stone between them. Instead, they held their hands up, palms pressed together, their hearts radiating the threefold flames they had seen on other occasions, often in the heart of a great master.

Now those flames began to spin together as even the minute separation between palms dissolved and they felt themselves merging as only twin souls are capable of doing. For here was the record of their origin, their infancy in a starry nursery where they had begun as a single ovoid of pure light substance.

The sensation lasted only briefly, though they would have sworn they had spent hours in a state of complete bliss. However long is the time required for timelessness, at the end of that interval each one looked across the great stone into the eyes of their eternal love.

Nothing had changed, and everything had changed. They released their hands from the stone and returned to where the devas continued to dance. Standing with their backs to the tall trees, they leaned into the gentle comfort they felt emanating from these presences. They gazed out across the stone circle and let the enormity of their experience sink into their consciousness until their inner sight showed them that Rory and Glenna were ready to return to their cottage at the resort.

No explanation was necessary. When Debbie and Jeremy walked up to the SUV where their friends were waiting for them, all was conveyed in the look of bliss that sparkled in the eyes of the two seers.

When they returned to their cottage, each couple went to their room until time for dinner. Fortunately, Rory and Glenna had been prompted to purchase take-out meals which they generously shared.

"As you can probably tell," said Jeremy with a misty-eyed grin, "our afternoon was beyond description. However, we would enjoy hearing about your adventures."

"We mostly just ambled around," said Glenna. "But we do have one story to share. It's quite remarkable. Tell them, Rory."

"We'd finished walking the town loop trail and decided to have a snack at one of the shops we'd passed earlier. There we were enjoying our tea and scones when who should walk in but Tim and Maggie O'Toole. Naturally, we asked them to join us. They wanted to know about our travels and how we were getting on as two couples touring together."

Glenna picked up the story. "Of course, we told them how we're all feeling very bonded, especially in our prayer work. We didn't feel it was our place to say anything about what we were working on, except that we had run into some heavy records from the past that we were praying about."

"They weren't at all curious," Rory continued. "In fact, I got the feeling they knew exactly what we were working on. However, I was curious about how we should come to meet."

" 'We love to visit Kenmare whenever we travel to this part of our homeland,' said Maggie.

" 'A little bird told us we might find you here today,' Tim chimed in. 'And sure enough, here you are.'

"They didn't stay long. In fact, I don't remember them having anything to eat. As they left they said to give you their love and best wishes and to be wary of challenges when you least expect them."

"Do you think Master K. H. sent them?" asked Jeremy.

"I'm certain of it," said Debbie. "Absolutely certain."

Forty-Two

Saturday was another rough night for sleep. Both couples awoke the next morning feeling as if they had been fighting a battle all night.

"My right hand feels stiff as if I'd been gripping a sword," said Rory.

"Mine, too," agreed Jeremy. "Does your left arm ache from holding your shield?"

"You're not alone," said Debbie. "Glenna and I remember chanting and holding our arms out for hours, focusing beams of light energy through our palms to roll back waves of darkness."

"I never imagined that being a mystic would be such hard work," joked Jeremy. "The book definitions don't say anything about being a warrior of the spirit."

"That's the fine print you don't see on the brochure when you join forces with the Great White Brotherhood," quipped Rory.

"And you wouldn't have it any other way, would you, *mo chroí*?" said Glenna, giving him a big hug.

"Oh, it feels good to laugh," remarked Debbie. "I had no idea that our sight-seeing in Ireland would take such a serious turn. Speaking of which, do you think our boat tour is on schedule?"

She was looking out the window of their cottage at the dark clouds that had gathered to the west.

"I haven't heard anything," said Rory. "We should act as if we're going and start getting ready. The dock's an hour away and they want us there early."

Just then his cell phone rang.

"Rory O'Donnell here. . . . Yes, I suppose we're not surprised. . . . Thanks for letting us know. . . . And you'll credit my card? . . . *Go raibh maith agat. Slán.*"

"No boat trip?" asked Jeremy.

"No boat trip," said Rory. "The man told me the seas are really rough this morning. Too rough even for their boat that doesn't try to land on Skellig Michael and that stays fairly far away from the rocks. They don't take any chances. We get a full refund, so there's no loss."

"Can I say that I am relieved?" said Debbie. "After last night's battle with whoever or whatever we were up against, I feel like we need to do extra prayers this morning."

"What shall we do after?" asked Jeremy.

"I've heard the hotel has a fine little library that I'd like to check out," said Rory.

"And I've been wanting to write some poetry," Glenna chimed in. "This hotel is known for the many famous authors and poets who have written some of their best works here. I'd like to soak up some of that inspiration. Plus, I'm getting some ideas for a children's drama program that I'd like to start at Fibonacci's. Feels like a day for contemplation."

"You know what I'd really like to do on this last day of our honeymoon," Debbie mused. "I'd like to spend the day at the hotel spa. Would you do that with me, Jeremy?"

"Gladly. That sounds much more inviting that bouncing around on rough waves in a small boat. I don't think we've cleared all of our sea-faring records. Staying on dry land seems like a much better option."

"Perfect," said Rory. "I do think we should have one nice dinner in the hotel before we leave. Our evening meals have been a bit sketchy, wouldn't you say?"

"Yes, I would." Jeremy playfully rolled his eyes and rubbed his stomach. "And there's a harpist playing in the lounge this evening. Listening to some ethereal music will be the perfect ending to a relaxing day."

"We'll have time for a morning hike tomorrow before we have to check out." Glenna reminded them of their itinerary. "It's only three hours from here to Shannon, so we can take our time getting there. We'll spend the night at that hotel across the street from the airport so we're already on site the morning of our flight home. I've read that they have a nice pub restaurant if we don't want to do any more driving, and we can have breakfast at the airport cafe."

"Glenna, you are a marvel of organization," said Debbie gratefully. "Thank you so much. And Rory, our intrepid driver. You've both been fabulous."

"We wouldn't have missed this trip," he said. "Now let's do our morning prayers. I do believe we've been saved from something by not going on the boat trip. Let's build on that with some mighty chants."

Spa day was a honeymoon dream come true for Debbie and Jeremy. They swam in the indoor heated pool. They soaked in the outdoor hot tub that offered expansive views of Kenmare Bay.

They spent several hours in the thermal suite, drifting between hot and cold, moist and dry therapies. They each had a massage. And they power-napped in an amazing wave system with vibrational frequencies to calm body and mind.

"I think my bones have liquefied," Debbie exulted with half-closed eyes when they returned to their cottage. "Just pour me into bed. I think I could sleep for a week."

"We have two hours before dinner. Time enough to pour ourselves into each other," suggested Jeremy tenderly.

"Perfect. You're perfect, my love. Thank you for all of this."

"I don't know how I ever lived without you," said her husband as he took her in his arms."

Thanks to a gentle reminder phone call from a very prescient Rory, the Maddens did manage to join their friends on time for dinner at the hotel. The meal was exquisitely prepared and served in the luxurious dining room with gorgeous views overlooking the bay.

"We're going to skip the musical entertainment tonight," said Rory as they finished their coffee and dessert. "We've had a full day of reading and writing. And we took a long walk after the storm clouds lifted."

"We need some snuggle time," said Glenna blushing. "We'll see you in the morning for breakfast and prayers, and we can decide on tomorrow's schedule then."

"Have a lovely evening, you two," said Debbie. Her eyes were still misty from the sweetness of her day with Jeremy. "My love, I'm not quite ready to go to the lounge. I want to change into something more casual. If you want to go ahead, that's fine. I'll meet you there in a little while."

"I can walk you back to the cottage," Jeremy offered.

"No, that's okay. Rory and Glenna won't mind if I go with them, and there will still be plenty of daylight when I walk back to the hotel. I know you really want to hear the music and it will be starting soon. I won't be long."

"Okay, thanks. Ever since hearing that incredible organ music at the cathedral in Galway, I've wanted to experience all kinds of instruments to notice how they resonate in my body."

Debbie kissed him on the cheek and left the hotel with their friends.

The harpist was tuning her instrument when Jeremy took a seat at the bar where he could watch the musician and where Debbie would see him when she walked in.

"Club soda and lime," he ordered from the bartender. He paid with a ten euro note. "Keep the change. I don't drink, but I know what it's like to earn a living."

"*Go raibh maith agat.* I wish all our patrons were as understanding."

"I'm a fortunate man," said Jeremy. "Life is being very good to me. I like to pass along the blessings."

"Enjoy the music, then," said the bartender and went back to serving other customers. The harpist strummed the first glissando on her beautiful instrument and heavenly chords filled the lounge.

Jeremy was immediately enthralled. He wished Debbie would join him soon. For a minute he thought she had, but then the scent of a heavy perfume told him that the woman who had taken the seat next to him at the bar was not his wife.

This woman was nothing like Debbie. She was voluptuous and obviously meant to broadcast that fact in her choice of a clingy, low-cut dress. Jeremy actually tried not to look at her, but when she ordered a cocktail, he could tell by the tone of her voice that she was distressed and had probably been crying.

Feeling his own heart so full of love, he couldn't help turning to her. "Are you all right?" he asked.

She swiveled on her bar stool and looked at him directly with eyes that were the deepest midnight blue Jeremy had ever seen.

"Oh, aren't you sweet to ask," she simpered. "I've just had the worst argument with my fiancé. I thought we were going to be married next week, but now I'm not so sure he's the right one for me."

"I'm sorry to hear that. Have you tried talking to him?"

"He doesn't talk, he just yells, and that kind of harshness wounds me so." Her eyes filled with tears and she stifled a sob.

Jeremy pulled a tissue from his pocket and handed it to her. "Here, there's no use in crying," he said compassionately. "I'll bet he's already sorry he upset you."

"A man like you would be, wouldn't you?" The woman leaned closer to Jeremy and touched him on the leg. She looked at his left hand and noticed his wedding ring. "I'll bet you never yell at your wife or make her unhappy."

Jeremy very purposefully took her hand and removed it from his leg. "I certainly try not to make her unhappy and I don't yell."

"What do you do?" purred the woman. "Do you make tender love with her? I imagine you are a gentle lover."

"Really, ma'am, that's none of your business." Jeremy was growing very uncomfortable and wasn't sure how to extricate himself from this conversation.

"Dear me, I've overstepped propriety, haven't I?" said the woman in a sing-song voice. "I'm always doing that. I suppose that's why my fiancé yells at me. I just don't seem able to control myself. Like now."

She leaned over and grabbed Jeremy's jacket lapels. She pulled him off of his bar stool as she slid from hers and plastered her body against him while kissing him seductively on the mouth.

Jeremy turned his head and tried to push the woman away, but she held fast with amazing strength.

"Oh, don't be like that." She wound her fingers in his hair and pulled him into another passionate kiss.

Which is what Debbie saw when she walked into the lounge.

Jeremy's eyes went wide as he managed to look past the woman who was practically writhing against him and saw the look of horror on his wife's face.

"Debbie!" He managed to push the woman away as the love of his life turned and fled.

"Whoopsie," the seductress giggled and released him. "Looks like wifey showed up. Then my work here is finished. Bye for now, Jeremy," she said with a wicked grin and sashayed out the other side of the lounge.

"Debbie!" Jeremy called as he ran after her. His legs were longer than hers and he caught up with her before she had gone past the hotel steps.

"Wait! Let me explain! Stop, so I can talk to you." He grabbed her arm, but she wrenched it away.

"Don't touch me!" she cried. Tears were streaming down her cheeks. "How could you? After our lovely day. The minute I'm not around, you hook up with some whore!"

"That's not what I was doing."

"What *were* you doing?"

"I was trying to fight her off."

"Right! Big strong Jeremy can't fight off a woman. Even if she was rather heavily endowed."

"It was weird. She was strong as a man. I mean it. She came after me like she knew me. She even called me by name when she left. I was just trying to be kind to her because she'd been crying and then, before I knew it, she had me in a lip lock. Why won't you believe me?"

"I know what I saw."

"No, you don't. Are you such a poor seer that you can't see through the truth of this situation? Don't you know me any better than to accuse me of betraying you with some floozy who throws herself at me?"

"I thought I did know you, Jeremy. Now I'm not so sure. I never expected you'd be capable of something like this."

"Debbie, I didn't *do anything!*" Jeremy was practically shouting.

"No, you didn't. You didn't do anything to stop her from kissing you. She kissed you twice. I saw that. You're a big man, Jeremy. You could have stopped her if you'd wanted to. I can't believe she was that strong."

"Then you'll have to believe what you want." Jeremy turned and strode off onto another path. He didn't care where it led. This was one woman he could get away from, if she thought so little of him.

Debbie stood where he left her, shaking, her eyes blinded by angry tears. She waited, hoping he would turn around and come back. But he didn't. It was growing dark and she didn't want to be out on the trail by herself. She stumbled back to the cottage and quietly entered their room. She lay awake for hours, but Jeremy didn't come back.

He did eventually return to their cottage, but he didn't go to the room where Debbie was sleeping. Or where he hoped she was sleeping by now. Instead he found some extra blankets in a closet and made up a cramped bed on the sofa.

That's where Glenna found him the next morning when she got up early to fix coffee for her and Rory. She had set the coffee maker to come on automatically, so the first cups were nearly brewed when she walked into the kitchen.

The sun wasn't up yet so she didn't see Jeremy until she turned on the light and yelped in surprise. At first she thought an intruder was in the living room, but an intruder wouldn't be asleep on their sofa.

"Jeremy?" She walked over and poked him to see if it was, indeed, her friend. He stirred and groaned. "What are you doing out here?" Glenna demanded. "Jeremy! Wake up! What's going on?"

He opened his eyes half-way and sat up slowly. He had slept in his clothes and was a rumpled mess.

"Big fight," he said groggily. "Debbie saw this sexy woman kissing me and blew a fuse."

"Why was a sexy woman kissing you?"

"I don't know. She came after me with some kind of power. I figured it out last night as I walked around the property. Good thing they've got the paths lighted. I didn't know where I was going. Just walking. Why wouldn't Debbie believe me?"

He was mumbling all of this to himself.

Glenna grasped his shoulders and shook him. "Jeremy, look at me! Something terrible has happened. This isn't like either of you."

She went to the counter and fixed him a cup of coffee. "Here, drink this. I'm going to wake Rory and you two are going to figure this out while I talk to Debbie."

Unable to argue, Jeremy did as Glenna told him. In less than five minutes an equally groggy Rory was sitting on the sofa next to his friend, drinking his own cup of coffee.

"I don't know what you did, brother, but Glenna says we have to go to the hotel for our breakfast. You're supposed to tell me exactly what happened last night. She'll try to make sense of what's going through Debbie's mind. She said she'd text me when we can come back.

"Hurry up and put on your shoes and your jacket so we can get out of here. I've never seen Glenna so fierce."

Forty-Three

Glenna knocked on Debbie's bedroom door but she didn't wait for an answer. Instead she entered carrying a tray with two mugs of coffee and some scones from yesterday's breakfast.

"Debbie, wake up," she said gently but firmly. "Something terrible has happened and we have to figure out what it is."

"Go away." Debbie moaned and didn't open her eyes.

"Wake up. I've brought you breakfast. Sit up, drink your coffee, eat a scone, and tell me what in the world happened to you and Jeremy."

Reluctantly, Debbie pulled herself up to sitting and accepted the mug Glenna put into her hand.

"I don't know what happened," she said weakly.

"Tell me what you remember," urged Glenna.

Debbie closed her eyes momentarily and the scene came back to her.

"I'd sent Jeremy ahead to the lounge to listen to the harpist. When I walked in about fifteen minutes later, he was locked in a passionate kiss with this woman who looked like a whore. She had on this tight dress with her bosom half hanging out and her body plastered against him. It was disgusting. I felt like I'd walked into an astral nightmare."

"I think you did, but this wasn't a nightmare. It was really happening, like the astral plane spilled into the physical. I don't know how to explain it. That's just what it feels like to me."

"That's exactly what it was like," sighed Debbie. "And I snapped. I was instantly furious with Jeremy. I couldn't see anything except him apparently enjoying having this woman all over him. It was like something came over me and I was blind except to this feeling of rage that he was betraying me right in front of my eyes."

"How do you feel now?"

"Like *I've* betrayed *him*. Oh. Glenna. What have I done? He kept saying, 'Why won't you believe me?' But I couldn't. I wouldn't. All I could say was, 'I know what I saw.' "

"But you didn't know what you were seeing, did you?"

"No, because it was an illusion. Almost as if somebody had created a cloud like the old druids used to do, but this was a false image and I believed it. After our lovely spa day together, my chakras were wide open. My guard was down and I walked right into that illusion.

"Jeremy kept telling me that the woman was so strong that he couldn't push her away. How can that be? Unless she was a demon or a witch or . . . "

Debbie and Glenna looked at each other, aghast, and exclaimed in a single voice: "*Una!*"

"Could it really be that Arán Bán's consort has showed up here and attacked you and Jeremy when you were most vulnerable?" Glenna brought a hand to her mouth as if she dared not give voice to this possibility.

"I think that's exactly what happened," said Debbie. "How could I be so stupid? Haven't I spent the last decade of my life on the spiritual path? And didn't Tim and Maggie send me and Jeremy the message to beware of unexpected events?"

"They did, yes," Glenna remembered.

"This is terrible," moaned Debbie. "How can Jeremy ever forgive me? *Will* he forgive me?"

"He will or I'll clobber him," Glenna blurted out, then reconsidered. "No, seriously. I'll text Rory that they should come back now. The four of us will talk this out. We'll pray about it, clear the energy, and move on. This entire situation is not real and we won't let it be. Okay?"

"Okay. I'm going to take a shower. My face must be puffed up from all the weeping, and I have an awful headache."

"You take care of yourself, Debbie. I'll intercept our husbands when they get here. I'll text Rory a bit about our discovery so he can prime Jeremy. Don't worry. You'll weather this storm and be stronger for it. I promise."

It was a very contrite Debbie and a very sober Jeremy who sat across from their two friends in their cottage living room. They couldn't look at each other and neither was ready to speak, so Glenna decided to do it for them.

"Since I'm the official bard among us," she began, "I'm going to tell you the story of what I believe happened to you last night. Having been on the receiving end of the venom of Arán Bán on the astral plane and then Ursula when she came to my play in Dublin, the plot seems clear. Feel free to jump in any time."

For whatever reason, other than their hatred of all of our twin flames, Una and probably Arán Bán have been tracking us.

I remember Kevin saying that Saint Germain explained how these people who used to have great light have the ability to track other people with great light.

None of us had been separated from our partners until last night when Debbie sent Jeremy ahead to listen to the harpist perform in the lounge. That was the opening Una was waiting for and she pounced.

I believe Jeremy when he says that she was so strong he couldn't push her away. I'm sure she's supported by demons who could do that. And we know that she's been a master of black magic for many embodiments. There's nothing to say she hadn't uttered curses against both of you in advance.

"That's it!" exclaimed Debbie. "Don't you remember, Jeremy? Just yesterday you said we were up against a curse."

"Of course." They were looking at each other now and clasping hands. "At the time I said that, the whole curse thing was kind of abstract to me. But now I see it was real. Una cursed us before she ever sidled up to me in the lounge and engaged me in conversation. It's like she was winding a coil of energy around me as we spoke and then I couldn't break free of it until she knew you'd seen her kissing me."

"That is diabolical," said Rory. "And it makes perfect sense."

"I was so angry at you, Jeremy, I was ready to curse you," admitted

Debbie. "Thank God something stopped me. Once I came back to our cottage, to this forcefield where we've been praying and chanting, the rage I was feeling dissipated. Then all I could feel was heartbreak. But I couldn't do anything about it except cry myself to sleep."

"My love, I am so sorry," said Jeremy. "I never should have gone to the lounge without you. I know you said for me to go ahead, and I did want to hear the music. But something told me I should come back here with you and then we'd go hear the music together. I didn't listen and we nearly lost each other. Can you forgive me?"

"Of course, if you can forgive me, my only love."

They were holding each other now. Seeing them embracing at last, Rory put his arm around Glenna. As she spontaneously began to recite the words they all needed to hear once more, Debbie was reminded of her remarkable bonding with Jeremy when they had found their stone only a day before. Never again would she take that blessing for granted.

> The quality of mercy is not strained.
> It droppeth as the gentle rain from heaven
> Upon the place beneath. It is twice blest:
> It blesseth him that gives and him that takes.
> 'Tis mightiest in the mightiest; it becomes
> The thronèd monarch better than his crown.
> His scepter shows the force of temporal power;
> The attribute to awe and majesty
> Wherein doth sit the dread and fear of kings;
> But mercy is above this sceptered sway.
> It is enthronèd in the hearts of kings;
> It is an attribute to God Himself;
> And earthly power doth then show likest God's
> When mercy seasons justice. Therefore,
> Though justice be our plea, consider this:
> That in the course of justice none of us
> Should see salvation. We do pray for mercy,
> And that same prayer doth teach us all to render
> The deeds of mercy.

Forty-Four

Late the next morning the Maddens and the O'Donnells were waiting for their daytime flight from Shannon Airport to JFK to start boarding when Debbie's cell phone rang.

"Debbie, it's Róisín. Are you all together and somewhere that you can put me on speaker phone? I have something to tell you and I want you all to hear the same message at the same time."

"Can you hold a minute, Róisín? There's an empty waiting area we can huddle in. Come on, everybody, this sounds really important."

They moved quickly and gathered around Debbie's phone.

"We're here, Róisín. What's going on?"

"I'll go straight to the point and don't interrupt me, darlin', until I've given you the whole story."

A. B. Ryan is dead. Tony was correct to suspect that the Argenti family might decide they couldn't leave the man alive.

After he confessed to having forced Rudy into setting the fire at Fibonacci's—which we believe was one last opportunity for mercy delivered by Master K. H.—he got so angry that he turned State's Evidence against the Argenti syndicate.

That's when they decided to get rid of him. Suicide is the official report, but no one believes that to be the actual cause of death. His jail cell was being improperly guarded. Anyone could have reached him.

So A. B. Ryan is gone from earth, but Arán Bán is raging on the astral plane. Or he was. Last night he attacked Lucky. He knew he was forbidden by cosmic law to attack either of us because of the position we hold in the Great White Brotherhood's hierarchy on behalf of Saint Germain.

But by this time he was consumed with rage that his one admission of guilt was not sufficient to save his soul if he did not surrender his human ego to the will and unconditional love of *An Síoraí.* So he defied the mercy he had been shown and sealed his own fate.

Archangel Michael's legions have bound him, so he can cause no further harm. But the reason I'm calling is that we need for you four to come directly to Fibonacci's as soon as you land. Kevin and Sarah will pick you up at the airport so your mandala is all together.

There is a trial taking place at inner levels, and the Friends of Ancient Wisdom are gathering. You are needed in your finer bodies to testify regarding your interactions with Arán Bán in any of the embodiments you've shared.

The trial could end in Arán Bán going through the second death, the final dissolution of his soul. The Brotherhood does not take that action lightly, which is why testimony must be given from actual witnesses to his deeds.

Saint Germain has sealed you four with a special protection for your safe travel home. Lucky and I will most likely already be giving our testimony when you arrive. The Twin Flames of Éire are meant to testify together as a mandala.

I feel your concern, but don't worry. My man is fine. Lucky is too tough to let an old black magician get the best of him. Especially one that was already weakened by your successful defeat of his attack on Glenna and Rory some months ago.

Now rest on your flight home if you can. You'll need your strength for what lies ahead.

One of the fascinating things about modern air travel is that when you fly from Shannon to New York, you arrive at nearly the same time by the clock as when you departed.

So it was that the MacCauleys were driving the O'Donnells and the Maddens to Fibonacci's with half a day's daylight remaining when the travelers had just spent half a day's daylight in the air.

Kevin and Sarah had greeted them with strong hugs and moist eyes.

"How are you?" asked Sarah urgently. She had both of Debbie's hands in hers and was looking intently at her friend and her husband. "We've been praying for you. Master K. H. showed us that you were going to face a major initiation. We knew we couldn't interfere, but we've been supporting you with our prayers."

"Thank you," said Jeremy sincerely. He had both hands on Debbie's shoulders. "I know that made the difference. Plus the kindness of these two stalwart companions." He motioned to Glenna and Rory. "I've never realized how much we need each other until this trip. I promise I will never take our mandala for granted."

"Well said," agreed Kevin. "I have much to explain to you. However, I'd prefer that we be settled at Fibonacci's before I give you the details. Meanwhile, let's all do some chants while we're driving."

"Wow! Look at how much has been accomplished," exclaimed Rory when the travelers entered the new Fibonacci's coffee shop.

"There's still lots to be completed in all areas," said Sarah, "but our volunteers and Brian's crews are true miracle workers. We are able to serve you a snack and some tea while we explain what's happening."

"That would be lovely," agreed Debbie. "We ate on the plane, but one of Róisín's invigorating teas would be much appreciated."

Sarah served them all at a table in one of the completely remodeled corners of the coffee shop as Kevin laid out the procedures for the trial.

"As I understand it, a group of cosmic beings known as the Four and Twenty Elders is conducting the proceedings. Solemn trials such as this take place at the Court of the Sacred Fire on the God Star Sirius, which is the seat of divine governance for our sector of the galaxy."

"It's also the brightest star in the Milky Way," said Jeremy.

"That's right," said Kevin, "and it's a very sacred place, as we are all about to experience. Master K. H. is handling instruction for how each soul is to proceed when they are called to testify. Tim and Maggie O'Toole are working with him to safeguard the bodies of those who are in the deep meditation required to reach the God Star in their soul consciousness."

"Don't worry. They will be with us while we are out of our bodies," said Sarah reassuringly. A look of concern had briefly flickered across the brows of her friends.

Kevin continued. "Several senior members of our community were called about an hour ago. I don't think any of us realized how many of the Friends hold important positions in the Brotherhood. Lucky and Róisín will follow them.

"We've not been told how long the trial will last. The Four and Twenty Elders are not troubled by such things as earthly time, so the proceedings will conclude only when they say enough evidence has been given."

"We're not certain when we'll be called," added Sarah, "but we do know that we'll all go in together because our experiences with Arán Bán have been so intricately interwoven since the days of Atlantis."

"I expect that every soul who has been harmed by Arán Bán will be given the opportunity to speak," said Kevin. "The Great Law is unconditionally fair, even to individuals who have blasphemed the Divine for eons. The light that remains in such a one is still divine energy and the Brotherhood will do everything possible to rescue that light."

"So we wait," Jeremy surmised.

"We do, but I don't think for long. Róisín wouldn't have asked Sarah and me to bring you straight here unless the timing was crucial for us all to be together now."

"Where are your babies, Sarah?" asked Debbie.

"With my parents. They're all moved in to their new home and they jump at any opportunity to take care of their grandchildren. It's very sweet and a big relief for Ivy and me."

She looked at Kevin, who nodded. "While we wait to be called, we'd love to hear any stories you'd like to share about your trip. Glenna, would you be our *seanchaí* and fill us in on your travels?"

"I'll get us started if everybody else will join in," Glenna agreed. "We've had more adventures than any one of us could possibly remember." She closed her eyes briefly, then began recounting the story that none of them would have believed if they hadn't lived it:

Once upon a time, there were two couples who were very good friends. They decided that a double honeymoon trip to Ireland would be a grand way to spend two weeks.

Others wondered if they would get along through so many days in each other's company. But by the time they returned, they had become even better friends than when they departed.

Forty-Five

Time passed quickly as the travelers related their most inspiring experiences along with those subtle clues about what might be coming upon them that they seem to have missed.

Somehow they were not surprised when Kevin and Sarah said they had been very concerned for their friends' safety on Sunday when they had planned to go on a boat tour around the skellig islands. They all agreed that the MacCauleys' prayers for the will of *An Síoraí*, the Eternal One, had probably inspired local elemental forces to raise up the rough seas and strong winds that canceled the tour.

After another hour Lucky and Róisín walked into the coffee shop. The light radiating from their auras was remarkable. Their eyes were glowing and they appeared to be not quite anchored in the physical plane.

"Come, sit and have some tea and something to eat," offered Sarah. Kevin and Jeremy brought chairs for the couple.

"Thank you," said Lucky as he and Róisín accepted some food. "We're fine, though testifying before the Four and Twenty Elders is an experience not soon forgotten. We'll rest here until you're called and before we head home." They all sat in silence until Róisín looked up and said, "They're ready for you now, my dears. Go directly to the ballroom."

The Twin Flames of Éire were greeted warmly at the ballroom door by Tim O'Toole. "Come in, friends. Maggie will seat you."

Maggie O'Toole was standing at the front of the ballroom where the altar had been completed. The golden sun disc had been polished and hung. Fresh candles had been placed in the tall, spiral candelabra.

"Come right in, dear ones," said Maggie, "and take your places in the chairs we have provided for you."

By now the group understood the seating matrix for their mandala with the Maddens in the center, the MacCauleys on their left and the O'Donnells on their right.

Master K. H. stood before the altar. His serene face, which many mistook for that of Jesus, bore his usual kind expression, though it was touched today with a solemnity they had not seen in him before.

He and the O'Tooles were all wearing the attire of the Brothers and Sisters of the Golden Robe.

As Tim lit the candles, the Master poured out his love to these twin flames whom he had come to regard as personal friends. When all the tapers were lit, he began his instruction:

> Dear ones, your presence is greatly appreciated by the Brother-hood. The Four and Twenty Elders are particularly interested in your testimony, as you of all our members have had the most direct interaction with the soul known as Arán Bán.
>
> He is being held where you will not see him, lest his behavior prove a distraction. He will hear your testimony, but he will not be allowed to respond until all witnesses have been heard and the Council charges him to give answer.
>
> These proceedings are different from the life reviews you have experienced at various times on your path. Therefore, they require additional preparation, which I will direct.
>
> Please sit erect in your chairs and close your eyes. We will chant the OM together to set our forcefield. Then follow my voice as I guide you to the Court of the Sacred Fire on the God Star Sirius.
>
> Once there, you will be in the presence of the Four and Twenty Elders. They will ask you questions and will request that you recount for them specific events in your many lifetimes in which you directly interacted with Arán Bán, particularly if you were harmed by him.
>
> Although some of those events may also involve his con-sort, for the purpose of this trial, please restrict your comments

to those details solely connected with the man himself.

You may be asked by the Council to confirm one another's testimony. If what they have said is true to your knowledge and your confirmation is requested, simply reply Aye. Let us begin.

OMMMMM. The Master and the couples chanted. Maggie and Tim joined in and unseen beings of Light could be heard chanting with them.

They kept their eyes closed as vibrant energy bathed their souls in sensations of great buoyancy. They felt their hearts burning with the threefold flames of love, wisdom, and power that expanded and intensified as the OM continued.

When the energy in the ballroom had grown to a tremendous intensity, Master K. H. resumed speaking while the unseen presences maintained a soft OM that acted as an underpinning of support.

Be at peace, dear ones, and allow your souls to rise, first from your bodies, now from this room. Follow me as we climb up through many planes of being.

We are leaving the earth now, continuing to accelerate above all emotional and mental substance, into the etheric plane. And now we rise even higher, into the upper etheric as we reach for the stars.

Open your eyes and see before you the Milky Way, a crystalline highway of Light, leading you to the God Star Sirius, the brightest star in the firmament, and your soul's home.

We enter now a vast, circular amphitheater, the Court of the Sacred Fire, where countless angels, masters, and cosmic beings are assembled in rings of presence surrounding the Four and Twenty Elders for the trial of the soul known as Arán Bán.

Step forward now and stand in all reverence before these great beings who welcome you with unconditional Love and gratitude for your service to the Light.

The voice of Master K. H. faded and the witnesses found themselves standing before twelve pairs of twin flames, each pair representing one of the zodiacal signs known as solar hierarchies.

All twenty-four beings were clothed in white robes that glistened with celestial light. On their heads were golden crowns that sent out rays of illumination, very much like the crown worn by the Goddess of Liberty in her statue.

As the Twin Flames of Éire listened, members of the Council spoke, though not as speech is conceived of on earth. Nevertheless, this is what they heard:

Sons and daughters of Light, the hour of judgment is at hand. As all individuals will be judged by their deeds, be they good or ill, you come today to bear witness to the actions of Arán Bán.

We charge you to speak truly that of which you have direct experience, for the fate of a soul hangs in the balance. Has he pursued the path of Light and Love and Divine Justice, or has he chosen the left-handed path of the brothers of the shadow, cursing the children of Light and working against their souls?

Kevin MacCauley, we would first hear your report. What is your experience with this individual?

Kevin's testimony would prove to be the longest of their mandala as he described to the Council Arán Bán's hatred for the soul of Ah-Lahn and the man's repeated attempts to destroy his fellow druid century after century. When the other members of his mandala were asked to confirm the murderous actions of Ah-Lahn's ancient adversary, they did not hesitate to say Aye.

Sarah told the Council how Arán Bán had manipulated her and tried to seduce her when she was his student, Alana, in first-century Ireland and again in this lifetime.

Debbie had somewhat to relate about the behavior of A. B. Ryan as an employer, but she knew that Tony had more direct experience, so she did not elaborate.

She and Jeremy had less to report about Arán Bán than others, as their confrontations had had more to do with his consort.

The testimony of Glenna and Rory was some of the most powerful, as it was also the most recent and involved not merely an attack upon their physical bodies. Arán Bán had actually tried to destroy their souls, literally cursing the Light within them.

Although the spirit beings assembled as witnesses to the proceedings held their peace, an awareness rippled through them that spoke to their conviction that such actions, if repeated through many lifetimes, were extremely serious.

When the Twin Flames of Éire had concluded their testimony and the truth of their words had been affirmed by their companions, the Council spoke:

> Thank you, sons and daughters of the Light. When all witnesses have been heard, you will be summoned once more. For all who bear witness are called to be present when sentence is given.
>
> Time and opportunity do expire for each soul. Let all be aware that each one's works are tried in the sacred fire. That which is of the Light will be preserved. That which is of darkness will be consumed.
>
> Understand that the dissolution of a soul is an act of the greatest mercy to that one and to Light itself. For even in a soul that has consistently chosen darkness over Light, cruelty over compassion, the ways of death over the ways of Life, tiny amounts of the divine energy remain imprisoned in that being and must be redeemed.
>
> We do not make the final decision. The Light itself is the ultimate arbiter. May you watch and pray and follow that Light to your own soul's glorious finale.

When the Council ceased speaking, Kevin and Sarah, Debbie and Jeremy, Glenna and Rory felt themselves whisking back through space and they were once more physically seated in the ballroom.

Master K. H. stood before them, gracing them with his most radiant smile. "You have done well," he said. "You are dismissed for now. Return to your homes and be ready to appear when you are called back for the final resolution of Arán Bán's case, which may occur quite suddenly."

Each couple departed wordlessly in deep contemplation of the remarkable scene in which they had participated. They suspected that more astonishing events were to come. And they would be right.

Forty-Six

When the three couples awoke the next morning, they were aware of the trial having continued at inner levels throughout the night. They expected to be summoned at any time, but were surprised by the nature of the call when it came.

"We're to meet at Lucky and Róisín's house for the next part of the trial," Kevin reported to Sarah when he got off the phone.

"Why is that?"

"Rudy is to give his testimony this morning. However, he is still under house arrest, so he can't go to Fibonacci's. K. H. has obtained a dispensation for him to travel in his finer body from Róisín garden room, which has a very high vibration."

"That is so kind," said Sarah. "I continue to be touched by the care K. H. takes of Rudy's soul."

"Yes, he is accomplishing more for the lad than I ever could."

"Are we meant to stand as support for Rudy during his testimony?"

"We are. This will be a new experience for him. K. H. wants us there to confirm that what he says is true. Of all of us, he has been the most cruelly manipulated by Arán Bán. Having to rehearse those soul-scarring experiences is likely to be unnerving for him.

"I understand from Lucky—that was him on the phone—that K. H. will join us at the Court because this is also a trial for Rudy. Time has not expired for his soul. This is an opportunity for him to give accounting of himself so he may receive mercy while he is still young enough to take advantage of it.

When the three couples arrived at Lucky and Róisín's house, they were amazed at the abundance of positive energy in their lush garden room. It was awash with light, the vibrancy of actual fruit trees and a Norfolk pine that reached nearly to the ceiling, and the vivid colors of bird-of-paradise and other tropical flowers.

Master K. H. was explaining to Rudy the procedure for his testimony and offering him every possible assurance that he would do well.

"Hey, Dad!" the lad called out when Kevin came in. He was putting on a brave face. He knew his friends were there to support him, but he couldn't help feeling embarrassed that he would be disclosing to cosmic beings the errors he had committed—never mind that many of them were instigated and forced upon him by Arán Bán.

"'Tis all right to be nervous, Rudy," said Róisín as she handed him a cup of calming tea. He was jumpy as a rabbit.

"We were all a bit unsure of ourselves before we testified to the Council," offered Jeremy. "But you know, I've never felt such profound compassion for the human condition. I could sense that they understand us better than we understand ourselves."

"And remember, your Uncle Tony has already given his testimony, so some of what you have to tell the Council will confirm his words," added Kevin.

"We'll all be with you," Sarah told him. "Just answer the Council's questions and give them the facts of your experience."

And so it was that the Twin Flames of Éire appeared once more before the Four and Twenty Elders. They would look back on the event and smile to think of themselves as acting like godparents for Rudy, for this was certainly the lad's baptism by fire.

He would tell them all later that he believed the time he had spent with them, with the Pythagoreans, meditating in the healing atmosphere of Róisín's garden, and being the recipient of much tutoring of his soul by Master K. H. had prepared him to speak the truth as he would not have imagined that he could speak it.

At the end of his testimony, the Council spoke to him:

Rudy Argenti, we have heard your testimony, and your friends have confirmed that you have spoken the truth.

Your courage in coming forward this day is noted. You are a fortunate young man to have the support of some of our best servants. That speaks well for the quality of your soul.

For that and other reasons, you are granted the mercy of this Court, which you will see manifest in coming days. Take advantage of this opportunity. Live a quality life, and show as much mercy to others as you have received this day.

You and your friends may now take your place as observers.

Rudy's eyes filled with tears as he bowed and said humbly, "Thank you for my life. I will not waste it."

K. H. motioned for him and his friends to be seated with the other observers in the vast amphitheater as the Council spoke in the most solemn of tones:

The hour has come. Arán Bán, step forward and stand upon the dais. You have heard the testimony of those with whom you have been directly involved for many thousands of years.

How do you respond to the charges that your persistent choice has been to oppose the Light in all whom you have met? That you have obstructed the purposes of the Great White Brotherhood. And that you have squandered the Light in your own heart of hearts?

What say you, Arán Bán?

Having known Arán Bán as gifted with a quick mind, a ready answer, and a glib tongue, those gathered expected him to mount a spirited defense of his own reasons for the choices he had been making almost since time began.

They thought he might even try to blame his victims, as they knew he had been skilled at doing in times past. So they were utterly astonished when the only sound that came from his mouth was a snarl. He was spitting and gnashing his teeth like a wild beast.

So completely had he been consumed by the darkness he had espoused, that he was reduced to a shell of existence that was not even human.

Without further discussion, the Council made its final declaration:

> Arán Bán, by free will have you arrived at this hour. Prepare to receive the mercy of *An Síoraí*, the Eternal One, whose unconditional Love will try the works of your soul.

Suddenly a shaft of living fire descended from the heart of the Godhead directly into the figure of Arán Bán. As thousands of witnesses watched in their finer bodies, his form disintegrated and the atoms of his soul were re-polarized back to the Source of all Life.

In an instant the identity of Arán Bán was no more.

Soon, the Friends of Ancient Wisdom found themselves back in their physical bodies, seated in a lovely garden room where the fragrance of violets, roses, and gardenias filled their auras with a vibration of sublime truth, beauty, and goodness—the likes of which they had never imagined possible.

Forty-Seven

At the invitation of Lucky and Róisín, the Friends of Ancient Wisdom remained in the garden room for several hours. Although their adversary had been vanquished for good, they felt no cause for celebration. The loss of a soul is a wound in the heart of *An Síoraí*, the Eternal One, and they felt that loss profoundly.

Quiet conversations were in process as individuals sought to make sense of the mystery of free will and its consequences.

"Kevin, can I speak with you and Sarah?" asked Rudy quietly.

"Of course." He had never seen Rudy like this. The lad was calm, self-contained, and humble in his speech. The three of them moved to another room where their conversation would be private.

"I understand," Rudy said simply.

"What do you understand?" Sarah was touched by the difference in his tone.

"All of it. Our relationship on Atlantis, the three of us. I see now that you did love me. Not as you loved each other, but as a true friend you would never betray. The High Priest lied to me and I believed him."

"We grieved for your death," said Kevin. "I still remember the look on your face when you died at the hands of that man. You thought I had told him where to find you, but I didn't."

"I know that now," said Rudy.

"How has this understanding come to you?" asked Sarah.

"It was being in the presence of the Four and Twenty Elders today. As I was giving my testimony about the terrible experiences my soul has endured with Arán Bán, somehow at the same time they were imparting to me the truth of each event. Truth that I'd never been able to see, or in seeing, I hadn't accepted."

"This is remarkable." Kevin felt his heart swelling with gratitude.

"It is," agreed Rudy, "and a relief that I didn't know my soul could feel. But I still have questions about why Arán Bán was my father in Ireland and then again in this life."

Kevin and Sarah looked at him with surprise. They had agreed not to tell him what they knew.

"I am aware of my parentage," he answered their unspoken question. "Uncle Tony told me about A. B. Ryan and my mother. But why Arán Bán in Ireland? And both times, he hated me and forced me into situations that put me in extreme danger, even though I was his own flesh and blood. Who knows? I may have been the High Priest's son on Atlantis."

"You may be right about that, Rudy," said Kevin thoughtfully. The pattern was certainly consistent. "You and Jeremy should compare notes sometime. I don't think he'll mind my telling you that his parents disliked him from the moment he was born. And I have known of other such instances."

"But why?"

"My only explanation is that souls of Light are often born to people who might be encouraged to return to the path of soul liberation. They volunteer to guide their families away from the brothers of the shadow. But often the parents don't want to be dissuaded, so they turn on their children."

"That makes sense," said Rudy.

"Another reason for your parentage is that Arán Bán would have owed you life because he took it on Atlantis. And then he perpetuated the cycle by manipulating your soul into the ways of death."

"But you've won, Rudy," Sarah assured him. "You're free now."

"I am, but I'm also alone," he said wistfully. "Uncle Tony has his own problems. And my mom is probably going to an institution. Lucky and Róisín are being great, but I can't stay here forever."

Rudy took a deep breath. This was the hardest thing he'd ever done.

"I know I'm practically an adult, but if I come out of this arson thing without having to go to jail, would you adopt me?"

"Oh, Rudy! Of course we will!" exclaimed Sarah.

"I have thought of you as my son since our druid days." Kevin's voice was thick with emotion. "I would be proud to make the relationship official. Then you really can call me 'Dad'—without the sarcasm."

The three of them laughed and Kevin embraced the lad as he had longed to do for two thousand years.

"We're not finished, are we?" Debbie said to Róisín as they finished setting out tea and sandwiches for their friends who were still discussing their experience at the Court of the Sacred Fire.

Róisín sighed and moved with her fellow seer to her kitchen's breakfast nook where the two of them could talk undisturbed.

"Not as long as Una is at large. Although she obviously scorned and manipulated Arán Bán, she will be furious that her twin flame has been eliminated. I'm sure she drew power by stealing energy from him. Now I fear she'll be looking for other targets."

"Do you think that's one reason she went after Jeremy? Because A. B. Ryan was in jail?"

"Possibly. And because of their extreme hatred of your mandala. I can see how the brothers of the shadow would have considered Arán Bán and Una useful tools in their ongoing war against the Brotherhood's mission for the union of twin flames."

"I do find it interesting how many of us in our mandala have had dealings with Una. Portents of things to come?" Debbie asked, though she already knew the answer.

"I'm certain of it. Be ready, my girl. The attack will come, and soon. This will be different because the ladies of heaven and earth must defeat the force that Una represents."

"How so?"

"Just as men must stand against the ones who would subvert the role of Father, we women must stand against the perversion of the Mother. If woman falls into the degradation of anger, resentment, and non-forgiveness, generations can be lost."

Debbie rested a hand under her chin, thinking.

"I remember Saint Germain telling us that the *shakti* can be more dangerous than her male consort because of the emotional power she wields and her ability to sway even souls of Light with sympathy."

"Exactly. Just as Una did when she attacked Jeremy. She portrays herself as a victim when really she is the perpetrator of enormous darkness practiced against the men she belittles or seduces. And against the children whose innocence she violates in the multiple ways she hinders the development of their souls."

"And in her cursing of our twin flames," added Debbie. "I was nearly overtaken by that force that wanted me to curse Jeremy."

"Had you done so, you would have been cursing your own soul because your beloved is the other half of you. The fact that you didn't proves that Light is stronger than darkness, but we must defend that Light in our loved ones and in ourselves at all times."

"Then we will fight when the time comes," said Debbie resolutely.

"I sense that time is upon us, so we must be prepared to respond in an instant," said Róisín. "For now you should go home and get some rest. I was hoping to retire myself, but apparently I have a message that needs my attention before I am allowed to be at peace."

They both rose. Róisín turned to go to her bedroom, then stopped and looked back at her adopted daughter with a tender smile that flooded Debbie with love. "Good night, darlin'. I'll see you in my dreams."

Debbie looked into her precious mentor's deep green eyes and saw an expression she could not identify. In that moment she felt a quaking in her soul as if a prophecy were about to come upon her. When no inspiration came, she walked over and kissed the woman's cheek.

"Good night, my dear Róisín. I'll see you in my dreams."

Forty-Eight

Dawn was beginning to rouge the eastern sky when Debbie, Glenna, and Sarah left their physical forms sleeping and began running in their finer bodies across the marble entry to the Temple of the One Light. Past the rose quartz fountain, past the exotic trees, past the baskets of fragrant flowers that were arrayed on tall pedestals surrounding the azure blue waters of still reflecting pools.

Lady Master Nada had summoned them, saying only, "Make haste to my etheric retreat." From the tone of her message, the three women knew that something was terribly wrong. They rushed into the inner pavilion and stopped suddenly, gazing in horror upon the scene that was playing out like a life review on a screen before them.

They could see their beloved Róisín lying on a cushioned divan in her garden room. She was barely breathing, her face pale as death. Maggie O'Toole was seated on a low stool beside her, bathing her forehead and praying softly.

Lady Nada had been standing next to the screen and came forward to greet the three young women who were all like daughters to Róisín and to this lady master whom they had known since the days of Atlantis.

"What happened?" they said together. "Is she all right?"

"Come with me, my dears, and I will explain." Lady Nada ushered them to a side chamber where they could be seated.

"You must calm yourselves, my stalwart ones, and be at peace for the challenge that lies ahead. Róisín's life is in the hands of *An Síoraí*, the Eternal One, and only the Divine knows her fate in this hour. Our dear friend has made a great sacrifice and we cannot know the outcome just yet. I will tell you the story."

Late last night Róisín received a message from Una saying that since her twin flame had gone through the second death, she realized she was beaten. Would Róisín meet her at a neutral location on the upper astral plane where she promised to beg for mercy and peace?

Suspecting a fake truce, and yet also knowing that Una might actually bend the knee to the Divine without Arán Bán's additional power behind her, our dear one put her physical form to sleep and ventured forth in her finer body, alone and undefended.

When she arrived, Una was already there, dressed in the somber robes of a pilgrim, appearing for all the world as a true penitent.

'You are so kind to meet me,' she said to Róisín in her most contrite tone. 'I am truly sorry for any trouble I may have caused. You must know it was Arán Bán who forced me to oppose you good people. I never meant any harm. You are all quite dear to me.'

'I appreciate your willingness to make amends,' Róisín responded. 'Although your name has been included on the list of souls who are under threat of the second death, the Great White Brotherhood extends to you opportunity to surrender your human ego to the Light of An Síoraí that lives in your heart.

'If you will also honor that flame in the hearts of all true children of the One Light, you will not face ultimate destruction of your soul. Are you willing to make that commitment?'

Una hesitated and did not speak, so Róisín repeated, 'Are you willing to turn toward the Light, Una?'

'I am NOT!' she screamed and threw off her pilgrim's garb, revealing herself in the seductive garments she usually wore.

She drew a circle in the air with her arm and pointed her right hand at Róisín. With the power of the evil High Priestess from Atlantis, she struck our friend with a ray of vicious energy that would have instantly killed anyone who did not have Róisín's attainment and ability to withstand enormous negative energy because of the great light in her own aura.

However, she was severely injured. The integration of her physical and finer bodies has been seriously disrupted. Una must have thought that her single blow was sufficient to kill her victim because she vanished, leaving our sister to die.

Many lady masters were instantly alerted. We rushed to Róisín's side and took her home. Her garden room contains the vibration of her own healing gifts and is the best atmosphere for Maggie to work with our dear one's Higher Self to repair the dreadful fragmentation that has taken place.

We have felt a flicker of awareness from her, so we know that progress is being made. We simply do not know how much.

I believe that the ascension may be what the future holds for our dear Róisín, but we will not know until she either re-covers or *An Síoraí*, the Eternal One, declares that her time on earth is at an end.

"How could she not know that Una was not to be trusted?" Sarah asked the question on everyone's lips.

"I believe she did know," replied Lady Master Nada. "However, by allowing Una to attack her, she assured the judgment of this one who has made herself our enemy for eons.

"I myself was once the victim of her machinations. I originally held the office of High Priestess in the Temple of the One Light on Atlantis. But this soul of Una, with the assistance of her twin flame who was the High Priest, precipitated my demise and usurped my position.

"What they did not know was that I had earned my soul's freedom from rebirth, which their murder only hastened. I soon returned as an ascended master, stronger and more powerful than ever. With the help of your twin flame, Sarah, I was able to render the evil High Priest and his minions powerless until many devotees of the One Light were able to escape before the final cataclysm that sank Atlantis.

"However, when dealing with beings who possessed great light, as did Una and Arán Bán, many cycles of opportunity are required before they can be brought to judgment—if that is the end they have chosen by their allegiance to the brothers of the shadow."

"Oh, Lady Nada, what are we to do now?" exclaimed Glenna. "You said we must be at peace for the challenge that lies ahead."

"And Róisín told me that we must be ready to respond in an instant," said Debbie, her voice choked with emotion. "She said she would see me in her dreams. Do you think she can see us?"

"That I cannot tell you," said Lady Nada. "But in this hour we are all called to respond with our most advanced mastery."

Great kindness flowed from her heart to these strong young women. She was confident of their determination. She prayed that their physical strength and spiritual attainment would match the initiation to which they were now being called.

She continued, "When Una attacked Róisín, she unleashed hordes of female demons, witches, sorceresses who all looked like her. This is how she is cloaked on the astral plane.

"The battle between good and evil in the age of the Divine Mother is on. It must be fought on the inner lest it spill into the physical where it will cause enormous harm to innocent people who would have no idea what has come upon them.

"Legions of our own feminine angels are sweeping through the ethers to bind Una's astral minions so her whereabouts can be revealed. Your task, dear ones, is to find her and defeat her.

"The lady masters of heaven are with you and will support you, but in this hour the daughters of the Divine Mother in embodiment must rise up to defeat the many faces of this beast whose intention is to separate twin flames and wipe the children of the Light from this planet and from the very universe itself."

"How shall we proceed?" asked Sarah, although she had a good idea. Alana and Ah-Lahn had had to fight Arán Bán on the astral plane.

Lady Master Nada read her thoughts. "Yes, Sarah, you are correct. We must descend to the astral plane, to Una's stronghold, where she has amalgamated her power and the forces of darkness she controls."

All three women took a deep breath.

"Never fear, dear ones. If you will look down, you will see that you have been clothed in a protective armor of light and armed with swords and shields that may appear as antiquated weapons, yet truly are the sacred Word and the shield of Light that your men are invoking for you."

Lady Nada directed their gaze to the hillsides that came into view as the Temple of Light disappeared and they found themselves standing on an open plain where grey clouds loomed overhead.

Arrayed on those hillsides were their men accompanied by legions of the Divine Masculine, all dressed in the white robes of ancient druids. Their hands were upraised and they were focusing great rays of light energy through their palms, creating a mighty shield that scintillated around each woman.

Debbie, Glenna, and Sarah now saw that they themselves were surrounded by vast numbers of female angels, ascended lady masters, and spirit beings who appeared to be waiting for their command to go forth. Also among them were countless women—nurturing mothers, teachers, midwives, nurses, professionals and artists of all kinds—who had joined the battle in their finer bodies to defeat the forces that oppose the union of twin flames and the Light of Love in their hearts.

"I will lead you, my dears," said Lady Master Nada. "Let us pray together and then we will be about our Mother's business."

O, Great Divine Mother, cosmic beings, lady masters, and mothers of the world, be with us this night as we seek the one called Una and those like her who would separate us from the beloveds of our hearts. Protect us, we pray, guide us in our efforts, strengthen our resolve, and fill us with your love of life that never fails.

"Amen," responded the hosts of Light as they swung into formation behind Ascended Lady Master Nada and Róisín's determined daughters. To their own astonishment, these three great friends now took on the appearance of Alana, Dearbhla, and Gormlaith—the women of mighty attainment they had been during their shared embodiment in first-century Ireland.

The Twin Flames of Éire were on the march!

Forty-Nine

"This must be the calm before the storm," commented Gormlaith as she, Alana, and Dearbhla followed Lady Master Nada toward a promontory of rock. Behind it was reputed to be another outcropping of stone and canyons. The sylphs who were acting as scouts had reported seeing activity in both areas, which suggested a place where Una might be hiding.

"I am trying to remember if I have ever been a soldier." Gormlaith pursed her lips as she considered. She was not feeling confident in her ability as a warrior.

"You will do fine, Gormlaith," Alana assured her.

"And what would Róisín be saying to you right now?" prompted Dearbhla. Not waiting for an answer, she focused her light green eyes in imitation of Róisín's deep emerald ones and declared, "Your man, Riordan, has been a soldier. Are you not one with him? Then call on his momentums, my girl, and prepare to fight!"

All three women laughed.

"Thank you," replied Gormlaith. "You are right. Riordan has been a grand soldier. And now I am remembering a skill I have that may be useful at some point."

"What is that?" asked Alana.

"Master Druid Óengus and I used to project our consciousness to each other between our *túath* which lay half-way across Ireland from each other. We became so proficient that we would swear the other was actually present.

"Once we find Una, perhaps I could do that. Make her think I am behind her, you know, so you can attack from the front."

"That is an interesting idea," said Lady Nada, who had been listening to their conversation. "First we must find Una. My sense is that she is in no hurry to reveal herself."

The lady master was correct. As the women and their cohort of spirit beings advanced, the atmosphere was eerily quiet until they came within one hundred yards of the promontory. Dearbhla thought it looked like a pyramid, but without a capstone.

Suddenly the air was filled with a great wind. The earth shook and an opening appeared at the base of the pyramid rock. Out poured waves of astral creatures, some appearing human, others horribly inhuman. And all resembling in some expression or physical feature Una herself.

The three women had never experienced anything to match the virulence and sheer number of demonic forces that rushed toward them.

"I believe we have stepped into the *Book of Revelation*," shouted Alana to her friends as they wielded their swords that were alive with the flames of spiritual fire that were each one's unique ability.

"Michael and his angels fought against the dragon; and the dragon fought and his angels, and prevailed not," quoted Gormlaith. "And the Woman Clothed with the Sun who wore a crown of twelves stars was seeking to save her child. We are all part of this great spiritual archetype of the Divine Feminine."

"And we have Michael's twin flame, Faith, fighting on our side to defeat the dragon's angels—Una's minions who have accused us and our twin flames since the beginning of time," Dearbhla declared.

The women and Lady Nada began to see a pattern in these forces. They were mercenaries, and feeble ones at that, easily dispatched by the angels who were arrayed in mighty phalanxes, ably meeting onslaught after onslaught until it seemed that Una's resources must be exhausted.

Unfortunately, they were not. The battle raged on, but without Una's appearance. Something must be done.

"Gormlaith," called Lady Master Nada, "your skills are needed now to flush Una from her hiding place. However, I do not want you using your energy to project your consciousness into her lair. That places you in too much danger.

"The Goddess of Truth will position herself to the rear of where we believe Una is hiding. As that wicked one has proved herself to be an enemy of Truth, she will not detect the presence of this cosmic lady master."

"Then what do you wish me to do, Lady Nada?" asked Gormlaith.

"I want you to sing, dear heart. Sing a new song as if your life, the life of your twin flame, and the lives of an entire universe of twin flames depend upon the power of your song, for indeed they do."

"I know just the one," replied the young bard.

"Excellent. Then stand beside me and we will project an intense vibration of Love and Light into the very teeth of hatred and death."

With the confidence of a seasoned performer, Gormlaith stepped onto the biggest stage of her life. As she began to sing, she felt Riordan's presence kindle like an enormous flame in her heart.

> Breathe me in as I breath you out;
> soul to soul, spirit to spirit
> one in the same—
> being in all being,
> beloved transfigured
> so beloved never dies.

She repeated that verse over and over until she could feel the radiation of pure Love breaking through the density and darkness of the astral beings whose pace began to slow slightly.

> Love me in you as I love you in me;
> my soul is yours—
> you live in the center
> of my body of Light
> where I surrender the secret
> of myself to you.

Gormlaith repeated these lines many times. And suddenly she was not alone, for scores of angels, lady masters, spirit beings, and elementals took up the song. In harmonies and tones that exceeded the ability of human throats they sang and sang, repeating both verses together until the hordes of darkness had stopped their relentless progress.

"Keep singing, Gormlaith!" shouted Alana and Dearbhla. "Give us the next verse. We are with you!"

> Touch your heart and feel my hand
> clasping yours—
> tangible, real,
> where you will always find me.

"Where you will always find me," answered the men on the hillsides with the hosts of the Divine Masculine. Twin flames one and all sang to their partners, melding their voices in a resounding chorus that shook the firmament when they all gave voice to the final verse in one mighty chord that proclaimed the reunion of twin flames for Eternity.

> I am with you forever, my darling;
> the radiance that shines
> out from you is also mine—
> we are luminous being
> in Eternity's kiss.

As the song continued echoing across the astral plane, the heavy clouds that had loomed over the battlefield parted. A shaft of golden sunlight pierced the gloom, illumining the amazing sight of waves of demons and other beings who had been under Una's sway weeping and falling to their knees.

For many that had been entrapped by her were actually twin flames of men and angels and spirit beings who were yet singing the song of Divine Love that was cutting them free from Una's oppression.

And that was enough.

Howling with rage, she appeared, standing on the promontory, raising up a wind that lashed her garments and caught her hair up in a wild chaos of tendrils that looked like Medusa's head of snakes.

Una stood hurling curses and calling upon dark forces to destroy her enemies. When she saw that her demonic minions were no longer obeying her, she changed tactics.

Thick clouds swirled around her as she summoned more elemental forces which she had imprisoned with black magic. She was commanding them to bring down bolts of lighting, torrents of rain, walls of fire, and hurricane-force winds upon the armies of Light that opposed her.

But all to no avail.

These evil manifestations did not touch the legions of Spirit who were surrounded with radiant spheres in every color of the rainbow—powerful manifestations of light energy for protection, illumination, healing, selflessness, purity, vision, service, and transmutation that are the gifts of the Divine Mother to her children.

Una was trembling with rage and shouting at a fevered pitch. The louder she screamed her curses, the quicker they fell back upon her until in a final desperate surge of energy, she turned to escape back into the dank canyons where she sought to hide herself again.

But that was not to be.

"Hold!" commanded the Goddess of Truth, who now made herself visible to Una and blocked her path.

"You shall not pass! I declare this day that you, Una, are bound by hosts of the Divine Mother! Your days of infamy are done! Your time of opportunity is up! Angels of Faith, come forth now, and remand this one to the Court of the Sacred Fire."

In a flash that left them breathless, the brave warriors suddenly found themselves assembled at that very Court, once again in the presence of the Four and Twenty Elders.

They were no longer clothed in armor and had returned to their modern appearance. Now joined with their spouses, Sarah and Kevin, Debbie and Jeremy, Glenna and Rory stood shoulder-to-shoulder with other pairs of embodied twin flames too numerous to count.

Debbie looked around the enormous amphitheater-like setting to see that Lady Master Nada, her sister lady masters, and hosts of feminine spirit beings with their twin flames were all seated as observers of the trial which was about to take place.

Although the warriors were desperately weary from the battle they had just fought, they knew they would do their duty and give their individual testimony upon which the Twenty-Four Elders relied when judging the fate of any soul.

However, the Council had a different idea. As cosmic beings who do not operate in a linear fashion, they declared:

> Hear us now. All twin flames of the human realm will simultaneously bear witness. Though you speak at once, we will hear you individually as you declare the truth of your experience with the one called Una. Please begin!

For a moment the many pairs of twin flames hesitated. They had never received such a command. Then an impetus as a ray of Divine Love from the heart of the Council of Elders surged through them and they began to give their testimony.

Men and women alike declared how they had been manipulated, scorned, abused, cursed, murdered, seduced, and bewitched by this soul. Though all tried to maintain their composure, many tears were shed as the myriad woes suffered at the hand of Una were unfolded to the Cosmic Council who listened with intense concentration.

In no time, all witnesses had spoken. Throughout this collective testimony, Una had been standing on the dais, where she heard every word. She was bound in chains and had continued muttering blasphemies, though her power was so depleted that her voice had been reduced to barely a murmur.

The Council spoke, addressing themselves to the masters, angels, elementals, and other spirit beings who had observed the testimony:

> Members of the Great White Brotherhood in Spirit, you have heard the witness of these embodied twin flames. Is their testimony true?

"Aye!" shouted the multitude.

The Four and Twenty Elders then turned their attention to Una and repeated a similar question as they had put to her twin flame only one day earlier:

> Soul of Una, you have heard the testimony of those with whom you have been directly involved for many tens of thousands of years. You are charged with attempting to thwart the purposes of the Great White Brotherhood in our best servants, and even in your own heart of hearts.
>
> How do you respond to the charges that your choices have consistently been to oppose the Light, most virulently in these twin flames? What say you, Una?

Having neither will nor ability to speak, Una curled her lips and spat upon the dais where she was bound. The Council did not hesitate:

> Una, by free will you have arrived at this hour. Prepare to receive the mercy of *An Síoraí*, the Eternal One, whose unconditional Love will try the works of your soul.

This time not one of the observers was surprised when a shaft of white fire descended from the heavens into the form of Una and dissolved her—body, mind, and soul.

Fifty

Friday morning dawned like a world reborn. Fingers of purple and gold and pink and blue flamed across the sky as if to announce a victory for the sons and daughters of *An Síoraí*, the Eternal One, in the overcoming of an ancient foe.

But in the garden room of Lucky and Róisín O'Connor there was no rejoicing. The Twin Flames of Éire, friends and fellow warriors, were gathered at the bedside of their beloved sister, mentor, and devoted disciple of the ascended masters, not knowing if she would live to see another dawn.

They had all returned to their physical bodies just before sunrise and had immediately gone to see Róisín and Lucky. When they arrived Tim O'Toole was sitting with the big Irishman next to the bed they had made for Róisín so she could be surrounded by the healing energies of her garden room. Lucky stood up to hug his great friends.

The room was filled with elementals and angels, each one radiating their special gifts of love and healing to the woman who had supported them with her prayers for many, many lifetimes.

"We sent Maggie home to get some rest," said Tim. "She was with Róisín all night. I told her I'd take over keeping the lad here company."

Sarah smiled. The two middle-aged men still called each other "lad." Indeed, they were young in each other's eyes.

"Were you here all night, too, Lucky?" she asked him.

"I napped a bit once Maggie told me Róisín was stabilized, but I couldn't leave my best friend." He didn't try to hide the tears that filled his bright blue eyes. "We always thought I'd go first, but she's going to beat me across the finish line."

"Do you mean she's . . . " Glenna couldn't finish her sentence.

"Yes, Glenna, darlin'," Lucky nodded. "Róisín is going Home. Right now she's working things out with the Great Lords of Karma who will determine the next steps for her soul. I'm not sure what they're talking about, but I've seen her with those exalted beings."

"What about Kuthumi and Saint Germain?" asked Kevin. "Have you seen either of the masters?"

"K. H. was here before Maggie went for her nap," said Tim. "He told us not to worry. Everything is in divine order. Our girl is completing her inner work for her next initiation. He was very kind and gave us each a blessing. He asked us to take a little break after your battle was over and he spent a good half-hour with Róisín. After that he said Saint Germain would be with her when the time comes."

"You mean when Róisín crosses over," murmured Debbie.

"That's right, darlin'." Lucky reached over and patted her hand.

"Has she gained consciousness at all?" asked Jeremy.

"Not physically, but her soul is very busy." Lucky gazed into the distance. "Before she went off to meet with the Karmic Board she was talking to me and Maggie on the inner. I could tell she really wanted to be fighting with you lasses, but Maggie made her stay put. Said she'd done her part in making sure old Una got what she deserved, though none of us ever wishes for the loss of a soul."

"It's a terrible thing to witness, isn't it?" said Tim, referring to the ritual of the second death.

"It is." All six twin flames agreed, and everyone was quiet as they contemplated the astonishing events they had witnessed in the past twenty-four hours.

"Lucky, do you have any idea how long Róisín will remain as she is now?" asked Sarah

"She's always been a big fan of Saint Brendan the Navigator. I have a feeling she'll take off with him on Sunday. 'Tis his feast day."

"Then can we relieve you over the next forty-eight hours?" offered Debbie.

"You can, and I think Róisín would like that. Tim and I are good for this morning. You six go home for now. Figure out your shifts and come back starting this afternoon. I expect our sweet girl will have some advice for you when you listen real careful-like."

Lucky's brogue was thickening as stress and fatigue were obviously wearing on him. Nevertheless, he was still their stalwart leader.

"Tim and I have a few things to work out. Kevin, I'd like for you and Sarah to take the first shift. And would you bring Brian with you? I need to speak with him while you're sitting with Róisín."

And so they carried on all day Friday and on through the night. Maggie returned later in the day, and other long-time members of the Friends of Ancient Wisdom took turns sitting with Róisín.

In fact, once word got out that she was making her transition, a steady stream of visitors came to sit with her for a while, to pray, to sing, to talk to her soul, and to tell her how much she'd meant to them. And to listen.

For this was a group of people who knew how to listen with the ear of the heart. And none were disappointed, for it seemed that everyone had enjoyed their own unique connection with Róisín. Which meant she had a special message for each one that she generously communicated to them on the inner.

Debbie and Jeremy were having breakfast in their apartment after covering an early Saturday morning shift in the garden room.

They had come away profoundly moved by the message Róisín had conveyed to them of her love and appreciation for the perseverance that had brought them together to complete the mandala of the Twin Flames of Éire. She was especially grateful for Debbie's adherence to the discipline she had given her and for Jeremy's courage in allowing his inner sight to open.

"You two are a great joy to me," she'd told them. "My precious seers. Debbie, I've told Lucky and Kevin that I want you to run the coffee shop for me. You'll see everything and everyone there, so you'll always know who needs your help."

"You know I will do anything for you, Róisín," Debbie had said, mustering a smile. "And I promise to keep your baristas in line. I can only hope to guide them with a love as profound as yours."

Róisín had treated her helpers with a mother's devotion that was forgiving, yet firm. She'd once commented that she was training souls. Debbie knew her mentor would expect that training to continue. She held Róisín's hand as her friend and adopted mother continued to speak.

"Jeremy, you take care of my Debbie, as you always have. A seer needs to be seen. Never lose sight of each other, dear ones. Embody the wisdom of your mandala, as Glenna and Rory embody its love, and Kevin and Sarah bring the power you will need to complete your mission. And don't worry. I'll be as close as a prayer."

A bright May morning was beaming outside, but neither Debbie nor Jeremy was motivated to go for a walk or do anything around their apartment. Today was a day for contemplation and maintaining an inner connection with the soul of their dear Róisín and with their mandala.

"You know the most amazing thing to me about the battle we went through?" Jeremy had his arm about Debbie's shoulder as they sat together on their living room sofa.

"The whole experience was beyond amazing to me," she replied. "Did something in particular stand out for you?"

He nodded, still remembering.

"The entire time I was positioned on that hillside with the other men, praying for you and your sister warriors and directing light energy to keep you strong and safe, the overwhelming vibration I detected from the lady masters, and especially from the angels, was forgiveness."

"Really? I guess I was too busy fighting. I could feel such a ferocity flowing through me. And a powerful determination to stay alive and roll back those astral hordes."

"That's understandable. I felt the same. With my entire being I was determined that you would be victorious. And all of your spirit cohorts were focused and fierce."

"They were. Fighting alongside legions of angels is not something I will soon forget. Not one of them ever entertained a possibility other than victory. They were completely uncompromising."

"I got that. And at the same time there was no anger in them. No sense of revenge or retaliation. None of that eye-for-an-eye consciousness of them being judge and jury."

"That's right," said Debbie. "Because of you're angry, you sink to the lower vibration of the ones you're battling."

"Exactly. Their response was almost mathematical, but not in a mechanical or unfeeling way. I could sense the power of their emotional bodies urging each other and all of you women to keep fighting. What I'm trying to describe is like what I go through when I'm balancing a ledger. In this case, they were stripping away darkness and adding light to tip a balance scale. Like setting right a situation that was out of kilter."

"I see what you mean," said Debbie thoughtfully. "They had a job to do and they were doing it. It was impersonal in a principle-based way.

"Right. As they conquered wave after wave of demons, witches, and sorceresses, I could feel them forgiving the energy that had gone astray and loving it back into alignment. It was as if every misqualified atom of energy was a wayward child of *An Síoraí*, the Eternal One, and they were guiding those children back home to a loving parent."

"What an amazing realization."

"I know. I'm still blown away. When many of the attackers began to weep and fall to their knees while we were all singing, I could feel the spirit cohorts rejoicing. I knew I was witnessing a true miracle of the Brotherhood's unconditional Love. And for the first time I was understanding what that really means."

"That is so beautiful, Jeremy. There's something else on your mind, isn't there?"

"There is. I've realized that I need to see my parents. I want to forgive them, and I hope you'll come with me. Will you?"

"Of course. When shall we go?"

"I'd like to call them now and ask them to see us today. I think that my offering forgiveness, adding a bit of that vibration to the world, could make a difference for the inner work that Róisín is doing while she makes her transition."

"Make the call, my love. I'll be ready whenever you say."

Fifty-One

Jeremy's parents didn't live far from Penn Station, so he and Debbie decided to take the Long Island Railroad into Manhattan.

"It's a good day to walk," he said. "The exercise will help calm my nerves and I can show you some of the blocks that were my favorite routes around the city."

"Like a full-size holiday train show, but without the trains." Debbie was trying to keep things light, even as they both kept their hearts tuned to Róisín.

"Exactly."

"What do you think you'll see when you greet your parents?"

"I'm not sure. But I know I won't be frightened."

Before leaving their apartment, they had prayed very hard to Archangel Michael to seal their third eyes against any negative energy.

"That's the other thing about the battle." Jeremy picked up his thoughts from earlier. "Watching those waves of demons, beasts, witches, and sorceresses, I was never frightened. I knew they weren't real. More like mechanized shells of negative energy that my compatriots and I had the spiritual power to dispel."

"That's a huge victory, Jeremy."

"It is. Let's see if this meeting will be as well."

The elder Maddens had moved into a smaller apartment once Jeremy and his sister had left home. She lived in another city now, was married with a child and a husband who apparently did not encourage visits with her parents. They would not be joining today's conversation.

"Hello, Jeremiah," said Josiah Madden when he opened the apartment door and indicated they should enter. Maeve Madden stood behind him, neither smiling nor speaking. She looked warily at her son and his wife.

Debbie immediately understood where Jeremy got his height. Both parents were taller than average. But unlike the robust good health of their son, they appeared wan, almost wraith-like, gaunt and grey.

"Father. Mother." Jeremy shook hands with his father and nodded to his mother. He could tell that she didn't want him to touch her. "Thank you for letting us stop by on such short notice. This is my wife, Debbie."

"Hello, Mr. and Mrs. Madden." She did not venture to shake hands.

"May we sit down?" asked Jeremy. "We won't stay long, but I'd like to talk to you." He was surprised at the lack of hospitality, especially from his mother. She had drilled good manners into him from an early age, but now was demonstrating none.

"Of course, be seated." Josiah gestured toward what proved to be a very uncomfortable brown fabric sofa while he and Mrs. Madden each sat on a straight-backed chair across from Debbie and Jeremy.

"What do you want?" demanded Maeve abruptly.

Debbie was watching the woman closely. She was surprised to realize that her only response was one of compassion. Mrs. Madden's aura was the murky color Jeremy had described with flecks of orange and red that spoke of irritation and anger. Most remarkable were the dark shades of fear and guilt.

The woman is afraid that her son has come to get even with what she knows she did wrong in raising him, thought Debbie. Nothing could be further from the truth.

"I want to set things right between us, Mother," said Jeremy.

Debbie could see that he was consciously using the vocal pitch and intonation of kindness and cordiality they had learned from spending time with F. M. Bellamarre and Master K. H. His aura was holding steady with a rosy-violet glow. That was a good sign.

"I came to tell you that I believe you thought how you raised me was the right away. I realized that if you never learned to love—as I suspect you didn't, knowing your parents—you would have had no capacity to love a child you didn't understand."

He paused briefly. There was no response, so he continued.

"I have found love in my wife and in my community. That love has dissolved the anger I felt toward you for most of my life. I want you both to know that I'm no longer angry at you, or about my life. Whether or not you can accept the forgiveness that I am here to extend to you today does not affect the fullness of love I feel for you in my heart."

Still no response. Jeremy's parents did not look at each other and he was not sure they were actually seeing him. Their eyes had taken on a glazed appearance that made him wonder if they were entirely present in consciousness.

"I don't know if you remember my telling you once that the universe is made of Love. I know that to be truer now than when I first encountered that unconditional acceptance of my soul. I hope you will believe me when I say that I forgive all of us for not being a family of mutual caring and respect. Some people just don't know how."

Debbie could feel the enormous effort her husband was putting forth to reach the souls of his parents. She visualized him surrounded in violet light to help him stay in a vibration of forgiveness.

"I leave it to you to decide what you were or were not capable of expressing. For me, all that is in the past. I'm working to make sure I don't carry resentment or anger into my marriage and the life that Debbie and I are making together."

He paused again. Surely they would have something to say after he had just poured out his heart to them. Then he remembered the time he did that after K. H. had taken him traveling to the stars. That's when they had decided to put him on behavior-controlling drugs. He would not let himself be disappointed this time.

"That's all I have to say, except that I always wanted to feel love for you as my parents. Now I'm pleased that I do."

"You were never an easy child," Josiah said quietly.

"I know," said Jeremy. "And you were never an easy father."

That brought a partial smile to his father's lips. "Fair enough."

That's probably the closet thing to an apology I'll get, Jeremy thought to himself, and realized that was enough. He hadn't come for an apology, but to forgive. He was about to be surprised.

"Jeremy," his mother began. She had never called him anything other than Jeremiah, and even then she had rarely said his name.

"Yes, Mother." He had to work to steady his voice.

"Jeremy, I am sorry." She appeared to want to say more, then thought better of it. Instead she stood stiffly and hurried from the room.

An expression of acute distress passed over Josiah's face. He started to follow Maeve, then sat back in his chair and looked pleadingly at his son and daughter-in-law."

"That's okay, Father. We'll let ourselves out. Go find out what she needs. Please thank her for me. What she said means a lot. Thanks for seeing us."

"You're welcome, son." Josiah stood and rather awkwardly took the hand of the young man he had never once called "son."

"It was good to see you and to meet your wife." He nodded to her. "Deborah."

Before exiting the room, he briefly shook Debbie's hand. She noticed it was damp. He had also been frightened. That fear had not shown as obviously in the muddy colors of his aura, and now she noticed a faint change in hue that might indicate a feeling of affection—if one were very generous in their observation.

Once they were outside, Jeremy and Debbie held on tight to one another, steadying each other until they felt grounded. When she reached up to brush a lock of hair from his forehead, he took her hand and briskly led her away from the dingy apartment building.

"Let's go to Union Square," he said as they walked. "It's not far and there's a café where we can talk. I need something to eat."

"I know the place," agreed Debbie. She said no more until they were seated with large mugs of coffee in front of them and a piece of apple pie that was big enough to share.

"Thoughts?" Jeremy asked her after he'd eaten several bites of pie.

"They are a completely different evolution from you, my love. I can see why they never understood you. And you have my undying admiration for surviving growing up in that atmosphere.

"I know you said they frightened you, and I can believe it. But I think they were more frightened of you. Or the dark spirits that inhabit them were intimidated by your light."

The look of gratitude in Jeremy's eyes told her he had been freed from another curse. She went on.

"Anyway, they certainly have nothing to do with who you are, even if they are the pair who birthed you. They are not the source of your life and certainly not of your light. I am so proud of you."

"Thank you." Jeremy breathed an enormous sigh and sat back to take a long sip of coffee. "I wanted you to experience for yourself what I've described. I didn't realize that I needed my recollections validated, but I did."

"Yes, I saw the truth of all you've told me." She looked into his eyes and furrowed her brow. "We don't have to go back there, do we?"

"No." He drew out the word and shook his head. "There's no reason for us to go back, because I'm free. I wasn't kidding when I said I love them. I could feel myself saying that to whatever vestiges of the Light of *An Síoraí* might be animating their beings.

"I don't know if they have souls. If they do, I can also love that part of them, however buried it may be. Whatever else they are, I leave up to the Divine. But my soul is free now to love my wife and my friends who are my true family."

Debbie's eyes danced as she gazed at this man she was falling more in love with every day.

"And now, do you know what I want?" said Jeremy with a grin. His aura began to sparkle as it hadn't all day.

"No, I can't imagine." Debbie returned his playful expression.

"That last bite of pie."

"You've earned it, my love," she laughed. "Enjoy your pie. Then let's go home. I believe we're being called back to Fibonacci's for whatever is next."

Fifty-Two

For several months before the great battle, Róisín had been referring to Glenna and Rory as her lovebirds. She had found their unabashed mutual affection entirely refreshing and important for the community of Friends.

"Don't ever lose your joy in each other," she admonished them on the inner during the hours they spent at her side in the garden room. "Others are inspired and nurtured by your example. Sing to them like the true bards you are, especially when days are dark. Offer them love songs and drive away the gloom.

"Your love is like water to thirsty plants, a balm to souls who are discouraged or depressed. I want you always to be a reminder to the community of how much I love them. They may not see me, but they will see you, and they will remember.

"Tell new students the stories of the lessons you have learned and of the adventures we have shared. That is how we will live on, long after Fibonacci's has become a wisp of memory. Our stories keep us alive, dear ones. Tell them and our love will go on forever."

"We will, Róisín, we promise," they vowed to her and to each other.

Kevin and Sarah were the last of the three couples to spend time with Róisín while her soul was communicating from inner planes. They were sitting with her in the wee hours of Sunday morning.

They had their nine-and-a-half-month-old babies with them. These two souls had let their parents know they also had a special tie with Róisín and should not be left in the care of others during her transition.

They were sleeping peacefully in their stroller, but they had been actively babbling to Róisín for quite some time. Now that they were asleep, Sarah and Kevin were paying very close attention to the figure resting on the divan before them.

"I can't help thinking she looks like Sleeping Beauty," observed Sarah. Yesterday she and Maggie had gently bathed Róisín's body and dressed her in a seamless silk gown that glistened whenever daylight or candlelight fell upon the delicate fabric.

"Yes, she does," agreed Kevin. Then a thought occurred to him. "I wonder if her twin flame is watching what's going on here."

"I would hope so," said Sarah, "but I don't know. Róisín has said only that he abides in the Great Silence as an ascended master. I don't know if such exalted beings can view the activities of earth from that plane, or if we are as invisible to them as they are to us."

"Knowing what I know about the heart connection of twin flames," Kevin looked lovingly at his wife, "I cannot imagine that he is not beaming his own radiance to Róisín across the silver cord that has surely connected them since the beginning."

Sarah felt her heart burn with love as she returned his gaze.

"I know she has worked very hard in these last few years to balance her own karma and fulfill her reason for being so she could join him at the end of this embodiment. She has hinted to Debbie, Glenna, and me that Saint Germain has been very generous in his instruction so she could win her ascension. I pray that her great sacrifice in the final undoing of Una's wickedness will be the deciding factor in her favor."

"Do you suppose that's what she's been discussing with the Karmic Board?" suggested Kevin.

"I wouldn't be surprised. But these are mysteries we probably will never know until it's our turn. Which I hope will not be for many years."

Sarah suddenly remembered the many incarnations in which she and Kevin had lost each other, one going out of embodiment much sooner than the other. *Please, An Síoraí, let us stay together to raise our children,* she prayed in her heart.

And then she heard her name called on the inner. Their friend and mentor was active again.

"Yes, Róisín, I am here," she answered.

"And I," said Kevin. He had heard Róisín also speak his name.

"My brave druids, a torch will be passed to you soon, my dears. Lucky will be retiring and I am on my way Home. Promise me that you will guide Fibonacci's with all the love and wisdom and right use of power you have gained. This is a sacred trust, my dears.

"Carry my love in your hearts as I will always carry yours in mine. You have been more precious to me than any children I might have borne.

"Raise your own children well. The hope of the future rests in them and their cousins and the babes who will join them. We of the Great White Brotherhood are more grateful than you can imagine that you came to us when you did.

"Be strong, dear ones. And remember me always."

She paused for a moment and somehow both Sarah and Kevin knew that this would be her last spoken communication with them.

"Wake my man for me, won't you darlin'?" she said to Sarah. "It's time I was on my way."

Sarah moved quickly to Lucky's bedroom where he was resting, fully clothed in case she or Kevin should call him. They had insisted that he go to sleep in his own room with the promise that they would wake him if Róisín's condition changed. Sarah gently knocked on the door.

"Lucky, it's time. You'd best come now. Róisín has asked for you."

He hurried to her side. As he knelt close to her and took her hand, she opened her luminous green eyes and whispered to her best friend and cherished soul mate, "*Go raibh míle maith agat, a chara dhílis.*"

Then she closed her eyes and slipped away.

While Sarah was waking Lucky, Kevin had sent a telepathic message to the other Twin Flames of Éire who were already sensing a shift in the energy at the garden room. Within minutes, Debbie, Jeremy, Glenna, and Rory arrived along with Tim and Maggie.

K. H. had appeared even before Kevin sent out the call to his mandala of twin flames. The Master was speaking quietly with Lucky as they sat beside Róisín's body, each holding one of her hands.

At the same time, all of those Friends of Ancient Wisdom who had kept vigil with Róisín since Friday received the message on the inner that their dear friend had crossed from this world to the next.

There had already been some discussion of when and how a memorial service might take place, so the Friends were not surprised when they received the prompting to immediately go into deep meditation and follow the direction that would come to them in their finer bodies.

A stillness settled over the entire community as each one entered into profound communion with *An Síoraí*, the Eternal One. These were the times for which they had prepared. They meant to do their utmost in support of Róisín and whatever action the Brotherhood planned to accomplish in this hour of her soul's final journey.

"You may come in now." K. H. summoned the four couples from the room where they had been waiting in order to give the Master and Lucky time alone with Róisín.

"I have explained to Lucky that our dear friend has earned the double victory of her ascension—the wedding of her soul to the Presence of the I AM that is her Higher Self and eternal reunion with her ascended twin flame. The Karmic Board has decreed that there be no delay in the ritual which we will witness on inner levels.

"Please arrange yourselves in the circle as we have done in previous rituals. Lucky will be positioned at Róisín's feet. I will be here at her head. Men on my right, women on my left. We will be seated for this ritual so you may be comfortable in leaving your bodies."

As soon as they were in place, K. H. explained:

As you are sensing, members of our Friends of Ancient Wisdom are now in deep meditation. The ten of us here plus the two babies will form an inner circle of oneness that will radiate out to them so that all may behold the ritual that will take place.

Please sit comfortably. Place your attention on your heart as we sound the OM together. Allow your consciousness to rise and do not be surprised by anything you see or experience.

You may feel a sensation of traveling. Please keep your eyes closed until I ask you to open them. Allow yourselves to flow with the ritual and participate if you are directed to do so.

OMMMMM, they chanted. Immediately they heard the voices of their community members joining on the inner, invoking great light. They felt themselves lifting from their bodies and traveling quickly. When the Master instructed them to open their eyes, this is what they saw:

They had entered a vast cathedral made entirely of crystalline substance that shone like diamonds. The walls were almost completely translucent so that soft, ethereal light flooded through them from all directions, creating rainbows that flickered and danced as if animated by the gentlest of breezes.

The cathedral was laid out like an enormous cross with entrances at the far end of each arm, so that anyone entering would be under the impression that they were walking down the main aisle of the sanctuary.

Seating for hundreds, if not thousands, was available in long pews that were richly upholstered in shades of violet, ruby, blue, and gold. All faced toward the center of the cross where a circular altar was raised with seven steps on each side.

Within the circle at the top of the altar was a dais created in the shape of a Maltese Cross, inlaid entirely in amethyst crystal with a disc of pure gold in the center.

Above the altar was an enormous dome that appeared to have been fashioned of gold and yellow diamonds. Around the bottom of the dome where it rested upon the walls of the sanctuary was a balcony. Here were seated the Four and Twenty Elders in their glorious white robes and golden crowns. They would be overseeing the ritual.

All of the guests were clothed in white. Some wore robes. Several of the women had donned white gowns, and their male escorts wore white suits. Many pairs of twin flames were in attendance, though not all guests were accompanied by their soul's counterpart.

Kevin and Sarah were seated close to the altar with their children, Gareth and Naimh, and the other Twin Flames of Éire. Lucky was with them, flanked by Tim and Maggie. There were many familiar faces in the congregation, which filled the pews on all four arms, and many more they did not know who had personal ties with Róisín.

Delicate harp music had been playing as the guests took their seats.

As soon as all was in readiness, the soul-stirring chords of the "Wedding March" could be heard coming from a magnificent pipe organ. Its numerous pipes were positioned around the perimeter of the dome so the exquisite sound came from all directions, enfolding the congregation in tones at once inspiring and transformative.

Everyone turned to see Róisín beginning her procession down the eastern aisle on the arm of Saint Germain. The solemnity and grandeur of the Master's Presence was breathtaking, and Róisín was as radiant as the most beautiful bride on her wedding day.

Indeed, she was dressed as a bride. Her seamless white gown had been transformed. It now included a long train and was embroidered with ancient Celtic and other occult symbols.

She was not veiled. Instead she wore a circlet of yellow diamonds in her lustrous white hair. She carried a bouquet containing a dozen violet roses which cascaded nearly to the floor.

When she and Saint Germain reached the bottom altar step, a young attendant received the bouquet from her. The Master lovingly placed his hands on her head and gave her a blessing that only she could hear.

Then the Four and Twenty Elders asked, "Who sponsors this candidate for the ascension?"

Saint Germain bowed and answered, "I do, my Lords. I present to you my faithful disciple, Róisín."

She raised her head as the Council of Elders spoke:

Daughter Róisín, we greet you and we bless you. By the grace of An Síoraí, the Eternal One, and your own perseverance, you have come to this hour. The Great White Brotherhood thanks you for your service and urges you to greater works that may flow from your many gifts. Are you prepared to take this final initiation to which you have aspired for many incarnations?

"I am," she responded simply.

Then step upon the dais as the sacred fire tries the works of your embodied soul. May you be found worthy of the ascension.

All in you which is of the Light will be preserved as that which is not will be consumed.

Standing in the center of the altar, Róisín spread her arms in total receptivity and lovingly gazed up to the heavens. A look of ecstasy shone on her face as a shaft of pure white light enfolded her form in a radiant shower that sparkled as it spiraled around her body.

As the ascension currents spun faster and faster in and around her, all vestiges of age disappeared until she bore the visage of a vibrant young woman in the prime of life.

This process went on for several minutes, Róisín's form becoming more and more translucent. At last the sacred fire diminished, leaving her standing in the same attitude, arms outstretched. But now her figure was no longer human. She had become a living flame.

In that moment, the roof of the great dome opened, revealing a golden firmament. More exquisite organ music could be heard, now accompanying angelic voices who announced the arrival of Róisín's twin flame.

A resplendent, white-robed man, with the golden hair and flashing emerald green eyes of eternal youth, was slowly emerging from the Great Silence to meet his bride in the air.

As he was descending, she was rising. They met at the base of the dome, where they hovered momentarily. Together they bowed to the Twenty-Four Elders and Róisín melted into the arms of her soul's own glorious twin.

Instantly they were surrounded by a sphere of blazing white light, so bright that the congregation could scarcely look at it, though every pair of eyes was fixed on the magnificent scene before them.

The sphere of light began to rise now, enfolding Róisín and her beloved. And as they were gradually carried into the heavens, her twin flame could be heard singing to her this song of Divine Love.

So perfectly joined are our two souls
that distance is a thing of the past
and separation an event
that never happened.

You are meeting me at last, my beloved,
at Home, where I have always been,
waiting for you to become one
with the fullness of my Love.

We shine as luminous starlight.
I bask in the radiance of your Presence.
We are one as we were always meant to be;
and I rejoice that now you know
with your whole body, mind, and spirit
the truth of our indelible bond.

Saint Germain had been standing off to the side of the altar. He now stepped forward to address the congregation.

Dear Friends, today there is a new star in the heavens, our own Ascended Lady Master Róisín. You are now free to call to her for guidance and support from the realms of Spirit, even as she has been caring for you in the physical these many years.

You may also call to her twin flame, although he has not yet released his name. He has promised to do so very soon for those who listen with their hearts.

May *An Síoraí*, the Eternal One, bless you each one in the unity of your own soul's twin. And may you know the eternal, unconditional Love of our Great White Brotherhood of Light which we bestow upon you this day in profound gratitude for your unfailing service.

Following Saint Germain's blessing, the Twin Flames of Éire plus Tim and Maggie and Lucky felt themselves gently returning to their physical bodies.

When they opened their eyes, K. H. was gone and so was Róisín's body. All that remained on the divan where she had lain for three nights was a bouquet of eleven of the dozen violet roses she had carried.

They all stood quietly for several minutes, staring at the flowers and inhaling the unmistakable fragrance of roses that filled the garden room.

Tim and Maggie were standing together, observing the scene before them. They had attended other ascension rituals, but Róisín's was the most deeply moving they had witnessed in many a year.

"I guess our dear K. H. took his rose with him," said Debbie, turning to gaze up at Jeremy.

"That leaves one for each of us, including the babies." He reached down and brushed back a lock of flaxen hair that had fallen across her brow.

"I think I'll press our roses when we get home," said Sarah softly. "I'm going to need a memento of this experience to prove to myself it really happened. And I'll want a tangible reminder for when Gareth and Naimh are older."

"Witnessing the incredible blessing that Róisín achieved gives you something to aim for, doesn't it?" said Glenna. She leaned back against Rory when he stepped behind her and put his arms around her waist.

Lucky nodded and began handing out the roses his beloved soul mate had left behind. "Yes, it does, darlin'. Yes, it does."

Fifty-Three

The next two weeks were a time of mixed emotions and round-the-clock activity for the Friends of Ancient Wisdom. Preparations for the grand re-opening of Fibonacci's bookstore and coffee shop were well underway and everyone was fully engaged in their responsibilities.

At the same time, all were profoundly aware of the physical absence of their beloved Róisín. They did their best to remind each other of the incredibly uplifting experience they had shared at her ascension service. And still, eyes welled up and tears were shed over the dozens of little reminders of the wisdom and love that had poured out to each of them in the course of simply being around her.

In these busy times, Lucky showed himself to be their masterful leader, a true adept in their midst. No one had more reason to mourn the passing of Róisín than her husband and soul mate. And there was no doubt that he did grieve. Yet, these days, he emanated an aura of joy and confidence in the rightness of her soul's path that raised the spirits of all who interacted with him—which appeared to be anyone who had occasion to stop by Fibonacci's.

Rather than secluding himself, as some thought he might, he seemed to be everywhere at once—inspecting final remodeling tasks, encouraging the workers, offering suggestions for the grand opening festivities, putting an understanding arm around a tearful friend, and assuring everyone he spoke to that all was well with Róisín.

Lucky had always maintained such a low profile around the bookstore and coffee shop that some of Fibonacci's more casual visitors had no idea of the man's deep connection with the ascended masters.

Yet it was this spiritual communion that sustained him now. And he generously shared it with those who were taking on more responsibility at the businesses he had opened in answer to Saint Germain's request for an outpost of the Great White Brotherhood on Long Island.

Three days after Róisín's ascension, he called a meeting of the Twin Flames of Éire, Tim and Maggie O'Toole, Brian Callahan, Cyndi and Phelan. As the ballroom remodel was complete, they gathered beneath the great sun disc that had been polished to gleaming and placed over a beautiful new altar.

"*A chairde*, my friends," Lucky began, "my heart overflows with gratitude to each of you. As you can imagine, my life is changing. And because we are all one, so is yours." His blue eyes were bright with humor. "I wanted you to hear about the changes as a group so you can reassure our Friends that all is in divine order.

"Since before our dear Róisín left us . . ." He blew out a breath and paused to collect himself. "Since before our dear Róisín left us, Brian, Kevin, and I have been working on plans for my future and yours." He pulled out a sheet of paper from a jacket pocket and read:

"First, Kevin will assume oversight of daily operations for both the Fibonacci's businesses. Rory will manage the bookstore. Debbie will run the coffee shop—which all of you dear ones have agreed should be renamed "Róisín's." The group applauded and many hands went to their hearts.

"Next, I am moving all of my assets into a trust with Tim and Kevin as trustees." This they had not expected. Lucky had certainly been busy.

"And I'm selling my house to Cyndi and Phelan, who have given me the massive privilege of announcing that they will be married as soon as Glenna can organize the ceremony!"

Everyone laughed and cheered their congratulations.

"Now, before you go thinking that I'm leaving you, the great Tim and Maggie have invited me to live with them, so they can keep an eye on me." He chuckled. "And so I can concentrate on a couple of projects the Brotherhood has assigned me before I can follow sweet Róisín's example and join my own ascended twin flame."

The room was silent as Lucky's friends wondered how long those assignments might take. They were in no hurry for him to leave them.

"Those are my announcements for today, my dears. We'll see more changes in coming weeks, but this should keep us busy for a while."

Grateful for his touch of mirth, they all laughed at the understate-ment. He read their thoughts and sought to comfort them.

"I can tell you that Róisín and her twin flame are looking upon you with immense gratitude for all you have accomplished and for all that *will* be accomplished here. I pray you will feel our love every single day. May *An Síoraí*, the Eternal One, bless you each one."

Excited conversation broke out as Lucky concluded his remarks. So many surprises and blessings had the group bubbling over with amaze-ment. The sale of Lucky's house to Cyndi and Phelan was one of the biggest surprises. It came about this way:

A day earlier Brian Callahan had asked Cyndi to come to his office. He wasn't looking forward to the conversation. He never liked to disappoint people, but this was likely to be one of those unavoidable instances.

"Thanks for coming in, Cyndi," he began. "I'm sure you've noticed that work has slowed on the remodel for your health food store. Now that only a few punch-list items remain to be completed before the grand re-opening of Fibonacci's, I was hoping we could speed things along. But we've hit a snag."

Cyndi had learned that Brian didn't like to be interrupted when he was laying out business details, so she let him continue.

"The signage came in for your store this morning, but instead of it reading 'Conroy's To Your Health' it says 'Conway's To Your Health'. I promise we'll . . . " That's as far as he got because Cyndi started to laugh so hard that tears ran down her face.

"Well, that's not the reaction I expected," declared Brian, clearly perplexed. "What's so funny?"

"All I can say is that *An Síoraí*, the Eternal One, works in mysterious and wonderful ways," said Cyndi, wiping her eyes with a tissue.

"How so?"

"I came in here not knowing how I was going to tell you that I've decided to sell my business."

"Really?"

"Yes. To my employee Stacey and her husband, Stan. She approached me the other day to say that she'd received a sizable inheritance from an aunt, and would I let her know if I ever wanted to sell the business. Stan recently lost his job and he loves the store as much as she does."

"Do you want to sell?"

"I do. Debbie and I have been talking about the coffee shop. She's going to be running it for Kevin, and I want to help her. If Stacey buys the store, I'll be free to do that and I'll have enough money for Phelan and me to purchase Lucky's house.

"Debbie said that one of us needs to maintain Róisín's garden room. Apparently, that's me. You'll like Stacey and Stan. They're very interested in the Friends of Ancient Wisdom, so they'll fit right in."

"That's great," said Brian, "but it doesn't solve the sign problem. I'll have to get on that right away."

"Yes, it does solve the problem, Brian. That's what's so funny."

"Why is that?"

"Stacey's last name is Conway!"

Other big changes were taking place in the lives of Lucky's friends.

Later that week, while Cyndi began transferring the health food store to the Conways, Glenna and Debbie were working together at Róisín's Coffee Shop. They were arranging tins of teas and coffees on shelves and preparing display cabinets for the fresh baked goods and lunch items that would fill them on opening day.

Glenna was humming happily and smiling to herself. Finally Debbie could no longer hold in the question she'd been wanting to ask for days. She stopped what she was doing and turned to her friend.

"Okay, my secretive Glenna, you cannot tell me now that you're not pregnant. You're glowing and humming what I'm certain is a lullaby. Fess up, darlin'—as Róisín would say. I promise I won't tell anyone, but I have to know. Do you have a little one coming?"

Glenna's face was a sunbeam. "Probably." She grinned and scrunched up her shoulders like a bashful schoolgirl. She set down her dust rag and perched on one of the bar stools. Debbie joined her.

"I wasn't going to say anything until I was certain, but I'm glad you asked. I have a confession and I didn't know how to bring it up."

"What could you possibly have to confess?"

"The night you and Jeremy were under attack from Una, Rory and I had our minds on other things." She blushed all the way to the tips of her ears.

"Glenna, that is so sweet."

"It was, and apparently we were successful, if you know what I mean. Anyway, for some time now I've wondered—if we hadn't been otherwise engaged—would we have tuned in to your needing our help?"

Debbie shook her head. "That's a very generous thought, but I don't think so. I'm sure that attack and our response to it was our initiation."

"That's what Maggie O'Toole told me," said Glenna. "I ran into her the other day and blurted out my question. She reminded me that each of us has to paddle our own canoe, even if the whole mandala is navigating the same river."

"Very true," Debbie agreed. "We support one another, but we're not responsible for each other's tests. We may go through certain initiations as a mandala, but this wasn't one of them—except for the brilliant way that you and Rory helped Jeremy and me come to resolution. We'll be forever grateful for your love and determination to stay with us while we talked things out."

"You know you are very, very welcome." Glenna reached over and took Debbie's hand. "We are family forever."

"So, did Maggie tune into your possibly being pregnant?"

"She did. That's the main reason I'm actually sure. She looked at my belly and said, 'You were right to keep your own timetable, my girl. You and your man. You'll make fine parents.' Isn't that kind of her?"

"It is. Then I'll wish you congratulations now, and I won't breathe a word to anybody until you're ready to announce your news."

"Let's get Fibonacci's opened and Cyndi and Phelan married first. Then we can talk about babies." Glenna laughed at herself. "I think I'd better start a new checklist."

"What if we just tell Sarah?" coaxed Debbie. Glenna smiled and picked up her cell phone to dial their friend.

Fifty-Four

At last Grand Re-Opening Weekend arrived. Public events were taking place all day Saturday through Sunday morning. Sunday afternoon was reserved for a private memorial service to celebrate the life of Róisín with her Friends of Ancient Wisdom.

On Saturday morning, when scores of customers poured through the doors of Róisín's Coffee Shop, Debbie and Cyndi and their team of baristas were prepared for the onslaught. Urns of regular and decaf coffee were full. Pots of hot water for tea were boiled.

Display cases were brimming with delicious baked goods. Dozens more servings and an abundance of lunch items were ready to bring out from the kitchen as needed.

Lucky was happily manning the new, longer coffee bar. He kept up a steady flow of jokes and conversation to entertain the large crowd that clustered around, simply to be in his vibrant aura. Tim and Maggie were bussing tables and having a grand time visiting with customers.

In the bookstore, Kevin, Rory, Jeremy, and Phelan were busy ringing up sales and answering questions about the new and used books that were discounted for the weekend. They were very encouraged that the esoterica collection, which was on full display in the expanded loft, was drawing a sizable number of genuine enthusiasts.

Later in the afternoon the Pythagoreans would be delivering a presentation on some fascinating aspects of their favorite philosopher's life and times. They looked forward to inaugurating the lounge which was now large enough for several dozen people to gather for lectures, book club meetings, and other community events.

Rudy and Tony were wending their way through the crowds, taking pictures, interviewing customers, sampling the food, and generally having more fun than they could ever remember having in their lives.

Tony had decided to open his own marketing and PR company with Rudy as his business partner. They were starting small, but today's event would certainly give them a boost. Brian was their first client and they were determined to impress him with their ability to capture the excitement at Fibonacci's and build on it for the future.

They got their best photos upstairs in the ballroom where Sarah, Ivy, Glenna, and Sarah's parents had assembled an indoor playground for children of all ages, including some adults who joined in the fun.

Patrick Callahan was leading kinesthetic activities with his grandchildren, Kerry and Kaitlyn, as eager participants. His wife, Eileen, was supervising jigsaw puzzles.

Ivy was facilitating a number of computer games. Sarah had designed some word games and was keeping an eye on the table she had established for children and adults who wanted to write. Glenna was teaching a group of little ones to sing and dance.

Later that afternoon, she and Sarah would be telling stories until dinner time, when the indoor playground would close so the ballroom could be re-set for the much-anticipated dance with Irish music they were holding that night. They expected a large crowd. Fortunately, the new, larger ballroom would be more than able to accommodate everyone who wanted to attend.

And so it was that Saturday flew by in a blur of food, fun, and fellowship. Everyone fell into bed that night, well spent and delighted with their first day in the new location.

By the time the last customer departed midday on Sunday, they knew the opening had been a rousing success. Everyone who had worked that weekend was assembled in the coffee shop to celebrate.

Lucky's aura was bright as the sun and his blue eyes were full of joy. "We've got a winner!" he proclaimed to loud applause, cheers, and mutual congratulations.

"You've outdone yourselves, my dear friends. I can't thank you enough except to say that the masters, Róisín, and I will never forget your hard work and your determination to bring Fibonacci's back to a newer and more abundant life.

"Now, if you lads will help me set up chairs in the ballroom, we'll be ready to welcome the many Friends who are coming to remember our darling lass."

Every seat was filled and every heart was full to overflowing with love for their friends, the masters who had established this outpost of the Great White Brotherhood, and for the woman who had embodied the spirit of community so naturally they had taken for granted that she would always be among them.

Now that she was not, they had all gathered to pay their respects, to honor Lucky, and to vow in their hearts to carry on the mission that Róisín and her devoted soul mate had so masterfully begun in an unassuming bookstore and coffee shop.

Kevin had invited everyone in the community to write something about their experiences with Róisín so their remembrances could be compiled in a book. A few long-time Friends would speak today.

Debbie and Jeremy were sitting toward the front of the congregation along a side aisle. She would be offering her thoughts about Róisín after the other Friends and before Lucky, who would close out the service.

Jeremy noticed that her aura was glowing with an unusual emanation. In fact, there had been something very different about her all day.

"Are you all right?" he whispered to her.

"I'm fine, I think. Do you know what day this is?"

"Sunday, May 30."

"More than that. It's Pentecost. How could we have forgotten?"

"Descent of the Holy Spirit. That's what you're feeling, isn't it?"

"I'm feeling something very different. And now I see it's my turn."

There had been laughter and tears, applause and deep appreciation in response to the other speakers. When Debbie took her place at the podium in front of the altar where the spiral candelabra had been lit, the room hushed.

To those who could see such things—which was nearly everyone in the congregation—her aura was as golden as her full-length silk dress that glowed in the candlelight. Her long, flaxen blonde hair flowed down her back and spilled over her shoulders. She looked like a goddess.

"I have been blessed with many teachers," she began, "ascended and unascended. And now newly ascended. Róisín was always more than a mentor who taught me invaluable lessons. She was my dearest friend and in many ways a second mother to me because my own had passed away several years ago.

"You all have described Róisín's many extraordinary qualities, so I will not repeat what you have so eloquently spoken. I will only add that I came to know her as a living flame of love. Especially in the last few months of her life, there were times I could see her etherealizing. At the time I wondered if she realized she was growing more and more light.

"I believe now that she did. Because when it came time for her to make the ultimate sacrifice, I saw in her only determination and the selfless love she gave to each of us. Especially to our darling Lucky."

She motioned for him to come forward. When he stepped to the podium, she gave him a big hug and turned to go back to her seat. But instead of letting her leave, he held her hand.

"Stay with me, darlin'," he whispered.

She thought he needed emotional support for what he was about to say. She would soon realize that it was she who would need his strength.

"My dear friends." Lucky's melodious voice rang out and touched every heart in the room with the vibration of his own accelerating consciousness and mastery.

"I have a special gift for you now. Rather than my telling you more stories about my sweet Róisín, she has informed me that she would like to address you herself. She says there is a ritual to be completed that only she can accomplish. So will you join me in chanting the OM as we make our attunement with her Presence."

OMMMMM.

The congregation chanted and quickly created a luminous resonance in the ballroom. Gliding in on that beam of sound and light, the Ascended Lady Master Róisín appeared with her twin flame at her side.

An awe-struck hush fell over all those gathered, and they lifted their hearts in welcome as she began to speak.

My beloved friends, thank you for being here today. Your words have touched me deeply. By the grace of *An Síoraí*, the Eternal One, and your determination to defend the Light, our community has won a great victory.

Each one of you is playing your part in the vast antahkarana that is uplifting our planetary home. Of course, more challenges will come, though not today.

Now, because of your love and dedication to the cause of soul freedom that Saint Germain first established at our original Fibonacci's, I am permitted to offer you an acceleration of consciousness and a special blessing to one among you which will be a boon to the entire community.

Debbie, please stand here before me.

As the young seer stepped forward to face her cherished teacher and friend, a torch that was burning with a brilliant golden flame appeared in the hand of the lady master.

"Oh!," exclaimed the congregation, for everyone could see it. What could it mean? they wondered as Lady Master Róisín continued:

My dear daughter, this day a torch of illumination is passed to you. For many years I carried this spiritual flame in my heart for the raising up of souls, the dispelling of ignorance, and the lighting of a path Homeward for all who entered our humble establishment.

The responsibility to shine this Light is yours now, my dear, if you will accept it. Gracious seer, will you carry this torch on behalf of our community, to illumine a world in darkness?

"I will." Debbie raised her arm and opened her hand to receive the torch that Lady Master Róisín placed there. Instantly she felt the weight of responsibility and also the protection the flame itself engendered in the one who bore it. The luminous lady master turned her around to face the congregation.

Let all understand that Debbie is our torch-bearer, yet the flame is for each of you to carry in your hearts—wherever you find yourselves in this world or the next.

May the peace and good will of *An Síoraí*, the Eternal One, bless you every day of your lives. The gratitude of the Great White Brotherhood goes with you.

For several minutes all eyes beheld Debbie holding the torch aloft. Gradually it dissolved into a golden mist, and the forms of their dear Róisín and her twin flame faded from view.

Lucky stepped to Debbie's side and motioned for Jeremy and the other Twin Flames of Éire to join them. As they stood together, everyone in the congregation rose to their feet.

Their reverent applause filled the room with profound gratitude, for the Friends of Ancient Wisdom now understood that a new chapter of Love, Life, and Light had begun at Fibonacci's.

Epilogue

Did you enjoy being a Wonderman for a while, my brother?" Saint Germain and his good friend Kuthumi were reflecting on recent events.

"I did. The experience brought back fond memories of my work with the organizations we founded in the nineteenth and twentieth centuries. Many of the same students are now Friends of Ancient Wisdom. They return, as do we, for the next dispensation. Much good will they accomplish in this age if they stay the course you have set them upon."

"And which you most ably reinforced as K. H. Many are wiser now and more at peace for your having nurtured them along the way."

"Yes, we have raised up a fine community who are becoming more of the True Self each day. And now that they have been reminded how to pray together and increase their spiritual attunement to contact us and work with angels and our powerful lady masters, they will continue to transcend their former selves."

"What do you foresee for them, now that the thread of contact has been restored?" asked Saint Germain.

"The blessings of community," replied Kuthumi. "Fellowship and family life. Children in abundance and financial well-being to sustain the quality of life that allows higher consciousness to be retained. Loss, of course. Life is finite in the world of time and space. But grief will be short-lived because our students understand the immortality of the soul and the ever-ascending spiral of Love from incarnation to ascension."

"As did our Róisín, and as Lucky will no doubt follow."

"I believe he will, after he completes one or two important tasks the Brotherhood has assigned him. Then he and his ascended twin flame will also assist the Friends of Ancient Wisdom from higher realms."

"I am pleased that he will be living with Tim and Maggie until then," commented Saint Germain.

"They are extraordinary souls," Kuthumi remarked thoughtfully. "A true son and daughter of the Light. I have suggested that they move into the Tower Room apartment after Lucky ascends."

"What about the Maddens?"

"Debbie and Jeremy will eventually need a house with a yard for the little boy who is anxiously waiting to be born to them. They are not quite ready to be parents and the lad's astrology is not optimal for another year. But when the time comes, it will be good for Fibonacci's to have the O'Tooles living there permanently. And their house will be perfect for the Maddens."

"Tim and Maggie do not age, do they?"

"No. They have been advanced initiates for many years. I have explained that they could take their ascensions and continue to serve from inner planes. But they said they enjoy working with our students in the physical, so they come and go on earth as unascended masters."

"Maggie is certainly correct about the O'Donnells being fine parents." Saint Germain's violet eyes sparkled as he spoke. "I am delighted for Glenna and Rory. I do hope our young actress will establish a drama school for children while their family grows."

"I am certain she will," said Kuthumi. "Rory will encourage her to remain involved in the academy, which I am pleased to know they have officially named 'Crotona'. He, Kevin, and Jeremy are streamlining their many duties so they will have plenty of time for teaching. Crotona Academy is a dream come true for all of them."

"And for you," added Saint Germain with a knowing smile.

"It is, indeed." Kuthumi agreed, vividly remembering his cherished school of the past.

"And what about our Sarah?" asked Saint Germain with a touch of amusement in his voice.

"I believe you already know the answer to that question, my friend."

"I do, because I secured the dispensation for her. She will soon begin work on her next book, which will help Lucky complete his mission."

"What a blessing that will be to the entire community."

Saint Germain agreed. "We need the stories about twin flames, and soul mates such as Lucky and Róisín, to continue. There are more steps on the path and an initiation that these couples must pass to help the world transition to the greater light of this age. They have overcome their personal adversary, but now an even more sinister enemy of the Great White Brotherhood lurks in the shadows, ready to pounce when our students least expect to be challenged."

"How soon do you anticipate that confrontation?" asked Kuthumi.

"Not for a while. The Friends of Ancient Wisdom have time yet to gain in mastery and raise up their children to be warriors of the spirit as their talented parents have become. I have plans for them."

"The children who have been born so far appear to be highly gifted."

"They are," agreed Saint Germain. He gazed off into the distance. "Yes, they are very gifted, as are the ones who are coming. We are going to see quite the conflagration of seers, healers, teachers, artists, professionals of all types, and musicians in years to come."

His aura began to radiate violet light.

"Speaking of music, Elder Brother. After listening to you play at Róisín's ascension service, I would be grateful to hear more from your magnificent organ in Shigatse. I believe we have kept you away from your retreat for too long."

"Then come with me, Holy Brother. I can hear the strains of a new composition calling, even as we speak."

The two ascended masters rested a brotherly hand on one another's shoulder. They turned toward the setting sun as a crystalline stairway appeared in their path and vanished with them the instant they began climbing up to the realm of Spirit that is their Home.

Glossary & Pronunciation Guide

Letters ch (written phonetically as chk) are pronounced as in loch.

Names	Pronunciation	Meaning
Ah-Lahn	ah-LAHN	*Var.* Alan, noble, rock
Alana	ah-LAHN-ah	Dear child
Arán Bán	rahn BAHN	White bread
Ciara	KEER-uh	Lovely dark features
Cormac	KOHr-mak	Son of the charioteer
Dearbhla	DAR-vla	Daughter of the poet
Finola	fih-NO-la	White shoulders
Gareth	GEHR-eth	Gentle, watchful
Gormlaith	GOORM-luh	Blue princess
Jarahnaten	JAH-ra-NAH-ten	Guard at Pharaoh's palace
Khieranan	KEER-uh-nahn	Atlantean Priest
Laoch	LAY-ochk	Hero
Lúcháir	LOO-chkah(ee)	Welcoming joy
Madwyn	MAHD-oo-en	Forthright, practical
Meke	MEH-keh	Pharaoh's daughter
Nhada-lihn	nah-dah-LIN	Original High Priestess
Naimh	NEE-av	Luster, sheen
Óengus	O-en-gus	Singular strength
Phelan	FEE-lun	Wolf
Riordan	REER-duhn	Royal poet
Róisín	roh-SHEEN	Little Rose
Saoirse	SER-shuh	Freedom, liberty
Tadhgan	TIE-guhn	*Var. Tadhg,* bard poet
Treylah	TRAY-luh	Atlantean Priestess
Una	OO-nuh	*Var. uan,* lamb
Víahlah	vee-AH-luh	Atlantean Priestess
Wyn	OO-en	Atlantean Priest

Place Names	Pronunciation	Meaning
Éire	AY-(rhe)	Ireland
Inis Cealtra	IN-ish KALL-truh	Holy Island
Tearmann	TAR-a-mun	Place of refuge (túath)

Endearments	Pronunciation	Meaning
A chairde	a-CHKAR-dyeh	My friends
A chara	a-CHKAR-uh	O friend, my friend
A chara dhílis	a-CHKAR-uh YEE-lish	My faithful friend
A ghrá	a-GHRAH	My love
A pháistí	a-FASH-tee	My children
Buachaill cróga	BUCHK-uhl KRO-guh	Brave boy
Mo chroí	mu-CHKREE	My heart
Mo mhuirnín	mu-WOOR-neen	My darling

Terms	Pronunciation	Meaning
An Síoraí	un SHEE-uh-ree	The Eternal One
Bealtaine (festival)	bee-YOWL-tin-ah	May 1, bright fire
Ceann-druí	KYAHN-dree	Chief Druid
Gaeltacht	GWAYL-tachkt	Irish-speaking areas
Imbolc (festival)	IM-bolk	Feb 1, St. Brigid's Day
Samhain (festival)	SOW-in	Nov 1, New Year
Seanchaí	SHAN-a-chkee	Storyteller
Taoiseach	TEE-shuchk	Chieftain
Túath	TOO-uh	Territory, like a village

Phrases with Pronunciation and Translation

Codladh sámh	KOD-luh sahv	Sleep well
Céilí	KAY-lee	Big Irish social gathering
Go hálainn	guh-HAH-luhn	Beautiful or great
Go raibh maith agat	GUH-ruh-MAH-hat	Thank you
Go raibh míle maith agat	GUH-ruh-MEE-luh-ma-HAH-gut	Thank you very much
Is mise le meas	Is mish leh mess	Sincerely yours
Oíche mhaith	EECHK-uh-wah	Good night
Slán	SLAHN	Good-bye
Teach na beannachta	TACHK-na-BAN-achk-teh	Home of blessing

About the Ancients

Many spiritual traditions have their own words and definitions for the manifestations of the Divine that mystics have been observing and experiencing for centuries. The following denote specific aspects of divinity as they are understood by the characters in the *Twin Flames of Éire Trilogy*.

An Síoraí, the Eternal One

Higher Self, I AM Presence, The Magic Presence
Individualized manifestation of the I AM THAT I AM
Soul's unique God-identity, God Self, Divine Monad
The soul's spiritual origin, source of one's divine plan
Spiritual Home to which the soul longs to return

Because *An Síoraí*, the Eternal One, abides in Spirit, the human mind requires a mediator to bridge the communication gap between Spirit and Matter. This "translator" is referred to as the True Self.

True Self

Higher Mind, Christ Self, Buddha Self, Real Self
Source of intuition, the still small voice
Inner Teacher, voice of inner wisdom

The True Self can be thought of as a personal, wise inner counselor who operates through the Higher Mind and communicates with both the Higher Self in Spirit and the human mind, which functions through the brain and does not have direct access to the I AM Presence.

In order to commune with *An Síoraí*, the Eternal One, the soul strives to become one with the True Self through various disciplines and practices designed to increase awareness of the Divine and dissolve limits of human consciousness.

Goddesses & Gods

Cosmic beings who can hold the consciousness of a certain divine quality, such as God of Freedom, God Harmony, Goddess of Liberty, Goddess of Light, Goddess of Truth, or God of Gold.

Adepts, Ascended Masters & the Great White Brotherhood

Adepts are men and women from every culture who have answered the call of *An Síoraí*, the Eternal One, passing many profound initiations, and bonding with their True Self. Some remain in embodiment for a time and others ascend, depending upon their calling.

Ascended masters are adepts who have balanced their karma, fulfilled their divine plan, and reunited with their Higher Self.

The Great White Brotherhood is a universal body of adepts and ascended masters who, like Saint Germain, have dedicated their attainment to the liberation of souls from the bonds of the lesser self.

"White" refers to the pure white light surrounding their forms. Certain devotees of the highest spiritual truth are also members of the Brotherhood, which is very much a Sisterhood.

Ascended Master Saint Germain

After making his ascension in the year 1684, Saint Germain was granted a dispensation by the Great Law to once again take on a physical body so he might guide the monarchies of Europe in their necessary transition to more democratic systems of government.

Widely known as the "Wonderman of Europe," he appeared for decades as a man in his early forties, dazzling those whom he wished to assist with his diplomatic skills, alchemical feats, incomparable wisdom, boundless grace, and loving-kindness.

Despite his monumental efforts, stubborn monarchists failed to heed his warnings, and many fell in the horrific reign of terror in the French Revolution. Finally, after Napoleon's betrayal in the early nineteenth century, Saint Germain declared that he would not be seen for a hundred years.

In the twentieth century, the Master once again contacted embodied individuals, this time empowering them as his hands and feet in the physical, and as his messengers to deliver his spiritual teachings.

The *Twin Flames of Éire Trilogy* novels are the author's musings of what might transpire, should our dear Saint Germain gain a new dispensation to appear in a physical form suitable for face-to-face communion with his friends of ancient wisdom.

Ascended Master Kuthumi

Known to students of Theosophy as the Mahatma (great soul) K. H., an abbreviation of his East Indian name, Koot Hoomi, Kuthumi ascended at the conclusion of his embodiment in the late nineteenth century.

Today he holds the office of World Teacher, with his own master Jesus, whom he closely resembles in appearance.

Master Kuthumi is said to have had many illustrious incarnations, including Shah Jahan, who built the Taj Mahal. He was also embodied as the great spiritual philosopher, Pythagoras, and as Saint Francis.

His connection with Ireland is not as well known, although he is suggested as the author of "The Dream of Ravan: A Mystery" which was published in *The Dublin University Magazine*, in 1853 or 1854.

Kuthumi is highly honored for his profound psychological insight and is loved for his unfailing kindness, although no student of the Light should ever mistake his gentle nature for lack of spiritual fire when the soul of one of his disciples needs the swift correction that will ensure the integrity of that one's path. He is truly a friend of wisdom, both ancient and modern.

Ascended Lady Master Nada

"The Rose Lady," as the Callahan twins Kerry and Kaitlyn call her, is said to have been embodied on Atlantis where she was a master of the law. As a member of the Great Karmic Board, she helps guide the progress of souls. She is known by students of the Light as a wise, compassionate, and profoundly loving advocate for families, individuals, twin flames, and soul mates who are striving to win their freedom from the rounds of rebirth.

Read the story that sparked the
Twin Flames of Éire Trilogy
and learn where the path of reunion began
for Sarah and Kevin . . .

The Weaving:
A Novel of Twin Flames Through Time
print: 978-1-7346450-4-0; e-book: 978-1-7346450-5-7

And don't miss any of the
sequels to *The Weaving* in the
Twin Flames of Éire Trilogy

Beginning with
The Ancients and The Call
print: 978-1-7346450-0-2; e-book: 978-1-7346450-1-9

Continuing with
The Water and The Flame
print: 978-1-7346450-2-6; e-book: 978-1-7346450-7-1

Concluding with
The Mystics and The Mystery
print: 978-1-7346450-6-4; e-book: 978-1-7346450-8-8

Available online or from fine bookstores everywhere.

Photo by Larry Stanley

Cheryl Lafferty Eckl has played many roles since she began her career in musical theatre—award-winning author, mystical poet, professional development trainer, life coach, inspirational speaker, and subject matter expert on end-of-life issues and grief.

These days, her favorite role is *seanchaí*. That's Irish for storyteller.

If you ask, she'll tell you that it's her love of Ireland—its people, language, land, and culture—that continues to inspire characters and stories in spiritual romance novels that follow the trials and triumphs of twin flames who sometimes struggle and often succeed in unlocking Love's mystery.

Learn more about Cheryl's books, and enjoy her extensive library of articles, audios, videos, and blogs at www.CherylLaffertyEckl.com.

CPSIA information can be obtained
at www.ICGtesting.com
Printed in the USA
LVHW041438181120
672004LV00001B/51

9 781734 645064